ONE *Lucky* COWBOY

CAROLYN BROWN

casablanca

Published by Sourcebooks Casablanca, an imprint of Sourcebooks, Inc.
P.O. Box 4410, Naperville, Illinois 60567-4410
(630) 961-3900
FAX: (630) 961-2168
www.sourcebooks.com

Printed in Canada
WC 10 9 8 7 6 5 4

To the Rucker Cyn's:
Graycyn and Madacyn

Chapter 1

SLADE TRIED TO INTIMIDATE THE PETITE, DISHWATER BLONDE with a glare meant to drop her stone cold dead on the spot. Even if it didn't work, she'd know exactly how he felt about the situation and that he wasn't buying into her act. The fair-haired con artist with pecan-colored brown eyes would be gone in twenty-four hours and that wasn't a threat; it was a solid promise. He might have just lost the first battle with his grandmother, but he'd be damned if he would lose the whole war.

Jane didn't blink when she and the tall, blond cowboy locked eyes. She needed a place to hide for six weeks and this was perfect. If he thought he could run her off, he had cow chips for brains. The opportunity had dropped in her lap at the bus station like an answered prayer from heaven. She could endure his cold accusations and he could damn sure live with the situation for a few weeks. She'd stay out of his way as much as possible. She'd just seen how the evil male brain worked, and it was scary.

Nellie Luckadeau, Slade's grandmother, could have danced a jig in a pig trough half full of fermented slop. Never had she seen Slade so angry. He was the cold, calm, collected, and slow-moving cowboy who never had a temper fit. She'd begun to think he'd never feel anything again and suddenly he was ready to chew up railroad spikes all because she'd brought home a stray, homeless girl. Well, praise the Lord and pass the biscuits, her prayers had been answered.

Slade shifted his big blue eyes to his grandmother. "I can't believe you drove to Wichita Falls. I told you I'd be here as soon as I could."

"Ellen wanted to get home this afternoon and she'd have missed her bus. Damned near did anyway, what with the wreck and all. Don't get your underbritches in a wad. I drove. I backed out into a car. I've got damned good insurance that'll pay for the damages and if I didn't, I expect I could handle the amount. I was lucky to be sittin' there when Jane got off the bus. Now I've got a driver and you can get on back to your ranchin' and quit your bellyachin' about me hiring her. She told me on the way from Wichita Falls that this was her lucky break. Well, I reckon it's mine, too. And if you'll admit it, it's your lucky break because damn it all, Slade Luckadeau, you don't have to worry about drivin' me anywhere long as she's here."

"She's not a driver, she's a con artist. I bet Jane Day isn't even her name. It's so close to Jane Doe that she probably picked it from the air when you asked her. It doesn't even show any imagination. She's here to swindle you, Granny. Wait and see. She'll end up with everything you own before she leaves." He stormed out of the house. His boots sounded like bolts of thunder and his spurs jingled like a wind chime as he stomped across the wooden porch.

"Don't worry about him, Jane. He's just got a burr in his britches. He'll get over it. Let me show you to your room. But before I do, look me in the eye and tell me you aren't a con artist," Nellie said.

Jane took a step forward, looked up, and met the tall older woman's eyes. "I am not a con artist. I'm not here to rob you of anything. I just need a place to stay for a few weeks. I'm grateful for the job and I'll work like a mule."

"That's all I need to know," Nellie said. "Follow me."

Jane picked up a stuffed duffel bag and carried it through a living room that looked seldom used, a dining room with a long table that could easily seat a dozen people, a den where most of the living went on by the look of the well-used, overstuffed sofa and recliners, and down a hallway. She would never have guessed she'd end up on a ranch south of Ringgold, Texas when she left Greenville, Mississippi two days before. But she wasn't about to look a gift horse in the mouth. Like she'd said, she'd work like a mule for six weeks and then go back home to settle matters.

"Old house started out as a two-bedroom frame back in the beginning," Nellie said. "My husband's father built it for his new wife. Then the kids came along and they added this wing with an extra three bedrooms. When my husband bought out his sibling's interest in the ranch and we got married, he added another wing for us. It's got a sitting room and a bedroom. Sitting room turned into his office and my sewing and quilting room pretty quick. My boys lived on this wing the whole time they was growing up. We saved the original two bedrooms for guests. Slade lives in this room."

She motioned toward a shut door. "Here's where you can toss your belongings and sleep at night. Reckon the rest of the time I'll keep you busy. Make yourself at home and get settled in. We serve up three meals a day.

We'll start dinner in an hour. That's for the whole work crew. Part of the deal we've always made on the Double L: a good salary and dinner at twelve sharp. Supper is flexible depending on what's going on. If Slade is cutting hay, we might not eat until eight or nine. If he's able to get in early, it's around six. It's not as big as dinner because the help all goes home to their families. Just the three of us at that time. You. Me. Slade. Sometimes my sister, Ellen. She spends a lot of time over here. Ignore Slade if he gets testy."

"Yes, ma'am. I'll be out there in an hour to help you," Jane said.

"Might want to stretch out. Don't reckon you got much sleep on that bus, did you?"

"No, ma'am, I didn't. And thank you," Jane said.

"And no thanks due. You'll work for the money I promised you and you'll have a room and board as long as you want to stay here." Nellie shut the door.

Jane threw herself on the full-sized bed, laced her hands behind her head, and stared at her surroundings. It had definitely been a boy's room at one time. Cranberry and ecru plaid curtains hung at the window. A piecework quilt using the same colors covered the bed. The iron headboard and footboard had been painted a soft buttery yellow. A mirror hung above a six-drawer dresser with family pictures arranged from the larger eight by ten sizes at the back down to small ones in the front. The light tan carpet had been replaced recently and still looked new. The walls were painted a soft antique white but were bare.

She glanced at the door. No lock. She shared a wing with the abominable grandson, Slade, with no way to keep him from sneaking into her room and smothering her to death at night. At least she would know there was a possibility she'd be dead by morning and it wouldn't come as a total surprise from the hands of the man she'd promised to love forever amen.

Tired beyond words, she couldn't be still. She popped up and opened the duffle bag. Three pair of jeans, three T-shirts, a dozen pair of underpants, three bras, two pair of Nikes, and a few pair of socks. She had the whole thing unpacked and put away in one empty dresser drawer and the closet in less than ten minutes. She could easily make do with that much for the next few weeks. If she needed anything for a special occasion, she could always purchase it with the money she'd be paid each Friday night.

That almost brought a smile to her face. Who would have thought a week ago that she'd be working for a hundred dollars a week plus room and board? It would have been the biggest joke in the whole state of Mississippi. Ellacyn Jane Hayes working on a ranch for a tiny fraction of her normal salary, without her fancy clothes, cars, and credit cards.

She dug around in her purse for her cell phone to call her best friend Celia and whined out loud. She had vowed she wouldn't miss her bank account or the credit cards she'd been wise enough to leave behind, or even her business, if she could just be safe. But she really, really did miss that cell phone.

"Damn you, John," she mumbled. She missed her friend, Celia, even more than all the clothing in her closets, more than the laptop computer that she relied on so heavily, even more than chocolate.

She'd thrown the phone out the window somewhere between Dallas and Wichita Falls when she found the tracking device hidden under the battery flap. Finding it had been a fluke. She'd dropped the phone on the floor and the back fell off. When she picked it up, she recognized the little shiny metal thing immediately. She'd slung the phone out the window into the tall grass along the roadside and berated herself for all the expensive subterfuge she'd already sacrificed. The plane ticket from Jackson to New York hadn't been cheap and had eaten up most of her cash. She'd left her Cadillac in the airport parking lot and taken a taxi to the bus station, where she'd bought a ticket to Dallas. No one would look for her on a bus.

She'd written a note that she had gotten cold feet and was on her way to New York for a few weeks to think things through. John would have gone there immediately if it hadn't been for that damned cell phone tracker. Oh, well, it had happened and it couldn't be helped. Now she was as safe as possible, hidden away on a ranch near Ringgold, Texas, population one hundred according to the history lesson Nellie had provided on the drive from Wichita Falls to the Double L Ranch.

She pulled the curtains back and got a view of Black Angus cattle just outside the fenced yard. Farther out she could see Slade on a horse rounding cattle into a huge semi truck. It was definitely a working ranch and Slade was a bona fide cowboy. He cocked his head toward the house and she dropped the curtain faster than if it had been on fire. Surely he couldn't have seen her, but that glare he'd settled upon her when he found out his grandmother had picked her up in the bus station like a stray puppy was enough to give her cold chills. On second thought, those blue eyes could most likely see well enough through trees, cattle hind ends, and glass windows to fry her where she stood.

To say that Slade was angry was the understatement of the century. He'd never been so mad in his whole life. Not even the day his mother shoved him crying out of the car and disappeared with her new husband in a cloud of Texas dust. Granny had no business driving more than thirty miles to Wichita Falls to the bus station in the first place. All she had to do was exercise a little patience and he'd have taken Aunt Ellen to catch the bus back to Amarillo. Damn it all, he'd have taken time to drive the feisty old lady all the way to Amarillo, if Granny would have given him a chance.

But oh, no, she had to take matters in her own hands and get behind the wheel even though she couldn't see jack shit. It had been a year since the doctor had told her about the macular degeneration and said she wasn't to drive anymore. Slade should have taken her license away from her then, but he'd thought she had more sense than to endanger her own life as well as others. Well, he'd been wrong but he'd see to it he had that license in his possession before nightfall. And that little blonde was going right back to the train station come morning. He'd never liked brown-eyed women and he could see through a con from a mile away on a foggy day.

Heat rose up from the ground in waves but he didn't notice it or the sweat pouring down his back, soaking the chambray shirt in big wet circles. It was June in north Texas and sweat was part of life.

"What you so mad about? Never seen you act like this," Vince Johnson asked. His father was the foreman of the Double L Ranch and the tall, gangly young man had worked for Slade in the summers since he was barely big enough to sit a horse.

"Granny drove to town, backed into a car, drug home a stray woman, and is acting like nothing happened," Slade said.

"It's the woman that's making you the maddest. Granny has driven to town before. She's had accidents before and you've never gotten in a snit like this."

Slade turned his horse to gather in another bull without answering. Damn kids these days. What made them so wise, anyway? He didn't remember being that smart when he was sixteen. So what if it was the woman that brought on the fury? Granny had no right to hire live-in help without consulting him. They had always talked things over, hashing through the pros and cons until an agreement was reached.

He pulled a bottle of water from his saddle bag and drank long and deep, frowning at the house the whole time. He'd never liked being reminded of his vulnerability where his mother was concerned and he'd hated the idea of being blindsided. Not that Jane Doe or Day or whatever fictitious name she pulled out of her ass was anything like his mother, who was a tall, gorgeous blonde and could put Marilyn Monroe to shame. Pretty enough to be a model. Trashy enough to entice men. Smart enough to know the difference between rich and poor men. These days she had her nails and hair done in Los Angeles and the line of ex-husbands was longer than his arm.

Jane Day was pretty in an impish sort of way. She had dirty-blonde hair cut in layers from her chin to her shoulders, big brown eyes with perfectly arched brows, and a wide full mouth that would appeal to some men but reminded Slade too much of the pouting Marilyn look. It was that mouth that reminded him of his mother and brought on the memories.

The resemblance ended there, though. He would give credit where it was due and admit she had some redeemable qualities in that short little body with a waist so small he could span it with his big hands. After all he wasn't blind. Nor was he dumb. The woman was after something, and she wasn't finding it on his ranch.

Jane found Nellie in the kitchen. A large pot of beans simmered on the back burner of the stove. Cornbread was in the cast-iron skillet ready to pop into the oven.

"You know anything about cooking for a dozen hungry men?" Nellie asked.

"Little bit. What can I do?"

"Got any skill at a Mexican casserole to go with those beans and cornbread?"

"I could do that," Jane nodded.

"Hamburger meat is in the fridge."

"Chips?"

"In the pantry right over there. You'll find every-thing else you need in there or in the fridge. Better make two pans full or they'll be whining about still being hungry."

"Dessert?"

"Get some frozen peaches out of the freezer. I didn't have time to make anything sweet this morning," Nellie said.

"How about some warm brownies to go with the peaches?"

Nellie's smile erased a few of the wrinkles around her mouth and deepened those around her blue eyes. "I knew I'd hired the right person."

Evidently that's who Slade had inherited his piercing blue eyes from—only Nellie's had softened with age. Jane couldn't imagine her shooting daggers like her grandson. When he was as old as Nellie, his eyes still wouldn't be soft. He'd be able to pierce steel instead of heal broken hearts and melt butter.

"Slade came to live with me when he was eight years old. That was twenty-two years ago, six months after my son, Thomas, died in a car wreck. Thomas was so smart it was just plumb scary. Finished high school over in Nocona when he was sixteen and had his first college degree before he could even buy a beer. Wound up with a doctorate in engineering and worked down in Dallas. He wasn't just smart. He was downright pretty. Looked a lot like Slade, only Slade has that tough angular look to his face that his Daddy didn't have. Yes, ma'am, Thomas was intelligent in everything but women," Nellie talked as she worked.

Jane listened.

"If I'd been picking a wife for him the one he got wouldn't have even been on the far bottom of the list. But he was damned and determined that he loved her. I called it the Knight-in-Shining-Armor syndrome. He thought he could ride in on his intelligence and save her. She was dirt poor, pretty, and didn't have two good brain cells in her head. They made it ten years before he died. Six months later she called me from a pay phone on the way here. Said she was bringing Slade to me to raise. She couldn't look at him without thinking of Thomas and besides she was getting married again."

"Oh, my," Jane mumbled. She didn't give a royal rat's ass that Slade Luckadeau hadn't had a perfect little life. She was the hired help, not his future psychiatrist.

"Hey, you're pretty good at stirring up those brownies. You got the recipe in your head or something?"

"Yes, ma'am. My momma taught me to cook. She said I needed to learn everything from the kitchen to the barn from the ground up," Jane said.

"I sure enough did the right thing when I hired you. God really did give me a lucky break when you got off that bus this morning."

Jane slid the brownies into the preheated oven and went to work on the casseroles. They'd follow the brownies into the oven in thirty minutes and be steaming hot when the crew came in from the hayfields for lunch. Cooking was her hobby and she was good at it. After all, she'd had the best teacher in the world for sixteen years.

"You want me to set the table while they're cooking?" she asked Nellie.

Nellie shook her head. "They'll eat out on the deck. Come on and I'll show you how to set things up for them."

"Why don't they eat at the table?" Jane asked.

"It'd take a week to fumigate the house with that much man-sweat coming inside. Winter time we only have a skeleton crew. They eat in the house. Rest of the time they eat on the deck. Besides, they like it that way. If they was to come inside and get all cool, it would give them a heart attack to go back out in the afternoon heat."

She led the way through sliding glass doors in the kitchen nook out onto an enormous deck. The deck covered the entire space between the two wings that made the U-shaped, one-story ranch house. Yellow and orange marigolds, purple, pink, and white petunias, multicolored lantana, violet vinca, and red impatients splashed color around the deck. Two ancient pecan trees and a hackberry provided shade for the yard and the deck.

Nellie opened two doors to a closet on the north side of the deck. Disposable plates, cheap cutlery, jelly glasses, and rolls of paper towels were all neatly arranged. "This is kind of like the tail end of a chuck wagon. Designed it myself years ago when I got tired of hauling everything in and out every day. We use paper plates but I've never learned to like plastic forks, so I bought some cheap stainless at the dollar store."

She handed a stack of divided Styrofoam plates to Jane and motioned toward an eight-foot table covered with a vinyl cloth. "We set it up buffet style on this table. They help themselves. We'll need bowls today for the beans and peaches; better open two packages. There's a blue plastic caddy I put the silverware in. Glasses go on the table with ice already in them. Four pitchers of tea, two of lemonade and two of water go down the middle of the table along with jars of picante sauce and salt and pepper shakers. It's a constant job keeping the liquid in the pitchers. They come in here with a big thirst after working all morning. Most of them carry a half-gallon jug of some kind that they'll refill before they head out again, so we'll make lots of tea and lemonade."

"How many glasses?"

"Twenty-four."

Jane whistled under her breath.

"Shame, ain't it? Used to take fifty men to do the work in the summer but with all this new-fangled equipment and those big, round hay bales, we get by with less than half that. Don't know if we're saving money or not. Equipment requires more upkeep than men."

"But it sweats less," Jane said.

"Smart as well as handy in the kitchen. I think I might be goin' to like you, Jane Day," Nellie said.

Slade heard the dinner bell sounding across the fields and rode his horse to the edge of the yard, where he tethered it to the fence. He pulled off his leather gloves and headed for the pump to wash his hands and face. The cold well water felt good but did nothing to appease the turmoil still rolling about in his heart and soul. Besides being upset with his grandmother, now he'd have to listen to Kristy whine and bitch about another woman in the house. While he dried off on a long length of paper towels, he sighed. Kristy had been looking for a job ever since she got laid off over at the leather factory in Nocona. She was going to pitch a real hissy fit when she found out Granny had hired someone right off the street and not her.

"You sick?" Vince asked.

"Might as well be," Slade answered.

"Can I have your share of the brownies?"

"Granny made brownies?"

"No, she said that new girl—the one she hired over in Wichita Falls this morning—made them. If you're too sick to eat, I'm layin' claim to your share."

"I'm not sick to my stomach but I'm going to be sick of listening to Kristy," Slade answered honestly.

"Well, shoot. They're fresh out of the oven and smell like heaven," Vince said.

Jane watched two dozen men wash up, dispose of their paper towels in a big trash can beside the pump, and load their plates and bowls to the brim with lunch. They sat at three eight-foot tables covered in the same red-and-white checked vinyl as the buffet table and talked about the work they'd gotten done as well as what they planned to do until dark.

"Slade, you need anything from the feed store or anywhere else in Nocona? I'm having Jane drive me over for groceries this afternoon," Nellie asked above the drone of the men's voices.

Slade shot Jane another mean look and nodded. "Sure, I'll make a list for the feed store, and would you go by the flower shop and send Kristy half a dozen roses? Sign the card, *Just thinking of you, Slade*."

Jane stiffened to keep from shuddering. How many times had John sent her roses with a similar note? In the six weeks they'd dated before he proposed she'd had fresh roses all the time. One vase-full scarcely had time to wilt before another arrived at her desk. In her mind roses meant a first-rate con job, not love.

Slade held up a tea pitcher. "This needs a refill."

Jane reached to take it from his hand. He held on tightly and whispered, "Pack your bags when you get back from the grocery store. I'm taking you to Wichita Falls as soon as supper is over."

"In your dreams, cowboy. You didn't hire me and you can't fire me."

"I can make you miserable."

Everyone stopped talking and silence filled the yard. Even the birds stopped their singing and the crickets were quiet.

"I've been made miserable before and by full-fledged professionals. I reckon compared to them you're just an amateur."

Vince chuckled. "I think you met your match, Slade."

Heat that had nothing to do with the thermometer crept up Slade's neck. "Why would you stay somewhere that you're not wanted?"

"Just call it determination. Nellie hired me. When she's dissatisfied with my performance she'll fire me and I'll leave. What you think or don't think of me doesn't matter a damn bit to me."

"Whew, she's spunky. You make these brownies?" A short Mexican man piped up right next to Slade.

Her eyes and face softened when she looked away from Slade. "Yes, sir, I did and the casseroles. Tomorrow we're having turkey and dressing with pumpkin pie for dessert."

"By the way, I'm the foreman of the Double L. Name is Marty. And if he fires you, honey, you come talk to me. I'll hire you right back."

Slade snorted. "Looks like I'm outvoted by a whole passel of fools."

"Enough bickering," Nellie said. "Jane is here to stay as long as she wants. If she proves out to be as good as I think she is, I'm thinkin' of going to Ellen's out in Amarillo for a week. So put that in your pipe and smoke it, Slade."

He rolled his eyes. Kristy would really go up in flames at that idea. Him alone in the house with another woman—that should throw ice on their budding relationship. They'd been dating for six months and he'd been entertaining notions of taking it to the next level. Granny wasn't real happy with that idea, but he was thirty years old and he wanted a family. Kristy came with two little girls. He'd have a jump start with those benefits.

He threw up his hands in defeat. "Have it your way but you're going to find I'm right when it's all said and done."

The men finished eating, threw their dirty plates and bowls in a trash can at the end of the buffet table, put the cutlery in a plastic dish pan, and lined the glasses up beside it. They claimed chairs, a spot of shade under the hackberry and pecan trees, or chaise lounges and shut their eyes—all but Slade, who toted the dishpan into the house.

Jane and Nellie each carried half a dozen glasses, waitress style, and followed him. The wind shifted and Jane got a solid whiff of Slade in all his musky, sweaty glory. She understood fully why Nellie wouldn't want two dozen like that in her dining room. It would take months to clean out that much testosterone. She wasn't sure there was that much air freshener on the market.

Nellie set the glasses down and headed back out to cart the bean pot inside.

"I'm serious. I'm not teasing. I do not want you here. It's going to complicate my life beyond words," he said.

"I'm here for six weeks. Sorry if it makes your life less than perfect," she said.

"She's paying you a hundred dollars a week. I'll write you a check for a thousand to leave tonight," he said.

"No thank you."

"Two thousand. Name your price."

"You don't have enough money to make me leave."

"Why?"

"That is my business. I'm staying right here for six weeks and then I promise I'll get out of your way. And darlin', don't worry about me causing a problem with you and your precious lady friend. I've sworn off all men for eternity. I'll tell her that if you want me to."

"What makes you think there's a lady friend?"

"The way you are actin' tells me there is. A woman would give you hell if another woman moved in on her property. Bring her around. I'll tell her I'm damn sure not a threat."

He pointed his finger at her. "You stay away from Kristy."

She slapped it away. "Don't be issuing orders. I'm not here to cause trouble. You stay out of my way and I'll be damn sure I don't get in yours. I'll tolerate your piggish ways and you can pretend I'm just a slave girl. I don't care how you handle it, but I'm not leaving."

Slade narrowed his blue eyes until they were little more than slits. "You are running from the law. That's why you're calling yourself Jane Day. What did you do?"

"Believe what you want. I've got to help Nellie. Conversation is over."

"I'm calling the sheriff of Montague County and seeing if you are wanted anywhere in the state," he said.

"Want me to dial the number for you?"

"You're bluffing."

"Then call my bet and see if the sheriff of Monty County has a thing on me," she threw over her shoulder as she disappeared through the doors.

He took a cell phone from his shirt pocket and dialed the familiar number. He'd grown up with the sheriff. They played poker the first Friday of every month together. Jane Day would be sitting in jail in an hour.

"Hey, Charlie, this is Slade. Got a little favor to ask. Granny hired a woman going by the name of Jane Day. Just picked her up at the bus stop in Wichita Falls this morning and come dragging her home like a stray pup. Please tell me you've got some warrant on her so I can get rid of her."

"Give me a minute," Charlie said.

Slade heard typing on keys and background noise of the deputies coming and going from the sheriff's office.

"Sorry old buddy. Haven't got anything new on anyone for the past three weeks. Did get a fax this morning about some rich broad over in Mississippi who might be headed this way. She run out on her wedding the night before the big ceremony. Her stepdad says it's not like her and he's afraid she might have been kidnapped. Her name is Ellacyn Hayes though. Twenty-four years old. Description says she's…"

Slade butted in. "That couldn't be this woman. She's working for a hundred dollars a week and room and board. This lady looks like she'd be pushing it to be nineteen and there's no way she's some rich broad from Mississippi. She don't have that kind of accent and she's wearing faded jeans and a T-shirt. Rich woman wouldn't be dressed like that. I figured her for a runaway from east Texas and was hoping she'd robbed a bank or a liquor store."

"Sorry old pal. How's things going with Kristy?"

"Fine until now. She's going up in smoke when she hears there's a woman living here."

Charlie chuckled. "Women! Can't live with 'em and it's against the law to shoot 'em."

"You got that right."

"Who are you talking to?" Nellie asked as she and Jane toted in leftovers.

Slade snapped the phone shut. "Charlie."

"This ain't a poker night," Nellie said.

"Would that be the sheriff of Monty County?" Jane raised an eyebrow. It was all she could do to keep from bolting and running. John would find the phone. He was such a smooth talker he'd have the sheriff out with a posse hunting her down for him.

"Montague County, not Monty," Nellie said.

"Yes, it was the sheriff. He's one of my friends." Slade narrowed his eyes and slowly went from her toes to her hair. Jane was certainly not a rich runaway bride. But kidnapping might be an option in the game. He could hire someone to nab her and keep her the six weeks she kept mentioning, then turn her loose. Whatever they would charge would be a small price to pay.

"Why were you talking to Charlie?" Nellie asked. "Slade, you weren't asking him about Jane, were you?"

"Yes, I was and it appears she's not wanted by the law. Only person they've got anything on right now is some runaway bride from over in Mississippi. Charlie says her father is looking for her." He watched Jane carefully but she didn't move a muscle; just kept running water to wash up the glasses and cutlery from dinner.

"You reckon your father is looking for you?" Nellie asked.

"My father died when I was ten years old. I don't suppose he's looking for me on this side of the Pearly Gates," Jane said honestly.

"Okay, Slade. Enough is enough. I don't give a damn what Kristy thinks of my decision to hire Jane, if that's what is sticking in your craw. The woman rubs me wrong anyway and she'd want to bring those two little girls to work with her every day and they don't do anything but whine about being bored. Besides she can't cook and I don't want to listen to her constant prattle when she drives me. Jane works for me. She doesn't work for you."

Nellie put the leftover beans in the refrigerator. Slade made a gun with his forefinger and thumb and shot an imaginary bullet at Jane while his grandmother wasn't looking. Jane pretended to catch it in her hand and toss it in the dishwater as she turned her back on him.

It wouldn't be as easy as she'd thought that morning when she sat down beside the elderly lady and caught the first lucky break since she'd run away from a deadly situation. The sheriff had already been warned to be on the lookout, so there was no doubt that John had located the cell phone. He'd turn over every stone between Wichita Falls and Heaven itself to find her. After all, he'd put six weeks into the venture and, even without the life insurance policy, she was worth thousands of dollars to him. Even more to her stepfather, Paul Stokes.

"Did you ever stop and eat dinner?" Nellie asked.

Jane's gag reflex went into fast gear at the thought of swallowing food. "No, but I'm not hungry."

"You're a big girl. You know where the groceries are. Eat when you get hungry. Heat ruins my appetite sometimes, too. But that casserole was so good today that I forgot all about the temperature. We'll get on over to Nocona and pick up groceries soon as you finish up with those dishes. I usually just wash up the dinner ones by hand and put the breakfast and supper ones in the dishwasher and run it before I go to bed."

"Thank you. I'm glad you liked my cooking. You sure about turkey and dressing tomorrow?"

"Yep. I want the boys to eat good to make up for just beans and casseroles today. Working men need lots of real food."

"Is Nocona where the county seat is located?"

"Heavens no. It's the biggest town in the county with around three thousand people. Montague is the county seat. Little bitty place that was bigger than Nocona at one time. What makes you ask?"

"Just wondered."

"You never have been in this part of Texas have you? Where are you from, Jane?"

"I was born in El Dorado, Arkansas."

"You want to tell me how you got to Wichita Falls and why you took me up on my job offer?"

"Not really."

"Well, that's your business. You ever want to talk about it, I'm right here. You don't, I could care less. You about done?"

"Just a few more glasses. And thanks, Nellie."

Chapter 2

THE WHOLE BACKYARD REVERBERATED WITH THE BIRTHDAY song as two strong men carried an enormous cake with seventy-five candles out of the kitchen. Nellie wore stretch denim jeans, a red-and-white seersucker shirt over a white T-shirt, and a great big smile. Her short gray hair had been styled the day before in a curly do that framed her wrinkled face. She sat in a lawn chair beside her sister, Ellen, who wore a stylish tiered skirt of every color in the rainbow and a long, gauzy tunic top belted with a wide gold belt. Her dyed-red hair was big enough to run Dolly Parton some serious competition.

Jane watched from the sliding doors. Ellen helped Nellie blow out the candles and the next generation of Luckadeau women served the cake. The yard was a sea of blond, blue-eyed people with kids to match running every which way. One tall, dark-haired man stood out in the midst of the crowd. A little girl stayed close to him and it was evident she was his daughter, with that white streak in their hair.

A short Mexican lady stepped inside the house and caught the quizzical expression on Jane's face. "He's really a Luckadeau. I asked Beau and he vouched for it. Said it was his mother's genes that surfaced. I could hardly believe it. I thought every baby a Luckadeau threw was blond-haired and blue-eyed. They seem to bypass all the dominant gene rules."

"He looks so out of place," Jane said.

Milli extended her hand. "I'm Milli Luckadeau. Married a year to one of those tall Greek gods out there."

Jane shook it. "I'm Jane Day. Nellie hired me to help out in the kitchen and drive her."

"I know. Gossip travels quickly in the Luckadeau family," Milli smiled.

"You don't match either," Jane said.

"Ain't that the truth. I remember the first time I was thrown in amongst all those blondes. I felt like a one-legged chicken at a coyote convention."

"How'd you…?"

Milli giggled. "It's a long story. The one standing over there by the tree holding the little girl with a pink bow in her hair is my husband."

"That's your child he's holding?"

"Yes, that little blonde-haired, blue-eyed child is mine. Hopefully the next one will look like my side of the family, but I wouldn't count on it. The Luckadeau genes are stronger than super glue. Anyway, Katy Scarlett was already born and Beau had no idea he had a child when I ran into him again. I had no idea he was living on the ranch next to my grandparents up near Ardmore, Oklahoma. It sure was a mixed-up summer. We'll swap details sometime when it's quieter. So what's your story?"

"I got off the bus in Wichita Falls and sat down beside Nellie. Half an hour later I was driving her home and working for her. That was a week ago."

"Be careful. Those Luckadeau men have a lot of charm."

"Slade hates me and has a girlfriend," Jane said. "And honey, it would take more charm than he's got to get me to fall for another man. I'm not so sure there's enough charm in the world for that."

Milli laughed again. "Been in that spot, so I can sympathize with you. Someday we really will find a corner and exchange stories. Looks like Katy Scarlett is giving her daddy fits. I'd better go rescue him."

Jane continued to keep an eye on the punch bowl set up beside the cake on the dessert table. She'd filled it five times already and it was down to no more than a cupful. She went to the kitchen and picked up another half-gallon jug of semi-frozen slush and a two-liter bottle of cold ginger ale.

She'd chosen her best pair of worn jeans and tucked in a chambray shirt. She'd cleaned her Nikes and did the best she could with her hair. It was all she could do without a curling iron and shopping and she doubted a hundred dollars would buy much in the way of finery, anyway. Besides, when Nellie said they were having a little family get-together for her seventy-fifth birthday, she hadn't expected every blue-eyed blond in the state of Texas and half those in Louisiana and Oklahoma to show up. She'd cooked a sugar-cured ham and made a large pan of hash brown casserole. Slade had said he was taking care of the cake so she hadn't made dessert. Thank goodness she'd made a triple batch of punch, thinking she'd keep extra in the freezer for later.

Ellen was first in line with her punch cup. "I'm so glad you hired on, honey. Nellie is ten years younger since you got here. And tell me—what is your secret ingredient in this punch? I could swear it has a bit of liquor in it."

"Almond extract. Two ounces for a gallon which makes two gallons when you add the ginger ale," Jane whispered conspiratorially.

"Well, I'll be damned. Almond? Would have never thought of it, but it does taste a bit like Amaretto. You'll have to make it again while I'm here. Nellie and I'll drink it for our afternoon tea instead of lemonade."

"I'd be glad to," Jane said.

"It's wonderful with that cake. Cuts the sweet." She carefully carried the cups back, mincing her steps to keep from spilling a single drop.

"She's an old hippy," Kristy said from behind her. "I heard she was the first one to burn her bra. She's younger than Granny and has always been the black sheep of the family. It's said she's had more lovers than a real hooker."

"Oh?" Jane finished the job and headed back to the house.

Kristy followed and looked down on Jane, who barely came up to her shoulder. There was no way the woman who'd caused her sleepless nights for a whole week could win a fight with a seasoned fighter, and Kristy held the Montague County trophy for verbal as well as real cat fights.

"You and I need to talk."

"About what?" Jane asked.

"Slade. I'll only say this once then I'll come at you with something more than words. Stay away from him. I intend to marry that man."

"Honey, you can have the man. I damn sure don't want him."

"Why not? You're nothing but a hired hand. Why wouldn't you want him? Besides, if you don't want him, why are you here?"

Slade slipped up behind Kristy and kissed her on the neck.

He shot Jane a mean look. "What's going on?" he asked.

Kristy gave Jane a you-are-informed-and-you-better-listen look, turned around and put her hands on his chest. "We were just talking about the recipe for this punch. It's got a lot of power for just punch, doesn't it sweetheart? Have you seen the girls? They were headed for the barn to see the kittens last time I caught a glimpse of them."

Kristy was decked out in skin-tight designer jeans that emphasized her wide hips and thick waist; a halter top made of eyelet lace that let her tanning bed skin show through the little holes right along with a back roll of cellulite begging to be released from a tight bra; high heeled shoes, and lots of chunky gold jewelry. Her dark hair was piled up on top of her hair in a style that was meant to look casual but had at least half a can of hair spray applied to keep every curl in place.

She'd certainly wasted nothing to look good but any fool could see when she looked at Slade she saw dollar signs. Poor old Slade; bless his heart. If Jane hadn't sworn off all men she might feel sorry for him, even though he had been a pain in the ass the whole previous week.

Slade kissed her on the cheek. "Come meet my cousin Griffin. You were saying that to be a Luckadeau you have to have blond hair—wait until you see him. He's got black hair with a natural white streak in it. His little girl has been playing with your daughters."

"Oh, my, I figured that child had something bad wrong with her and her hair grew back all crazy," Kristy whispered.

"Nope, born that way. Griff inherited it from his mother. His sister is as blonde as the rest of the Luckadeau clan."

Jane looked out the window. Only two pieces of cake remained. The punch bowl was half full. People were gathered in groups from two to ten and kids ran every which way. It was the very kind of family gathering she'd always imagined she would love and here she was in the midst of it feeling as out of place as a hooker on the front row of a holiness tent revival meeting.

"So this is how the hired help feels," she mumbled as she made her way into the den and flopped down in a recliner.

She leaned her head back and shut her eyes. Today she was supposed to be in Cancun on her honeymoon. John had offered her a choice of anywhere in the world she would like to go. Exotic places. Mountain tops. Italy. France. Remote islands. But she'd opted for a suite in a beachside hotel in Cancun. Later they'd vacation and see the world. She had wanted beach, sun, water, wine, and romantic evenings for their two-week honeymoon.

Instead of choosing just the right sundress from her extensive trousseau for dinner, she'd gotten up that morning and had a choice between three pairs of faded jeans. Why couldn't she at least have thought to bring a few decent things when she packed?

"Because..." she muttered as she finally allowed the memories of that horrible day to flood into her mind.

❖ ❖ ❖

It had been a glorious day at the ranch. The wedding planner was crazy with last-minute details. Her step-father, Paul, was very supportive and attentive. John, the tall, dark and very, very handsome groom, was off making millions of dollars and setting everything in order at his business so he could be away for two weeks. There was the bridesmaids' luncheon and then the manicurists arrived to do mani-pedis on everyone. After that, there was the last fitting of the dress, a custom creation she'd had made locally from a picture on a romance book she'd kept stashed in her file cabinet since she was sixteen.

Then boom, it was time for the rehearsal. The yard had been transformed into something from *Brides* magazine. Celia walked down the aisle on John's arm and pretended to be the bride. After all, Jane wasn't taking any chances with bad luck. They went through the basic ceremony three times, finishing just in time to pile into the limos to take them to the rehearsal dinner at the conference center in Greenville.

John's sister, Ramona, was serving as best man and the jokes centered around her not looking anything like John—or a best man. She was a tall redhead with no freckles and a lithe figure that looked wonderful in the shimmery silver silk dress Jane had chosen for her. Jane had asked her to serve as one of the bridesmaids, but John had insisted she stand on his side, since she was the only family he had left. She'd jokingly said she'd wear a pink tux but they'd all finally agreed that she would wear a dress identical to those chosen for the bridesmaids.

❖ ❖ ❖

Jane's reminiscing stopped cold and she opened her eyes when someone came through the back door. Ellen waved, her gypsy skirt swishing around her ankles as she headed toward the bathroom.

"Too much punch. It packs a wallop, all right, but in the bladder instead of the brain," she teased.

Jane smiled and shut her eyes again, trying to get away from the most horrible day of her entire life by thinking about grocery lists or the recipe for potato chowder or even doing laundry. It didn't work. Her mind was determined to play out every painful memory.

"So be it. Let's get it over with. And then I'm not thinking about it again," she mumbled.

"What?" A thin little voice came from her elbow.

She sat up so fast, her head swam for a minute.

"Who are you talkin' to?" The little girl asked.

"Myself. Why aren't you outside playing with the other children?" Jane asked.

The child was hauntingly beautiful, with the clearest blue eyes Jane had ever seen. A pure white forelock at the front of her otherwise jet-black hair looked like a dollop of whipped cream on a chocolate cake.

"My name is Lizzy and I don't want to play with those two girls. They called me a skunk."

"Who did?"

"One of them is Kayla and the other one is Keely but they aren't twins. I asked them. Their mommy is Kristy."

"Did you tell your mommy that they were being rude?"

"I don't have a mommy but I told my daddy and he said to renore them."

Jane smiled. "Well, that's what I'd do. I'd just renore them the whole rest of the day and find someone else to play with me."

Lizzy smiled brightly. "Okay. I'll go find Tim and Richie. Sometimes I get tired of playing with boys, but at least they don't call me names."

She took off in a dead run out the back door yelling for Richie the whole way. Jane leaned back again and for a split second wished she was Lizzy's mother. Then she would have a good reason to go snatch Kristy bald-headed for raising her daughters to be as rude as she was.

The minute she shut her eyes, the incident with Lizzy faded and she was right back in the middle of the memories.

The toasts had been made, with John giving the longest one declaring that he'd been a self-proclaimed bachelor and never intended to marry until he met Ellacyn Jane Hayes. He must have liked the sound of his own voice because he talked a long time about how they'd met when he walked into the Ranger Oil Company to convince them to purchase a piece of art from a recent collection he'd acquired, only to find true love instead of a sale.

She remembered every word verbatim of his toast to her but it was only as she relived it on a ranch in Ringgold, Texas that she also realized that he hadn't looked at her while he talked. Rather he'd made eye contact with the guests and his sister.

"Sorry bastard," she whispered.

"That's a dirty word," Lizzy whispered back from the other side of the chair where she was rolled up into a ball, her blue eyes the only thing visible from the shadows.

"It just slipped out," Jane said.

"Sometimes a dirty word just slips out of my mouth, too," she whispered.

Jane cocked her head to one side and raised an eyebrow.

"That's the way Daddy looks at me when he's going to give me a talking to."

Jane giggled. She didn't mean to, but she couldn't keep it in. It was the first time she'd laughed in a week and it felt so good she didn't want to stop. "You are funny, Lizzy. Want to be my friend?"

"I don't want to be Kayla and Keely's friend. Or Tim and Richie's neither. They all ran away and told me I can't play with them. Kayla said Tim is her new boyfriend. Yuk! She's crazy. Boyfriends are for big girls, not little girls like us. My daddy said so."

Jane tried to put on her serious adult face. "Your daddy is right."

"I might be your friend if you don't tell them I'm hiding from them."

"It's a deal."

Kayla, a freckle-faced, brown-haired child, yelled from the back door. "Hey, maid lady, have you seen Lizzy? She's got hair like a skunk and we can't find her."

Jane dropped her hand down beside the chair and Lizzy grabbed it. "Why are you looking for her?"

"Because..." Kayla searched for a lie.

"Because she was mean to us and we told our mother and she's going to tell Slade and he's going to tell her daddy and she's going to be in big trouble," Keely gushed.

"What did she do that was so mean?" Jane asked.

"She…" Kayla started again.

"She took our friends away from us and said if they were her friends they couldn't be ours." Keely was evidently much more experienced at the game than her younger sister.

"Are you sure she said that to you, or did you say that to her?"

Kristy walked up behind the girls. "What is going on? I told you to go play and here you are pestering the maid."

"We're hunting for Lizzy. Remember Mommy, we told you she was a mean little girl who looks like a skunk. Her daddy looks like one too, and I bet her mother does too. She's weird and we don't want to play with her but we have to find her even if she's not our friend. What if she went off somewhere and died like a skunk on the road?" Keely said.

Lizzy squeezed Jane's hand.

"That isn't nice to call Lizzy that name. I think her hair is beautiful. It's like she's been kissed by the leprechauns and that's really a lucky streak in her hair. I bet wherever she goes she brings good luck to her friends. Maybe she ran off to play with Tim and…" Jane couldn't remember the other name.

"Richie," Lizzy barely whispered.

"Richie," Jane said. "They probably are hunting for a black kettle of gold, which only a little girl with a white streak in her hair can find."

Kristy grabbed each of them by an arm. "Come on, you two. I don't have time to listen to nonsense from the hired help. Go play with someone else and stay out of my hair. One more ounce of trouble out of you and you'll wish you'd been good. I'll take away your television, video games, and the trampoline for a month. You'd better listen to me. If you embarrass me in front of Slade again, you'll be washing dishes until your hands wither up like prunes." She was still hissing out threats when her voice faded and blended in with the buzz of the rest of the party.

Lizzy poked her head up over the edge of the chair. "I don't want a mommy after all. I thought I did, but that lady scares me. I feel sorry for Kayla and Keely even if they are sorry bastards."

Jane covered her mouth but it didn't stop the laughter.

"What's so funny?" A little snaggle-toothed boy asked as he made his way through the breakfast nook and into the den. "Hi, Lizzy. Kayla said you could help us find a pot of gold. She said because of the white in your hair you are special and you can find gold. Want to go on a treasure hunt with us?"

Lizzy grinned. "Where's Richie?"

Tim hung his head. "He's keeping Kayla and Keely out there. I'm supposed to beg you to play with us. He says you might if I ask."

Suddenly the little girl who'd been the ugly duckling had a use. Weren't kids a total hoot? She wanted a dozen of them, starting with a little girl exactly like Lizzy. She wouldn't even care if she had a white streak in her hair.

"Okay, but no more calling me names," Lizzy said.

Tim crossed his heart with his fingers and held up two in a serious gesture. "We promise."

"I'm sorry you all don't have a lucky streak and I can't promise there's a pot of gold out there. Sometimes the little elves hide it on a ranch and sometimes in a castle, but I'll help you hunt for it if you don't be mean to me," Lizzy said.

"Okay," Tim grinned.

Lizzy hugged Jane tightly. "You really are my friend."

"Thank you," Jane said past the lump in her throat.

They ran off to play and she shut her eyes again but kept her ears acutely aware of anyone else sneaking in to hide beside the recliner. The memories started again like a movie that had been put on pause.

John had finished his speech. Before his fanny hit the chair, Ramona was on her feet with a raised glass. She began by telling how fortunate she'd been to have John look after her when their parents died and how much it meant to her to finally see him happy. She accredited Ellacyn for the glow in his eyes and hoped that she'd always be a part of their lives.

"Yeah, right," Jane said and promptly popped her eyes open to see if there was a child right beside her. "Lousy bitch," she said when she knew the coast was clear.

The memories went on.

John danced with her all evening, whispering the sweetest and also the sexiest things in her ear the whole time. She wore a cotton halter sundress with big red roses on a white background and red high heeled shoes.

He told her that she was the single rose in his vase of life and he would cherish her until death parted them.

He was speaking the gospel truth and that's exactly what would have happened in Cancun if she hadn't been in the wrong place at the right time. She couldn't sleep that night. Excitement from the whole day and anxiety for the up and coming one combined to keep her wide awake. At two o'clock in the morning, she finally tiptoed to the kitchen for a glass of milk and a handful of cookies.

Those in hand, she carefully slid open the door to the deck and slipped out to the far corner to look at the full moon. At that same time tomorrow she would be in the bridal suite of the hotel in Jackson for the first night of her life as John's bride. The next morning they'd fly to Cancun. If she didn't stop thinking about it all, she would have bags under her eyes for her wedding.

That's when she heard the voices from the other side of the hedge surrounding the deck. Whispers, actually, with a few panting moans thrown in. Surely Celia and that groomsman who'd been flirting all day weren't actually having a midnight rendezvous on the grass. Not when Celia had a king-sized bed in the room she used at the ranch.

"Oh, Jonathan, darling, I can't bear to think of you with her."

That got Jane's attention in a hurry and she dropped down on her knees on the deck, pushed the hedge back enough to create a peep hole, and saw John and his sister making out, right there before her eyes.

"I hate this as much as you do, darlin', but just remember the whole time I'm with her I'll be thinking of you and that wonderful life insurance policy. I promise I'll try to get out of it but remember, even if I do sleep with her, it's only sex and it's worth a million bucks," he said.

She laid her head on his shoulder and sighed. "Knowing that is the only thing that keeps me sane."

"Don't think about it. Once this job is over, what do we do next?"

"You get to play my husband in Germany. I need a good cover to get in close to a couple. We'll get ten times what Paul is paying us to create an accident for Ellacyn. You were a genius to think of the insurance policy. We might do that again if I can get past the idea of you sleeping with another woman."

"She is a pretty little thing and it hasn't been hard to pretend to fall in love with her. Paul has no idea that I'm the hired gun. That's the beauty of it. He knows the accident will happen in Cancun and he'll pay the other half when it does. She'll be dead before her twenty-fifth birthday and that puts the oil company totally in his name. He'll own it all and he can play the heartsick stepfather. We'll console each other. And he'll never know he paid me to be the grieving widower."

"Isn't that double dipping?" Ramona asked.

"Yes, it is. Genius, isn't it? But we both get what we want. He gets a dead daughter. I get a dead wife. He gets a company. I get to collect on the life insurance I insisted on buying for each of us. She's my beneficiary and I am hers. The minute we say 'I do' they go into effect. Everyone gets what they want and everyone feels sorry for us."

"I don't feel sorry for you," she said.

"Yes, you do. I'm sleeping with someone other than you and pretending to enjoy it. You have to feel sorry for me for doing such a sweet little deed."

"I won't be there, so let's go over it again. No way it can be a suicide?"

"I've got it under control. There's no way there will ever be a question to void that insurance. She's going to drown very accidentally." And he went on to tell her every detail of the scuba diving accident that could never be traced back to him.

Jane's blood ran as cold in Ringgold, Texas at the Double L Ranch as it had that night. She couldn't believe what she'd heard and for a while she had almost convinced herself she had just had a horrible, horrible nightmare.

But after blinking a dozen times and seeing her groom removing the woman's bra and kissing her so passionately it left no doubt that she was most certainly not his sister, Jane faced the cold hard truth.

She'd been duped; not only by her fiancé but also by her stepfather, Paul. The oil company was hers by inheritance. It had belonged to her great-grandfather, passed down to her grandmother and then to her mother. Paul had been the CEO when her father was living and as she sat there in the den, replaying the events of her life, she wondered what had really caused her father's private plane to crash when she was a little girl.

The next step had been getting back into the house without alerting John and his cohort. It had taken forever for her to quietly gather her glass and check for cookie crumbs. She had eased inside even more quietly than she'd gone out and had gone straight to her room.

Without turning on a light, she had packed, written John an email in the dark, sent another one to Celia, and before daybreak been in her car on the way to the Jackson airport.

She'd lived in mortal fear that John would be waiting at every bus stop and had spent most of the next day and a half looking over her shoulder. She'd be twenty-five in six weeks and the company held in trust until that time would be hers on her birthday. At that point, Paul would be at her mercy—if she could survive. She had no innocent illusions that John would stop looking for her or that Paul would call off the contract on her life. She was worth far more dead than alive and until midnight of the eve of her birthday, they'd turn over every single rock searching.

A hand touched her arm. In that moment, she expected to look up and see either Ramona—or whatever the hell her name really was—or John, but instead found herself gazing into the eyes of Lizzy again.

"Are you really my friend?"

"Yes, I am," Jane said.

"Well then, would you play with me?"

"I sure will. Shall we take a walk and find a pot of gold?"

Lizzy's chin quivered. "They said I wasn't magic because I didn't find it fast enough. They said I was a skunk after all and they held their noses and ran away from me."

Jane came up out of the chair in an angry flash and took her hand. "I think they are wrong. Let's me and you go hunt for it and when we find it, we won't even tell them."

They played a game of hiding from everyone as Jane suggested next moves until they reached the barn. Behind this tree. Over to that rose bush. Under the fence so fast no one could see them. Now behind the barn doors. Once inside she listened carefully and put a finger over her lips to keep Lizzy quiet.

"The rainbow comes first. We have to see the rainbow because it leads to the pot of gold that only you can find because you are special and have a lucky streak in your hair. Now be very quiet and shut your eyes tightly and imagine a rainbow of purple and blue and yellow and pink. Can you see it?"

Lizzy's nose as well as her eyes puckered up. "I can see it in my head," she whispered.

"Okay, now what do you hear?"

She grinned. "Baby kittens?"

"Where is Lizzy?" Griffin Luckadeau asked Tim and Richie.

"She ran away because…"

"Where did she go?"

Griffin was beginning to get that prickly feeling on the back of his neck. Something was very, very wrong.

"I asked you boys to tell me where she went."

"She and the maid went sneaking off. We went to find her in the house because that's where she went the first time she ran off and then we saw her and the maid running away. The maid was playing a game with her and they were hiding," Richie said.

"Yeah, and the maid told us a lie. She said that Lizzy's hair was a lucky streak and she could find a pot of gold with it but she can't. She's just a..." Keely stopped in the middle of a breath.

"A what?" Griffin asked.

"They said she was a skunk, but we didn't say it," Tim said.

Keely pointed a finger at them. "Yes, you did. You said it first."

"Where did the maid take her?" Griffin asked.

"To find the gold but she's just a crazy old maid 'cause there ain't no gold," Keely said.

Griffin hopped up on a picnic table and yelled. "Everyone, Lizzy has gone missing. The kids say she was with the maid. Anyone seen her?"

"I think they went to the barn," Slade said. "Come on, I'll go with you."

"But Slade, darlin'," Kristy said.

"I'll be right back," he said.

"I hope she doesn't hurt the child. Who knows what she was before she came here? She was probably a child molester or a kidnapper. Maybe that's why she wanted a job here, so she could kidnap one of our kids for the ransom," Kristy said loudly enough for everyone to hear.

"And you are full of shit," Ellen said. "That girl wouldn't hurt a fire ant."

Kristy glared at her.

The two men started off in a trot toward the barn.

"Lizzy!" Griffin called out from the door.

"Shhhh," he heard her over behind a stack of square hay bales.

He and Slade practically tripped over each other's feet getting around the corner of the bales only to find Jane and Lizzy facing each other with a litter of yellow and white kittens between them.

"I found the gold, Daddy," Lizzy whispered.

"What?"

"Jane is my friend. She is playing with me because I have a lucky streak and no one else wants to play with me. Kayla and Keely said I was a skunk and that I stink, so Jane and me went hunting the rainbow where the gold is and we found it. Jane says that gold isn't always money. This time it was yellow kittens. Ain't they cute, Daddy? Look at this one. It's all furry."

Griffin sat down beside his daughter, heaved a sigh of relief, and began to pet the kittens in her lap. "I'm glad to make your acquaintance, Jane. Any friend of Lizzy's is a friend of mine. Thank you for helping her *find* the gold."

Slade wanted to slap his cousin or strangle Jane. Everyone thought she was the sweetest woman in the world—even his cousin, who had no time for women since his wife ran off and left him with a baby to raise. But he knew different. She was playing a game for some reason, and by damn he'd find out what it was, or else.

"I'm sorry those kids were rude to you. I'm going to tell Tim and Richie's mom and I bet they won't act like that again," Griffin said.

"Neither will Kayla or Keely," Slade said.

"Yes, they will. Their momma said they'd have to wash dishes for a month and all kinds of other things if they made you mad, but they said they would call me a skunk forever because they don't like me. It's all right,

Uncle Slade. They can't help it if they are sorry bastards. Their momma is just as mean as they are."

"Lizzy!" Griffin exclaimed.

Jane laughed aloud.

"Sorry Daddy. It just slipped out."

Slade set his jaw. "I can't imagine Kristy's little girls saying such a thing."

"Monkey see, monkey do," Jane said.

"Don't you have things to do in the house?" Slade growled.

Jane slid the two kittens she was holding into Lizzy's lap and stood up slowly. She saluted Slade smartly. "Sir, yes, sir. I'll get right in there and do my work, sir, just as you say, sir."

Chapter 3

JANE HAD NEVER HAD A SINGLE ARGUMENT WITH JOHN. FROM the time he'd walked into her office at the oil company until the day she'd walked out on the marriage, he had been attentive, kind, considerate, and generous with his time and finances. Of course he'd had an ulterior motive, but all the same she'd never fought with him.

Now it was the exact opposite side of life. Every single morning she awoke wondering how long it would be before she and Slade began slinging verbal mud at each other. They broke the record the day after the birthday party. The argument started before his hind end hit the kitchen chair for breakfast.

"What you drug home sure ruined your party yesterday, didn't it, Granny? I told you she was bad news."

"Pass the eggs and quit your bitchin', Slade Luckadeau," Ellen said.

"I'm stating fact."

"You are angry and taking it out on Jane, who did nothing wrong. You're going to have your hands full with those little demons Kristy is raising if you decide to stay with her. I always wanted a daughter or a granddaughter, but God was probably looking out for me. If He'd have given me two kids like that, I'd have sold them into slavery. Thank God I got three boys," Nellie said.

"They're just little girls. They need a father," Slade said.

"They are clones of their mother," Nellie said.

"Kristy is not childish. They were just playing kid pranks. Griffin and Andy and I used to play tricks on each other when we were kids."

"Tricks are one thing. Mean is another," Ellen said.

"Lizzy is just a little girl who needs a mother, and she doesn't act like that," Jane said.

Slade pointed at her. "You don't have a say in this."

Jane's brown eyes danced as she slapped at the air around his finger. "Don't you point that thing at me. Since I was the culprit who was accused of kidnapping and perhaps even child molestation, I will take a say whether I have one or not. Your argument isn't valid. Those little girls are merely mimicking their mother's actions. They see her act ugly and they act the same way."

Nellie and Ellen both stopped eating and waited.

"You are wrong and I'll prove it."

"How? By asking her to marry you so you can spend the rest of your life trying to fix her mess? Go right on ahead and do it. Cut off your nose to spite your face. Now if you'll send the biscuits to this end of the table, I would appreciate it," Jane said.

He passed the bread basket and then the gravy and watched her routine. One biscuit cut open and covered with sausage gravy. One cut open and filled with butter, then with a fine sprinkling of sugar and black pepper when she got ready to eat it. It was the very same every morning without change.

"Thank you," she said.

"I'm not ready to get married and if I were it wouldn't be because you goaded me into it with your smartass remarks," he said.

"Don't call me a smartass. That would be the pot calling the kettle black," she said.

"Hey, anyone who puts sugar and pepper on their biscuit instead of honey or jelly has to be a smartass or a dumb ass. You choose."

"My grandmother came through the depression. She learned all kinds of tricks. One is sweetening the breakfast biscuits with sugar and pepper. Don't knock it until you've tried it."

He opened the biscuit he'd already buttered and followed her lead, expecting to gag on such a concoction. Surprisingly, it wasn't half bad. Couldn't hold a candle to homemade plum jam, but it wasn't disgusting.

"So?" she asked.

"I'm adult enough to admit that it might have worked during the depression, just like all kinds of substitutes for coffee did during the Civil War, but if there's jelly I wouldn't use it," he said.

"Fair enough. Now what's on our agenda today, ladies?" she asked Nellie and Ellen.

"We're going to cook dinner like always. Fried chicken and the works. Then afterwards I've got a doctor's appointment in Nocona and while we're going that way, we thought maybe you'd drive us on over to Gainesville to the outlet mall so we could do a little shopping. Ellen doesn't have nearly enough clothes," Nellie rolled her eyes toward the ceiling.

Ellen put up her hands. "One of my three weaknesses. Clothing. Good-looking men. Fast cars."

Slade rolled his eyes. "You are both—"

"Old women? Of course we're old, son. But we ain't dead. When I die I'm going to slide into heaven on Nellie's coattails a-screamin', 'open the doors and let me in. I've used up every bit of my strength livin' and lovin' every minute of it.' And I'll go out knowin' I didn't waste a single minute. I'm going to wear fancy clothes and chase men right up until they put me six feet under. I'd drive fast cars, but you know that story."

Nellie finished breakfast and sipped at the last of her coffee. "Lord, yes, I know that story."

"Don't we all," Slade said, glad to be in on an inside story that Jane had no part of.

"I don't," Jane said.

"You tell her, Slade, while we wash up the dishes. Go on with him out to the barn and he'll tell you all about his wild aunt. We'll get the potatoes peeled for potato salad, and you can make it when you get back," Nellie said.

Ellen pushed back a strand of dyed red hair, the gray roots beginning to show, and grinned at Jane. "I'm not wild. I just don't let inhibitions rob me of life. You two get on out of here. Enjoy a little free time. Watch Slade do some work. Maybe he'll even let you ride one of those horses. Of course, I'd rather drive a Corvette down a Texas highway. And don't worry about dinner fixin's. I can cook as well as I can drink and honey, that's damn good."

"Jane can't ride," Slade said.

Jane looked right at him. "Want to place a side bet on that?"

"Twenty dollars says you can't saddle up a horse. Fifty says you'll be begging to be taken back to the bus station by noon if you ride all morning. I'm riding fence today to make sure everything is still tight. You really want to bet with me?"

"You're on if the ladies can put dinner on the table by themselves," she said.

"Oh, honey, we work together in a kitchen just fine. You run along and ride the fence with Slade. Just don't either one of you kill the other," Ellen said.

He combed his blond hair back out of his eyes with his fingertips and picked a straw hat from the hooks beside the back door. He motioned toward the others. "Take your pick. You'll burn without a hat."

"Mine is the old weathered one with a red bandana hatband," Nellie said. "You are welcome to it."

Jane settled it on her head and followed him out the back door. It had been months since she'd ridden, but she was no stranger to it.

When she was eighteen she'd gone away to college. For the next five years she'd studied hard, partied a little, loved a few good men. Then she came home and went to work at the oil company. Paul had an apartment on the top floor of the building, so he seldom came home to the ranch. She drove ten miles to work in the morning, put in a twelve-hour-plus day, and drove home. There was little time except on Sundays for riding and she seldom visited the stables, so it had been a while, but by golly she could still saddle a horse and ride all morning.

"Molly or Demon?" he asked when they reached the horse barn.

"Names any indication of what they'll do?"

"Molly is mean as sin. Demon is a bucker. I intend to win the bet."

"Who are you riding?"

"Oh, no, you can't have Blister. He's been my horse for ten years. I don't share."

"Didn't ask you to share. I'll take Demon."

He nodded toward a saddle and she was scarcely less than a minute behind him in the unspoken race.

"I guess you have saddled up a few times, but I still don't think you can keep up with me all morning. If I'd thought of this before, you'd already be on your way to Wichita Falls," he said begrudgingly.

"Twenty down. Fifty to go. I need the seventy dollars. I'll stay with you and I don't whine. Hell couldn't keep my ass from sticking to this horse until dinnertime."

They had barely cleared the barn doors when Demon reared up on his hind feet and tried to toss the weight on his back across the county line. Jane was not prepared for it but she hung on until he came back down, reined in tight, and leaned down to talk to the animal.

"If you do that again, you sorry bastard, I'll shoot you between the eyes and feed your carcass to the coyotes. That is a fact, not a threat, so you *will* behave."

"Think you are a horse whisperer, do you?"

"Not me. He almost bucked me over the house. I'm surprised I could even hang on. I should have listened to you and ridden Molly."

That took him aback but he kept his silence.

"So you are supposed to tell me this big story. That's the whole reason I'm here and not in the kitchen," she said.

"What kind of job did you have last?" he asked.

"What do you think?"

"I think you were a cook in a restaurant. Not a burger joint but maybe Cracker Barrel or Applebee's. If you were a rich person you wouldn't be here doing this kind of work for less than minimum wage. You're poor and you are running from something or someone. How old are you, anyway?"

"How old do you think I am?"

"Nineteen on a good day. Twenty on a bad one."

"Thank you. Do I really look that young?"

"If you are a day over twenty-one and can prove it, I'll double our bet," he said.

"I'm twenty-four and that's admitting a lot. Ladies don't usually tell their age. We are allowed to lie about our age by five years and our weight by twenty pounds without going to hell. And I don't have to prove shit to you, so we'll keep the bet where it stands."

He actually chuckled. "Aunt Ellen would say the age by twenty years and the weight was nobody's damn business."

"She's a good woman. Now tell me this story about why she doesn't drive."

He sat the saddle well—tall and handsome. His blond hair curled up on his shirt collar and covered half his ears. His blue eyes were shaded beneath the hat but Jane had no illusions that they would be looking at her nicely. No sir, if she could see them, they would be shooting darts at her main arteries.

She couldn't imagine John riding a horse. Not in his custom-made, Italian silk suits. She sure couldn't see him in scuffed up old cowboy boots or spurs. Or her stepfather, either. They were cut from the same mold. If Slade wanted to see con men up close and personal, he should meet those two.

Jane's mother, Susan, had been the ultimate rancher. They'd lived in town until her paternal grandparents had died and left them the horse ranch. Her father had hated ranching and loved the oil business, but Susan had found her soul on the ranch. She was the one who'd dressed in faded jeans and scuffed up cowboy boots. She was the one who'd taught Jane everything from the ground up. She'd always said that someday Jane might find herself in a situation where she'd need to know how to do things for herself and not depend on anyone else. Until that moment, Jane hadn't realized that her mother was a prophet.

"So?" she finally prompted.

"Okay, about five years ago Aunt Ellen had a boyfriend. One of a long line of many boyfriends. She's somewhere around sixty-nine now—no one knows exactly how old she really is. She's even made Granny promise to lie on her obit when she dies. Her feller drove this vintage 1964 Corvette. She loves 'Vettes and speed in a convertible is the most wonderful thing in the world to her. She used to own an old Caddy and she'd drive it like a bat set loose from the bowels of hell. She'd get a wild hair in her under britches and here she'd come to our house to visit. It was always a party for me, because she was so unpredictable. She and that old Caddy might take me and Granny to Six Flags or over to Wichita Falls to a hockey game. One thing for sure, she never sat still or drove slow. Only trouble was, she likes her booze almost as well as fast cars and good-looking gentlemen. She got caught one damn time too many out drinking and driving under the influence and they took her license away for good."

"That can't be the whole story."

"No, remember now she's with her feller in his car. A vintage 'Vette. He gets out at a service station to go to the men's room and Aunt Ellen, who has done a major amount of damage to a fifth of Jack Daniels whiskey, decides to pull a practical joke on him and drive away. She got about half a mile down the road when she lost control on a patch of gravel. It threw her out and they had to peel the car from around a tree."

Jane laughed aloud. "Please tell me she wasn't hurt."

"Not even a broken bone. Wouldn't have even messed up her makeup if she hadn't landed in a cattle pond. She came up sputtering and spitting filthy water and cussin' about getting mud and cow manure on her new boots. The owner of the car had called the police and reported his vehicle stolen and his girlfriend kidnapped. When they arrived a few minutes later, she was sitting beside the car with what was left of the bottle of Jack in her hands. She did offer them a drink for coming to her aid."

Jane laughed even harder.

"It wasn't so funny back then. She was drunk and had no driver's license. She spent the night in the county jail and called Granny when they let her get to a phone. Granny paid the fines, for the car and the whole shebang. Ellen was hungover but she found the energy to flirt with the judge. She still bitches because he never called her, even though she left her phone number on the table right in front of him. So now she has to rely on busses or taxis. When she comes over here, I take them wherever they want to go."

"Why doesn't she just move here?"

"Because the men aren't as plentiful."

Jane got another case of giggles and a severe bout of hiccups. Slade passed a canteen full of water to her. "Ten sips without taking a breath."

"Sounds like my grandmother's advice."

"What was her name?"

She'd gotten so relaxed that she almost spit it out before she clamped her mouth shut. One minute in front of the computer and he'd have enough information about her family to cause a major catastrophe.

"Guess," she said.

"One thing I know is it wasn't or isn't Day. That's not your real name any more than Jane is. A couple of times it's taken you too long to respond when someone calls your name," he said.

Astute little cowboy, ain't you? she thought.

"Maybe I didn't hear them. What do you think my name is?" she asked.

"I wouldn't have any idea but I'm a damn good judge of a person, so I know Jane is not your name," he said.

"Then by all means, entertain me with your version of who and what I am," she said.

"Gladly," he nodded. "You have worked around wealthy people and you've picked up a few of their mannerisms. The way you hold your fork and put your knife just so on the plate after you use it. The way you dab your mouth with your napkin rather than wiping at it like a field hand. Little things like that tell me you've been around moneyed people. But you have limited clothing and were riding a bus, which tells me you grabbed what you had and ran away from someone. You didn't have a vehicle and you were traveling the cheapest way possible. You took a job for low pay, so you have no money."

"My, oh my, you are a genius, Slade Luckadeau."

"Now tell me how you are in trouble," he said.

"Me, in trouble? You're the one fixing to marry a shrew with two little clones of herself. I'd say you're the one in trouble."

"I'm not marrying Kristy and she is not a shrew and how could you say that about two innocent little girls?" He raised his voice loud enough that two buzzards left their armadillo breakfast and took to the nearest pecan tree.

"You don't have to yell," she said.

"You'd provoke Jesus, Himself," he declared.

"Probably. Fence is busted or cut. Third wire from the bottom. Looks like someone might have cut it to slip through. You going to fight with me or fix it—or do I need to show you how to stretch barbed wire to win the bets?" she said, changing the subject.

She made him pay up what he owed her before they left the barn to go to dinner. Seventy extra dollars that she'd not counted on meant she could buy a dress and maybe even a pair of cheap sandals. Not that she was planning on a date, but she'd proven in the past week and a half that anything was possible. Maybe that handsome, dark-haired Griffin Luckadeau would come around and ask her out.

"Great God in Heaven!" she exclaimed.

"Yes He is and yes He does live there," Ellen said from the doorway into her bedroom.

"I just had a far-fetched idea that caught me by surprise," Jane admitted.

"Happens more and more as you get older. Even when I'm sober, I get these crazy notions that have me wondering if I'm sane."

Nellie appeared from her bedroom and caught the tail end of the conversation. "It's a female thing. We're able to do what Oprah calls multi-tasking. Some folks think that's just a physical thing. Like cooking beans and a cake at the same time. It's also a mental thing. Like putting on our jewelry and figuring out how to talk your sister out of some silly idea and suddenly remembering a verse out of the Bible that has nothing to do with either."

"Nellie Luckadeau, you are not talking me out of the Silver Saddle on Thursday and if you start quoting scripture, I will, too. Thou shalt not lie to thy sister."

They bickered back and forth, spouting off verses all the way to the pickup truck. Jane opened the back door of the club cab Silverado and both women crawled inside without missing a single beat. Nellie dug around in her worn, tooled-leather, saddle-shaped purse. She pulled out the keys and tossed them over the headrest into the front seat.

Jane had to hop up into the seat. She fastened her seat belt and started the engine.

"Bet this old tank won't do more than eighty, not even on a straight stretch," Ellen said.

"You will not goad her into driving fast," Nellie informed her sister.

"Don't know until you try," Ellen said. "It might have worked if you'd have been quiet. She's young and she probably likes speed and good-looking men, too. I'm surprised she wasn't out in the yard at the party staking a claim on one of those tall Texas Luckadeaus."

Color filled Jane's cheeks.

"And don't make her nervous so that she drives faster to get us there in a hurry to get away from your smart mouth," Nellie said.

"Wouldn't think of it. I just hope this doctor doesn't have a room full of squalling kids with snotty noses or take forever checking your blood pressure and pulling out some blood. I want to find a new outfit for the Silver Saddle on Thursday."

Jane reached the end of the lane and turned right. She drove through the small town of Ringgold, which was only a handful of houses sitting three or four miles from the Red River, and made another right-hand turn. The first sign said it was thirteen miles to Nocona. The land wasn't so very different from her part of the world in Mississippi—take away the pine trees and add mesquite, make the hills just a little more rolling.

"Is Amarillo like this?" She tried to steer the conversation away from whatever the Silver Saddle was and toward something less controversial.

"No, honey, it is not. It's flat and sandy and I love it. The sunsets are spectacular and the men are gorgeous. You should come on out there and stay with me and see for yourself. It's a haunting beauty. I'll pay you double what Nellie is giving you to come live with me and be my driver."

"Don't you be trying to steal her. I found her and she's mine," Nellie snapped.

"Oh, don't get your granny panties in a wad. I was only teasing. What do you mean you found her? I figured she was someone's kid you knew from around Nocona."

"I found her in the bus station after you left to go back to Amarillo."

"You picked up a stranger in a bus station and took her home? God Almighty, no wonder Slade is in a snit.

She could be a serial murderer or a suicide bomber. Are you on a holy mission to kill everyone in Ringgold?" Ellen leaned forward to stare at Jane.

"No ma'am, just needed a place to stay and a job," Jane said.

Nellie slapped the air beside her sister's arm. "Don't get your red silk thong in a wad. I know people better than you do when I meet them and besides, how many men have you picked up in bars and taken home with you? Any one of them might have been a serial murderer or a suicide bomber just waiting to level your place in Amarillo. I bet there's one casing the Silver Saddle right now, hoping you'll pick him up so he can put another notch on his walking cane."

Jane giggled.

"If you hear the bed springs on Thursday night you can put an extra plate on for Friday morning break-fast. *I'll* be carvin' an extra notch on the bedpost," Ellen said.

Jane suppressed her laughter. She had no idea if the bickering had turned to arguing or if they were still teasing. She had certainly never encountered two elderly women who acted like Nellie and Ellen. Nellie, with her chaste gray hair cut in a short, stylish do that took very little upkeep, usually wore jeans, T-shirts, and sneakers. Today she had on cute little blue capri-length pants with a matching knit shirt and sandals, but that was as dressed up as Jane had seen her.

Ellen's red hair had been ratted up into a big hairdo that took a ton of hair spray to keep in place. She wore bright red spandex capri pants with a loud, floral gauze shirt over a bright yellow tank top. Her yellow sandals laced around her thin legs and had neat little bows an inch below the hem of her pants.

"If I hear bed springs on Thursday night after we come home from the Silver Saddle, I'm not going to worry about it. They'll only be noisy five minutes, tops," Nellie finally said.

Jane bit the inside of her lip. Ellen had goaded her sister into admitting they were going to the Silver Saddle.

"Maybe so, but I'm damn good. In an hour they might squeak for another five minutes. What are you buying today to wear? Can I pick it out?"

"God, no. You are not going to start dressing me. I have a seeing problem, not Alzheimer's," Nellie said. "Turn right at the next street. It'll take you right back to the clinic and hospital."

"Then can I pick out your dance partners?" Ellen asked. "You might not see well enough to know which one is a homeless reject and which one is a rich oil man."

Jane had to admire the sister. She was digging in deeper and deeper until pretty soon Nellie would think the whole idea of going dancing at the Silver Saddle had been hers. Before it was all over, Nellie would probably let Ellen pick out a new outfit for the night. Jane parked the truck in a space close to the front door but before she could open the door for the ladies, they were already out and marching arm in arm toward the clinic—Nellie, the tall one in her conservative clothes; Ellen, a head shorter, in her Hollywood hooker outfit. Both of them giggled as they shared a story in whispers.

When they reached the door in the corridor, Nellie and Jane entered, while Ellen broke away and went to the ladies' room. Nellie went to the desk and checked in with the receptionist then joined Jane in the corner, where she'd chosen three seats.

"You're thinking I let her talk her way around Thursday night but just for the record, I didn't. Sometimes I let her win one just to keep things interesting. Besides, I had to get her off onto something else so she wouldn't drive you crazy with questions about why you were in a bus stop and who you really are," Nellie said.

"You're really good."

"Lots of experience. One time a baby kitten came up to my back door. Wild as Saturday night sin. Bit the fire out of me when I tried to pick it up. Took me six weeks to tame that critter with food and love. She's the mother of those kittens out in the barn. A good mouser. Wonderful pet. Good addition to the Double L. Just took a little persuasion to get her to see things the right way."

Jane cocked her head to one side and frowned.

"Think about it. It'll come to you when you least expect it. Kind of like a Bible verse when you're thinkin' on stranglin' your sister."

"I don't have a sister," Jane said without thinking.

Nellie smiled and patted her hand.

Ellen swept inside the waiting room. It wasn't so much an entrance as a force entering the room. "They haven't called you to go back there yet?"

A nurse opened a door and peeked out into the nearly empty room. "Nellie Luckadeau?"

Nellie followed her and Ellen took her chair.

"I worked that real good, didn't I? She didn't even see it coming. Now we're going dancing on Thursday night. She doesn't get out enough. Cooks for the crew on the ranch and devotes her life to Slade. He was a good boy, just like his daddy. That Thomas couldn't be beat. Was so smart it was scary—and good-lookin'?" Ellen fanned her face to put out the imaginary flames.

"He looked just like his daddy, Lester. Now there was a man who could have gone out to California and give them men movie stars a run for their money. If I'd been a little older, Nellie wouldn't have gotten him. If she hadn't been my sister I would have seduced him just to see if he was as good in bed as I imagined. Only difference was, Lester was smart when it come to women. He married Nellie and adored her right up to the day he died of a heart attack before he was even sixty. She raised Slade from the time he was eight and his sorry momma dropped him in her front yard. His momma, Terra, sends Slade a card on his birthday and Christmas and drops in to see him for a day a couple of times a year. Never spends the night. Nellie says it's awkward. Slade doesn't know what to do with her and Nellie wants to shoot her and throw her out on the back forty for the coyotes."

Jane wondered why Ellen was telling her so much. Was she expecting Jane to open up to her and share her story?

"Anyway, Slade's daddy had some of my blood, because he married that woman. He should've just had an affair with her and went on to the next hot little girly. But oh no, he had to marry her. I can't say much. I've had to marry for love four times. At least when I left the feller each time I came out a little richer instead of poorer. Poor old Thomas was about to go to the bankrupt court by the time Terra finished with him. If he hadn't died in that car wreck, they'd have been living on the streets or back at the ranch with Nellie, and Thomas hated that ranch with a passion. So does his brother, Robert. Robert lives down in southern Texas. He's got two sons, both of them blonds like the Luckadeaus, but they're adopted kids. Turned out Robert couldn't have kids because of a late dose of mumps. Those boys both hate the country as much as their father. Always have. It's a chore for them to come home for a weekend once or twice a year. Now Tim, he liked it but that's another story. Tim got killed in Vietnam and we still don't mention him in front of Nellie. Slade's momma had enough insurance money to get her by for six months until she could twitch her tail and catch a rich man. Who, by the way, did not want an eight-year-old boy in his life."

"Oh my," Jane mumbled.

Nellie came out with her arm bent up to hold the cotton ball in place. "All done."

They met a young mother with four kids coming in as they were going out.

"Saved by the grace of God," Ellen said when they reached the pickup.

"Ellen!"

"Well, we were. He was good to us today."

"You don't like kids?" Jane asked.

"Love 'em. Wished I would've had a yard full of them. But since God saw that I was unfit and wouldn't let me have them, I don't want to look at other women with them and wish they were my grandkids."

Nellie fastened her seat belt. "You are full of shit."

"Yep, I am. God didn't think I was unfit, Jane. But He was wise in not giving me kids. First time I married I was too young to be a mother. Married and divorced before

I could legally buy a bottle of Jack Daniels. Looking back, that's why I married him. So he could buy it for me. Second time around I was twenty-four…"

By the time they reached Saint Jo, Jane had heard the whole tale of the four marriages with commentary by Nellie. She felt as if she'd just watched a movie, complete with the gag reel at the end.

"If you'd turn here and go up to Illinois Bend, you'd find Griffin Luckadeau's ranch. Want to go visit him?" Ellen asked.

"We could blow off the whole shopping trip and run up there for a glass of cold tea," Nellie said.

"No, thank you. What would either of you wear to the Silver Spur on Thursday if we didn't shop?" Jane said.

"Silver Saddle," they said in unison.

"So didn't you find him handsome with that white shock in his hair? He does stand out amongst all those blond Greek gods, doesn't he?" Ellen asked.

"Very, very handsome, but I'm not in the market for a man," Jane said.

Ellen raised both eyebrows. "Now or ever?"

"I'm not gay. I've just come out of a very ugly relationship and right now I wouldn't trust anything that wore pants…" she thought about Ramona, "… or a skirt, either. Only people I trust in this world right now are you two."

She didn't see Nellie wink at Ellen or Ellen squeeze Nellie's leg. She had no idea that Nellie had just gotten the second bit of information from her. Number one: she had no sister. Number two: she'd had a bad relationship.

"Where to first?" she asked when they reached the mall.

"Burke's. I love that outlet store. They have the best prices," Ellen said.

It was the first time in her life that Jane had shopped in an outlet store. She bought two sundresses and two pair of sandals with the seventy dollars she'd won from Slade. Even though she was saddle sore and her hind end felt bruised, she considered the morning's work well worth it for the things she carried to the cashier's counter.

Ellen purchased a flowing, tiered silk skirt with huge yellow flowers on a turquoise background, and a white knit tunic with the same color flowers embroidered across the top. She chose a thin blue belt to rope it in to her still slim waistline and matching flat leather sandals.

"Used to dance in high heels but they hurt my feet. I'd rather dance more and look less sexy," Ellen said with a wink.

Nellie let Ellen talk her into a lovely full denim skirt with the frayed seams on the outside of each tier. She matched it up with a chambray shirt that had embroidery and fake jewels on the left side of the breast. They picked out a gold belt and gold sandals to match.

"So now you two are ready for a night at the Silver Saddle?" Jane asked.

"Yes, we are. And you'll be wearing that pink-checked, halter-top sundress and those cute little white sandals, right?"

"Oh, am I going?"

"We got to have a driver," Ellen said.

Chapter 4

JANE'S HAIR NEEDED A TRIM AND SHE'D ONLY BROUGHT THE very basic makeup—the kit she carried in her purse, to be exact. She had a tiny spray bottle of perfume that was barely half full and she hadn't even thought about a curling iron or straightener when she fled from her murdering son-of-a-bitch fiancé.

"I don't expect many near-sighted men with artificial hips are going to be noticing that my hair isn't perfect or that my mascara is a little lumpy," she said to the reflection in the mirror. She did feel semi-pretty in the dress, the first she'd worn or had occasion to wear in two weeks, and was more than a little amazed that she was actually excited about going to the Silver Saddle with Nellie and Ellen.

Slade shaved, being careful not to nick the very slight dent in his chin. He combed his sun-streaked blond hair back and even used a touch of hair gel to keep it in place. He dressed in a white knit shirt with three buttons and heavy starched Wranglers. He pulled a tooled leather belt through the loops and fastened the big silver buckle engraved with the Double L brand. He shoved his feet down into black eel boots polished to a high shine.

He took one look at the finished product in the mirror and smiled rakishly.

*That'll do for the ladies at the Silver Saddle. It'll
please Granny and Aunt Ellen to walk in with me and
then they'll go off in search of a distinguished gentleman
to flirt with. I'll spend the whole evening at the bar
nursing a long neck beer and watching whatever is on
the television set. But they'll be happy. I could shake the
liver out of Jane for insisting on an evening off. She was
hired to drive Granny wherever she wanted to go.*

They arrived in the den at the same time.

Jane had never seen him dressed up for an evening
out on the town. He smelled wonderful and looked even
better. She stood there staring as if he were some kind
of movie star who would disappear if she blinked. No
doubt about it. Kristy was flirting way out of her league.
That man could have any woman on the face of the
earth… except Ellacyn Jane Hayes.

Slade really did want to shake Jane when he saw her
all dolled up for an evening away from the ranch. Just
who was she going out with and when had she met him?
A flush of green jealousy shot through his heart. She
was lovely in that get-up and any man would be the envy
of the whole party if they arrived with her on his arm.
Was it his cousin, Griffin? Was that the man she was
going out with? Griffin could at least have consulted
him about asking her out before he did it.

As if on cue in a Broadway play, Nellie entered the room
and gushed, "Well, what are you doing all dressed up?"

"Taking you to the Silver Saddle," Jane said.

Ellen made her entrance. "You got a date tonight with
that Kristy witch?"

"No, I'm taking you two to the Silver Saddle. Remember, Granny, you said Jane needed a night off. It wasn't right to take up every waking minute for what you paid her and blah, blah, blah. You know what you told me, so I don't need to repeat it."

"Guess we got our wires crossed. Ellen asked Jane and I thought she might want a night off and insisted you drive us."

Ellen shrugged. "What's the big problem? You are both dressed and look mighty fine so we'll all go. It's no big deal."

"I'll stay home," Jane said.

Slade frowned. "No, I will. I can call the Kristy witch and see if she wants to go for ice cream without a big notice."

"Don't be silly. You both got prettied up and you're going," Nellie said.

Ellen shook her head. "Besides, the Kristy witch would need an hour or two to get all dolled up to match you. And honey, there ain't a woman alive who'd want to go for ice cream with something that looks like you and her lookin' like leftover oatmeal."

"Well, that's settled. Let's go. I don't want to miss any of the fun," Nellie said.

Neither had a choice if they didn't want more shenanigans. They stiffly and wordlessly headed toward the truck. Both women chattered about who might be there, who they'd dance with and who they wouldn't. It was as if they were going to a debutante party and they were the belles of the ball in their new finery.

Slade opened the doors for his grandmother and aunt and got them settled into the backseat, then started around to do the same for Jane, only to find her already in the passenger's seat. She looked as though she could chew up railroad ties and spit out Tinker Toys. It had been a simple mix-up; she didn't have to act as though she was going out with the scum of the earth. Damn it all, it wasn't a date. They were simply going to a senior citizen's dance and evening at a club. He'd sit at the bar nursing a beer, and she could find a corner and play nice.

The Silver Saddle was a hot spot on Friday and Saturday nights for the younger generation but the owners had agreed with the local senior citizen's groups to open the doors on Thursday nights for the oldsters to do a little bar hopping. It had started a month ago and Ellen had just talked Nellie into trying it. Slade didn't know how she managed to perform that trick but he was glad she had, because Nellie seldom ever got away from the ranch.

He fired up the engine and drove west. The club was located between Jolly and Wichita Falls, about half an hour away. Silence prevailed in the front seat. The party goers in the backseat kept right on with their discussion and paid no attention to Slade or Jane right up through the time he parked in the near empty lot.

"Looks like we might be the only ones here," Nellie said, disappointment in her voice.

"I don't think so. Folks our age are being driven and left like teenagers at the movies," Ellen whispered.

A burly guard in a three-piece suit stood beside the door outfitted with a red velvet rope complete with a golden clasp on the end. "I'll need ID, please," he said.

"From us?" Nellie asked.

"That's right sweetheart. No one under fifty-five goes through the velvet tonight and you ladies sure don't look fifty to me," he said.

"But—" Jane started to argue.

"Sorry darlin', I can see that you ain't nowhere near that age and you ain't either, sir. So you can come back at midnight and pick up the two Cinderellas, or you can wait in your pickup truck. Don't make me no never mind, but you ain't goin' through the gate. This is for seniors only. Tomorrow night you can all four come back. We don't have an age limit then. If you're twenty-one, you can dance and drink. I have my doubts about you, young lady, so you better bring a license or ID."

Nellie's grin was a bit too big and fake when she turned to face Jane and Slade. "Sorry. See you at midnight. Go have some dinner and see a late movie. Ain't no need for you to sit in the parking lot all evening. You'll kill each other."

"Listen to that music," Ellen enthused. "Is that Elvis? God, I'm going to love this place. I may come to Ringgold every week on Thursday." Ellen pushed her sister on inside and left Slade and Jane standing speechless.

"What just happened?" Jane asked.

"I think we just got rinky-doed by two old ladies."

Kristy appeared from the shadows of an older model black Lincoln Continental. "What in the hell are you doing here with her?"

"I might ask you the same. What are you doing here with him?" Slade shot right back. He was already stunned and anger was setting in quickly. He didn't need Kristy to start on him, too.

"He is my uncle who wanted to come to senior night. I drove him and will come back and get him. But it's pretty damned evident you thought this was a night you two could come dancing. I thought we were an item."

Kristy had her hair slicked back in a ponytail, wasn't wearing a bit of makeup, and her T-shirt with Betty Boop on the front had seen better days. She wore rubber flip-flops and tight, cut-off jean shorts. And her voice was so high and shrill it would hurt a deaf man's ears.

She took two steps forward, stopping only when she could see the whites of Jane's eyes. "Well, since he's evidently tongue-tied, what have you got to say for yourself? I told you Sunday he was my territory and to stay away from him. Remember I promised that the next time wouldn't be with words. It appears that a low down, white-trash bitch like you don't have much sense."

Jane had heard of honky tonk, parking-lot cat fights. If she'd been told on the eve of her wedding that two weeks later she'd be standing in the middle of one, she would have had the person doing the talking committed. She wasn't sure how she was supposed to respond, but no one was calling her white trash. She stepped into Kristy's invisible wall of space, doubled up her fist, and connected solidly with the woman's chin in an upper cut. When the tall oak of a woman started to fall to her knees, Jane caught her again in the stomach. She bent over clutching her gut and screaming that she was going to kill Jane.

"I told you Sunday I wasn't moving in on your territory and this fight isn't for Slade. It's to teach you never to call me white trash. Either get up and quit threatening me or go home. I don't give a damn which one you do."

Kristy slowly got up and shook her fist toward Jane, but she didn't get close enough to take or give any more punches. "I'll file assault charges on you."

"Bring it on. I keep enough cash in my purse to pay the fine for assault at all times. It's insurance against anyone who calls me names or thinks they can intimidate me."

"You going to let her talk to me like that, Slade?" Kristy edged in close to his side.

"I'm not your territory, Kristy," he said through clenched teeth.

"You can both go to hell. Don't call me and don't come around my place any more. Consider us broken up," she shouted and stormed off toward the Lincoln. She fired it up and laid enough rubber on the parking lot to deplete the life of the tires by at least twenty miles.

Jane glared at Slade. "Don't you say a word. I'm hungry and I'm still mad. So feed me or take me home and I'll cook."

Slade glared back. "Why didn't you tell me she was making threats to you?"

"Why should I? It was between me and her."

"But it was about me."

"So?" She headed toward the truck, glad that she was wearing flat sandals and not high-heeled shoes because both heels would be broken the way she stomped.

"Steak?" he asked when he started the engine.

"For my stomach or her chin?"

"She can take care of her own chin," he said gruffly. He didn't like Jane, but he sure didn't want Kristy acting as if they were already engaged and on the way to see the preacher. The woman had shown her true colors that night and he was glad it was over. Maybe he had inherited too many of his father's genes that drew him to trashy women and thought he could be the knight in shining armor and change her. That could be the reason he wasn't the least bit attracted to Jane, who was classy even if she was poor.

"Then steak is fine. A big one with a stuffed baked potato on the side," she said.

"Anger makes you hungry?"

"Yes, it does. When my mother died I went through all the stages of grief. When I got to anger I gained ten pounds," she said.

And it loosens my tongue. I shouldn't have said that about my mother. I shouldn't be getting close to Nellie and Ellen because I'll have to disappear in four short weeks. I already love both of them like they were my favorite aunts and leaving is going to be painful.

Slade kept his silence and drove to McBride Land and Cattle Company, one of his favorite steak houses in the area. Thursday night was fairly slow so they were shown to a table immediately. The waitress handed them both a menu and asked what they'd have to drink.

"Coors on tap," Jane said.

Slade nodded. "The same, please."

Jane perused the menu for a few minutes. "What do you recommend?"

"Ribeyes are my favorite," he said.

By then the waitress was back with their drinks. She set them down and removed an order pad from the pocket of her apron. "Are you ready or do you need a few more minutes?"

Jane handed her the menu. "Please bring me a salad with ranch dressing and bread on the side to start with. After that I'll have a ribeye, rare, another salad with my meal, baked potato with everything you've got in the kitchen to stuff it with except anchovies, and another Coors."

Slade wiped his forehead in a mocking gesture. "Whew."

"If you can't afford my appetite, then tell your woman to stay at home and keep her mouth shut," Jane said.

Slade smiled up at the waitress. "Give me the same as she ordered. Extra ranch dressing on the salad and extra bread."

She wrote it all down and disappeared toward the kitchen.

Slade picked up the glass of beer and looked across the table at Jane. "Anger makes you hungry. Hunger makes you mean. I'll have to remember that."

"Why? I won't be here in a few weeks and you'll forget all about me," she said.

"Yes, but you could mean me to death in a month or break my bank account if you get really mad," he teased.

"I think women make *you* mean, and then when the mean is gone, you are almost civil. You almost smiled at me right then. This could work for both of us. I won't get mad if your women don't call me white trash, and you will be happier without someone who's marking you for their territory like a tom cat pissing on a tree."

"You don't mince your words, do you?"

"Never been accused of it."

"Who are you, Jane?"

"I'm Jane Day to you, and I'm glad to see food coming right now."

She went at the salad and bread like she hadn't eaten in weeks as she tried to appease the rage in her heart. When the food was half gone, she picked up the mug of Coors and downed half of it before coming up for air.

"Can you hold your liquor, or am I going to have to carry you out?" Slade asked.

"I could drink you under the table any day of the week."

"Don't make statements you can't back up with actions," he warned.

"I've never been accused of that, either." She went back to the job of polishing off her salad before the entrée arrived.

"So tell me what we're supposed to talk about for four hours," he said.

"First we'll talk about ranching and good steaks, then we'll go to a movie where we won't have to talk. This isn't a date. We don't have to find out intimate little details about each other."

"What is it?"

"A big mistake," she said.

"Well, praise the Lord and pass the ribeye, you finally spit out the truth," he said.

The waitress brought their steaks and they both lit into them. Jane made all the appropriate noises as she ate, telling him it was the best steak she'd ever put in her mouth and wondering why there wasn't a McBride's in every town in Texas.

By the time they'd finished she'd had three beers and was about to order another one when Slade said it was probably time to get on to the movies if they were going to be on time.

She didn't stagger a bit when she walked out the door. He began to wonder if she could indeed drink him under the table like she'd said. Just who was this woman who wasn't a bit interested in him or his ranch? Every woman he'd dated for the past fourteen years got all swoony-eyed when they heard how big the Double L actually was. What they didn't know was that they'd have to sign a pre-nup stating that the ranch wasn't up for grabs if Slade and fiancée ever divorced. They would receive ten thousand dollars in cash and he would be responsible for child support should there be children born of the union, but the Double L could never be part of a divorce settlement.

Just last year that very same kind of pre-nup had kept Beau Luckadeau from making a hell of a big mistake and marrying the wrong woman. The fate that put him and Milli together was the biggest stroke of luck Beau ever had. Noted for his luck with anything he touched except women, he'd finally gotten lucky in love as well. Milli was a wonderful woman, born and raised on a ranch. That was the kind of woman Slade wanted in his life. Too bad Beau had gotten to Milli first at their cousin's wedding over in Shreveport.

"Penny for your thoughts," Jane said.

"My thoughts aren't for sale," he replied.

"What's showing tonight?"

"Don't know. Hadn't planned on going to the movies. I figured I'd be sitting at the back corner of a bar sipping on beer and watching old folks dance to Elvis music."

"Me, too," she said.

"Do you think it was an honest mistake, or that they played us?" he asked.

"Who knows what goes on in Ellen's mind? God, I hope I grow up to be just like her," Jane finally smiled.

"Aha, the food is working," Slade said.

"For a little while. I might want popcorn and candy at the movies."

"You are an expensive not-date."

"Like I said, you got to pay the bill when you can't control your woman."

"She's not my woman anymore, so you can quit eating," he said.

He drove to the first theater only to find that anything they wanted to watch was already sold out. The second was the same but finally the third was playing an old movie, *The Bucket List* with Jack Nicholson and Morgan Freeman. Jane would have watched Tom and Jerry cartoons to be able to sit in the dark and not have to talk to Slade anymore, so she readily agreed when he suggested they watch it.

She had no idea what it was about and was surprised to find herself enjoying the banter between the two men's characters when they found out cancer was going to kill them within a year. Nicholson played an irascible billionaire and Freeman a scholarly mechanic, the two as mismatched for friendship as a hungry feral cat and a field mouse. They made a list of everything they wanted to do before they died and set about doing it.

Jane laughed until tears rolled down her cheeks when they went sky diving and felt her own heart pounding when they tore around a race track, Freeman in a Shelby Mustang and Nicholson in a Camaro. She sobbed at the end when their ashes were put in the same place and didn't even care if Slade heard her. He wasn't a date and she'd never see him again after her twenty-fifth birthday, so what did she care if he heard her blow her nose five times into the paper towel the concession stand lady had given her with the popcorn?

It was eleven o'clock when they walked out of the theater—an hour to kill before they drove the magic pumpkin to the Silver Saddle and picked up the two meddling Cinderellas. Jane was convinced that they had indeed known what they were doing and had done it on purpose. They couldn't have known Kristy would meet up with them in the parking lot, though. Or could they have engineered that, too? They knew everyone within a thirty mile radius who was going to the bar. No doubt about it, they knew Kristy's uncle would be attending.

"So what now?"

"Wal-Mart. I could do a little shopping," she said.

"For what?"

"Personal items that couldn't be found at the Gainesville mall yesterday," she said.

He almost blushed. Heat started up his neck and had almost reached his face when he got it under control. The movie had come nigh onto making him shed a few tears, especially when he heard Jane whimpering. He blamed his acute sensitivity on that rather than her comment about personal items.

"Okay. I could look through the electronics aisle while you shop," he said.

She bought makeup, a bottle of shower gel, one of Tylenol, tampons, and a jar of moisturizer. She winced when she thought about paying for it with her hard-earned money. She really frowned when she tossed the tampons into the cart. She'd left a six-month supply of birth control pills in the bathroom medicine cabinet. That morning she'd taken the last one in the packet in her purse.

Not to worry, she thought. *Why would I need them, anyway? I'm certainly not going to be having sex in this place.*

She bumped the back of her hand into the cart when Slade walked up beside her. "Ouch," she said.

"What? Did you run over your toe?"

"No, it's my hand," she held it up.

All four knuckles were turning purple.

"Good grief, woman, did you break your hand when you hit Kristy?"

She wiggled her fingers and flopped her hand back and forth. "It's just bruised."

He grabbed her hand and held onto it. There was a slight cut on the middle knuckle which had no doubt taken the brunt of the blow. "You act like you've done this before."

"Couple of times, but I was just a kid," she said.

Bite your tongue off and quit telling things.

Speak or even think of the devil and he or she shall appear. That was the first thing that came to Jane's mind when Kristy stopped her cart beside Jane's so fast that the wheels actually squealed just slightly. She still wore the same clothes she'd had on in the club parking lot and they didn't match the purple bruise under her chin.

"Are you following me everywhere I go?" she snarled.

Slade dropped Jane's hand as if it were a hot branding iron fresh from the fire.

"I'd think you were following us. Your cart is empty and mine is full, so I've been here longer. Is the whole Wal-Mart store your territory, too? Did you piss on all four corners?" Jane asked.

"Don't get mad. We don't have time to eat again," Slade groaned.

Kristy threw up her hands in disgust. "What are you talking about? Damn it all. I'll never know what I saw in you in the first place. I think you are touched in the head, and I intend to make it my mission to tell every woman you date that you are an idiot."

"Be careful. I can fight with either hand and my left one is still good. I can give you a bruise on the other side of your chin that Cover Girl will have a hard time covering up," Jane whispered.

"Go to hell," Kristy muttered and marched back to the hairspray aisle.

"Does she just rile you wrong or do you have a problem with all women?" Slade asked on the way back out to the truck after she'd paid for her items.

Jane fastened the seat belt and crossed her arms over her chest. "I have trouble with bullies, especially right now, so it would be best if she stays away from me."

She'd never displayed such low-class manners in her whole life. Her mother would be appalled if she were living. Her grandmother, who'd been a rounder in her day, would go into apoplexy if she was alive. Ranger women didn't act like white trash.

Yes, they do when they get their hackles up, and mine have been up for two weeks. I think I just hit the anger stage of this thing with John. It was denial at first. Surely I made a mistake, or else it was just a practical joke they were playing because they knew I was there. Maybe it was even a test to see if I loved him unconditionally. At least that's what I told myself the first night on the bus. Then I realized I wasn't crazy; it was real and survival mode took hold. Now it's anger. He'd better keep his distance or we'll see who gets planted six feet down. I'd do it without a contract or payment and eat half a steer afterwards.

The ladies were waiting at the door when they arrived and came right out to the truck. They were visibly completely worn out, still excited and rattling on and on about who they'd danced with and seen. They didn't hush all the way home.

Slade parked the truck and they crawled out whining about sore feet and leg muscles and declaring they'd do it again the next week, so someone could just get ready to drive them again. Slade rolled his eyes at Jane. They might never know for sure if they'd been hoodwinked that time, but it wouldn't happen again.

Or would it?

It hadn't been such a horrid evening. Slade had had many worse dates that were real dates and he felt more alive than he had in years and years, perhaps in his whole life. But he wasn't giving Jane credit for that. It was simply the circumstances.

Jane told them good night and went straight to her room, where she peeled out of the new dress and slipped a nightshirt over her head. She checked the hallway and made a beeline for the bathroom, took a quick shower, and hurried back to her room. She'd shut the door and was about to crawl into bed when she realized there was another body between the sheets.

"What the hell?" she exclaimed.

The covers flew back and two heads popped up—Ellen with her red hair wrapped in layers of toilet paper; Nellie's cap of gray poking up every which way.

Ellen was in a bright red silk teddy; Nellie in a white cotton sleeveless gown.

"We can't sleep. Tell us a story," Nellie said.

"You've both had too much to drink," Jane said.

"Probably, but I'm not drunk and I didn't wreck anyone's car and no one came home with me to make the bed springs squeak, so I want a story," Ellen said.

"I'm tipsy," Nellie admitted. "But I always wanted a daughter or a granddaughter and all I got was three old boys and three grandsons. And two of them hate the ranch and country life so I don't even hardly know them. So tonight you are my granddaughter and you're going to have to fill in."

"Tell us about punching old Kristy's lights out," Ellen said.

"And start it with 'once upon a time' like a real story," Nellie said.

"If I do, will you both go to bed? We've got to get up in less than six hours. You're both going to have headaches in the morning," Jane said.

Ellen crossed her heart with her hand. "We promise."

"Okay," Jane grinned. This really was fun. She'd never known two old women who lived life like this. Every once in a while her grandmother would show a rowdy side, but not often, and she'd died before Jane was fully grown. She'd be willing to bet that both Ellen and Nellie really would slide into Heaven screaming and yelling, their lives used up with experiences. Just like the two characters in the film she'd seen this evening. Not one moment wasted on wallowing around in self pity or fear.

They both hugged their knees to their chests and listened, eyes aglitter, breath smelling more than a little of Coke and Jack Daniels.

"Once upon a time, there was a poor little orphan girl who ran away from home and ran into a fairy godmother in a bus station," Jane started.

"I'm not a fairy godmother," Nellie declared.

"This is my story. I'll tell it the way I want and you have to listen like good little girls and then go to bed."

"Yes, ma'am," Nellie played into the role.

"Now she was trying to decide where to go next and how far she could get on her last twenty dollars, when this fairy godmother—who was gorgeous, by the way, and not at all like the fat little godmother in the Cinderella story—sat down beside her."

She kept the story going for a good ten minutes and told about the godmother taking the orphan to the pink castle and adopting her. They shopped and ate in fast food joints and had lots of fun.

"And she and her fairy godmother lived happily ever after," Jane ended. "Now go to bed."

"Not until we hear about how the orphan decked the bad witch," Ellen protested.

"She called me a white-trash bitch and my anger got the upper hand. I just proved she was probably right by hitting her," Jane said. "It wasn't ladylike and it wasn't the proper way to act."

"How'd it feel?" Ellen asked.

Jane grinned. "Better than jumping in the swimming pool on a hot day."

"Better than eating chocolate?" Nellie asked.

"Much better. Then she was in the Wal-Mart store and accused us of following her. She'd said that Slade was her territory so I asked her if she'd pissed on all four corners of the store to mark her territory there, too."

Both women doubled up in laughter.

"My momma and granny would put me in the corner for a month if they were still alive," she said.

Nellie wiped at her eyes. "I'd get you out and steal you away. God, I hate that Kristy. She's just after Slade's money."

"And the ranch," Jane said.

"Can't have the ranch. It's not up for grabs. All Luckadeau brides have to sign a paper that says they can never have the ranch. Somewhere way back there in Louisiana history, a Luckadeau must have lost his property to a gold digger. It won't ever happen again."

"Does she know that?" Jane asked.

"Probably not, but it don't matter. It's over, praise the Lord," Ellen said. "And now we'll be good little girls and go to bed. Thanks for a wonderful evening. Want to top it off with a snort of Jack? I'll go get the bottle."

"I had three beers with supper. Better not mix what's left with whiskey or I'll have a worse headache than you two in the morning. Someone has to be sober enough to cook breakfast. Why don't you leave it to me and y'all sleep late?"

"Sounds like a good idea to me," Nellie yawned.

Jane ushered them out the door. "It's a deal, then. I'll cook and you can eat when you get up. Sleep in and I'll hope like hell your heads are pain free."

❖❖❖

Slade barely got his door shut before he heard his aunt and grandmother slipping down the hall, giggling the whole way. He'd spent the last hour with his ear pressed to the door, listening to the stories Jane fabricated and the one she told about decking Kristy. Why in the world couldn't he find it in his heart to like the girl?

It was as plain as the nose on his face that his grandmother loved her, his aunt adored her, and it was so damned convenient. She was right there in the house, the next door down from his bedroom. It didn't get any handier than that arrangement. But down deep in his heart there was still a little voice that told him that if he fell in love with Jane he'd lose the independence he'd fought so hard to win after his mother left.

It wouldn't be like loving Kristy. He could give her only the portion of his heart he wanted her to have and keep back the rest of it. She could produce an heir for him and even if she didn't stick around, he'd still have a child. Jane wasn't like that. She'd insist on having it all or none, and Slade wasn't ready to give that much. Besides, how did a man fall in love with an illusion? That's all Jane was… just a wisp of smoke fading fast as it spiraled toward heaven. She had no past and no future and lived only for today and whatever lurked ahead after another month. He had to protect himself from such a woman.

He laced his hands behind his head and shut his eyes but it was a long time before he fell asleep.

Jane was too wound up to sleep. She paced the floor and stared out the window at the bright stars twinkling in a sky that looked like a bed of velvet. In the big cities like Los

Angeles or even Houston the stars didn't shine like they did in Texas. And in those places it wasn't so quiet that the sound of crickets and tree frogs could be heard through a closed window, either. Police sirens, ambulances, and road noise were constants. In Ringgold, if a siren went past, every phone line in the western part of Montague County would be busy finding out if someone was hurt or if they got a speeding ticket or just a warning.

It reminded her of ranch life in Greenville as opposed to the corporate life her stepfather, Paul, enjoyed and she had to participate in more often than she wanted. Greenville wasn't such a huge town. Not like Houston, where she flew in and out to take care of oil business. Or Los Angeles, where she had to conduct some of the offshore business. Or even hot, humid Biloxi, where the oil company kept an office.

She was always eager to get back to the peace and quiet of the ranch. So what on earth had made her think she'd be happy in the big city of Chicago with John and his art distribution business? She'd been so close to the forest she couldn't see the trees. He'd been a professional con who'd swept her off her feet and into the clouds of make-believe. Now she had her head on straight and, though she refused to be one of those I'll-never-trust-another-man-because-he-did-me-wrong women, she would be careful in the future and weigh the pros and cons before she let her heart overrule her good sense.

Finally she set the alarm and stretched out on the bed. She fell asleep as soon as her head hit the pillow, only to dream of John holding her under the deep blue waters in Cancun. She awoke five minutes before the alarm went off, her chest aching from holding her breath, and her heart pounding.

Chapter 5

JANE HAD BEEN IN SALE BARNS BEFORE, BUT NOTHING AS HUGE as the one on Beau and Milli's ranch. It was as big as a medieval coliseum. Any minute she expected to see the crowd below her clear out, the lions let loose from the far end, and a couple of gladiators, or Christians—oh hell, whatever it was the lions had for supper—tossed out into their midst.

She'd found the way up to the catwalk when she opened the wrong door looking for the restroom. After a quick trip to the bathroom, she'd returned and found a quiet corner in the shadows where she could look down at the party from an eagle's standpoint.

Nellie and Ellen were sitting at a table with four or five other people about their age. They laughed, nodded their heads in agreement, shook them in disagreement, and seemed to be enjoying the evening. Ellen had said on the way to the barn party that she was staying in Ringgold for at least a month on this visit. She was even considering using her savings to buy a small trailer house and parking it somewhere on the ranch.

Slade fit right in among a sea of blond, blue-eyed cowboys. All of the Luckadeaus slipped into the stereotype mold so well that they could have made television commercials. Tight fitting Wranglers, western cut shirts, and boots. Put them on a horse or standing beside a barn with a beer in their hands and the beer company would have to increase production. Or let one of them prop his leg up on a bale of hay and show off a fancy boot and the boot business would have to double their employees.

"They'd have to get rid of the hat hair, though," she said.

It was true. Most of them had a rim around their blond hair where their hats had set just moments before they entered the barn and hung them on a row of hooks on the wall just inside the door. That was a cowboy trademark as much or more than the boots and spurs on working days.

Slade stopped by the table and spoke to Nellie. She said something that made him scan the barn and then he shook his head. Ellen pointed her finger and gave an order and he shrugged. Then he asked a tall, blonde lady to dance with him. The woman wore dark jeans that hugged up to her voluptuous figure, a pink sleeveless western shirt, expensive boots, and big gold hoops in her ears. She and Slade were close to the same height and danced well together.

When that dance ended, Ellen caught him on the edge of the floor and shook her finger some more. He scanned the barn, even looking up at the catwalk. The blonde pulled him back out to the floor and they melted into each other's arms for another slow dance.

Where did that woman come from, anyway? She couldn't be a Luckadeau. Girl relatives didn't press up against boy cousins like that. They didn't whisper in their ear and nibble on the lobe just slightly. They sure didn't twirl the hair on their dancing partner's neck. One thing for sure, kin or not, she was a blatant hussy.

Beau and Milli took the floor on the next song and in less than ten seconds everyone had stopped dancing and formed a circle around them. They danced as if they'd taken lessons together for years, never missing a beat or a step. It was so smooth that it bordered on artistically beautiful. Hells bells, they would have won if they'd ever been on that *Dancing with the Stars* show.

Jane was so taken with watching the performance that she didn't hear Slade approaching until he sat down beside her.

"You startled me," she said.

"They're about to panic down there. They're afraid you've bolted again," he said.

"Just staying out of the way. They only brought me because—"

"They asked you to join us because they like you, Jane. God knows—and He's the only one who knows—why, but they do. Unconditionally. They don't have to know your past or what you're going to do tomorrow. They like you today. Kind of like that movie we watched the other night."

"Living for today," she said.

"I can't do it. Unconditional like that," he said.

"Tell them I'm not going to bolt. I'm just watching from up here and—"

"And they'll cut down a pecan tree, build a cross, and crucify me right outside the barn door. Oh, no, honey, you're coming down to the dance floor, and I've been commissioned to dance with you."

"So you don't want to but in order to keep peace you will?"

"Don't fight with me tonight, Jane. Just consider it a nice gesture for two old ladies who like you. Kind of like telling them a bedtime story when they were tipsy."

"How'd you know about that?"

"Birdie told me."

He stood up and held out his hand.

She took it, amazed at the heat it produced. There had been a warm fuzzy feeling in her heart when John held her hand as they crossed a street or when he kissed her. But nothing like the boiling steam Slade's touch provoked.

She tried to shake off the feeling. She refused to be out of control ever again. She'd proven that when she left Mississippi, and she'd prove it again when she was twenty-five and could go back and fire her stepfather. She wouldn't allow herself to be physically attracted to Slade. She'd fight it forever because he'd just said he could never love unconditionally and that's what she intended to demand from any man before she fell for him.

He led her down the stairs and out to the middle of the dance floor. She felt out of place in her sundress and sandals when the rest of the women wore starched jeans and western cut shirts. The female singer did a fine job of singing "This Side of Good-bye" by Highway 101.

Before long the crowd had stopped dancing and circled Slade and Jane like they'd done when Beau and Milli danced. Jane kept the appropriate distance from him and followed his lead, knowing instinctively each step he'd make. The singer talked about heading out on the open road and seeing neons flashing vacancies. She talked about miles behind her and all the reasons fading into her memories this side of good-bye. Jane could relate to almost every word, especially the ones about reaching out again.

When the song ended with a fading guitar run Slade dipped her low, her circular dress tail sweeping the dirt floor. Everyone clapped and whistled.

"More, more," Beau yelled.

The singer started up another Highway 101 song in basically the same tempo. "The Bed You Made For Me" had another message for Jane's heart as she enjoyed another dance with Slade. The singer asked if he'd told the other woman that she was sleeping in the bed he'd made for her. She thought about Ramona for less than a minute before tossing the memory out into the darkness along with those of John. Jane had made a big mistake in judgment. That didn't mean she'd do it again. Life was meant to be lived and she wasn't going to miss another moment—or dance.

When the song ended, the male singer picked up the mike and started, "The Dance" by Garth, a slow waltz, and Slade didn't miss a beat. He drew her a little closer and kept dancing. At least until the blonde tapped Jane on the shoulder and cut in. She stepped back gracefully only to find herself in the arms of another cowboy, who hugged her close and told her his name was Kevin. He wasn't nearly as smooth as Slade and twice he stepped on her toes, but he kept her laughing the whole time with his humor.

The next dance started the minute "The Dance" ended and Kevin kept her in his arms. Halfway through the song, Ellen tapped her on the shoulder. "Let me at him, darlin'. I think I can teach him some better moves."

Jane laughed and stepped back only to find herself in Slade's arms again. The crowd didn't part to watch them and she enjoyed the dance even more without the attention. The band kept the songs coming with no time in between. It was easier to play to a live crowd who danced, clapped, whistled, and yelled out requests than to a bunch of folks who were content to sit around tables and drink.

At one point Jane felt a tap on her shoulder and turned to find Kristy standing there in her skin-tight jeans, sleeveless western shirt, full makeup, hair all piled up on top of her head, and a grin on her face. "Mind if I cut in?"

"Have at him," Jane said and turned to be swept into Beau's arms.

"Who is that?" Beau asked. "Slade looks mad enough to kill something."

Jane shuddered.

"I didn't mean he'd really kill a woman, but he is pretty angry. I don't remember Milli mentioning inviting someone like her. Oh, now I remember, that's the lady Slade brought to Aunt Nellie's birthday party a couple of weeks ago. She had two little girls who were mean to Lizzy. Milli was ready to pinch her head off and feed it to the buzzards by the time we got home. If anyone ever treated Katy Scarlett like those two little girls did Lizzy, Milli would be hauled up for whippin' someone else's kid with a peach tree switch," Beau said.

When the song ended, Jane slipped away to a corner. She didn't want to cause a problem with Kristy and ruin the party, so the best thing for her to do was stay away from Slade. Evidently he had the same idea, because he finished the dance with Kristy and left her on the dance floor while he went to the bar.

Kristy squeezed up tight with another man and Slade headed for the bar and downed half a bottle of beer before coming up for air. That could mean a couple of things, Jane decided. He was mad either because she was there or because she was glued to another man and he was jealous. Lord, that beer looked good. She sucked in a lung full of air and made her way to the bar. No one, Slade or Kristy, was going to put her in the corner and keep her from having a good time.

Ellen wasted no time getting to the bar at the same time Jane did and standing between the two. "How did that hussy get here?" she asked Slade.

"I wouldn't know. I didn't bring her. You sure you and Granny didn't have something to do with it just to watch the fireworks?"

"I promise. I wouldn't do that to Milli and Beau for anything. Wouldn't be right, causing a scene at their barn dance."

"Guess she crashed the party," Jane said.

"I'd like to crash her head," Ellen said.

"Here comes your chance. Looks like she's hauling Mr. Clumsy Feet over here for a drink," Jane said.

"Who?" Slade frowned.

"That man. I don't know his name, but he doesn't dance as well as you do," Jane said.

"I'm leaving. Can't trust myself around that hussy. She's trouble on wheels," Ellen said.

"Could you mix me up two martinis with double olives?" Kristy asked the bartender. "Well, looky here. The two little sweethearts of the dance. Bet they make y'all prom queen and king."

"Who's your friend?" Jane asked.

"That would be Kevin Felder. He's the brother of the man who owns a ranch up near Springer. Brother got invited. Kevin was visiting so he came along. He's from McKinney. Has a dry cleaning business down there."

"Well, tell Kevin Felder that I'm voting for you two to be prom celebrities. I got it back in high school and I don't think you can have the honors twice," Jane said.

"You come with him?" Slade asked.

"Of course not. I crashed the party. Marty and my uncle were at the feed store at the same time and Marty told him y'all were coming up here tonight, so I crashed it. I was going to tell everyone that you invited me but now I'll just let them think I came with Kevin, since I intend to go home with him as soon as we drink these martinis."

Jane threw her hand over her heart. "And miss getting the plastic crown? I'm shocked."

"Honey, what I intend to get will be much, much better." Kristy talked to Jane but looked Slade right in the eye. "And what he is going to get is going to make him the happiest little prom king in Texas."

"You going to get him over the state line before you buy him a candy bar?" Jane asked, all wide-eyed and innocent.

"Oh yes, all the way to that hotel in Gainesville and darlin', it'll be sweet and he can unwrap it, but it won't be chocolate," Kristy shot right back.

Slade crossed his arms and watched the cat fight. It was amusing, really, and Jane wasn't losing an inch of ground. He should be at least a little sad or jealous since he'd been dating Kristy for three months, but all he felt was relief.

"Have fun. Want to dance, Slade?" Jane quickly switched her attention from Kristy back to Slade.

"Think I'll sit this one out. How about we grab another beer and find a table?"

Jane nodded and followed him, leaving Kristy to wallow in happiness, since she felt she'd gotten the last word. They'd no more than sat down when Nellie and Ellen joined them.

"What did she say?" Nellie asked.

"She said she's going home with that fellow over there that is not so slick on his feet, that she crashed the party to make me mad and Slade jealous, and that she'll let everyone think she came with the other man," Jane said.

"Good," Nellie said. "Milli works hard on her parties and I wouldn't want any trouble."

"That mean I can't follow her outside and snatch her bald-headed?" Jane teased.

"That means you can, but bury her cold dead carcass and don't let anyone know what you did. Beau keeps a shovel in the tack room," Ellen said.

"You ever do that?" Jane asked.

"I'm layin' claim to middle-aged dementia. Can't remember what happened back in my heyday. 'Course it might have been that Jack Daniels fogged my memories a bit," Ellen answered.

"Middle-aged. Hummppph," Nellie snorted.

"I am middle-aged. Old age begins at seventy."

They began to banter back and forth. Slade and Jane finished their beers at the same time and he held out his hand. They disappeared in among the dancers and left the two ladies to discuss the finer points of aging.

❖ ❖ ❖

Jane tiptoed out to the deck and sat down on a lounge chair, tugging the bottom of her knit nightshirt down over her drawn-up knees. She couldn't remember the last time she'd had so much fun: the dancing, meeting new people who had no idea who she was or how much money she was worth, yet treated her with respect and kindness—even the cat fight with Kristy. The excitement kept her awake like afterglow following good sex.

Dark clouds drifted over the moon, giving it an eerie look. She wondered where John was in his search for her. Had he counted his losses and given up? Had Ramona consoled him for the loss of the money he'd paid on an insurance policy he'd never be able to cash? She didn't feel anger anymore, just a foggy sense of detachment.

She had a lot of decisions to make in the next three weeks. Perhaps fate had sent her to Ringgold, Texas to show her what was important and what would make her happy. She'd gone to college with the understanding she needed a degree in business to aid her in running the oil company when her time came to take over but looking back, she'd done it out of necessity, not because she loved the job.

Ranger women did what they had to do and she needed to run an oil company. Her father had inherited a ranch from his father and her mother had loved it. She had managed to run it and the oil company. Maybe Jane could do that, but she decided in that moment that she didn't want to do both. She wanted out of the oil business, and she wanted to devote more time to ranching.

So should she hire a competent, trustworthy CEO to run Ranger Oil, or should she sell it outright?

"Not to Paul. He's not getting his hands on one single penny of what is mine," she whispered.

"Who's not getting what?" Slade asked from the doorway. He wore a pair of knit pajama bottoms with John Deere tractors printed on them and no shirt or shoes.

"Just thinking out loud," she said. "Having trouble sleeping?"

"A little. You'd think as much as we danced we'd be asleep like kids after a long day of running and playing," he said.

"Adrenaline settles down faster in little kids," she said. "No wonder Nellie and Ellen have trouble getting to sleep after a big night. Theirs must take forever to level out at their age."

"Shhh. If they hear you even thinking they are getting old, they'll string you up from the nearest oak tree with a worn-out rope," he teased.

"That should make you happy. At least I'd be gone," she taunted.

He ignored the barb. "You see that tall blonde I was dancing with this evening? I'm thinking about asking her out to dinner next week. What's your opinion?"

She almost choked. Surely she'd heard wrong. Maybe he wasn't even standing in the doorway and she was dreaming. She slapped her leg. "Ouch," she said.

"Mosquito?" He moved to another chaise lounge and stretched out.

"Big one."

"Well?"

"I saw her and my opinion doesn't mean jack shit. You don't even like me, much less respect my opinion on any given matter."

"We danced good together, didn't we?" he said, changing the subject.

"Yes, but two trained monkeys could two-step together."

"Think we might be friends?"

"Are you drunk?"

"Sober as a judge."

"Whatever changed your mind about me?"

He couldn't tell her that the minute he'd touched her hand, all kinds of indecent thoughts sped through his mind like a class five tornado on its way to tear up a row of tar paper shanties. That his mouth went dry and his palms began to sweat. He couldn't tell her that holding her in his arms during the dances felt so right. After the way he'd acted ever since she'd arrived on the ranch, she'd think he was certifiably goofy.

He wasn't sure he wasn't ready for the boys in the white jackets to come and take him away. After thinking about it since they'd gotten home, he'd come to the conclusion that she could be his friend and give him girl-type advice about his other women. That should erase any crazy notions of physical attraction right out of his mind.

"You hunting for an answer, or didn't you hear me?" she asked.

"Truce. Let's bury the hatchet and at least be civil for the next few weeks. After that, you'll leave and never even look back or remember us. So are you going to answer me? What do you think of me asking her out?"

"Did you ask Kristy? She's already marked you as her territory. You don't belong to me. I didn't hike my leg on your boots."

He chuckled. "I think Kevin is busy helping her forget all about me right now. Maybe she's marking new territory."

"Poor Kevin."

"So?"

"I'm to be your little sister, then?"

Lord, why hadn't he thought of that? Instead of a friend she could be the sister he never had. He couldn't be attracted to his sister; that was just plain repulsive.

"Friend. Sister. Confidant. Whatever."

"Never shut a door God opens. That's what my granny used to tell me. God opened a door and let you meet Elaine tonight. If you liked what you saw and she liked you—though that does make her a complete idiot—then ask her out. See what happens. Don't expect miracles but don't throw ice water on her if she holds her fork wrong or snorts when she laughs."

"Wow! I had to drag it out, but you aren't bad with the advice. I'll call her tomorrow morning and ask her out for Friday night."

"Good luck."

"Thanks, Jane."

"I'll be damned. Miracles do still happen. You said thank you to me."

He slapped at the air above her bare arm. Sparks flew from the almost-contact. He had to get over this attraction to Jane. He had no intentions of a serious relationship with Elaine because she was too clingy, but at least he would forget Jane for a few hours.

"Don't expect me to be nice just because we are burying the hatchet. It's not my style," he said.

"Nor is it mine. I tried nice once and it blew up right in my face. I'm not sure I'd live through any more nice."

"Want to talk about it?"

"Not on your life, cowboy. You want to tell me all your deepest secrets now that we've planted the ax?"

He shook his head. "I'm sure Granny and Aunt Ellen have told you most of them, but the ones they don't know… the answer is no."

"Then we're even."

"I'm going back to bed. Got hay ready for baling tomorrow morning soon as it dries up. I'll be cranky without any sleep."

"You'll be an old bear. Cranky is for sweet little children who've eaten too much sugar and have a tummy ache."

"Whatever," he snapped and left her sitting alone.

She watched the dark clouds shifting and moving. It was a symbolic sign of what was tormenting her soul. Her life was shifting from what it used to be and moving toward something to make her happy.

She straightened out her legs and headed back inside. "Enough deep analyzin'. Like Scarlett O'Hara said at the end of the book, 'Tomorrow is another day.' I've got time. John hasn't found me yet and he won't. I'm hidden better right here than any other place on earth."

The nightmare surfaced again that night. In it, John held her head under the water and she couldn't breathe. She awoke to the sound of the alarm, her chest aching and gasping for air. She stumbled out of bed and was still clutching her chest when she opened her bedroom door.

Slade came out of the bathroom, took one look at her, and reached out to catch her when she dropped into a pile of loose bones.

He picked her up and carried her back to her bed and gently laid her down. Her eyes fluttered open and she grabbed her chest again.

"What in the hell? Jane, what is the matter? Are you having a heart attack?"

"Nightmare. Can't get enough air in my chest," she gasped.

"I'll get Granny," he said.

"No!" She grabbed his hand and sucked in a lung full of fresh air. "I'll be fine."

"You're as white as snow."

"It was a scary nightmare. It's gone now. It's all right. I can breathe."

"What happened to you?" he asked.

"Go on and get dressed. I'll have breakfast ready in thirty minutes."

"You'll lay right here. I can make myself a bowl of cereal. You ladies can eat when you get up."

She shook her head. "It's my job and I need to get my mind off the dream. I'm fine now. Thanks for catching me."

He nodded curtly and left her alone. He'd heard that pregnant women fainted. Was Jane expecting a baby and that's why she was hiding out? Did it have something to do with a sorry husband or boyfriend abusing her? A million thoughts chased through his mind as he dressed. One minute he was ready to put on his armor, mount his white horse, and go take care of the sorry culprit who'd hurt her. The next he was furious with himself for caring a whit about the woman. She'd be gone in a few more weeks, and he doubted he'd ever know what happened to her after that. She'd been damned secretive about her problems and what she was running from ever since she got to their place. Maybe that's what she did. Simply went from one job to another. Saved her money and bought bus tickets until the money ran out and then used her little girl innocent look to get someone to take her home.

The smell of bacon and coffee wafted down the hallway as he made his way to the kitchen. She couldn't be pregnant or she'd be upchucking at those mixed aromas. And when they'd gone to dinner, she'd ordered beer without hesitation. She'd drunk five or six in the course of the previous evening. He would give her credit for having enough sense and loving children enough not to drink if she was expecting a baby. He didn't know he'd been holding his breath until it expelled with a whoosh into the kitchen.

"What brought that on?" She looked up from the stove. She wore one of her three pairs of jeans and a T-shirt that had been pink once but had faded to almost white.

He thought she was beautiful, barefoot and with her hair in a ponytail.

"I didn't want to crawl out of bed this morning. Then I had to catch this broad who faked a faint just to see if I'd be nice," he said.

"I wasn't faking," she protested.

"Looked like it to me. You sure recovered fast."

"I told you it was a dream, damn it."

"Your momma know you cuss?"

"My momma could put a sailor to shame when she got mad. I'm told my grandmother could out cuss and out drink any man who worked on her…" she stopped dead.

"On what, Jane?" He helped himself to a piece of bacon.

"Nothing. Fried or scrambled this morning?"

"Scrambled with cheese. What did your grandmother do? She worked outside the home at what?"

"My grandmother was a lady. She would wash my mouth out if she caught me using dirty words. She did a few times. I think her words were for me to do as she said and not as she did. And that's all you are getting, Slade. So sit down and I'll bring your plate to the table."

Ellen appeared with one eye still closed. "Just toast for me this morning and lots of black coffee. God, I'm glad we aren't making fried chicken today. Jane, put something in the oven and open some peaches. Like Danny Glover said in *Lethal Weapon*, 'I'm too old for this shit.'"

"You admitting something like that? Can I tell Nellie?"

Ellen came to life enough that both eyes opened. "You do and I'll cut your tongue out with a rusty pocket knife, one that Slade used to castrate hogs."

"You are a vicious woman," Slade said.

Ellen nodded. "Little girls are all born vicious, darlin'. We just don't let the boys know it. It would hurt their little egos. Eat your breakfast and get on out of here. I'll be human by dinnertime."

Slade dug into his breakfast without a word.

Ellen sipped her coffee. "So what did Kristy do? Did she finally leave with that loser?"

"Isn't a loser, according to Kristy. She said he owns a dry cleaning business in McKinney and she was going to make him very happy. I think she was just trying to make Slade jealous, but he's too stupid to know it. She probably went right home and cried her little eyes out. With good reason. He's asking the big blonde bimbo out on Friday night. They're doing dinner and a movie. Maybe she'll make him very happy," Jane said as she buttered Ellen's toast.

"You don't keep secrets worth a damn," Slade said.

"Oh, was it a secret? You didn't tell me not to tell Ellen and Nellie. If it's a secret, next time let me know ahead of time, and I'll tell you a secret. Guess what it is? I don't keep secrets worth a damn."

Jane didn't know why she was baiting him. He'd played nice. Picked her up when she'd fallen in a heap at his feet. Told her she could stay in bed and not prepare his breakfast. Maybe it was because she didn't like the feelings he evoked when he touched her.

He finished his eggs and carried his plate to the sink. "You are one of them vicious little girls."

"Oh, did I hurt your little ego? I'm sorry. Maybe Elaine will puff it all back up for you on Friday night. I could have a nice little chat with her. Where's her phone number?"

"You stay away from her. You are horrible. I'm not going to be your friend after all."

"Well, praise the Lord! I thought for a minute He didn't even listen to my prayers last night."

"What is all this bickering about? It's too early to be fighting," Nellie said as she entered the room.

"She's vicious. I'm going to work."

"He's mean."

Nellie smiled. "I remember when me and Lester first met. We fought like two cats with their tails tied together and thrown over a clothesline. I thought he had a big head because he had this ranch and he thought I was a city girl who didn't know chocolate cake from cow shit."

"What happened?" Jane poured a cup of coffee and joined Nellie and Ellen at the table.

"They killed each other. Of course they called it marriage. That just meant it was a long, slow, painful death," Slade said. He almost made it out the door before Ellen's coffee cup hit him in the back.

"You are all mean women. You can't go to any more parties," he yelled back as he slammed the door, leaving behind a broken cup.

"What happened is that we fought for six months. Reason we did it was that we knew right off we were attracted to each other and neither of us wanted to give in and admit it. I wasn't going to be tied down to cows and a stupid ranch. He wanted a girl who'd been raised on a ranch who'd be his equal. Guess what? Neither one of us got what we wanted."

"Tell me more," Jane said.

"The passion of the fight carried us through forty good years of marriage. We loved just as passionately as we fought. And heaven help the person who thought they could divide us."

"Ain't that the truth? Remember Aunt Minnie?" Ellen said.

"What happened?" Jane was all ears.

"She tried to get between them when they were fighting. She said Nellie didn't have to put up with him and could come live with her. She didn't have to live on a stinking farm with a jackass for a husband. Nellie set

her straight with about ten words. Something about not
getting in her business or her marriage."

"So, you and Slade fighting because you hate each
other, or because you're afraid of what you do feel?"

"He says I'm like his sister or a friend. He asked my
advice about taking Elaine out on Friday. I'd say he's
not afraid of anything about me," Jane said.

Both Ellen and Nellie laughed so hard they had to
cross their legs to keep from wetting their pants.

Jane couldn't figure out what was so damned funny.
The ladies needed to go back to bed and sleep off the
effects of the alcohol from the night before.

Chapter 6

SLADE DRESSED IN BLACK WRANGLERS, POLISHED COWBOY boots, and a blue plaid, western cut shirt that had been tailored to fit his wide shoulders and narrow waist. He'd found time to get a haircut that week so the curls over the tops of his ears and on his neck were gone. The aroma of shaving lotion permeated the house for an hour after he left.

Slade whistled in appreciation when Elaine opened the door. She wore a black and white floral sundress with just a hint of cleavage. Freshly painted red toenails peeked from white sandals. Blonde hair begging for a man to tangle his fingers in the softness flowed to her shoulders.

She smiled and picked up her purse from a table right inside the door. "I'll take that as a compliment. I'd invite you in for a drink, but I wouldn't be responsible for my actions if I drank on an empty stomach. I might not be any more responsible later on when I do intend to invite you in. If I could whistle I would, but I can't, so I'll just tell you outright. You are one damn handsome piece of eye candy."

"Thank you, ma'am."

He opened the door for her and settled her into the seat, making sure the hem of her dress was safely inside. A vision of Jane sitting in that same place just last week deflated his puffed up ego pretty quickly. She'd never told him he was a handsome piece of eye candy. She'd fought with him on every issue and wouldn't tell him a thing about herself.

He opened the driver's side pickup door and said, "So tell me all about yourself, Elaine. Why isn't a beauty like you already married with a couple of kids?"

"Been there. Done that. Didn't like it. I graduated high school from Whitesboro ten years ago. Stop figuring my age in your head; it's not polite to ask a woman her age or to figure it up from something she says," she smiled, showing perfect teeth. It must have cost someone their calf crop to pay for the braces.

"Yes, ma'am," he smiled.

She was funny. Jane wasn't funny; she was biting. All the time sparring back and forth with barbs meant to sting, not make him laugh.

"Anyway, I went on to college over at Midwestern in Wichita Falls. Met a fellow there in acting class. God, he was good-looking. Not as handsome as you, darlin', but movie star pretty. You're rugged, like Clint Eastwood in his younger days or Robert Redford back when he was thirty. Jeff was downright pretty and determined to be the next big Hollywood star. Name in the tabloids—the whole enchilada. I got pregnant. We got married. He said it ended his career and he never forgave me for it. He became a high school speech teacher and we moved to Alvord, Texas."

Jane hedged around every question and Elaine was telling him her life story, when all he had wanted to know when he asked the question was what kind of movies and food she liked. He shook his head to remove the picture of Jane in that sundress the night they'd been forced to go to dinner.

"We had a son and then another one the year after Jeff started teaching. Last year they were three and five. There I was, living on his teacher's salary and my job as a bank teller, unhappy as hell, making ends meet most months, but not having a damn thing I was used to. I was about to suffocate to death. So I told Jeff we needed some time apart. I liked it so well I filed for divorce. It was final three months ago."

He parked the car in front of Applebee's in Gainesville. "So does your ex have the boys this weekend? I didn't hear anyone in the background at your house."

"My grandmother left me that house when she died last year. I've always loved it and I wanted Jeff to move to Ardmore with me. He refused. But to answer your question, yes, he has the kids this weekend. Next weekend is mine. I get them second and fourth weekends through the school year and two weeks in the summer. I could have had them four weeks, but two is enough."

"You mean you don't have custody?" Slade asked.

"No, darlin', Jeff is much better with them than I am. Besides, just think of all that child care I'd have to pay out. I love my boys, but I don't want to live with them twenty-four seven. You know what I felt when I walked away from them and Jeff? Pure relief. I don't think we would have ever married if I hadn't gotten pregnant."

Slade was stunned into silence.

"Let's see, that's the dark side of my life. This past year I went on back to college and finished my degree. I work as an accountant at an oil company in Ardmore. I'm happy and I don't intend ever to marry again. So the pressure is off you, darlin'."

Slade didn't feel any kind of relief. He parked the truck at the steak house and went around to open the door for Elaine like a gentleman. He'd make it through the night, but it was damn sure going to be a long one. If Jane knew all about Elaine and had pulled a trick on him, he swore he'd get even.

Elaine took his arm as they headed toward the restaurant door. "Now let's talk about you and that woman you had at the barn dance the other night. Did I tell you how I got there? My older brother owns a ranch near Healdton and is cow-buying buddies with Beau. I went with him and his wife. It was either that or they were going to ask me to babysit their four kids. I'm not fond of dirt and barns, but it was better than changing diapers and reading *Sleeping Beauty* for a bedtime story."

The hostess seated them and Slade fought the impulse to go to the bathroom, crawl out the window, and go home. He opened the menu and willed himself to sit still.

"I think I'll have the rib eye topped with garlic and mushrooms, baked potato, dinner salad, and iced tea," he said. There was no way he was trusting a single beer in his system. Even if he was eye candy, he didn't intend to go past the front door of the woman's house.

"Not me. I never eat steak. Let's see. I'll have the Cajun lime tilapia and a Margarita."

The waiter disappeared with their orders.

Elaine propped her elbows on the table and propped her chin on the shelf made by turning her fingers inward. "Now let's talk about you. You are about thirty. You have never been married and you have no children."

"Pretty much sums it up," Slade said.

"Oh, no, it barely gets the ball rolling, darlin'. Now we're going to really talk. Why haven't you been married? My guess—and I'm a good judge of people—is that you don't want to be. You like your ranch and you have your grandmother to take care of. A wife would interfere with both. Right? Of course I'm right. I know you already even though we've only danced a few times and ridden half an hour to Gainesville from Ardmore."

Slade took a deep breath. "I'd like to have a wife someday. Someone who loves ranching as much as I do and gets a smile on her face when a new calf is born." He hoped that would let all the helium out of the balloon she was floating with his name on it.

"Honey, they don't make women like that. If one says she likes living out on a remote ranch south of Ringgold, Texas, you pull up your Wranglers and go on home because you've got a lyin' bitch in bed with you. And a smile when a baby calf is born. Yuk! That would be even worse than smiling after childbirth. It might happen, but it's fake. Be careful of those kind of women."

"You are full of advice," he said.

Their drinks arrived. Slade stirred three packages of sugar into his tea and Elaine seductively licked the salt from one side of her drink. He remembered the way Jane had downed half a mug of beer.

Elaine cocked her head to one side, obviously trying to be coy. "On to the children issue now, since I was right about the wife business. You are an only child, and you know nothing about children. Probably never been around very many in your life unless it was up at your cousin Beau's place a few times a year. I understand he comes from a big family. Too damn bad he's already taken. I might have set my cap for him. But don't worry. I don't go after married men when there're plenty of good-looking single ones struttin' around."

He thought, *I'm on my way to the courthouse tomorrow morning with the first woman I see after I let you out of the truck tonight, and from now on I walk like an old man using a cane.*

He said, "Well, that's a good thing. Milli would scratch your eyes out if you looked cross-eyed at her husband. I heard she flattened one of his old girlfriends with one good right hook." That brought back the memory of Jane's "good right hook" under Kristy's chin. He wondered if Milli and Jane had sprung from the same family tree root. It didn't look possible on the outside, what with Milli being a Mexican. However, there was that little bit of English coming from her maternal grandmother, so she and Jane could have possibly shared the same DNA from a thousand years before.

"That's why I steer clear of married men. So tell me, am I right about you?"

"I love kids. Hope to have a yard full of them someday."

She giggled. "You almost had me. For a minute there I thought you were serious, but you have a dry sense of humor. I like it."

Jane picked up the book Ellen had given her. A fat romance by an author she didn't recognize, but Ellen promised it would have her swooning before the end of the evening. She read the first five pages and didn't feel a sudden urge to rush out and kiss the first man she encountered. She made herself sit still and read the next ten pages. Interesting, but not enough to hold her attention.

She tossed the book aside and pulled back the curtains to look out at the moon. They'd be finished with dinner by now and off to see a movie. Was he laughing as hard as he did when they watched *The Bucket List*, or was it a chick flick? Was Elaine sniffling and Slade yawning?

To get away from her own thoughts, she wandered down the hall, through the den and dining room, and into the living room, where Ellen and Nellie had set up a card table. Two other older ladies from near Alvord had come to play bridge. They had arrived about the time Slade left, tossed their purses in a recliner, and sat down to play some serious cards. Myra was short, stocky, and wore her gray hair in a frizzy do that would rival Kizzy Jane in the old *Roots* series. Jeannie was tall, thin, and had a little gray bun on top of her head. They both wore jeans, T-shirts, sneakers, and serious expressions.

Jane had escaped to her room with Ellen's book as soon as the introductions were over. Her attention was held by the book for a few minutes, by the twinkling stars a little longer, by the waning moon—until she blinked a couple of times, and then she found herself wandering back through the house.

"Want to play?" Ellen asked Jane.

"I'll raise you ten," Myra said.

"I'll see your ten and raise you twenty. Jane, honey, be a dear and mix another blender of daiquiris for Ellen and bring in three beers for the rest of us," Nellie said.

Jane's eyes widened. She was sure she heard Nellie tell Slade to go have a wonderful date, that she and

Ellen had invited a couple of friends for bridge. Didn't look like bridge to her. She rolled two limes on the countertop until they were squishy, then squeezed them into a measuring cup. She poured two ounces into a stainless steel shaker, added three ounces of Bacardi, two teaspoons of powdered sugar, and a few ice cubes and shook it until the outside of the container was cold.

"Cuban. My favorite," Ellen said when she sipped it.

"What's the difference?" Nellie asked.

"Have a sip. It's just different than those sweet strawberry or the new peach ones," Ellen said.

Nellie tipped it up. "Good stuff. Make a whole pitcher full and bring us some glasses. Girls, you're going to love it. Now, I'll see your five, Myra, and raise you ten. You're bluffing."

"We'll see," Myra laughed.

"I thought you were playing bridge," Jane said.

"So did our husbands for the past forty years. They had poker night and we started out playing bridge like good little wives. We chased babies and changed diapers. Exchanged recipes. All those kind of things," Myra explained. "Then the kids were grown and none of us wanted to play cards on Friday anymore until Ellen came visiting and taught us to play poker. That was twenty years ago."

"But why not just tell Slade the truth?" Jane asked.

"He's not man enough to take it. Men folks tend to think poker is their game. Want to sit in on a few hands?"

"I'll bartend."

Ellen finished off the daiquiri. "You don't fool me, girl. You know how to play Texas Hold 'Em and you'd own this ranch if you played. I can see it in your eyes.

Nellie can't stand losing so she'd wind up putting the ranch up on a bet and you'd own it. Sure you don't want to play, just to see Slade's face when he walks in and finds out he's working for you?"

Jane smiled. She didn't want to play for a very good reason. If she just made drinks all evening, Myra and Jeannie would go home and only remember her as the new maid slash driver slash bartender. They might talk on the drive back to Bowie about how Nellie had done good when she hired some help, but the next time they came to play poker she would be gone and forgotten. If John came looking and she had whipped them all soundly at poker, they'd remember a lot more about her.

"I'll just make daiquiris. Who's the designated driver?"

"I am. Put extra rum in mine," Jeannie laughed. "Honey, I could out-drink, out-bluff, and out-cuss a sailor. I won't wreck the pickup or get a ticket on the way home, I promise."

Jane thought Ellen and Nellie were a rare breed. She could scarcely believe that there were two more unusual elderly women in the same neck of the woods. Had her mother lived to be an old woman, would she have been like this foursome? Was her grandmother the same kind of woman when she wasn't wearing a black suit and sitting at the head of a conference table in the oil company?

"You know who I miss?" Myra said. "Ouch, why'd you kick me?"

Nellie shot her a dirty look. "Foot jerked."

Myra glanced at Jane, who'd headed for the kitchen. "Oh! Oh, my! Now I understand. Well, I'll see your twenty and raise you thirty."

"See what?" Jeannie asked.

Ellen tilted her head toward the kitchen and winked.

"I still don't see. Betcha if…" Her eyes widened and she shook her head. "Well, I'll be damned. Talk about fate. If that don't beat all. You going to tell her?"

"Not yet. Ellen and I are waiting for her to tell us," Nellie said.

Jane returned with a pitcher of daiquiris and three glasses on a tray. "Where do you want it?"

"Put it on the end table. Ellen can reach it and keep us refilled. Sure you don't want to play?" Nellie asked.

"No, I think I'll sit out on the deck for a while. You ladies get too tipsy, I'll drive you home and you can claim your car tomorrow," she said.

"Ain't happenin'," Jeannie said. "I could take a bath in beer and still be able to drive. I don't have Indian blood like Myra, who can't hold her liquor. She'll drink a beer and one daiquiri and have a hangover. It's in her genes. I come from a long line of Scottish cattle rustlers."

Jane shook her head in disbelief. With her gray bun and veined hands, Jeannie looked more like the offspring of a holiness Sunday school teacher than the descendant of cattle rustlers.

"It's the truth, sure as I sit here," Myra said. "My great-grandpa was one of those Taovayas Indians from up around Spanish Fort. Did you know that town used to have several brothels, two or three banks, and enough churches to keep the patrons of the brothels and saloons out of hell? Anyway, rumor has it that my great-grandpa stole one of the ladies right out of the brothel and married her before his parents knew anything about it. She was part Taovayas, too, so I've got the blood that doesn't do well with drinking. Jeannie can drink and doesn't have the headache, but she's a mean drunk, so I'll keep her from having too many."

"Hey, I've got an idea. Why don't you all go home with me to Amarillo for a week? Jeannie, you could drive, since Nellie and I aren't allowed. We could shop and party and play cards. Maybe hop over the line at Randlett and play a few hands of blackjack at the tables."

"You're crazy," Nellie said.

"Maybe not," Myra said.

Jane headed for the deck. Nellie would never go home with Ellen. She wouldn't leave the ranch during the busy season—or Slade, either, for that matter. Ellen had told her earlier that week that Nellie never went anywhere.

She kicked off her sneakers, removed her socks, and stretched out on the chaise lounge. Wiggling her toes, she noticed the nails were chipped. She hadn't had a pedicure since her wedding day. That left a bitter taste, and she decided right then that she would never paint her toenails pale pink again. They might even be natural the rest of her life.

At eleven o'clock she heard the ladies leave. Jeannie slung a little gravel when she peeled out but Jane figured that was to make Myra squeal and Nellie and Ellen giggle. They'd only been gone a few minutes when Slade slid open the glass doors and joined her on the deck.

"Where did you come from? How'd the date go?" she asked, hoping her voice didn't betray her feelings.

He wore his knit pajama bottoms and his hair was still wet from a recent shower. Crimson crept up her cheeks as she imagined what had happened that he'd need a shower the minute he got home.

"I drove up about the same time Jeannie peeled out. That woman will be the next one to get her license taken from her. The date went fine."

"Are you calling her again?"

"Probably not."

"Then it didn't go fine."

"Oh, yes it did. It was very fine, as a matter of fact. She called me handsome eye candy," Slade argued.

"She was just buttering you up. What'd she want?"

"Nothing except to be right about everything," Slade admitted.

"Then it wasn't a fine date," Jane said.

"Yes, it was," he argued.

"How can you say that when your tone said you were disgusted about the way she had to be right about everything?"

"A fine first date is when you come home absolutely convinced that you either want to see the woman again or you don't. I don't want to see her, so it was a fine date."

Jane's heart skipped a beat before that little niggling voice called a conscience reminded her that Slade didn't want to take her out even on a first date. Therefore, Kristy and Elaine had gotten considerably further with him than she had. Not that she wanted him to ask her on a real date anyway, but it was a bit of a blow to her faltering ego to know that he didn't want to do so.

"Tell me something," he continued. "If you were one of those psychic people or you could read palms or whatever those people do that know all about a person without knowing them, what would you say about me?"

If I was a psychic or palm reader, I wouldn't be here right now. I would have seen through John and Ramona from the beginning. So that's a crazy question.

"What would you say about me?" she asked.

"No fair. I asked first."

She held out her hand. "Give me your palm."

He laid his hand in hers. The warmth went all the way to his toes and curled around his heart.

"Oh great moon, please shine upon this man's hand and tell me his past and future so that he will be a happy little boy," she intoned. Actually she was amazed that she could utter a word with his big hand searing hers. She wondered what it would be like to crawl between the sheets with him, both of them naked as the day they'd come into the world. They'd probably set the sheets on fire so quickly the fire department wouldn't find anything but ashes.

He jerked his hand away. "I'm not a little boy. I'm a thirty-year-old man."

"Okay, then I will tell your fortune from what I've learned about you in the few short weeks I've been here. Oh, great moon, please don't bother shining on this man. He's not a little boy and I can't fool him into believing a lie; I'll have to tell the truth," she said.

"Enough shenanigans already," he growled.

"Okay then, seriously, here goes. You are kind and considerate—except with me, of course, but then I'm a con artist you have befriended in hopes that I won't steal your ranch or rustle your prize cows. So I don't matter. That's why you argue and fight with me on every issue, including my calling upon the great moon since I don't have a crystal ball."

A smile tickled the corners of his mouth but he didn't let it materialize. Jane thinking he was kind and considerate was even better than Elaine calling him eye candy.

"Do you think I'll ever marry? I mean, I am thirty and that's evidently past the prime bull age."

She stuck out her lip in a pout. "Did the big old blond bimbo say something ugly? Of course you'll marry. Some woman will come along that loves ranching as much as you do, who loves Granny even more than you do, and she'll make you a fine wife."

Her heart turned to stone at the thought of him with another woman. Why in the hell did she care if he married or not? She couldn't imagine being married to such an egotistical, set-in-his-ways, chauvinistic man.

"Thank you," he said seriously. "Children?"

"What about them?"

"What's your take on my relationship with kids?"

"You love them. They gather around you like ducks on a pond at the family get-togethers. I'd say you'll be a good father, but you'd best be gettin' on with the job. If you're going to have a big family, you got to remember you won't be eye candy much longer. Pretty soon all your blond curls will fall out and you'll be bald. Your arms will get too short and you'll have to purchase reading glasses. Your prostate will—"

"Whoa! Your predictions are getting too personal," he said.

"My turn," she said.

"For what?"

"The same thing. You have to tell either my past or future. Since you haven't done too good a job on the past, maybe you'd better stick to the future."

"Oh, I can do the past. You are the child of a gypsy couple who never stayed in one place more than a month. You are self-educated and on one hand, you'd love roots, but on the other, there's that wandering gypsy blood that keeps drawing you to the next bus station. The future is easy. You'll drift out of here and find another place to light until the itch begins and then you'll do the same thing, because the wanderlust is greater than the desire for roots."

"You got it," she said.

"Which, of course, means I didn't come anywhere near it."

"I wouldn't burst your bubble."

"Oh, yes you would. You'd just love to prove me wrong," he grumbled.

Ellen and Nellie joined them on the deck before she could think of a quick comeback. Ellen wore a flowing cotton lounging robe with big roses splashed around the full circle hem. Nellie had on pink seersucker pajamas. Both wore towels turban-style around their heads and carried daiquiris.

"Want a drink? We'll share. We just didn't want to waste a single drop of these. You ought to marry this girl, Slade. She makes the best daiquiris this side of Cuba," Ellen said.

"I'll pass on both," Slade said.

"It's the powdered sugar. Just a teaspoon per recipe to sweeten it up—and I'm glad he passed on both. I'd hate to have to break his heart," Jane said.

"Hmmphh," he snorted.

"You could do worse. Almost did with that Kristy. How was the Elaine trial?" Nellie asked.

"Are you the jury?" he asked.

"Could be. Jane can be the judge. We'll be the jury. Was she all clingy, telling you how handsome you are? Did she try to talk you into coming inside for one more drink at the house? Did she assure you that she was on the pill so you didn't need protection?" Ellen asked.

"Sounds more like you are the prosecutor," he said.

"You going to answer?"

"Your honor, I'll answer one of the questions," Jane played along. "She told him he was eye candy."

Ellen guffawed. She didn't giggle or chuckle or even laugh. She actually snorted daiquiri out her nose and stomped her bare foot on the wood deck until it looked as if she might start tap dancing.

"Good God, am I that ugly?" he asked.

Nellie joined in the laughter. "No, she's that stupid."

"Why?"

"I bet she talked about herself all night, didn't she? One little compliment and the rest of the evening was all about her," Ellen said.

"We need to start a school to teach women how to catch a man," Nellie said.

"I'm so sure you'd have a line of women beating a path to your door," Slade said.

"He didn't have a good time, Nellie. That's why he's out here crying the blues to Jane. Bless her heart, she's a sweetheart to listen to him. What he needs to do is beg her to make him a drink, count his losses, and forget the woman. Did you tell her you'd call her?" Ellen asked.

"I did not," he said.

Nellie pulled a five dollar bill from her pajama pocket and handed it to her sister. "How did you know? You only saw her at the dance for a little while."

"I can spot one a mile away," Ellen said.

"What?" Jane asked.

"A conniving bitch," Ellen answered.

"Hey, now that doesn't say much for my taste," Slade said.

"Exactly," Nellie said.

"But we didn't come out here to talk about you. Although I'm glad you learned something with Kristy and didn't let this conniving bitch take up three months of your time. You are over thirty and it's time for you to settle down," Ellen said.

"We came out here to tell you that I'm going to Amarillo with Ellen tomorrow morning. Myra and Jeannie are going, too. Jeannie is driving and we're all staying in Ellen's apartment. We're going to shop and party at the senior club she knows about, and we're going to hit a casino on the way. We'll call every night so you won't worry," Nellie said.

"You can't leave during the busy season," Slade said.

"Oh, but I can. Jane is familiar with the kitchen. If you get in a bind, she can saddle up and ride with you. She can go to the grocery store on Monday, pick up whatever she needs to do the cooking for the week, and—"

Jane's mouth dropped wide open. "You're going to trust me with keys to the truck?"

"Of course, you haven't robbed me blind yet. I don't expect you'll steal my truck while I'm gone—not that you'd be getting such a good deal if you did. The old bucket of bolts is fifteen years old and not worth enough for it to be a felony if you did run off with it."

"Thank you," Jane said.

"She can't keep up with the cooking," Slade said.

Jane pointed a finger at him. "Don't you underestimate me."

"Don't come begging me to peel potatoes," he said.

"I wouldn't think of it. I'd buy instant before I asked you to pick up a paring knife," she said.

"I can smell instant and I hate them. Don't you dare serve instant potatoes while Granny is gone." He glared at her.

Ellen and Nellie slipped back into the house and left them to their arguing. They high-fived each other just before going into their bedrooms.

"The menu is my business. You take care of the ranch and leave the cooking to someone who knows how to do it," she said.

He folded his arms over his chest. The woman was a fighter, most definitely not a lover. Lord, she'd probably tell him how to make love to her and then tell him he did it wrong if he ever did get close enough to kiss her without getting his lower lip bit clean off.

"If Granny is gone then you are working for me. If you even bring instant potatoes in this house, I will fire your ass," he said.

"And the rest of me?"

"What are you talking about?"

"The rest of me. If you fire my ass, then it can't work here. Can my hands work or my brain or any other part of my anatomy?" she asked.

He threw up his hands with a one-word utterance, "Women!"

"Can't live with us and it's against the law to drown us," she said with only a slight shudder.

"I'm running for Congress and changing the law," he declared on his way into the house.

She sat there awhile longer feeling quite pleased with the evening's bickering. It had been fun and she'd found out even more about Slade Luckadeau. She got misty-eyed again at Nellie trusting her with her home, the job of cooking alone, and her truck. She'd been on the Double L less than a month and for the older woman to put that much faith in her was touching enough to bring tears to her eyes.

Slade's bedroom window looked out onto the deck so he pulled the curtain back slightly and watched Jane. She wiped at her eye at one time. Did something in her past make her sad? There was so much he didn't know and suddenly he was interested. Not enough to get involved with her, for heaven's sake, but his curiosity was piqued.

At first he'd only thought about her in terms of getting rid of her, but Granny trusted her and Slade was slowly changing his mind. Either she was truly on the up and up, or she was the best damn con artist in the world.

Finally she stretched like a lazy cat on a summer afternoon, did a couple of toe touches and in a few moments he heard her padding barefoot past his door. He listened to the shower running and imagined her wrapped up in a towel, sneaking back across the hallway to her room.

He still couldn't believe his grandmother was leaving the ranch in the middle of the summer. It wasn't like her at all to delegate authority. The kitchen had always been hers and some of the time she laid claim to the hay barn or a new baby calf. Either she'd been bitten by the crazy bug and needed to see a psychiatrist, or else she knew something about Jane she wasn't telling.

He sat straight up in bed and held his head. Everything had been insane since Jane came into their lives. The peace was gone with the arguments. The routine was askew with her in the kitchen. Kristy had broken up with him. He wasn't willing to give Elaine a second chance. Lord, if only he could catch a lucky break now and then—but he never had and probably never would.

"She knows something," he said aloud. "Granny knows something and she's not sharing. She knows who Jane Day really is and I don't think Jane is even aware that she does. That's the only way she'd put so much faith in the girl. What in the hell is she hiding?"

Chapter 7

SATURDAY WENT FAIRLY SMOOTHLY. NEITHER SLADE nor Jane really thought Nellie would leave with the ladies, but she did. Every time Jane heard a noise that morning, she thought Nellie had changed her mind and come back to the ranch. Slade was so busy making hay that he scarcely had time to think about the issue and figured that Nellie would be there at dinnertime. She was playing a trick to see how he'd take it and simply gone off shopping with her friends. He'd come close to giving half his kingdom, known as the Double L Ranch, to discover what she knew about Jane.

Jane made lasagna and hot rolls, a corn salad, and cinnamon rolls for dessert. Keep it simple, she kept telling herself. No fried chicken and mashed potatoes would be served that week. Pot meals or casseroles so one person could handle it in the kitchen. After the dinner mess was cleaned up and put away, she did laundry, folded towels, put away linens, and ran the vacuum.

Just after five o'clock she stepped out onto the deck for a breath of fresh air and noticed the black clouds gathering in the southwest. Lightning split the sky in long, crooked streaks. No thunder followed, so the storm was still miles away. The house phone rang and she trotted back to the den to catch it, thinking it would probably be Nellie telling her that she'd won enough to buy a third world country or at least dinner at Cracker Barrel at the casino.

"Hello," she said.

"Hey, there's a storm brewing. Marty says the weatherman on the television at his house says it's coming our way. We still got the small square bales on the ground. We can use every hand we can get to put it in the barn before the rain hits. You mind driving a truck?" Slade asked.

"You got anyone else who can see over the dashboard that can drive?" she asked.

"I won't beg," he said coldly.

"I'm not asking you to beg. I can handle a set of hay hooks as good as you can, so if you can get someone's kid to drive, I'll help load. Where are you?"

"Not far. I've got a pickup ready to unload. Meet me in the barn where the kittens are."

"I need gloves."

"Granny's are on a hook inside the back door, right beside her hat. You might want to wear that, too."

By the time he reached the barn she'd moved the kittens to a safer corner, the momma cat following along behind, meowing loudly. He backed the truck into the barn and Jane grabbed a set of hooks and began to unload. They worked side by side until the bales were stacked uniformly, then she hopped into the bed of the truck and he drove back to the field. When the truck came to a stop, she wasted no time before getting out, but left the hooks in the seat of the truck. She could load twice as fast simply by picking up the baling wire and tossing it to the hired hand, who had gotten ready to catch it. Next time she'd do the easier job of organizing the hay in the truck to make the most of the space. It was a switch off. The one who threw the bales for one load organized the next time around to prevent exhaustion. As it was, every muscle in her body would ache at bedtime and the next morning it would be a miracle if she could move.

It had been years since she'd worked the hayfield, but she remembered the hard work. Her father had tried his best to talk her mother out of making her learn everything about ranching from the ground up, saying that a girl would never need the knowledge. Her mother did not share his viewpoint and she'd won the argument. Ellacyn Jane spent time in the hayfield, mucking out horse stables, planting a garden, canning green beans and corn, making jelly, balancing a checkbook—and then she went to college to learn how to run a business.

They were running two trucks that evening. When Jane's truck was finally loaded and the driver started back to the barn, she hopped up on the empty one just returning and got ready to stack. On that load, Slade threw and she stacked. The rhythm was fast-paced and kept her hopping to stay up with him. She could have asked him to slow down slightly but there was no way she would give him the satisfaction of knowing she couldn't match his speed.

"That's it. We got it in the barn before the storm hit," Slade said when they reached the barn with the last load.

He'd barely gotten the words out when the first drops of rain hit the metal barn roof. Along with the thunder right overhead, it sounded worse than it really was. Slade leaned against the side of the still-loaded truck.

"You lived on a ranch, or at least grew up on one. No one knows how to do that unless they've spent a lot of time ranching," he said.

"I never said I didn't know anything about ranching," she said breathlessly. "Help me get this off the truck and go have some supper. I'm starving."

"You are avoiding the issue," he said.

"I am not. I admitted that I'm hungry. Now are you going to unload or do I have to do it all myself. Maybe I played you out in the field, huh?"

He grabbed a set of hooks and fought hard to keep up with her as she tossed the bales. By the time it was all stacked the storm had passed, the rain had stopped and the stars were just beginning to twinkle. Jane inhaled the fresh clean scent of rain and shut her eyes. For a minute she was sixteen and back on the ranch in Mississippi, her mother standing beside her, both of them exhausted to the point of giggles after a long day working beside the hired hands.

"What were you thinking about?" he asked softly.

"Old times," she said.

"Want to go out for supper?"

"No thank you. I want a shower, my soft old nightshirt, a good movie on television, and food. Not necessarily in that order. How about omelets to start off with?"

"With cheese and ham and bacon?"

"All of the above, plus fresh tomatoes on the side and hash browns. No biscuits because I'm too tired to stir them up. Toast."

"So I wore you out with just two little truckloads, did I?" he grinned.

"Little ole gypsy city girl like me who's not used to working hard would get tuckered out with just a couple of truckloads, wouldn't she?" Jane put on her best fake Southern accent.

"You're not ever going to tell me about yourself, are you?" he asked on the walk to the house.

"That answer would be 'no.'"

"I wouldn't think less of you," he said.

"You can't know that. What if I told you I'd murdered a bank teller in a robbery or shot an old lady on the street to make my bones in the gang I wanted to join?"

"But you didn't. You couldn't live with yourself if you'd done those things," he said without hesitation.

"If you really, really think that, then everything else doesn't matter. You'll know I'm a good person and that's enough. You want onions in the omelet?" She tugged her filthy dirty shoes off inside the back door and tossed them toward the washing machine along with her socks.

"Yes, and I'll help," he said.

"Ahh, a man in the kitchen. That should be amusing."

"I can cook. Granny made me learn the basics. She said there would come a day when she was gone and by damn, it has come. I didn't think she'd go. I thought she'd be back at dinnertime with some big hoo-raw about how she'd scared the hell out of us with her tale of leaving for a whole week."

Jane opened the refrigerator and removed eggs, green peppers, onions, cheese, bacon, and ham. "Why did she make you learn to cook? I thought in this part of the world, men were men and women were women."

He pulled out the wooden cutting board and chose a sharp chef's knife from the drawer. "I suppose she didn't want me to starve."

She fried bacon. He chopped vegetables and shredded potatoes for hash browns. She made toast. He made coffee and set the table. She made the omelets and he put butter and jelly on the table.

"Did you see that? We made supper without killing each other and there was a knife right handy," he said.

She passed him the platter with the potatoes and eggs. "A knife isn't my weapon of choice. Too much blood."

"You prefer a gun?" he asked.

"Poison," she said with a twinkle in her eyes. "Did you watch every single move I made in the kitchen? I could have put arsenic in your half of that omelet."

He turned the platter around and took the half closest to her. "Now the poison belongs to you. Who do I call when you fall dead on the floor in about twenty seconds?"

She loaded her plate and picked up her fork. He was one sneaky son of a gun and she was dog tired. She'd have to watch her tongue or she'd spit out a name so quick even she wouldn't know where it came from. "Just roll me up in a blanket and toss me off the back of the hay truck in the nearest bar ditch."

He helped wash dishes and gave her first chance at the shower on their wing. While he cleaned up, she picked out a movie from the stash beside the television set in the living room. She chose *The Shooter* starring Mark Wahlberg. It had been a toss up between that and *Runaway Bride*. She loved Julia Roberts and Richard Gere, but didn't think she'd find the movie quite as humorous as she had the first time she saw it.

"So what chick flick have you picked out? Not that I care. I'll be asleep and snoring before the first scene is over," he said.

"It's between *Shrek* or *Shrek Two*. I thought I'd let you decide," she said.

He rolled his eyes and glared at her.

She grinned.

"Are you teasing? I never know whether you are serious or not," he said.

"Keep 'em guessing, that's what my grandmother said," she teased.

He sat on the other end of the sofa as far away from her as possible. "Oh, you had a grandmother? I thought you sprang from an egg somewhere deep in the forest, that you were sent here from a flat UFO that landed just outside the bus depot in Wichita Falls."

"Shhh. The mother ship will hear you and call me back home," she whispered as she pushed a button on the remote control and the movie started.

He actually smiled when he realized what she'd chosen. "I love this movie. Haven't seen it but once, but it's a good show."

"Well, I haven't ever seen it so don't tell me anything," she said.

"Only thing I'll tell you is that you won't fall asleep."

"Hand me a pillow and hush."

He fulfilled the first request but she learned that evening that he was not quiet when he watched movies in his own house. He voiced opinions, swore at the bad guys, and rooted for Mark's character, Bob Lee Swagger. Bob Lee had been pressed into service to help the government officials prevent an attempt on the president's life, only to find that he had been double-crossed. The real target was an African who was about to tell the truth about atrocities related to an oil line.

While the adrenaline was still pumping, Slade grabbed Jane in a bear hug when Bob Lee finished the job at the end of the movie. She wasn't ready for him to pick her up off the sofa and dance around the living room with her while the credits rolled. Her feet didn't come close to touching the floor and she felt dizzy.

Suddenly Slade realized what he was doing and set her down abruptly in the middle of the floor. He kept his arms on her shoulders for a moment until she was steady. He was mesmerized as he stared into her chocolate-brown eyes waiting for them to focus and lose the glazed look.

He bent forward.

She tiptoed up to meet him.

Their lips met in a whirl of emotions that shocked them both, but neither wanted the kiss to end.

Finally, at the same moment, they each pulled back.

Jane was shaken and wiped her forehead, trying to make light of the kiss.

"Whew. Thanks for holding me up until I could get my bearings. It wouldn't do for us to watch an action film like that in the theater, would it?"

"Not hardly. But I do try to refrain from too much live commentary when I'm in public. I'm off to bed. Want to go to church with me in the morning?"

Maybe some good old hellfire and damnation would preach out the hot desire that had surged through his body the moment his lips touched Jane's.

"Where do you go?" she asked. Surely she'd dreamed that kiss. One minute she was floating away on a wave of sensation, the next they were talking about church. She reached up and touched her lips to see if they were as hot as they felt.

"Methodist over in Nocona. Granny and I haven't been in a month, with the busy season on us, but the hay is in and we could take a day of rest, I suppose," he said.

"What time?"

"We don't often attend Sunday School, so eleven for church." He wanted to retract the invitation. Everyone in the church would think they were a couple. Lord, if he shared the hymnbook with her, they'd have him standing in front of the preacher within a month.

"I'll be ready," she said.

She immediately realized her error and didn't know how to bow out of it gracefully—or at the least without Slade demanding an explanation. She'd have to go or else he'd want to know why. There would be that many more people who might remember her if John did appear on the scene. That many more who could point a finger to the Double L Ranch, and she wouldn't put Nellie… or Slade… into harm's way for all the gold in Fort Knox.

She fell asleep thinking that she wanted out of the oil business if there could ever be an ounce of truth in the Bob Lee Swagger story. Did people actually commit such atrocities out of greed for oil? Of course they did. A company as small as Ranger Oil had caused Paul to be greedy and to put out a contract on her. Maybe it had been an omen that she had watched that particular movie tonight.

Sunday.

She wore one of her two sundresses and sandals. She shaved her legs and used the last of her perfume. Slade was quiet on the way to church and kept his distance. The kiss must have been nothing more than the surge of adrenaline brought on by the movie. She sat in the air-conditioned comfort of the pickup truck and wondered what she would have done if Slade had kissed her because he wanted to and not because he was hyped up on the action film. The refrigerated air couldn't keep up with her hormones and she had to cough to keep from actually panting a little.

He was dressed in his Sunday best. Shiny eel boots. Black Wranglers. White shirt unbuttoned at the collar. Hair combed back perfectly. Shaving lotion applied to send a woman's senses reeling.

Once they were in the sanctuary and sitting in the Luckadeaus' normal pew, two from the back on the left side, he was careful to keep his hymnbook in his lap and a foot of space between them. She did the same. She wasn't totally ignorant of the ways of the religious. Sit close enough together to share a book and the old ladies went home to start a double wedding ring quilt. It sounded old world, maybe even a bit Amish, but her momma had taught her more than how to stack hay and make lasagna.

The preacher's sermon was from the twelfth chapter of first Corinthians. He went on and on about the aspects of love and what it produced in the lives of Christian people. Jane thought about asking the preacher if he taped his sermons so she could buy one to send to her stepfather and ex-fiancé.

After services she was introduced to a multitude of people. Gray-haired ladies who'd tipped the dye bottle a little too much and turned their hair lilac, young women who no doubt thought Slade Luckadeau was a whole dishful of eye candy, old men who slapped Slade on the back and winked, young men who slapped Slade on the back and winked.

"So where are you going to feed me?" she asked.

"What makes you think I'm going to take you out? We can go home and eat there."

"You have to take me out or else get singed by hellfire. It's biblical."

He led the way to the car and was very, very careful not to let their hands touch. One infraction would be reported to his grandmother so fast it would create a tornado between Nocona and Wichita Falls. Every woman in the church had been hunting for a bride for Slade since he'd turned thirty. Folks evidently thought that he was near death and an heir to the Double L was in danger. Didn't they remember that his Uncle Robert had two children? Granted, they weren't one bit interested in ranching, having been raised in the big city of Houston where Robert worked for NASA, but it didn't mean Slade was the last chance to keep the Double L in Luckadeau hands.

They reached the back of the truck at the same time and she hurried around to the passenger's side. She didn't need him to open doors for her. She was quite capable of doing it herself, thank you very much. If they were on an actual date, then she'd expect it, but he could scarcely tolerate her. The exception being when they watched action films—and that was an adrenaline rush and simple physical attraction.

He got in, started the engine, adjusted the air conditioning and said, "Quote me verse and chapter that says you should go out to eat on Sunday."

"Matthew five, verse six. Blessed are they who hunger after righteousness for they shall be filled," she intoned.

"What has that got to do with Sunday dinner?"

"Do you want to be blessed or not? It says we will be blessed if we are hungry after righteousness, as in going to church. And He promises we shall be filled."

He fought back the smile, determined that she wouldn't see that he was amused with her answer. "That's stretching the verse until it breaks."

"So?"

"So I'll feed you dinner. Dairy Queen, Sonic, or Subway. Your choice."

"Fried chicken, potato salad, dinner rolls, and maybe a bean burrito," she said.

"I thought you said you weren't cooking."

"I'm not. They sell all that at the grocery store. We can take a picnic to the park."

"Are you kidding me?"

"No, sir. I do not tease when it comes to food or a park. I love the swings and the slide."

The Nocona park was located on the south side of Highway 82. It had a small tennis court, basketball hoops, swings, slides, tetherball, and enough sports equipment to keep a whole classroom of kids busy for a whole day. It also had a pavilion with picnic tables and benches where Slade and Jane spread out their grocery store bounty and had lunch.

Slade couldn't believe a little woman could eat so much and stay so small. She barely reached his shoulder, so she was probably five foot three inches at best. Her waist was small, hips rounded, a little small in the bosom—though there was enough to fill out the top of the sundress with no problem.

"And now we put away the leftovers for a mid-afternoon snack when we get home, and we go play. I brought shorts and a T-shirt. I'll change in the truck and you'll keep watch." She announced as she finished off a chocolate donut complete with sprinkles on top.

He pushed her on the swing and her laughter rang throughout the park like church bells. She climbed on every jungle gym, raced from one ride to the next, and dared him to see-saw with her. She'd been eleven years old the last time her mother took her to the park in Greenville. It wasn't nearly as big as the one in Nocona nor did it have as many toys. Her mother had played with her and it had always been one of her fondest memories.

It was late afternoon when they got back to the ranch only to find a message on the machine from Nellie, saying that she'd won five hundred dollars at the poker tables the day before and Ellen had won four hundred. Myra had lost and so had Jeannie but they'd sworn in blood they wouldn't tell how much. Sunday they were skipping church and hitting the shopping mall at one o'clock right after lunch at the Cracker Barrel so she wouldn't be calling again until Monday or Tuesday. They had her cell phone but by damn if they called for anything other than blood, guts, or a similar emergency they'd have to deal with her when she got home.

Jane and Slade had an afternoon nap and sat on the deck reading the rest of the evening. Jane had the urge to kiss Slade on the cheek when they reached his door at bedtime but she hesitated and the moment passed. She was tired enough to sleep soundly—at least until morning when the nightmare awoke her again. The only variation in the horrible dream was that Slade was there. John was drowning her in the clear water and Slade was hitting him with his fist. When she awoke she wondered what a dream interpreter would make of that?

Monday.

Jane expected a routine Monday.

She didn't get it. Dinner came off without too much trouble. She made banana pudding and a double batch of brownies for dessert while a pot roast complete with potatoes and carrots cooked in the oven. Biscuits and green beans with ham hocks and thinly sliced onions finished off the meal. The men ate with gusto, leaving just enough leftover roast to slice for barbecue sandwiches that night.

It was after dinner that things got hectic. One of the older Mexican hired hands had a heat stroke in the one-hundred-plus degree weather. Another one took him to the emergency room at the Nocona hospital. That left Slade shorthanded and he needed to get the hayfields plowed under and readied for another crop.

Jane had the cookbooks down, intending to make a couple of Bundt cakes for the next day's dessert, when the phone rang. She picked it up on the second ring.

"Hello. Luckadeau residence."

"Who's speaking?"

The hair on her neck stood straight up. Chills chased down her spine in spite of the heat. "Who would you like to speak to?"

"Nellie Luckadeau, please."

"May I ask who is callin'?"

"This is Ramona Farris."

"Well, ma'am, you'll have to call back. Miz Luckadeau has gone off on a little visit. Will anyone else do?" Jane exaggerated a Mexican accent, hoping that Ramona wouldn't recognize her voice.

"Slade Luckadeau?"

"He's off on a tractor. I don't reckon he could come to the phone right now," Jane said.

"Would there be a young lady in the house by the name of Ellacyn Hayes?"

"Used to be."

"Where is she now? Out shopping with Mrs. Luckadeau?"

"No, ma'am. Miss Ellacyn stayed a week with us and took off one night in the middle of the night. Just disappeared after she got that first paycheck. I liked the girl just fine and she was a hard worker. This new one Miz Luckadeau hired ain't got nearly the spunk."

"Do you know where she went?" It was clear Ramona was getting bored with the conversation.

"Yes, ma'am, I surely do. It was my job to see to it she worked in the kitchen helpin' fix up the menfolks' dinner. They get hungry out there a-workin' like dogs in the heat so we have to feed 'em good. So we got to be good friends, me and Miz Ellacyn did. Strange name, that is, ain't it?"

"I don't care about her name. I want to know where she went," Ramona snapped.

"Lady, I don't have to be givin' out no information to you." Jane hung up the phone. She counted to ten and tried to breathe normally. It would ring again because Ramona needed the information.

It did.

"Hello, Luckadeau residence." Jane said.

"This is Ramona Farris again. I'm sorry I was rude. It's just that Ellacyn is my sister and she's got psychological problems. She's escaped from the institution where we keep her and she needs her medicine or she might do harm to herself. We've been looking for her for a month. Anything you could tell me would be a great help."

"Yes, ma'am. Like I said, it's a strange name. I'm right sorry to hear that the poor little thing ain't right in the head but you know, I kinda thought that when she was here that week. Miz Luckadeau, she give her a hun'erd dollars for that week's work and I don't reckon she earned but about half that much. Stayed in her room and looked scared most of the time. Would that have been a-cause she didn't have her medicine?"

"Oh, yes, I'm sure it was. Now could you please tell me where she said she was going?"

"Be right glad to tell you seein' as how the poor little thing needs to be put back where they can take care of her. You never know about all the crazy people out there in the world. Why, any man could come along and talk her into doin' ugly things for a few dollars to keep her alive."

Ramona sighed and Jane smiled.

"She packed up her bags on a Saturday morning when Miz Luckadeau and Slade was off to the grocery store. The foreman here on the ranch said he was going over to Gainesville to get a part for a tractor and she asked if she could go along with him and would he drop her at the bus stop. Said she was headin' on north for a spell. Maybe Tulsa or Miami. That's a town on up past Tulsa in the corner of Oklahoma. I figure she'll go to Miami. No reason except that she kept talking about liking the beach. I didn't know there was a beach there. Did you?"

"Maybe she was talkin' about Miami, Florida," Ramona said.

"Never thought of that. I bet she was. But why would she go to Tulsa first? Maybe she's got relatives there who she wanted to see? She didn't mention anyone but one distant cousin and she didn't say if she lived in Tulsa or not. Sorry I can't be of no more help to you. Poor little ole thing out there all alone."

Ramona hung up without even saying good-bye.

The phone rang again and Jane's nerves about snapped.

"Hello. Luckadeau residence." Jane was still using her fake Mexican accent.

"Jane, is that you?" Slade asked.

"It's me." She changed back to her normal voice.

"What are you doing? Playing jokes in case Granny calls? Never mind. Don't tell me. You'd beat around the bush until it was stripped bare of leaves. I need someone to drive a tractor and plow until dark. You ever done that?"

"Where are you?"

"Remember when you rode the fence line with me?"

"Yes."

"Go all the way to the second section line and turn left. You'll see the dust before you get to me. Pull in and park the truck anywhere."

She followed directions, crawled up into the cab of a John Deere tractor, and fired up the engine. All afternoon she plowed and worried that Ramona might have seen through her story. If not, maybe she bought herself a few more days and they'd be off on a wild goose chase to Tulsa or Miami... Oklahoma or Florida. She didn't care as long as it kept them away from the ranch and out of her sight.

❖ ❖ ❖

Tuesday.

She cooked all morning. Two Bundt cakes. Vegetable soup. Ham and cheese sandwiches on thick slabs of her own homemade bread. Chips and picante made from her mother's recipe.

She plowed all afternoon, stopping just long enough to drive back to the house, make sandwiches, refill the tea jug, and carry his meal to Slade at suppertime. She ate while she drove the truck back to the field and didn't sit around jawing with him while he swallowed his food. She got back inside the cab of the tractor, fired it up, and turned on the lights. At ten thirty that night they stopped and dragged themselves to the house. They didn't have energy for anything other than showers, and were asleep five seconds before their heads hit their pillows.

Wednesday.

Lord Almighty, but she'd be glad when Nellie got home. She missed her so bad that morning as she laid out chicken to barbecue in the oven that she could have wept. She whipped up two pecan pies and a double recipe of peach cobbler for dessert, then made baked beans and potato salad.

Slade and the help talked about moving cattle that afternoon from one pasture to the next. They debated whether to get out the semi and load them up, or round them up by horseback and herd them from one section of land to the other.

"Hey, Jane, you want to ride this afternoon? We could use another person. You ever worked a herd?"

"I expect I could learn fast enough," she said, glad for anything to pass the afternoon so she wouldn't be so homesick to see Nellie and Ellen.

She whispered threats into Demon's ear as she saddled him. She stuck a foot in the stirrup and hefted herself up and over in one graceful motion. He must have believed her about the cat food industry because he responded to every touch of the rein the rest of the day. She brought up the rear and would have had to eat a fair amount of dust had they been driving the cattle in anything but pasture grass. But to her notion she had the best seat in the house.

The cattle dogs were a big help in keeping the cows together but often a calf would get lost and start bawling for its mother. During the afternoon when they rounded up a straggler and brought it back to the herd, she and Demon flushed a dozen rabbits that skittered off away from the cattle hoofs. Slade had trained his dogs well, though, because not a one of the four took off after the rabbits. She could almost see the desire to chase them in their eyes, but they obeyed when he whistled.

Would he expect his wife to jump like the dogs when he hollered?

"None of my business, is it, Demon?" she mumbled as she adjusted her hat.

They hit the house that night at dark and ate leftover chicken straight out of the pan, standing at the kitchen bar. They wiped their fingers on paper towels and Slade called for the first shower that night. She didn't see him again until morning. She was too tired and sore to dream about anything that night. There was surely not time for fretting about what could be or would be on a ranch.

Every waking minute was taken up with work. Not that she was complaining. She was down to two weeks until her birthday on July eighteenth. Then Paul was going to find out what it felt like to be on the street without a job. And John could abandon his plans to marry slash kill her and go on back to sleeping with his pseudo sister.

Thursday.

Jane moaned when she crawled out of bed. Her legs were going to be permanently bowed if Slade asked her to ride all afternoon again. He'd already eaten breakfast and was going out the back door when she reached the kitchen.

"Got to get at it early today. We're branding the late calves. Should be done by noon. Sorry to hurt your feelings if you've got a thing for seared flesh," he said.

"Only yours. Bring the iron on home while it's hot. I can always put the brand on you," she said.

He picked his hat from the rack and settled it on his head. "I bet you would, too."

"It was a promise, not a threat."

"Actually, I'm not sure I'd want you to brand me. Isn't that what you women say when you catch a man and haul him kicking and screaming to the altar?"

"Just leave it at the corral. If that's what it means, I damn sure don't care anything about it," she said.

He left with a chuckle and a wave.

She put on an old Conway Twitty CD she found in the rack beside the television and listened to music as she cooked. She swayed with an imaginary dance partner when Conway sang, "Hello Darlin'." While she made a batch of chocolate chip cookies to go with the fruit salad for dessert she listened to "I See the Want To in Your Eyes." He sang about seeing a sparkling little diamond on her hand and that it was plain she already had a man but he could see the want to in her eyes.

That drew her up short. Had she met Slade when she was engaged to John, would he have seen the want to in her eyes? Would it have even been there? She was finally willing to admit she enjoyed the bantering they shared. That he was handsome was never a question; that he would ever find her attractive had six question marks behind it.

By the time she started making meatloaf, Conway was crooning "Tight Fittin' Jeans." He sang about a woman trying to hide the kind of woman she truly was by the denim clothes she wore and that he saw right through her tight fittin' jeans. Lord, she truly hoped Slade never saw through her tight fittin' jeans and found out that she was worth a fortune. Conway's song said there was a tiger in the tight fittin' jeans and they'd gone through a lot of beer.

Maybe Jane really was a cowgirl if all it took was jeans and a love for good old cold beer to make her one. She made up her mind before the song ended that she was selling the oil company for sure. She'd fallen in love with ranch life. Maybe she could even talk Nellie into coming to Greenville for a visit occasionally.

Conway started singing an old favorite of her grandmother's: "I'd Love to Lay You Down." Her skin began to tingle as she pictured Slade singing that song to her.

"Now where in the hell did that come from?" she grumbled. "He'd never sing that to me, especially when he finds out that I really have duped him all this time. He thinks I'm a poor vagabond gypsy. He'll feel like I made a fool of him when he finds out the true story."

"Who are you talkin' to?" Slade opened the back door and started singing with Conway about how he'd love to lay her down and there was so many ways her sweet love made the house into a home. He mentioned her standing in the kitchen in her faded cotton gown.

"You singing to me?" she asked.

"Just singing with the old Twitty bird." He grabbed another pair of gloves and was gone again.

That set him to thinking about how he had liked to see her in the kitchen in her faded nightshirt that came to the top of her knees. And how she had stepped right up to the task and taken on the running of the house all week.

He shook his head to clear such idiotic notions out of it and went back to work.

The next song on the CD was "Don't Call Him a Cowboy." When Conway said not to call him a cowboy until you've seen him ride, Jane's face turned scarlet. Then he sang about fancy boots and a Stetson hat that didn't tell what's inside and if he wasn't good in the saddle, she wouldn't be satisfied, and the high color in her cheeks actually burned.

That set off a whole string of visuals of Slade in a saddle that was not on the back of a horse. She had no doubts that he'd make it through more than a one-night rodeo like Conway mentioned. Lord Almighty, folks went on and on today about the innuendos in the songs on the market. Conway alluded to as much or more than the new singers.

She wished she could erase the pictures in her mind, but they wouldn't go away. At noon she avoided Slade like the plague and was very glad he didn't need her help that afternoon. She caught up on laundry, cleaned house, scrubbed bathrooms, and made six pies for the next day's dinner. Still, every time she turned around she was humming that song about not calling him a cowboy until she'd seen him ride.

"Oh, he's a cowboy, no doubt," she giggled.

"What's for supper?" He hit the door at seven thirty that night.

"Potato soup is on the stove. Bread is sliced and in the Tupperware container. Cookies are beside that in a plastic bag. I'm off to read a book until I fall asleep."

He ate alone and wondered if his singing had offended her.

Friday.

Jane awoke with a song in her heart, but it didn't have words and Conway Twitty had never sung it. Nellie was coming home and she was as excited as a five-year-old with a fistful of money in a candy shop. She hopped out of bed and headed for the kitchen only to be met with the aroma of bacon and coffee wafting down the hall.

Slade, cooking breakfast? Had the world come to an end or had hell frozen over?

Nellie was flipping pancakes. "Good mornin'. How'd things go while I was gone?"

Jane crossed the room and hugged her fiercely. "You're home! I missed you so much."

"I enjoyed the trip and the fun but I'm glad to be back," Nellie said. "Ellen says she's sleeping in this morning."

"You brought her, too! It gets better and better," Jane said.

"What?" Slade said sleepily from the door jamb where he'd been leaning the past few minutes. Jealousy rattled through him that Jane showed such emotion for Nellie and was so angry at him for singing that she wouldn't even sit down to supper with him.

"Nellie is home," Jane sing-songed.

"Glad to have you back. Please don't leave me with that shrew again," he said, pointing at Jane.

"Shrew! Me! You've got cow shit for brains! He was mean to me, Nellie. Made me work like a dog all week. I had to drive a tractor, herd cattle, and haul hay. Took me to church and was going to make me come home and cook dinner. I had to produce Bible verses to get a piece of fried chicken."

"She stretched that verse so thin even Jesus would have sent her to hell for using it like that," Slade yawned.

Nellie beamed.

Things were going right in her world.

Chapter 8

Jane had never been to a small town fireworks display before. She'd always seen the big one in Greenville or back when her mother was alive there was always a big Fourth of July celebration at the ranch. They would barbecue a steer and at least one hog, invite everyone in western Arkansas and eastern Mississippi, and at the end of the day there would be a spectacular fireworks display from a boat in the river on the back side of the ranch.

According to Nellie, in Terral, Oklahoma, population 386, they roped off a section of the main street, sold hamburgers right off the grill and snow cones made while you wait, and turned the children loose with their personal firecrackers and other fireworks. At dark they put on a show for everyone. It was a bring-your-own-lawn-chair, eat, and visit affair.

Five miles and the Red River separated Ringgold, Texas and Terral, Oklahoma. Terral was almost four times as big as Ringgold and actually had a Mini-Mart that sold bread, pizza, milk, and gas, as well as a small grocery store. There were two cafés: Doug's Peach Orchard, specializing in catfish and calf fries; and Mama Josie's, where a person could dine on Mexican food, hamburgers, or steaks in an old lumberyard-turned-café. Nellie had insisted they stop at Doug's for catfish. She rode to the celebration with Ellen, Jeannie, and Myra. Since it was Friday night and they'd have to postpone their pseudo-bridge game, they'd all decided to go together. She'd insisted that Slade take Jane in the truck with him so everyone could be more comfortable.

The Peach Orchard was a small restaurant with the menu on the wall at either end of a dining room decorated with real branding irons. Nellie laid claim to a table for six and motioned for the waitress, who brought a note pad and asked them what they'd like to drink.

"Coors for me," Slade said.

"I'll have Miller Lite," Ellen said.

Jeannie looked at the menu and held up two fingers. "Make that two Millers."

"I'll have the same," Myra said.

"Nellie?" The waitress asked.

"Iced tea tonight. I might have to drive these drunks home."

"You can't drive," Slade said.

"Better to be caught driving blind than drunk," Jeannie laughed.

"Sweet tea for me," Jane said. Already the evening was shaping up to be fun. For a second she let the idea of John and Ramona flit through her mind, then reassured herself that they were in sunny Miami combing the beaches for her.

The waitress returned with drinks and took their orders. Jeannie, Myra, Nellie, and Ellen all had catfish and it was on the tip of Jane's tongue to order the same when Slade said he guessed he was the only one with enough nerve to eat calf fries. Jane picked up the gauntlet and grinned.

"Bring me a full order of calf fries and please add a Coors to that order. Maybe I'll join the ranks of the drunk after all," she said.

"Do you even know what calf fries are?" Slade asked.

"Of course, they're like chicken fries. Little pieces of veal rolled in some kind of special batter and deep fat fried," Jane said.

A wide grin split his handsome face and she noticed the dimple on the left side for the first time. His blue eyes twinkled prettier than the stars in a midnight velvet sky. "You are exactly right."

"What are you two fighting about now?" Nellie asked.

"We missed it," Ellen said. "Do the fight all over again."

"Well, damn, I've got to learn to keep my mouth shut," Myra said.

"You all are the real Ya-Ya Sisters, aren't you?" Jane laughed.

"You bet we are. They probably made that movie about us and just changed the names to protect the guilty," Myra told her.

Ellen pulled a mirror from her purse and fluffed up her hair. "When we were growing up, there were five of us. What one of us couldn't think of, the other four did, and we barely stayed a step ahead of trouble all the time. You all remember when we were kids. Of course I was the youngest one and they all got me in trouble. They're probably the reason I turned out the way I did."

"What about when we were kids? Hell, Ellen, you were the wild one. You had your bra off and headed for the bonfire before any of us could unhook ours," Myra said.

"Y'all were old and floppy by then, anyway," Ellen teased.

"What story were you going to tell?" Jane asked.

"Don't encourage her," Slade moaned.

Ellen pointed a perfectly manicured, bright-red polished fingernail at him. "You can hush or go over there and eat by yourself. The story goes like this: we were all staying at Jeannie's house. Her momma was the least nosy of all and we could sneak out easier there. All five of us went skinny dipping in old man Massey's farm pond and honey, those minnows nibbled at more than our toes. We damn near got caught by the local deputy. Of course, if we had, I fully intended to divert his attention while the older four got dressed."

Jane laughed right along with them. Slade pretended he wasn't a bit interested but he had that twinkle in his eye that told Jane he was amused as much as she was.

"So what were you fighting about?" Nellie asked.

"He dared me to order calf fries. So I did."

"I did not dare her and when she turns up her nose at them, I'll eat her portion," he said.

"Do you know what calf fries are?" Nellie asked.

"Granny!" Slade exclaimed.

"Of course, they are little bits of veal, rolled in batter and deep fried to a golden brown," she said.

"Slade?" Nellie lowered her head and looked up over the top of her eyebrows.

The waitress brought their food before Slade could explain. She set a red plastic basket in front of each of them. French fries covered the top. Fish or calf fries were on the bottom. A platter of bread, tartar sauce, sliced onions, and pickles was set right in the middle of the red-and-white checkered vinyl tablecloth.

"Napkin?" Slade used his manners and handed the roll of paper towels sitting upright on a wooden holder to Jane.

"Don't mind if I do. Maybe I'll just have three or four. I might be a messy eater," she said.

"Dig down deep and get one of those calf fries. See if they're as good as the ones you got over in Arkansas. That is where you are from?"

"I was born in El Dorado," she said.

"And grew up there?" He was already popping one into his mouth and blowing out at the same time because it was so hot.

"Hey, I found one hiding under all these scrumptious lookin' fries. And don't worry about where I grew up, Slade Luckadeau. Just eat your bull balls and hush while I enjoy mine."

He jerked his head around. "You said..."

"I said they were little bits of veal, which they are, and they were rolled in batter and fried, which they are, so don't be sending me to hell with that look. I didn't blow the bottom out of the ninth commandment about bearing false witness."

Jeannie nodded. "Want to join our Ya-Yas and be our number five?"

"Maybe. Can I have a fancy hat or go skinny dipping in a pond? These are wonderful. Almost as good as Momma made. And don't ask me her name, either, Slade, because that's all I'm saying."

"Honey, if you'll make it a moonless night so all our cellulite and baggy skin don't show, we'll gladly go skinny dipping with you, but you'd probably have a better time if you went with Slade," Ellen said.

Slade blushed. "No thanks."

High color filled Jane's cheeks. "Chicken?"

"No, just protecting your young innocent eyes," he said.

It was near dark when they finished eating and drove a mile up Highway 81 to the Mini-Mart, where they turned right and parked in the first available place. Everyone lined up at the back of the truck to claim a lawn chair and then carried them past the post office, the fire station, the old Methodist church, and to the center of town.

The four ladies lined their chairs up in a row and commenced to talking about the past Fourth of July celebrations they'd attended together. Slade and Jane sat behind them on the steps of the old Methodist church, which had been boarded up for years.

Jane loved listening to them talk, even when various people stopped by to visit a spell. They discussed the weather and wondered if it could get any hotter and people not start dropping like flies; who died; who had babies; who moved away; the fire in 2005 that almost wiped out Ringgold; the watermelon crop and whether there'd be enough to last through the festival in a few weeks.

"What festival?" Jane asked.

"Watermelon. They've had it for as long as I can remember. Granny first brought me when I was eight. They set up tables and give away ice cold watermelon all day. Vendors come and line the streets with their wares and there's games and contests. It used to be bigger and then it fizzled for a few years. Now there's a committee that oversees everything and it's growing again, only now they call it the Terral Festival or something like that," Slade explained.

"Hey, what happened to number five? I just realized y'all mentioned there being five of you. Where's number five?" Jane asked in a lull when there were just the four of them.

"She died about ten years ago. It was a sad day for us. She got married and moved away when we were all about nineteen. At least they were all nineteen. You got to remember I'm a lot younger than these old girls," Ellen said.

"I'm sorry," Jane said.

"She came back every year about this time and we'd have this big party at Jeannie's momma's old place. It was just a little frame house and her momma had been gone for years, but Jeannie kept it just like it was back then. It had beds and a full kitchen and a living room and this wonderful old gazebo out back," Myra said.

"And we'd all get together for a few days, get drunker'n old women ever should, and remember all the good times we'd had," Nellie said.

"In Ringgold?" Jane asked.

"No, in Chico."

"You told me you were going to a friend's house for Bible studies," Slade said to Nellie.

"I was. Jeannie's momma had a Bible on the coffee table," she told him bluntly.

"Anyway, when number five died, we put her picture on a little raft we made with Popsicle sticks, set it on fire, and pushed it out into the pond where we'd skinny dipped," Jeannie said. "It was truly a funeral worthy of a queen."

"Did she have children?" Jane asked.

"One," Nellie answered.

"Oh, look, they're about to start the big show," Myra said.

Jane hopped up. "I'm going for a snow cone before it starts. Anyone else want one?"

"Blue coconut," Slade said.

The rest declined and she headed toward the stand at a trot so she wouldn't miss any of the show. She ordered a blue coconut and a salty dog and was on her way back when she stepped on a piece of paper and saw two elderly women pointing at her at the same time. She stopped and looked at the paper stuck to her sandal and there she was, in living color, wearing a white robe and looking like pure hell. For a moment she wondered if the picture was computer generated. She'd never worn a robe like that except when she got out of the pool.

Maybe she hadn't caught a lucky break after all when she got off the bus in Wichita Falls. Maybe she'd just prolonged a really unlucky streak.

Another look and she remembered John taking it with his digital camera. It had been an issue because she didn't want him to snap it. Her hair was wet and limp and hanging in her face. Her makeup had long since washed off and she'd just jerked the robe on to cover her bikini. She looked exactly like Ramona had described her on the phone. Drugged out and slightly deranged. The white robe could easily be mistaken for hospital attire. How very convenient. She picked up the flier and read what she could by the low lights.

Ellacyn Jane Hayes had escaped from an institution, blah, blah, blah. The same story Ramona had told her on the phone.

When Jane looked up several other people were holding the fliers and looking around the grounds. Evil had come to their little town. The insane lunatic might be hiding behind the trees ready to jump out and nab a child while a firecracker was being popped to cover the sound of the screams.

"Have you seen this woman?" Ramona was asking the snow cone operator. "We had word she was last seen working for Nellie Luckadeau at the Double L Ranch."

"Can't say I have. Nellie don't usually hire help, though. Wait a minute. She does look familiar. No, I'm wrong. I'd remember someone that helpless lookin'," the lady said.

Jane's heart raced, blood pumping through her veins so fast and furious that she got dizzy. Her stomach clenched up into knots. She made herself pretend to study the poster as she carried the snow cones in one hand toward the pickup truck. Thank goodness she still had the keys in her purse and she'd brought it along to buy the snow cones.

She tossed the snow cones along with the flier at the last minute and was about to crawl into the truck when a hand touched her shoulder. Adrenaline rushing and flight mode kicking in, she doubled up her fist and drew back to begin the fight. She might wind up dead but they were going to have a hard job. A big fist closed over her hand in mid air.

"You about to steal my truck?" Slade said.

"Yes, I was. But I was just going home in it."

He shoved a flier in her face. "Got anything to do with this horrible picture of you?"

She nodded.

"Damn, I hate to miss the fireworks show, but I guess we'd better get you out of the limelight. Folks around here wouldn't cotton to you stealing their thunder tonight. They put on a fine show. If the FBI was to handcuff you and lead you off to the unmarked black van which is sitting across the street, that's what the folks would talk about for a month. No one would remember much about the show." The whole time he talked he was leaning in toward her ear as if he was propositioning her.

"What in the hell are you doing?"

"Nod."

She did exactly as he said.

He pulled out his billfold and handed her a dollar bill.

"Fold it up and stuff it into your bra, then get in the truck. Don't slide all the way over. Stay in the middle and put your hand on my neck and toy with my hair while we drive away. There's a man in the van and he's looking right at us," Slade said.

She did.

"Want to explain what the hell is going on that the FBI is looking for you?"

"FBI?"

"They're flashing credentials back there. That is you on the flier, isn't it?"

"It is, but I'm not deranged and I've never been in an institution. Why would the FBI want me if I wasn't in my right mind?"

"That's what Ellen asked them. They said you'd witnessed a murder and they needed you for testimony.

Granny whispered I was to take you home and wait for her to get there. She doesn't want to leave for fear she'll cause them to follow her."

"I'm so sorry and believe me, those two are not FBI agents. That's just a scare tactic."

"You know them? By the way, you can scoot over now and you can stop playing with my neck," he said.

She blushed. "I don't know where to start, but I damn sure don't want to tell this story but once, so I'm waiting until Nellie gets home to do it."

Ten minutes later they were sitting in strained silence in the living room. Half an hour after that, the four ladies came rushing through the door, all of them talking at once.

"Okay, here's the deal. Your grandmother was Olivia Ranger, right?" Ellen said.

"How did you know that?" Jane was stunned. Besides, what did her grandmother have to do with what was happening right then?

"Fate. I believe in fate, Jane. I always have and always will. If Slade had been able to take us to the bus station that morning I wouldn't have been driving. If I hadn't been driving I wouldn't have been so shook up that I had to sit awhile after I put Ellen on the bus back to Amarillo. That's the reason I was sitting there to begin with and you got off that bus and sat down beside me. At first I thought I was seeing a damn ghost," Nellie said.

"Then she called me when she talked you into going home with her," Ellen said, "and I came back as soon as I could. Myra and Jeannie had been out of pocket so we couldn't play poker like we usually do on Friday nights, so we didn't tell them, but they figured it out on their own last Friday night."

"Poker?" Slade looked stunned.

"Keep your eye on the big picture, son," Nellie said.

Jane still didn't understand.

"Here," Nellie pulled a photograph from a drawer and handed it to Jane.

"Who are these people and what has it got to do with... oh, my, that's my grandmother isn't it? And there is Ellen and Nellie and... she's number five. You are JoNell. Grandmother talked about her friend, JoNell. And Ellie and Jean and Myra. But I always thought she was saying Mara."

"We just want to know, what you are running from?" Jeannie said.

Jane nodded. It was time to 'fess up, so she began, "There's two of them posing as FBI. John was my fiancé. He pretended Ramona was his sister, but she's not. My stepfather put out a contract on me. If I'm dead before I'm twenty-five, Ranger Oil goes to him. When the assassin saw me, he decided to put a play of his own into effect. He insured me for a million dollars. After we were married he'd kill me, collect the insurance *and* the contract fee. My stepdad would be the grief-stricken father who'd lost his last link with his dead wife; I'm not so sure he didn't have something to do with her death and my father's. My fiancé would be the poor widower who'd lost his wife on their honeymoon."

"Good God," Slade exclaimed.

"He is that," Jeannie said. "He sent you to us to protect. And by damn we're going to do it. Didn't you know your grandmother was from these parts?"

"No ma'am. I just knew she was born in Texas and moved to El Dorado when she married. My mother and I were both born there. Then we moved to Greenville when I was a little girl to run the oil company office there."

"Slade, pack a bag. You are taking a much-needed vacation and you are leaving your truck here. You'll be driving my Caddy."

"I'm not going anywhere." He crossed his arms over his chest. He'd been right. By golly, he had been right when he said there was something not kosher about that girl. Just look at the mess she'd drug his family into. No sir, he wasn't going to step foot outside the door with her.

"That's where you are wrong, son," Nellie said.

"I'm so sorry I've brought this to you all. If you'll take me to a bus station I'll go somewhere else," she said.

"You'll do no such thing. Slade is taking you and protecting you for the next two weeks. Slade, you go open the safe and load up a briefcase with some cash. Credit cards leave a paper trail. Get one of those little cell phones that you can use once and throw away or better yet, mail it to Alaska so if they can trace it like they do on CSI, they'll be following a cold trail. Call me every other night and get rid of the thing. We'll keep them here as long as we can. They'll be showing up on my doorstep probably tomorrow morning but I reckon I can spin a few lies," Nellie said.

"And if she falls down on the job, I swear I can blow the damn bottom out of that commandment about not tellin' lies," Ellen assured them.

"Granny, this is ridiculous. Just call the sheriff and tell him to come on out here. We'll explain it all and the government will crucify them for posing as FBI," Slade said.

Nellie ignored him. "A rolling stone is a hard target. You'll be staying in a place no more than one night. Always check in the hotels under a different name than you used the last time. Luckadeau is a name they'd spot a mile away. You surprise me, Slade. I figured you'd have enough of your father in you to want to be the knight in shining armor."

"Jane is not a damsel in distress, Granny."

All four women turned their eyes on him.

"I'm not caving in. I'm staying right here. Give her your Caddy if you are so sure she's telling the truth. Maybe she really is a deranged crazy who only appears sane at odd times."

"She's Ellacyn Jane Hayes, one of my best friend's kin and in Texas, that ain't no jokin' matter," Nellie said.

Slade wasn't being railroaded into two weeks in the confines of a twenty-year-old Cadillac with Jane Day or Hayes or whatever her name was. The whole sordid tale she'd told sounded like something an institution escapee would tell. When the ladies thought about it for a while they'd realize they were caught up in the moment of playing detective. He wouldn't call the FBI number on the flier and that's as much leeway as he intended to give.

"Good night ladies. Good-bye, Jane. I'll see you at breakfast in the morning, Granny."

When he was out of hearing range, Nellie told Jane to pack her duffle bag. "We'll figure something out."

"Don't blame Slade. If I heard that story I wouldn't believe it, either," she said.

Tears of frustration, fear, and pure old sadness streaked down Jane's face as she put her meager belongings into her worn bag. She'd made it this far, so she had no doubt she could outrun them for another two weeks. She'd head to Miami and work her way up the eastern coast and across the northern part of the United States. Nellie's advice about not being able to find a rolling stone made sense. Nellie would loan her enough money for the trip and she'd repay her as soon as she was back in Greenville and officially twenty-five years old.

Slade dialed the Montague County Sheriff's office and asked to be patched through to Charlie. It would satisfy his curiosity at best and he'd sleep easier knowing he was right.

"Hi Slade. Why are you calling me at this time of night?"

"I need a favor and it's a big one. You got a number for the FBI?"

"Not in my back pocket. I was putting my hyper kids to bed. They'll see fireworks in their dreams. But I could call the office and get it for you. You going to be right there for five minutes?"

"I will, and thanks, Charlie."

"Want to tell me why you need it?"

"Not right now. Maybe later, if I'm right."

Exactly four minutes later Charlie called back with the number. Slade felt more than a little stupid when he dialed it and almost hung up when the automated voice came on telling him to press one if, press two if, and three because. He went through the procedure, finally talked to a real person, and explained the situation.

"I'm sorry sir, but I can't divulge any information. I'm not an actual agent, just a secretary."

"Are you free to tell me if this number is actually for FBI agents working on a case? Can you at least tell me that much?"

"No, sir, I can't tell you anything," she said. "I can give this to my superior and he can check it for you and give you a call in a couple of days if it's something to be concerned about."

"Please do that," Slade said. He picked up the flier and studied it, then dialed the number.

A female voice answered.

"Hello, this is Slade Luckadeau. I've got the woman you are interested in."

"That is wonderful. Would you please hold her until we can drive over there and pick her up?"

"How do you know where I am?"

"Your phone call is coming from Ringgold, Texas. Is that right? And you live at the Double L Ranch. It's our job to know where Ellacyn was last seen."

"I'll see to it that she's hidden so far you'll never find her if you set foot on my ranch. My grandmother is elderly and I don't want that kind of grief. Jane or Ellacyn or whatever her name is wants to run so I'm taking her anywhere she wants to go. I want to be two days out away from this place before I hand her over to you. I'll be in touch with my grandmother daily, so she'll tell me if you snoop around the ranch. If that happens, you just remember that this is a big world and there's lots of places to hide."

"Two days is fine. Do I call you or will you call me?"

"I'll call you. Is there a reward?"

"Oh, yes, a thousand dollars."

"I didn't catch your name. It wasn't on the flier you flooded Terral with."

"Ramona. My name is Ramona and my partner's name is John."

"Thank you, Agent Ramona," Slade said.

"What? Oh, yes, thank you, Mr. Luckadeau."

He snapped the phone shut and drug a dusty suitcase from the back of his closet. With a moan he began to pack. It would be the longest two days of his life and he didn't look forward to a single minute of it. However, he would be the knight in shining armor his grandmother mentioned. Only he wouldn't be protecting the fair maiden in distress. He'd be riding his white horse away from four old poker-playing ladies who thought this whole episode was an hour of CSI on television.

They'd never know that he'd kept them from being harassed at the least. Or killed at the most, if Jane was telling the truth and Agent Ramona wasn't FBI at all. He shuddered when he thought about what a hired assassin might do to Granny. But then he reassured himself that if the tall tale was bona fide gospel truth, they wouldn't be after Granny and hurting her would only blow their cover. They'd never be hired to do another job if their faces and names got run in every major newspaper in the world. He picked up a laptop computer. There would be time in the evenings to do some research. Did the FBI even get involved in runaway cases?

He frowned. Maybe she wasn't telling the truth at all. Had she been put in an asylum as part of a witness protection program until she could testify about some corporate crime? Was she terrified that she'd be killed anyway even if she did testify? The questions spun like a kid's merry-go-round in his head, but they had no answers.

Chapter 9

SLADE HAD DRIVEN FIVE HOURS AND SAID NO MORE THAN three words to Jane the whole two hundred and fifty miles. She had said her piece in Ringgold and had nothing more to say. Nellie had handed her a throw pillow from the sofa as they walked out the door and commanded her to sleep as much as possible. That was very little. Every time she dozed, she saw that horrid picture of her on the flier.

In Sherman, Texas, he said, "Hungry?"

She shook her head.

In Paris he pulled off Highway 82 into a Love's store. "Need gas."

She said nothing but did go into the store and used the ladies' room.

When he stopped at a Day's Inn in Texarkana, he went inside and returned with two room keys. He tossed one to her and hauled his suitcase out of the backseat of the truck, leaving her to fend for herself. The truck was the one stipulation he made when he changed his mind about going with her. He refused to drive a bright red 1952 Cadillac all over the country. He declared that it would be like putting a Mallard duck on a pond and telling all the bird hunters not to take a shot. Jane had to agree with him, though it came nigh onto giving her the vapors to do so.

She lugged her duffel bag up to the second floor and opened the door to find him standing in the doorway connecting the two rooms with his arms folded across his broad expanse of chest.

"Why?" she asked.

"Because if I'm to be your bodyguard, then I need fast access to you in an emergency."

"No. I don't care if there's a door between our rooms. I'd even trust you to sleep in this other bed." She pointed to the extra queen-sized bed in her room. "I want to know why you changed your mind."

"Who says I did? Tomorrow we decide whether to go on east, drop down south, or go straight up."

"Do I get in on the decision or is it yours?"

"I'll sleep on it and let you know. Checkout is at eleven. Breakfast is in a room off the lobby from six to ten. Don't go alone. Good night, Jane."

"Whatever your reasons are, thank you."

"I bet that hurt like hell to say, didn't it?"

"You will never know the pain of it. Now that the shock is over you can always go on back home. Loan me some money, which I will repay in triple in two weeks, put me on a plane or a bus, and I can make it on my own," she said.

"I'm not loaning you shit, Jane Day or Ellacyn Hayes, or whoever the hell you are," he said.

"Okay then, but don't bitch and whine like a little girl because you have to spend the time with me," she snapped back.

"Good, we got that out of the way. I'm not here because of some underlying gene inherited from my father that says I have to protect the damsel in distress. Truth is I'm here because if you aren't at the ranch, then those FBI agents will be out lookin' for you and not harassing Granny," he said. He was physically exhausted and emotionally wired.

So was Jane. "I'm going to bed. Tomorrow I'll decide whether I'm staying with you or kicking you out on the curb."

Slade let her have the last word. He went to the bathroom and ran a hot shower. It was after two a.m. on a Saturday morning. If all went well, he could be back on the ranch by Tuesday. If not... well, it was going to be one hell of a long two weeks.

It was three o'clock when Jane came out of the shower and turned back the covers on the bed away from the door. She stared at the ceiling a few minutes, but her mind was as numb as her body. She fell into a deep sleep with no haunting dreams.

Slade awoke with a start at ten o'clock, jumped out of bed, and opened the door between the two rooms. He half expected her to be gone and had himself prepared and even hopeful that she would be. He could deal with her disappearance far better than if she was lying to him.

"No such luck," he moaned.

He kicked the edge of her bed. "Hey, rise and shine. Checkout in an hour. We missed breakfast, so we'll get something on the way."

She stretched like she'd done that night he watched her from his window—a catlike movement that mesmerized him. "Did the boogerman find us? Which way are we going? I'm hungry."

She sounded so childlike that he bit the inside of his lip to keep from smiling and reminded himself that the devil reappeared in all kinds of forms. No one said he had to be sporting a forked tail and horns. That morning old Lucifer himself could be a woman in a faded cotton nightshirt with blonde hair and sleep still in her pecan-colored eyes.

"No, we're still a step ahead of the boogerman. I haven't decided which way we are going yet. And we check out in one hour. After that we'll find breakfast."

She jumped to her feet, clicked her bare heels and saluted sharply. "Yes, sir."

"Drop to your face and give me twenty push-ups for sleeping too late," he said before he thought.

It was a serious situation and he had no intentions of teasing or being teased. The whole matter wasn't funny, and he wasn't out on a lark. He was protecting his grand-mother, his aunt, and their two friends. So where in the hell did that bit about push-ups come from, anyway?

"Kiss my naturally born white ass," she said and headed toward the bathroom. He'd made fun of her attempt to lighten the mood so he could drop graveyard dead in a pile of fresh cow shit for all she cared.

"Get ready or I'll leave that naturally born white ass right here in this motel," he snapped.

She turned so fast that all he saw was a blur and came back to tiptoe so she could get even closer to his face. "Just do it. Leave me here, Slade. Go on home and consider your good deed finished. I don't need you. I can fly anywhere in the world and I just bet the front desk will call me a taxi that will take me to the nearest airport."

"What are you going to use for money, Miss Independence?"

"I've got a purse full of credit cards. Even though I've been scared to death to use one of them, they are there.

I can stay a step ahead of them for two weeks, surely. What do you think? Thailand or Mexico City? Think I could get lost for a few days in one of those places?"

"Why didn't you do that to begin with instead of riding the busses from Mississippi to Wichita Falls?"

"Shock. Acute fear. Then plans made in a hurry hoping to throw them off course. Of course it was all in vain because he'd put a tracker in my cell phone. Now that I know I wasn't hearing things that night and I've had time to think about the whole mess, I can outrun them."

"We'll check out and have breakfast and then discuss which way we are going."

"Don't threaten me again," she said.

"Don't offer me kisses that you don't intend to provide," he answered.

"What?"

He winked. "Something about kissing your naturally born white ass?"

She blushed.

They breakfasted at McDonalds. With food spread out all over the table, they discussed which way to go. Jane had never been on a road trip. When she and her family traveled, it was by plane. She'd seen the major tourist attractions: Washington D.C., New York City, Disneyland and Disneyworld, the Grand Canyon, the Redwood Forest, and big cities galore on several continents.

"So what do you want to see? I'll be content to look at the scenery and listen to music all day."

Slade studied the issue for a while. "We don't have to make the itinerary for the whole trip right now, do we?

Why don't we go where the whim takes us each day? Where do you want to wake up tomorrow morning?"

In my bedroom in Ringgold, Texas, she thought.

She said, "In Montgomery, Alabama. I want to go see the cemetery where Hank Williams is buried."

"Thought you didn't care anything about sightseeing."

"Didn't think I did, until that popped into my head. You ever been there?"

He shook his head.

"Then let's make a pact. We can't go anywhere or do anything unless it's new for both of us. I choose one day and you can choose the next."

He nodded. It sounded like a good idea. She could choose that day. He'd choose tomorrow. Then he'd hear back from that FBI agent and he'd go home to Ringgold.

They finished breakfast. She insisted on a receipt for the meal and filed it away in a compartment in her purse. She'd reimburse him for expenses plus his time if he kept her alive for two weeks.

The temperature was already close to a hundred degrees by the time they reached the pickup truck, and a gust of hot air blasted forth when they opened the doors. He hurriedly started the engine and turned the air conditioning up on high. While she took off her shoes and settled in for a long, long drive, he pulled his laptop computer from the backseat and checked the mileage. Ten hours from Texarkana to Montgomery, Alabama. Go south to Shreveport and catch Interstate 20. They'd get there by bedtime if they kept after it steady. But then that was the name of the game. Stay on the move and dodge bullets.

She unzipped the duffel bag and brought out a thick paperback; the cover featured a red-haired woman draped out on a bed with a near-naked man holding her. She wore a yellow slip of a dress. Even the picture inspired pure sexual heat. Jane wasn't a bit surprised that Ellen would have read such a novel.

"What have you got?"

"It's called *Master of Pleasure*." She held it up so he could see the front.

"Who's the author? Nora Roberts?"

"No, a newcomer. Ellen knows a friend of her mother's or something like that. Her name is Jessica Trapp and she lives down in southern Texas."

"Looks like something Ellen would read," Slade said. The woman actually looked like Jane would if she had red hair. Thank God she didn't! Jane was fiery enough with that dishwater-blonde mop on her head.

Jane read for a while and nodded at the words.

"And what are you agreeing with?" He was already bored with the drive and wished he could turn around and go home.

"Page fifty-nine, the heroine is refusing to behave like a lapdog. She's very sassy and the hero isn't going to win every time with this girl. Want me to read it out loud to you?"

"Lord, no. I'd fall asleep and wreck my truck."

"Not with this book, but it's just as well. If I read some of these passages to you we'd have to stop at a local brothel just so you could sleep tonight."

"Okay, okay. I won't ask any more questions about your pleasuring master book."

She went back to reading and he put a Martina McBride CD in the player. It was one she'd made several years before; a tribute to the old country singers.

It started off with "You Win Again." Appropriate to the idea of going to Montgomery the next day, since it was an old Hank Williams tune.

The tinkling piano and strum of the acoustical guitar had him tapping on the steering wheel and enjoying the scenery. They were in the tall pine country with trees reaching to heaven. If he'd been with anyone else he would have considered this road trip a wonderful vacation, but being forced into taking care of a con artist put a damper on his mood.

Martina began singing, "Today I Started Loving You Again."

"Who recorded this first? Dolly?" Jane asked.

"You like country music?" Actually, he'd been surprised to walk into the kitchen and find Conway on the CD player earlier that week. He'd have figured her for a rock music enthusiast.

"Love it. My grandmother listened to it all the time. And Momma was a big fan. She loved George Strait and she would have flown halfway around the world to see Travis Tritt in concert. I really like Billy Ray and Blake Shelton. But you didn't answer me. Who did this the first time? Didn't Willy write it for her?"

"No, Merle and his wife Bonnie wrote it. Recorded it, but it didn't light up the charts."

"Then Dolly did it?" she asked.

"No, Kenny Rogers."

"How do you know so much about it—or are you lying to me?" She eyed him carefully but couldn't tell if he was bluffing. Slade Luckadeau damn sure wouldn't do to play strip poker with, no siree! With his ability to keep that stone face, she'd lose everything but her dignity before the night was finished. On second thought, she might just string him along and see what he had hidden underneath those tight fittin' jeans.

"I read the leaflet inside the CD case when I got it. I actually thought Hank recorded it. It was written back in the early 70s, so neither of us was even born then. Dolly did record it. So did Emmylou, Waylon, and Conway. And you'd never guess who did it the most recently."

"Blake?"

"No, Buddy Jewell."

"You're kidding me," she said. Buddy Jewell had been on American Idol and gotten a lot of publicity with his singing there.

"Nope, he really did."

"Do you realize we just had a five-minute conversation without a fight?" she asked.

"You'd better go back to your sexy book. We'd be pressing our luck to try for anything longer than that."

"You got it," she said. But instead of reading, she propped the pillow against the window, curled up in a ball, and went to sleep.

Slade listened to the CD a couple of more times before he put it away and turned on the radio. Every few minutes he looked his fill of Jane and tried to figure out by staring if she was innocent or the best damned actor in the whole world. If those two people really were FBI, he could be arraigned on charges of aiding and abetting some kind of criminal. If they weren't, he could be wearing cement shoes at the bottom of a deep body of water right along beside her. Neither option was very appetizing.

She didn't awake until suppertime. He exited at the next available off-ramp, headed for the Arby's drive-by, and ordered sandwiches, fries, and Cokes while she dashed inside to pee. By the time the order was ready, she was already back in the truck. She squeezed sauce on his beef sandwich while he drove and situated the French fries between them so they could share.

"Want me to drive for a while and let you catch a nap?" she asked.

"Not on your life. We'd end up in Montana or Mexico," he said.

"Just because I've never been on a road trip doesn't mean I can't follow signs. It's interstate the whole way. And besides, what difference would it make? You just have to keep moving with me for two weeks so they don't catch up to us. Which reminds me, pull over at the next exit, half a mile down the road."

"You already got to pee again? Girl, your bladder ain't big as a thimble."

"No, I saw a sign that said a restaurant was right next to Wal-Mart. They sell those go-phones in there. We can pick up one and call Nellie tonight."

He caught the exit and they bought the phone. He charged it in the cigarette lighter as they drove. When they checked into the hotel in Montgomery at ten o'clock that night, they called Nellie before they unzipped their suitcases.

"Hello," she answered cautiously.

"Granny, is everything all right?" He held his breath. Her voice didn't sound a bit normal.

"Oh, it's you. Yes, everything is fine. I just had one of those telemarketers trying to talk me into a credit card.

I hung up on the woman when she demanded that I give out personal information on the phone. She even wanted to know if I had children or grandchildren who lived here with me and their names. It might have been those loony bins after Jane. I should have given her some kind of spiel, but I was spooked."

"You did a good job, Granny. We are fine. We're in Alabama. We'll call you again tomorrow night. Do you really think we should dispose of this phone? Seems a waste."

"Not if they've found a way to bug my phone and use it to find you," Nellie said. "From now on, don't even tell me where you are. Just that you are fine and having a good time. You are, aren't you?"

"I'd rather be branding cattle," he said. "Hell, Granny, I'd rather be shoveling fresh shit out of horse stalls. Just remember I'm doing this whole thing for you."

Nellie ignored the comment. "Let me talk to Jane."

"Hello," Jane said.

"Darlin', are you havin' a good time?"

"The best in the world, thank you very much. And tomorrow we're sightseeing a bit before we take off again. I love Hank Williams and…"

"Don't tell me where you are or where you are going, in case they've got ways of listening."

"It's so good to hear your voice, Nellie. I miss you," Jane played along with the detective stuff but smiled the whole time.

"It's nice to be missed. Now get off here and get some sleep. Make Slade eat right. He'll live on junk if you let him. Make him stop and eat real food instead of hamburgers and ice cream."

"Yes, ma'am," Jane said. "Good night."

"Same to you. Tell Slade to toss the phone."

Jane handed the telephone back to him and he pushed the right button to disconnect. "She said to tell you to toss it. There's no way in hell they can trace a phone like that, is there? I mean, it's pay as you go and it goes dead the second the minutes are all used up."

"I'm just a country boy. You're the big, hotshot, rich oil baroness. You tell me," he said.

"I want to call my friend before you get rid of it," she said.

"What's her name?"

"Celia."

"I don't think it would be a good idea but it's your naturally born white ass that will be in trouble if you do," he said.

She made a face at him and closed the door between their rooms but she didn't call Celia. She wanted to hear her voice, learn what was going on and what kind of stir it had caused when she ran away, but something kept her from it. Probably that smartass remark from Slade.

She awoke the next morning at seven o'clock. Her first thought was that she was late and Nellie would already have breakfast ready. Then she realized where she was. Day two of the two-week ordeal. A part of her wanted to sneak out of the hotel, catch the next plane to the most populated city in the world, and get lost in the middle of it. The other part said she was doing the most sensible thing, even if it did mean constant battles with Slade.

They ate breakfast in the hotel dining area and gathered up area attraction brochures from a display near the checkout desk. They found Hank Williams' boyhood home, a one-story, white frame house that displayed some of his clothes, documents, photos, and other mementos of his life. Jane was in total awe and hummed "You Win Again" the whole time they were there.

Next they sat in the old pews of the Mount Olive West Baptist Church where Hank said that he had begun his career at the age of five or six years old sitting on the organ stool beside his mother, Lillie, and singing louder than anyone else in the church. Jane hummed "I Saw The Light."

They grabbed a burger on the way to The Hank Williams Museum, where Jane squealed over the 1952 Baby Blue Cadillac convertible, then said in awe, "That's where he really breathed his last. His spirit could still be in that car. Do you feel it, Slade? Can't you just feel all the pain and sorrow plus the joys in his life that made him write those wonderful songs?"

"You believe in all that folderol?" Slade asked.

"I don't disbelieve in it. I do believe in fate since all this happened in my life. I didn't used to, but I do now. Something drove me outside where I heard John and Ramona discussing their plans. Something sent me to Wichita Falls. I could have bought a ticket to Houston out of Dallas. I had enough cash on me. Call it fate. Call it destiny. I don't care. It exists on some level."

"You going to start telling fortunes?" Slade frowned.

"Nope, just appreciating that God is taking care of me."

"Well, thank you very much but honey, I'm not God."

"I didn't say that you were," she said through clenched teeth.

"You said God was taking care of you. It's me taking care of you, so you called me God."

"You are full of shit. And don't call me honey," she snapped.

"Believe me, it wasn't an endearment," he told her. "And I think it might be wise for you to make a trip to the bathroom before we leave. That way we won't have to stop in ten minutes."

"Hey, my bladder isn't as small as yours," she taunted, but she headed toward the bathroom all the same.

She stopped in the first stall and parked her fanny on the potty. She heard the door open and someone humming a tune she didn't recognize. It sounded somewhat like the wedding march and then the door opened again.

Maybe someone was getting married in the museum. Big fans of Hank's, no doubt. She wondered if the groom would wear a copy of one of Hank's suits she'd just seen on display. Perhaps they'd have their first married picture taken by the blue Caddy.

She finished the job and went to the sink to wash her hands and came close to fainting stone cold unconscious on the floor. One of the fliers with her picture was taped to the mirror right in front of her.

That had been Ramona humming.

Jane panicked and ran back into the stall. She sat down, put her head between her legs and took great gulps of air. Finally everything stopped spinning.

She only opened the door a crack to make sure the bathroom was clear before she ventured out. She eased open the door to the museum even slower. Slade was waiting patiently not three feet away.

"Pssst," she whispered.

He looked around, finally spotting her. "What are you doing? You want to see the cemetery, we've got to get going."

She put a finger over her lips and handed him the poster she'd ripped from the mirror. His eyes widened and rage boiled up from his boots to his blue eyes. The only way those people got to Montgomery so damn fast was because they'd bugged something at the ranch. It was a violation and by damn he'd have their hides tacked to the barn door before this thing was over. His grandmother had been right—again!

He edged over to the door and whispered. "I'll be right back. Don't move."

Tears flowed down her cheeks and fear ran through her veins like ice water. She went back into the stall and leaned against the cold metal door.

Slade went to the gift shop and purchased a pair of oversized sunglasses, a package of hair things that she could use to make a ponytail, and a big gaudy pink cowboy hat with a plastic fake diamond tiara for a hatband. On the way to the checkout counter he bought a pink bandana.

The ten minutes Jane leaned against the stall door lasted three days past eternity. When the door opened, she pulled up her feet and held her breath.

"Jane, where are you?" Slade asked.

She slung the door open and rushed out, nearly knocking him over.

"Put these on and then hang on me like you're half drunk and hum 'I Saw the Light.' Don't you miss a single note."

She flipped her hair up in a ponytail, stored the rest of the elastic holders in her pocket, crammed the funny hat on her head, and wrapped the bandana around her neck. She took his arm and began to hum. They walked right past Ramona, who was busy talking to the sales clerk.

He pointed toward the ladies' room and said, "I saw that girl but she looked better than that. She went to the restroom a few minutes ago. She's been in here quite a while. What did she do that the FBI is lookin' for her? Do we need to evacuate the building? Is this a terrorist thing?"

Jane's stomach did so many flip-flops that she feared she'd lose everything she'd eaten that day. She kept humming as if her life depended on it all the way to the truck, where Slade picked her up like a bride and put her inside. Then he took his own good time walking around the hood and slowly crawling inside.

"Go! Get out of here," she said.

"You don't want to go up there to that Malibu and kiss your sweet fiancé on the lips? You might surprise him enough that he won't kill you."

"Great God in heaven, is he really parked that close? Just get us out of here, Slade. I don't think I've ever been so scared in my life."

"If he's the same man that was in the van in Terral, he is—and are you admitting that you might not be so good at staying ahead of them all on your own?" Slade started the engine and pulled out slowly. Ramona rushed out the front door of the museum and went straight to the silver Malibu, gesturing frantically. John got out and followed her back into the museum.

"Let's go see the cemetery now," Slade said.

"Let's go to China," she gasped.

"We came to see where old Hank is buried and pay our respects so we'll do it. We don't have to sling snot and weep over his bones for an hour and those folks are going to be lookin' under every piece of sheet music in that place, so we've got a few minutes," Slade said.

"What if—"

"You know, I'd kind of like to face off with that city slicker and what better place than on top of old Hank's grave? I might be a cowboy with only a set of fists and a pair of tough boots, but I kinda like to think I could whip his ass. He might be good at killing women, but we could see how he'd fare in an honest fight," Slade drawled in that slow Texas accent that weakened her resolve never to trust another man.

She giggled nervously. "He's an assassin. He'll know tricks you couldn't even think about."

"I'm a barroom brawler."

"When did you ever fight? I didn't think you ever left the ranch long enough to get into a bar fight." She began to breathe easier.

"Lots of things you don't know about me."

She shook her head slowly from side to side. "Sorry, I still can't see you as a brawler."

"I was about twenty and went through a rebellious stage. Saturday night drinking was part of it. Fights come with the territory. But that's enough about my ornery days. We're here." He pointed to the cemetery sign and drove up to Hank's grave.

They got out and stood in front of the tombstone. Jane had finally stopped shaking and her heartbeat had settled down to an even rhythm.

"Why'd you make me hum?" she asked.

"To keep you busy so you wouldn't faint. You were pale as a ghost. That man really has got you spooked, hasn't he?"

She gulped and nodded. "I hate to admit it. I've never been afraid of anything in my life but my blood runs cold every time I think of what he and my stepfather planned. Both are going to be mad as hell that they haven't gotten the job done yet. The time is getting close to my birthday."

"We're going to see to it that you have that birthday, Jane. You ever been to Pensacola, Florida?"

She shook her head.

"Less than two hundred miles. We'll be there in time for supper and to watch the sunset on the beach."

"Have you been to Pensacola?" she asked.

"Nope, never have. Looked it up on the net last night. Thought about Nashville, but I want to see the Grand Ole Opry and it's only playing on Friday and Saturday nights."

She followed him back to the truck wishing she had the nerve to reach out and take his hand. "So much for just riding and stopping, huh?"

"Might as well see a few things and make the trip enjoyable, hadn't we?" he said.

"Got to admit, it does help with the nerves."

"So Miss Tougher-than-a-cougar has nerves?"

"And every one of them are raw, so you'd better watch your mouth, cowboy," she smarted off.

They were back in familiar territory.

"So, does this mean I have to feed you again? I didn't know if nerves affect you the same way as being angry."

"Give me an hour to think about Ramona being that close to me. By then I'll be able to do damage to the menu at McDonald's."

She watched the scenery speed by the first hour and then, true to her word, she got angry and hungry. He stopped at a McDonald's and when she leaned across him to order at the drive-by window, traces of the scent of her shampoo filled his nostrils and he wanted to tangle up his hands in her hair and kiss her again.

For the past two days that's all he'd been able to think about. He attributed it to being cooped up in close quarters with no one else to talk to. No way could it be because he was falling for the girl. No sir, he wasn't his father and she wasn't a damsel in distress. Well, she was, but not the kind of poor girl who needed saving from poverty kind of damsel in distress. If everything Jane had said was the pure gospel truth, she was as rich as Midas.

They checked into a cabana room with a kitchenette in a beachfront hotel long before dark. He booked one room with two queen-size beds and hoped she was truly sincere when she said she wasn't averse to sleeping in the same room with him. She looked around the room for the connecting door and back at him.

"You said…" he started to defend himself at the look she gave him.

"It's all right. Actually after today, I'd feel safer," she admitted, although it went against her grain. That episode in the museum had taught her right quick that she wasn't nearly as tough or ready to die as she'd thought. "By the way, who are we tonight?"

He grinned. "Hiram and Lillie Williams, who else?"

She managed a weak laugh.

"And now while it's still light let's go find a place that sells bathing suits and shrimp," he said.

"Beer, bait, and ammo? We might be a little too far south for a redneck place like that," she said.

"All of the above and bathing suits, too, unless you want to do what Ellen suggested and go skinny dipping." He wiggled his eyebrows.

His cell phone rang.

She froze. Nellie wouldn't be calling on his real phone so that meant that John and Ramona had found his number. With that they could probably track them, and damn it all, she'd wanted to go swimming and eat shrimp.

"Hello," he answered it cautiously.

"This is Agent Riley August of the FBI returning your call from two days ago concerning a lady by the name of Ellacyn Jane Hayes and a flier that is out stating that she is a runaway."

"Agent August, would you please state your secretary's name for me?" Slade asked.

"That would be Brenda Levi. She's the one who passed on the information."

Slade let out a whoosh of air. There was no way either John or Ramona would know that information. "Did she relay the whole story to you?"

"She did and we have looked into it. Ellacyn Jane Hayes is a runaway bride. She left a note on the eve of her wedding day and ran away. The note said that she had second thoughts and needed some time to think. That's all we can find on her. She is the owner of a big ranch in western Mississippi and heiress to a large oil company. At least she will be on her twenty-fifth birthday which is… let me check… July 18. The pair posing as agents, John and Ramona Farris, do not belong to us. Also, the phone number on the flier is a private cell phone number. It's not one of ours either. Does that help?" Agent August asked.

"Tremendously. If I sent a picture of the two of them, would you be able to see if they are in your database?"

"Yes, I would."

"Thank you for your time and efforts, Agent August. What's your fax number?"

Slade picked up the hotel pen and wrote a number on the pad beside the phone. He flipped his phone shut and turned to find Jane still standing in the same spot.

"Breathe. Hum again. Do something before you turn to stone," Slade said as he took two steps toward her. She was going to faint at any minute and hit her head on the dresser. He'd come too far to allow her to be killed by a silly accident.

She began to hum.

"Who was that?" she asked and then went on humming.

"The real FBI. I called them before we left home to see if we could find out about the ones posing as FBI. They have no idea who they are, but if I send them a picture they can look them up on their database. You got any pictures with you?"

"Hell no!" The humming stopped.

"You a good enough artist to give me a composite?"

"Hell no again! I have trouble drawing stick people." She sat down on the side of the bed.

"Leaves only one thing." He flipped open his phone and dialed his grandmother.

"Hey Granny, what's goin' on there?" he asked when she answered.

"Slade Luckadeau, I've got caller ID and I know you are using your cell phone. What is the matter with you? Have you lost your mind?"

"No, but I lost my curls and got a tattoo today. Blame Jane when we get back home. She got one, too. A rose, right between her boobs. I got a white tiger on my arm and had my head shaved. Don't worry, I bought a do-rag to wear so I don't sunburn this white globe. Jane loves it. She says tomorrow we might get something pierced while we are in Pensacola. There's a tattoo parlor right down the street from us. I'm thinking of a gold earring and she's looking at a diamond nose ring. What do you think?"

"God Almighty, are you drunk?" Nellie shouted into the phone.

"No, but I will be in a little bit. There's another shot of Jack Daniels in the bottle and it's calling my name. Jane has been drinking Jim Beam all day. I keep telling her Jack is better but she's stubborn as hell. She's even saying we might have some champagne sent up here to the room. Says she didn't get to drink her bottle in Cancun where she was going on a honeymoon with that son of a bitch fiancé she had."

"But…" Nellie had a scalding lecture on the tip of her tongue when she remembered that Jane hated whiskey and the only time Slade ever drank it was mixed with Coke. Most of the time they both preferred cold beer.

"Don't come home until your hair is grown out. I can't do nothing about that tattoo, but if you get your nipples pierced I'll pull them off you with pliers, I don't give a damn if you are twenty-five. I can still whip your ass, boy. And tell Jane to go easy on the champagne. It'll knock her on her butt."

"See you in a couple of days. We're going to hole up here. Ain't no way the FBI will find us in this place," Slade said.

"I mean it. Until your pretty curls are grown back in, don't you darken my doorstep," she said.

"Yes, ma'am. Go have a shot of Peppermint Schnapps and think of me. We've outsmarted those fools."

"Sober up. Good-bye." Nellie said and hoped she'd said the right words.

Jane looked at him as though he'd lost his mind. "What in the hell was all that about?"

"Let's go find bathing suits and I'll tell you on the way. They won't get here until late tonight."

She shivered all the way to her toenails.

While they drove to the first souvenir shop on the strip he explained. "I told her all that shit so they could hear it and they'll be looking for a bald man with a new tattoo on his arm. And a lady with one on her boob."

"Did she believe you?"

"Not at first, but then it dawned on her what was going on and she let me know she understood. She's a grand old gal, ain't she?"

"Grander than you'll ever know."

Chapter 10

JANE SAT AT THE EDGE OF THE WATER, BUTT IN THE SNOW-white sugar sand, toes in the surf that drifted in and out, sloshing against her bare legs. She'd chosen a brown floral tankini at the souvenir shop. She'd tried on a bikini but suddenly went all shy in the dressing room.

Slade wore a baggy blue suit. His chest was broad and muscular, his arms as big as piano legs and firm as an oak tree. What would it be like to have those arms wrapped around her in the middle of the night when she had nightmares? Would they keep her from waking up in a cold sweat? Would just knowing someone that strong was beside her keep the dreams at bay? Suddenly a different thought skipped through her mind. She wondered briefly if indeed he could whip John's ass in a barroom brawl.

"Of course he could," she mumbled. In a real fight he'd be no match for Slade. But he was a devious man and in that Slade was no match for him. John would kill him without raising a finger or giving Slade a black eye. He'd do it with sly poison or a sniper's rifle from a block away. John wouldn't think of fighting fairly.

In the old western movies, John would be the evil cowboy on a black horse and wearing a black hat. Slade, the painfully honest man who said what he thought without considering the consequences it would bring, would wear the white hat and ride the white horse. In present-day movies, John would be the terrorist. Slade would be the man who brought justice and thwarted John's plans.

Slade plopped down beside her. "Who are you talking to now? I'm beginning to believe maybe you *are* an escaped crazy. You have a funny look in your eyes like you are planning a robbery or a killing."

"I'd probably be happier if I was. At least a killing. It could be self-defense if I shoot him before he kills me. It's so peaceful here, it's hard to believe there's someone out there who'd kill anyone for money. It's so far removed from anything I've ever known that sometimes I think I might be insane, Slade. Then I shake my head and realize that I really did hear that conversation and he's really going to assassinate me if he can. And all for money. He was with me every day for six weeks. He got down on one knee and proposed to me. We wrote wedding vows. Is nothing sacred? I feel like a fool for being so duped."

"Evidently nothing is sacred to that man. But don't feel bad. You must have fallen in love with him and that's what makes you so mad. Oh Jesus, Mary, and God all rolled into three. Are you going to want to eat a steer?"

"Not right now. I'm just going to sit here and not think about any of it. This is the most peaceful place in the whole world. I may buy this beach someday."

There was sand, ocean, and sky with a glorious sunset that covered every spectrum of color in the palette. The biblical Noah didn't have a thing on Jane that evening. The day he stepped off the ark he saw a lovely rainbow. She doubted if it was one bit more spectacular than the sun setting that evening both in the sky and reflected in the water.

Slade picked up a broken shell and drew pictures in the sand. "What are you going to do when this is over?"

"I'm going home and cleaning house," she said.

He stopped drawing and looked at her. "As in dusting and scrubbing the bathrooms?"

"No, as in getting rid of people in my company who want to do me harm. As in a full-scale investigation and audit to see how much my stepfather has embezzled through the years. I might not even have a viable oil company left to put on the market, but it won't take long to find out once I boot his sorry ass out on the street."

"Remind me never to put a contract out on you. You really going to sell your oil company?" Slade asked.

She'd said it aloud. She was going to put the oil business on the market. That idea brought as much peace in her heart as watching the sunset.

"Yes, I am," she said with conviction.

"It's your inheritance. How can you sell it? I could never ever sell the Double L. It's as much my life and blood as Granny is."

"The oil company has been good to my family. I have my grandmother's pearls and my mother's memories. I don't need a company to remind me of them," she said, turning her attention to what he was drawing in the sand.

First he made a stick house. Three sticks down and one across to close it up. Three more for the roof and a square for a window in the front plus a door. She picked up broken shells and lined the sidewalk up to the door. He gathered a few bits of sea oats as foliage on the outside of the sidewalk.

"Who lives here?" he asked.

"A young couple very much in love who haven't been jaded by the evils of the world. It's 1955, back when my grandmother and Nellie were young women and young brides. Grandmother lived in this house with her new husband and they... no, that's not right. Grandmother had money and she moved into a semi-mansion in El Dorado when she married my grandpa, who also had oil money."

"Did they combine their resources?" Slade asked as he kept planting sea oats around the base of the house.

"Oh, no. Grandmother's money came from the Rangers. Her father founded the oil company and she was the only child. It was set up to be passed to her oldest daughter and then to the next oldest daughter. In those days women didn't run oil companies. They stayed home and had babies. She told them all to go to hell and she ran her company. She swore that the time would come when a woman could do everything a man could and she wasn't going to be around so she'd do it in her day. Some years she made more money than grandpa. It didn't make him happy but she did it anyway."

"And you're putting it on the market? Maybe nothing is sacred anymore."

"It's a material possession. Sacred has to do with life and morals—not an oil company. My grandparents and my mother gave me those things as well as a sense of morality. Yes, I am selling it. It's provided for generations but it's time for it to get swallowed up by the big companies. I want a little house like this, not a mansion," she said.

He looked at her as if she was spitting green goo out her mouth and had sprouted scaly skin and a set of horns. "You've got to be kidding. You *can* live in a big house and still be in love."

"Maybe so, but I don't want a man who'll marry me for my money or who'll take out a million dollar life insurance policy on me, either. I want someone who loves me in my jeans and T-shirts and with my hair in a ponytail and who'll live in a little house with me. Like Nellie's grandpa. They only had a little house and they built on to it as they needed it."

"That was necessity," he argued.

"Then I want necessity," she shot right back.

"You are crazy. Your stepfather would be right to commit you," he said.

"Then take me to Mississippi and turn me over to him."

Slade shook his head. "I don't think so. I'd have to whip his ass and today I'm too tired from all the driving."

"Slade, I'm scared about tomorrow but I'm damn sure not crazy. And I'm sick to hell of this conversation. So stop talking about it. I've had the big house—own it now. Plantation style with a cook, two gardeners, horse trainers, ranch hands, all of it. It don't bring me one bit of happiness," she admitted.

"How do you know *not* having it will make you happy?" he asked.

"I don't, but I'm willing to give it all up to see. And that scares me, too, if you want to know the truth."

"Good. You are human. For a while there I thought you were ten feet tall and bulletproof."

"*Me?* I thought you were Superman. I figured if I ever saw *you* without a western shirt and jeans you'd be wearing a red and blue outfit with a big old S on the front."

"Yeah, right! I'm not Superman. I'm just an old dirt farmer who hasn't got enough sense to stop farming. Ever hear that story about the man who won the lottery? He told his friend that he'd give him a million dollars of the winnings, but the friend would just ranch it all away. That's me. If I had money, I'd just ranch it all away because it's what I love," Slade told her.

"That's what I want. Something I love so much I'd put my money and life into it. You've got something worth more than money can buy, Slade. Don't ever give it up."

"Oh, honey, I wouldn't. Couldn't. What would I ever do or be without the Double L? But listen up, don't be afraid about tomorrow. We'll be in public places where they'll be afraid to do something stupid. All I need is a picture. You hide once you point them out to me. They won't knife you or shoot you in a public place. They'd get caught or someone would see them and remember their faces. That would end their profession. Think of it as a lark. We're out to ruin them so they don't kill another innocent bride."

"Honey, you have no idea what they'd do to collect that money. They're good and mad. It's a matter of principle now. I bet Ramona would do me in just out of anger over losing all that insurance money. And if I'm dead, who'd ruin them?"

"It ain't happenin' on my shift. I'm the bodyguard, remember."

Thank you Lord for that, she sent up a silent prayer but didn't say anything aloud. They were actually getting along and that was miracle enough. She didn't want to jinx it with any more admissions.

"Ready to go in for the night?" he asked when the sun finally dipped low enough there wasn't even a hint of orange left in the sky.

"I suppose. Don't you love the salt smell of the ocean though? I'll always remember this night, Slade."

He didn't think he'd forget it too soon either. The picture of her sitting there in that modest bathing suit with salt water in her hair, silhouetted against a setting sun, was branded on his brain for eternity. He might marry some day, but he'd always keep that memory and return to the days when he was a knight in shining armor and rode in to save the damsel in distress. He was the one who was ten feet tall and bulletproof when he walked side by side with Jane through the sliding glass doors into their room.

He turned the air conditioning on high cool and sat down in a chair, propped his feet on the side of one of the beds, and turned on the television. Basically, he didn't watch much TV but rather liked to read. Mysteries were his favorite: John Grisham, Sandford, even Grafton. Then there was Randy Wayne White and Carl Hiaasen that reminded him of the old writer, deceased for several years. What was his name? Slade frowned trying to remember.

"John D. MacDonald," he finally said aloud.

"One of my favorites." She came out of the bathroom, her nightshirt damp where her hair hung down her back.

"Really? My dad read him and I found the books when his things were shipped home to the ranch."

"My dad loved him, too. I've read everything he wrote."

"How about Hiaasen?"

"He's a hoot, isn't he?"

"That he is. Want to watch old reruns of *Law and Order* or CMT? Nothing much looks good."

"*Law and Order*," she said. She fell asleep before the first one finished.

He stayed awake for a couple of hours and watched her sleep. It would be so easy to fall hook, line, and sinker for her but he couldn't. He'd always wonder if she really loved him or if it was simply because he'd saved her "naturally born white ass."

Chapter 11

JANE STARED AT THE LIST OF TEN TATTOO-PIERCING establishments listed in the yellow pages in the hotel phone book. According to what Slade pulled up on the computer the previous night, Pensacola made brags that it was the tattoo capital of the whole area. Which one would John and Ramona go to first? She wanted to get this done and over with on the first try and not play cat and mouse all day long, running from one parlor to the next seeing if they could catch them in a picture and hopefully not get caught or dead.

She pulled her hair up in a ponytail, wrapped it tightly into a bun, and slipped the wig liner over that. Once she had the curly auburn wig in place she set a hot pink sun visor on top of it, pulling some of the curls out to cover the elastic piece at the back of her head. She applied too much eye makeup and bright red lipstick. She snarled her nose when she looked at the outfit on the bed. It had seemed like a good idea that morning; Slade had assured her that no one would notice such an outlandish outfit. She'd look as if she wanted to draw attention to herself and consequently, no one would look at her.

She pulled the spandex, Hawaiian-print miniskirt on and topped it with a hot pink tank top cut low in the front to show the absence of tattoos peeking out from between her breasts. According to Slade, Ramona and John would be looking for Jane with a tattoo on her boobs keeping company with a fellow with a freshly shaven head and a tattoo on his arm. He wouldn't be searching for a red-haired bimbo hanging on the arm of a blond cowboy. For the grand finishing touch she slipped on big sunglasses with twinkling rhinestones around the lenses.

He whistled through his teeth when she came out of the bathroom. "I do believe we could make a few dollars if you'd stand on the street corner tonight."

"You offering to be my pimp? You'll have to get a black Italian suit and one of those honking big necklaces to hang around your neck. And at least one ear pierced with about a three-carat diamond stud in it."

Slade shuddered.

Jane giggled. "I thought you might change your mind. It's not fair that you get to go dressed like that," she said.

He wore sandals, a pair of baggy shorts, and a tank top that showed nothing more than a farmer's tan. Definitely a cowboy farmer in town for a vacation who'd picked up a local lady.

"You've got the list, so which one do we start with?" he asked.

She shut her eyes and pointed. It was a silly way to make a decision but made as much sense as any other. "Hula Moon."

"Okay, then Hula Moon it is."

Half an hour later they'd checked out of the hotel and were hunting for a parking place close to the Hula Moon. A receptionist with blond, pixie-cut hair and big brown eyes looked up from behind a desk. She asked if they had an appointment and Slade told her they were just shopping around and trying to get up the nerve to actually get a tat.

Jane gasped when she looked down on the receptionist's desk and saw a picture of herself on a different flier than the one she'd seen in Terral, Oklahoma. The new one was a head shot of her taken the day she and John had engagement pictures done. Her hair was freshly done and her smile bright and beautiful.

"Who's that?" Slade asked.

"Don't know her. A couple came in about twenty minutes ago. Asked if we'd done a tattoo on this woman in the last two days. Even said it was between her breasts. They said she might be coming back for a piercing today. I'm to call that number if I see her," the lady said.

"Why are they hunting for her?" Jane asked.

"I didn't ask. Guess she's been kidnapped or something."

"I saw her yesterday at the Psychedelic Shack. She was with some big old bald-headed fellow," Slade said.

"What a lucky break. They said if I helped them find the woman, they'd give me a reward."

Slade slipped his arm around Jane. "You ready, honey?"

"Yeah, I think I'm about to change my mind. It's going to take a whole bottle of Jim Beam before I let them hit me that many times with a needle."

The receptionist smiled. "It's really not that bad. We have pain-free now. But maybe you'd like to try a temporary, one that only lasts a few weeks; see how much fun it is and then come back for a permanent one."

"I'll think on it," Jane said.

When they reached the Psychedelic Shack, John and Ramona were sitting in the waiting area looking through magazines. They were the only two people in the room and both looked up when Slade and Jane walked inside. It didn't take them long to turn their attention back to their books.

Slade whispered. "This isn't going to be easy. I was hoping for a whole crowd of people."

"I'm getting hives and this wig is hotter'n hell," Jane whispered.

He leaned down and whispered in her ear. "Well, here goes. Play along with me."

She nodded and took a deep breath.

"Honey, are you sure you want a rose on your hip? I think Tweety bird would be better, and right below your navel. Just think of all the times I could kiss his little beak," he said loudly.

Jane didn't have to fake the stereotyped hooker giggle. She was so nervous it came out easily. "My Daddy will have your wild hide tacked to the barn door if he knows you're talkin' like that. He says only whores and white trash get tattoos and I wear a bikini when we go to the lake. So it's going to have to be a rose on my butt so he can't never see it."

"If he knew what we been doin' in his barn for the past six months, he'd have my wild hide in the church sayin' weddin' vows," Slade said.

He turned to John and Ramona. "Hey, y'all must be in here for a tat or a piercing. I bet you're about to get your belly button done, ain't you?" He looked right at Ramona trying to memorize every detail to tell Agent August if he didn't get a picture.

She shrugged.

"Come on. Y'all give us an opinion. A rose on her hip or a Tweety on her navel?"

Ramona wore black slacks, a black shirt, a pissed-off look on her face, and Ray Ban sunglasses. John had on his signature dress slacks, a white polo shirt, and sunglasses that matched hers perfectly, his black hair combed back like a television preacher.

They both lowered the glasses at the same time and looked at Jane.

"The rose," John said.

"I agree," Ramona said.

"Hey, Pun'kin, come look at this picture," Jane said.

"You find something else you like better? I'm willin' for about anything but them wild mushrooms you were talkin' about," he said.

"No, the picture of this woman right here. Says there's a reward if these people at this number find her. Didn't we see her at the Pensacola Tattoo place this morning? Remember, that was the one where she come in with that bald-headed fellow and they were looking for a piercing?"

Both John and Ramona whipped off the sunglasses in unison and tucked them in their pockets.

"You saw her where?"

"You the people we'd be calling?" Jane asked.

"That's right," John cocked his head to one side and drew his eyes down. He remembered seeing that man somewhere before. Something about the way he stood and held his head looked familiar. "How long ago did you see them?"

"That depends on how much the reward money is. I expect it ought to be worth a hundred dollars. That'd pay for most of my Tweety bird—or my mushrooms, if I can talk this old redneck into it."

Slade laughed. That accent she used was part Mexican and part pure Ellen.

John whipped out his billfold and handed Jane two fifties.

"Ten minutes ago," she said.

They took off so fast that he left the briefcase sitting beside the chair. She waited until they were at the silver gray van before she opened the door and whistled loudly. "Hey, y'all forgot something."

Slade stepped up behind her, pretending that someone had called and holding the phone up to her ear, all the while shooting over her shoulder with his cell phone as fast as he could click the button. He managed to get several pictures of John coming back for the briefcase and three of Ramona waiting beside the locked van.

Jane waited until they were in the truck to start humming and kept it up the whole time she removed the wig and wiped the excess makeup from her face.

"I hope you got something you can use because I'm not doing that again. I can't believe he didn't recognize me and kill me on the spot," she said.

"It's the eyes. A picture is worthless if the person is wearing sunglasses because the eyes are the windows to the soul," Slade said. "That's why I wanted a picture without them. Barely made it before Ramona stuck hers back on. I think I got several good ones of John. Next roadside rest or place where we can pull over for a few minutes, I'm sending them to Agent August."

She tugged at the miniskirt. "How do we know he's not in on the deal, with a name like that?"

He stared at her trying to cover her knees with barely enough material to keep her underpants from showing.

"Gut instinct," he said hoarsely.

"Don't look at my legs," she said.

"Why not? They're good-looking legs and you're covered every bit as well as you were on the beach last night. I can't understand why a woman will parade around in a bikini and then feel naked in a miniskirt. Just don't make a bit of sense to me."

"There's an exit with a McDonald's. You can get your job done there and I can change into jeans."

"You wouldn't make a good hooker anyway," he said.

"And you'd make a terrible John."

They began to laugh at the same time at the obvious pun.

He parked the truck as close to the door as he could and fetched her duffel bag from the backseat.

"I expect we'd better be sure the hotel we stay in tonight has laundry facilities. This is lighter than your dirty clothes sack."

"That would be a good idea—or else we could buy some new things and disguise ourselves as two executives from... let's see, maybe an oil company. I'd like to see you in an Italian suit and dress shoes," she said.

He chuckled. "That's one thing you won't never see. I'm a boots and jeans man."

"But as a disguise?"

"I'd rather be a pimp," he said.

She picked out her last clean pair of jeans, a T-shirt, and sandals and carried them inside to the bathroom where she changed and finished cleaning her face. She left the miniskirt and tank top slung over the door of the bathroom stall. Maybe someone would be glad to find a free hooker outfit.

She smelled fried apple pies when she got back inside the truck.

"Coffee?" she asked.

He nodded and passed a cup to her along with a pie in a small box. "Thought you might like something to put the butterflies to rest."

"What butterflies?" she asked as she sipped.

"Those that are still fluttering around in your stomach. You started humming when we left the tattoo place. That might help cure them."

"Butterflies nothing. I've got buzzards the size of gorillas flying in my stomach. I've never been so damned scared in all my life," she said.

"You were cold as snow in there, girl. I was proud of you and your Ellen impersonation. I swear you could have been a girl right off the farm dressing up in what you thought was pretty clothes."

"You sayin' I was overdressed? Man, you sure know how to bust a girl's fashion bubble. God, this tastes good. Did you only buy us one each?"

"No, I bought a dozen. Considering what we just did, I didn't want to ride with you very far without food. Oh, and there's a couple of those cheap little chicken sandwiches in there that you like so well, too."

They hadn't driven an hour when his cell phone rang.

"Hello," he said. "Well, I'll be damned. If that don't beat all. Thank you and please keep us informed."

"What?" she asked.

"They've never seen or heard of John or Jonathan. His picture didn't come up on anything they've got."

"He must be very good then. This wasn't an amateur hit, was it? He's one of those horrible men who only do a job right and that's why he's still after me, because I'm the only one who got away and can identify him." Her voice had a hauntingly hollow sound.

"Not at all. It's Ramona slash Amanda slash Lisa slash a whole bunch more names they were surprised to see. She's the good one. She's been in business for years and they've never gotten close to her. Got one picture from a surveillance camera when she assassinated a United States senator a few years ago. But Interpol and the FBI and every other agency are after her. It's their thinking that she has a new boyfriend slash protégé. She was hired and gave him the job to help him make his bones in the profession. Killing you was supposed to be a clean, easy job and he's botched it, so now she's got to clean it up."

Jane felt as if someone had just flushed her veins with ice water. "What are they going to do?"

"Catch her."

"Today?"

"Actually, we'll be making a few more calls to Granny if they don't get her in Pensacola."

"I'm bait!" Her voice echoed in the truck as though it was a volcano she was yelling into.

"Maybe you better start humming again. I'll stop at the next exit for more food."

Jane consumed both chicken sandwiches, three pies, and all her coffee before she could trust herself to speak. She stared out the window at the scenery. They bypassed Mobile and she was still silent. They made it to Biloxi, Mississippi before she could find words.

"Are they calling you when they get them?"

"Yes."

"It's my turn to decide where we stay. Why are we going west? I want to go to Savannah, Georgia."

"Can't. I've been to Savannah."

"Then New York City."

"Been there."

"What in the hell were you doing in New York City?"

"Would you believe I was chasing women?"

She ignored him and they kept going west.

In the middle of the afternoon he took an exit into Baton Rouge. He stopped at a service station for gas and asked her where she wanted to stay for the night.

"Right here. I'm tired of riding already. I want a shower, a few hours with my book, some time beside the pool, and a television movie tonight."

"They don't offer all that in a service station. You could take a spit bath in the bathroom, read your book on the way, and maybe get the rest in St. Charles," he said.

She shot him a go-to-hell look.

"Okay, you win. I'm not riding in a truck with those looks all afternoon; a motel it is. I saw a sign back there for an Embassy Suites. Will that do for a minnow?"

"A what?"

"A minnow. Think Jane. Minnow. Bait."

He got another look that should have left nothing but a greasy spot on the floor mats.

"With a pool."

"Yes, ma'am. I can almost guarantee it at the Embassy."

"How do you know so much you can make that kind of guarantee?"

"Chasing women in my past wild days."

She really didn't know Slade Luckadeau as well as she thought. There were as many layers to him as a good big Vidalia onion and she'd only gotten the first one peeled back. "Then take me there and book us for two nights. I'm tired of outrunning them. Send the FBI right to the hotel. Call Granny and tell her exactly where we are and I'll either walk out in two days or you can come to my funeral in three."

"What makes you think I'd go to your funeral?" he remarked with a sly grin.

"Drive," she demanded.

"Dead or alive in two days, huh? Well, I got to admit that sounds like a winner. You want two rooms this time so when they do you in, I'm not included, or one so that when they *try* to do you in, their blood gets on the wall? Remember, I still think I can whip his sorry old ass. I might just do it for all the trouble he's put me through here in the middle of hay season."

She let him park in front of the hotel before she answered. "One room or suite if they have it."

He nodded.

They were given a room on the seventh floor at the end of the hall in a suite that included a private bath and bedroom with two queen beds, and a small living area with a second television and seating arrangement. It also offered a desk with one of those ergo chairs Slade hated, but he'd manage for two days. Then the ordeal would be over and she could go her way and he'd go his. She could read her romance novel and he'd get caught up on his sleep. The FBI could lurk around reading papers—or whatever they did these days in an attempt to fit in with their surroundings—and catch the assassins. John would rat out Ramona, who would rat out the stepfather, and all would be solved.

Jane would go home to her oil company and dude ranch. It couldn't be a real ranch, because no genuine rancher would leave his or her property on a whim with no one to run the cattle or make hay at this time of year. At least he had Marty, who was overseeing everything for him, and Nellie, who knew as much about ranching as anyone in the whole state of Texas. Jane probably didn't know squat about what her foreman was doing. He could be robbing her blind if her own stepfather could rinky-do her into thinking he was taking care of her business while he was putting out a contract on her.

He threw his suitcase on the sofa, went into the bedroom, and flopped down on one of the beds. "Does this suit her majesty?"

"If you are talking about me, yes, it does. Now call Nellie and tell her the hotel name and address."

"You sure about this? We can stay on the go and they'll catch them soon enough. You don't have to put yourself in danger, Jane."

"I was in danger this morning. I don't like the feeling one damn bit, Slade. Matter of fact, I hate it. I hate not being in control of my own life. I hate the fear. I'm putting an end to it right here and now."

The phone rang.

She jumped.

He grabbed it. "Hello?"

"This is Agent August. We have the woman in custody. But the man going under the name of John Farris got away. Woman is not talking. Where are you?"

"Could I call you back in ten minutes?"

"Sure. Problems?"

"Decisions."

"I understand," Agent August said.

Slade turned to face Jane, who'd sat down on the edge of the bed.

"Okay, here's the deal. They've got Ramona but John is still out there. You still want to stay here two days, or stay on the run until your birthday?" he asked.

"What's the story she's telling?" Jane asked.

"I have no idea other than she's not talking," Slade answered.

"I want to stay here and get it over with," she said with a sigh.

Slade punched the right numbers and gave Agent August the information, then listened for a while. When he hung up, he took a deep breath and began to talk.

"Ramona says that she and John were old friends and that your stepfather was concerned when you went missing. She claims she runs a P.I. business and that checks out to be legitimate. She says that John was heartbroken so, being an old friend, she took him with her. They were simply using any means possible to locate and return you to your worried stepfather."

"Bullshit."

"If it smells like bullshit, looks like bullshit, and came out a bull's butt, I expect it is bullshit. And that smells like it, looks like it, and came out of something similar to a bull's ass. I agree it must be the real stuff," Slade said.

"What do we do?"

"We go about our lives for the next couple of days like two people on vacation. Swim, eat in the hotel restaurant—which I'm told has excellent food—read books, be lazy. It will drive me crazy." It was his turn to sigh.

She grinned. "Then I love it."

"You are just downright mean. Kristy don't have a damn thing on you."

"Don't you be comparing me to her or I'll…" She couldn't think of anything bad enough to do to him short of killing him.

"You will what?" he egged her on.

"I'm not sure but I'll figure something out. Now tell me the rest of it while I think about something ugly to repay you for saying that I'm like that two-bit bitch you were in love with," she said.

"I didn't say you were like her. I said she didn't have a thing on you when it came to being mean. And I wasn't in love with her," he defended himself.

"I'm not a gold digger and I don't treat people like shit," Jane said.

"Have to agree with you there, even though it pains me to do so," Slade said. "Now listen up: two FBI agents will check into the hotel tonight. We won't know them, but they'll be around. It's best, according to Agent August, that we aren't aware of who they are."

"I'm putting on my swimsuit and going to the pool. What are you going to do?"

He picked up the remote and, using the stand-up guide to the channels, flipped to the *TV Guide* station to see what was playing. After four days of tension and riding in the truck with Jane, a little mindless television might settle his nerves. Not that he'd ever let her know how she affected him. Lord, that would be the mistake of a lifetime. That he was so attracted to her that all he could think about was making passionate love to her would set her into a fit of laughter.

"*Cowboy Way!*" she squealed when she saw the title roll up. "Let's watch that. I can swim later. I love Pepper."

"Who?"

"Pepper Lewis, the part that Woody Harrelson plays. I haven't seen this in ten years. Hurry up and find the right station. It's coming on in two minutes."

She kicked off her shoes, grabbed all the pillows from both beds, propping them against the headboard in two piles, jerked her duffel bag open, and pulled out a knit nightshirt. By the time the movie opened with two little boys playing with guns and stick horses, she was out of the bathroom, settled in beside Slade on the bed, and already smiling.

Early in the movie, a grown-up Pepper came out of his house wearing nothing but his boots and a black felt hat in a very strategic place.

"Bet you couldn't hold up a hat like that," she said when Pepper let go of the hat and it stayed in place.

"You are blushing," Slade said. "Three good long kisses and darlin', we'll see if I couldn't hold up my hat just like that."

The blush deepened. Kiss Slade? Gladly! Just to get the itch out of that place so deep in her soul she couldn't scratch it. And when his body responded like Pepper's, she'd gladly take care of that, too.

In the movie, the lady Pepper had in his house stepped to the door and offered to let Sonny, played by Kiefer Sutherland, come inside and play with them. Sonny reminded her she was married.

"So are you going to play games after you get married?" Slade asked.

"Don't reckon I'll have to worry about that. I'm not sure I'll ever trust a man enough to marry him after all this."

"Don't be lettin' one rotten apple spoil your life," Slade told her.

They settled into the movie, laughing until they cried at the stereotyped characters and enjoying the antics of two fast friends, angry with each other at the beginning of the movie but back to sharing a lifelong friendship by the end. When it was over, she rolled up next to Slade until their bodies were touching from neck to toes. Just when he thought she was about to kiss him three times just to see if his hat would stay on with no hands, she reached for his cell phone and scooted across the bed to her half.

He thought the old man in the movie, Nacho, had made her think of Nellie, so he was surprised when she said, "Celia? Hello, this is Ellacyn. I've missed you so much," Jane said.

"Well, I've missed you, too, but I'm more than a little aggravated at the way you ran out and haven't even called me," Celia said.

"It's complicated. I'm in Baton Rouge and I couldn't tell you a thing because it was too crazy. I'm at the Embassy with my... I guess you'd call him a bodyguard."

"John is here beside me. You do owe him an explanation, you know. He's been crazy with worry," Celia said.

"John is there with you right now? Celia, you are in danger. Hang up and call the police. Get out of town. Do something!" Jane was shouting loudly and turning pale.

Slade stood up and reached for the phone.

"Celia, hush. Don't tell him anything. He's the very person I'm running from," Jane said.

"Why would you be running from him? You say you're at the Embassy in Baton Rouge?"

Jane's hands shook. "Celia, listen to me. You are my best friend. Would I run away from my own wedding if I didn't have good cause?"

"He just ran out the door and jumped in his car. Are you telling me the truth? I think I just made a mistake. What do I need to do?"

"Nothing. There's nothing you can do."

"Ellacyn, I'm sorry. I mean it, but why are you running from John?"

"It's a long story. I've got to go now. I'll call you when I come home."

She flipped the phone shut, handed it to Slade, rolled up in a ball and sobbed.

He touched her shoulder but she shrugged him away.

"Shut up and let me cry. It's been a long time coming and I don't give a damn about why, I just want to cry."

He moved away and folded his arms across his chest. He ached for Jane and wished he could help, but before he could do that, she had to realize she needed him as much as he needed her.

His heart skipped a beat and hung for a moment before it picked up again. He needed Jane about like he needed a thirty-eight slug planted between his eyes. Life with her would be a constant emotional roller coaster.

Life with her would be living, his conscience screamed. *There would be no dull moments in or out of bed. The woman has more passion in her toenail than most women have in their whole body.*

It was his turn to blush.

Finally she sat up, dried her eyes on the corner of the pillowcase, and set her jaw. Slade had seen that look for the first time when he had confronted her about being a con artist that first day—and every day since, in some form or fashion.

"We're going to catch that son of a bitch, Slade. I'm not running any more. And then I'm staying out of Greenville until my birthday. On that day, I'm burning down the house just like Bob Lee did at the end of that movie we watched—*The Shooter*."

"You mean for real or are you speaking in the figurative?"

"Paul is going to think his ass is on fire. Do you know a damn good lawyer that I can trust with my life?"

"I do."

"Get him on the phone. I want to talk."

Chapter 12

JANE TALKED FOR MORE THAN AN HOUR IN THE SITTING room outlining everything she wanted to do with her oil company. A few times James Massey asked her to slow down while he caught up on the notes he was taking. He read them back to her; asked her if she wanted to press charges after the audit; if she was truly sincere in selling the entire oil company or if she'd want to keep stock since it had belonged to her grandparents; and if she wanted him to fly into Jackson, drive up to Greenville, and go with her to the first conference. She told him exactly what she wanted done with Paul and he said he would see her in ten days.

While she talked, Slade watched CMT videos in the bedroom. When she opened the door and handed him the phone, there was a purposeful look on her face he hadn't seen since she'd arrived at the Double L that first day. The fear he'd seen recently was gone. Determination that even the devil in all his forked-tail glory couldn't intimidate had replaced it. His Jane was back.

That thought shook him to the soles of his feet. She'd never been *his Jane* and would never hold that title. She was too independent for Slade Luckadeau. He had no doubt she could fend off a forest fire with eight ounces of water. Hells bells, she might scare it into submission with one of her evil glares.

"What now?" he asked.

"I'm hungry. Hand me that room service menu."

She ordered the biggest steak on the menu, French fries, a garden salad, corn on the cob, and strawberry shortcake, and then handed the phone off to Slade, who simply told them to double the order and add a six pack of Coors to it.

"So you're hungry, too?" She poked buttons on the remote until she found the TV Guide channel.

"Not particularly, but by the look on your face, I bet not a morsel of the food goes to waste. Why didn't we just go to the restaurant? Maybe they'd have a buffet bar and we could wipe them out?"

"Or they'd have a real bar and I could get drunk," she suggested.

His blue eyes glittered. "I thought you didn't get drunk. That you could hold your liquor. Want to go for that brag you made about drinking me under the table?"

She shook her head. "Not today. Maybe later. Right now I want to eat and then lie beside the pool so John can find me when he arrives. I've been run into a corner and it's time to stand up and fight. Besides, I hate the me that's scared to death. I'm ready to get this damn thing finished. Could you get that Agent August on the phone? I'd like to talk to him."

Slade hit the buttons on his cell phone and handed it to her.

"Mr. Luckadeau?" a deep voice answered.

"It's Ellacyn Hayes. Since I'm the bait in this trap, I want to ask a favor."

"And that would be?"

"Before you carry him away I want to talk to him. I don't even have to be alone with him, and I don't care if he's cuffed or hog-tied."

"You got it."

"Thank you—and one other thing. I called my best friend. She's aware that I'm in Baton Rouge and John was in Greenville, Mississippi when I talked to her. So I'm sure he's on the way. When are your agents going to be in play?"

"They checked in ten minutes ago."

"Thank you," she said.

"No, it's me who's thanking you. If he talks, we get Ramona."

"If he doesn't talk, what do you do with him? Does that mean he's still a threat to me? After all, it's just his word against mine."

"You won't have to worry about that."

"Then good-bye, Agent August."

"Good-bye, Ellacyn."

Slade looked across the room. "Which reminds me. I understand where the Jane came from; it's your middle name. Where'd you pick up Day?"

"I stuttered when Nellie asked me my name. I started to say Hayes and wound up stuttering out the name Day instead. It worked. I was just glad she never asked to see my driver's license for verification."

Slade slapped his bare leg. "Damn it all to hell on a silver poker. That's where I went wrong. If I'd snooped in your purse, I could have gotten rid of you that first day and I wouldn't be laid up in a hotel room when my hay needs baling."

"I don't imagine the ranch will shrivel up and die while you are gone. Matter of fact, I bet they don't even miss you. Nellie can run that place better than you can any day of the week," she said.

"Same back at you. I bet the oil company and your ranch didn't miss you either," he said through gritted teeth.

"You are right. Both can run smoothly without me. I'm sure Paul is ripping off millions just like always, but his days are numbered. The ranch has some fine hired help that's always run it efficiently. I can't wait to get back and be a bigger part of it."

He was speechless.

"No comebacks?" she asked.

He shook his head. The thought of going home to Ringgold without her left a hole the size of a crater in his heart. He'd admitted to a physical attraction. Hell, any man who didn't give her a long second look must either be gay, blind, or both. But an attraction was something a man could get past; a hole in his heart left him dead.

"Hey look, they're playing *Double Jeopardy* next. Want to watch it while we eat? Then I'll go lie by the pool, maybe even do a few laps to work off part of the food."

He nodded and swallowed hard past the grapefruit-sized lump in his throat.

The movie had been playing for ten minutes when the food arrived. She pulled up a chair to the table where the young man put the food and began to eat without missing a single scene. Ashley Judd's character was framed for murdering her husband, slimy character that he was, and went to jail, leaving her son in the care of her best friend.

Slade ate and realized why Jane looked so familiar. She was a ringer for Ashley, except that her hair was a few shades lighter and her eyes a different color. The mouth was the same. The cheekbones and chin similar; the same general build. He'd been wrong when he thought she looked like his mother or Marilyn Monroe. It had been Ashley all along.

The character she played in the movie reminded him of the spunk Jane had. She'd argued with him as much as Ashley did with Tommy Lee Jones. Wasn't it the most ironic thing in the universe that he'd finally realized that Jane was the very kind of woman he wanted to spend his life with, only to find out that she was rich beyond his league and would never be interested in someone who sweated and worked everyday for a living.

You just said she was too damned independent for you, his conscience reminded him. *Make up your mind and either go after her or get over her. You can't have it both ways.*

When the movie ended, she looked over at Slade. "Would you ever do that? Would you let your wife go to prison just to save your financial sorry ass?"

"When I have a wife I'll love her more than money," he said.

"Fair enough. Let's go swimming. It's been five hours since we checked into the hotel. I reckon John has had time to race his double-crossing sorry ass down here. Let's go take him down."

"So I've got a financial sorry ass and he's got a double-crossing sorry ass? What's the difference?" Slade asked.

"Depends."

"On what?"

"You figure it out. I'll get changed in the bathroom. Or I can strip down right here and you can cover up the family jewels with your hat," she teased.

Damn that crazy *Cowboy Way* movie anyway. The image of Slade in nothing but scruffed-up boots and a black felt hat hanging much lower than the top of his head kept playing over and over in her head as if the replay button on the remote had gotten stuck.

"You take the bathroom, then, and I'll hurry. Wouldn't want to damage your innocent little eyes," he said.

They rode the elevator down to the pool area and Jane stretched out on a lounge chair. She wondered which of the people arriving not long after she did were FBI agents. Surely not that elderly lady in a black one-piece bathing suit. Granted, she didn't have an ounce of cheesy cellulite on her legs and that gray hair could be a very good dye job, since there were few wrinkles in her face. She kept company with a younger man that could possibly be her son with those streaks of silver in his temples. Or was he just posing as such? Ramona had posed as John's sister. It was difficult to know what was real and what was an illusion. She didn't know if she'd ever trust anyone again.

The gray hair reminded her of Griffin Luckadeau and she wondered what Lizzy was doing that day. Was she playing in a blow-up swimming pool or riding her pony in the pasture? Were her cousins calling her a skunk because of those two bratty kids that Kristy birthed?

"What happened to Lizzy's mother? Did she die?" she asked Slade, who'd claimed the chair next to hers.

"No, she married Griffin and then decided she wasn't cut out for ranching. She had signed the pre-nup saying that she couldn't have any part of the ranch and said she didn't care about the ranch. She just wanted to be married to Griffin. I think she just wanted to be the

star of a big fancy wedding. Then she got pregnant six
months after they were married. She'd promised Griff
she'd stay home with the babies when they got around
to having a family, so she quit her job at the bank in
Saint Jo. She was quite a bit younger than Griff and she
wanted to party and chase around with her friends. A
baby puts a damper on that real quick. When Lizzy was
about two months old, Dian came in and said she was
leaving for California and taking Lizzy with her. Griff
bought her off. Wrote a check for fifty thousand dollars
if she'd give him complete custody of his daughter."

"Is that legal?" Jane asked.

"They call it a settlement. She went with her friends
and has never come back."

A man slipped between the two chairs and squatted.
Slade felt something hard and cold press against his ribs
and looked down to see a gun under a linen napkin.

The man held the gun steady and looked at Jane.
"Hello, darlin'."

"Well, hello to you. So you finally found me," she
said. "Where's Ramona? Up in the room sleeping off a
romp in the king-size bed?"

"Ramona is taking care of business. Your little call to
Celia let me know where I could find you. I was right.
You might give up your credit cards and your phone, but
you couldn't stay away from your best friend so I stuck
to her like glue. It didn't take you long to find another
man did it, Ellacyn?"

"Cheating fools are a dime a dozen. You can kick any
bush between here and the Pacific Ocean and a hundred will
come running out willing to sleep with you for a million
dollar life insurance policy," she said in a calm voice.

John ignored the slam and kept his own tone soft and sweet. "Paul is worried out of his mind. How could you run out on me like that?"

"How could you have sex with your sister on the night before you were to marry me?"

"She's not my sister. She's my friend. If I'd told you I had a friend so close that I wanted her to be my best man you'd have had a fit, so we decided to lie about her being my sister," John said.

"So it wasn't incest. It was still unfaithful, wasn't it?"

Slade pretended he didn't feel the cold metal on his bare skin and let the scene play out, hoping the whole time the man didn't have a hair-trigger finger. Nellie might be sorry she'd guilted him into this trip if the next time she saw him he was lying in a casket with his hands crossed over his chest covering a bullet hole in his heart.

John chuckled. "You got me on that one, but it's time to go home and face the music. We'll be leaving now. Your friend is going to stand up at the same time you do and I'm going to follow you out the front door. When you are in my car, I'll take this gun away from his liver."

"Kill me here. I'm not going anywhere with you and Slade could take that gun away from you and make you eat it if he wanted to. He's just playing with you like a cat with a mouse," she said.

"Why would I kill you, darlin'? I still plan on marrying you. So what if you had a little lapse in judgment and got angry because I was fooling around with Ramona? I promise it won't ever happen again. Paul and I have been talking. We'll have a simple little ceremony at the courthouse. He's already rescheduled our honeymoon in Cancun. We fly out tomorrow morning right after the wedding. I'll see to it you don't run again. It's either that or an insane asylum for the rest of your life. Paul has that kind of power, or didn't you know that? Now, stand up or he dies. Or better yet, I shoot him, shoot you and how ever many others I can hit before I run out of ammunition. I can get away with no problem and they'll call it a random shooting. I rather like that idea. Paul will still pay me for the assassination and they'll never get the man who killed that cute little dark-haired girl over there in the kiddy pool."

"I heard you and Ramona that night talking about how you were going to kill me and collect the insurance money."

"And you heard right. Don't take it personal, darlin'. It's just business. Don't cross me again," he said.

A waiter appeared in front of Jane with a cell phone. "Miz Ellacyn Hayes?"

She nodded slowly. Where were those damned FBI agents, anyway?

"Phone call from your friend, Celia."

"I don't want to talk to her. Go away," she said.

"You tell her that. It's my job to bring phones or messages, not deliver news," he said gruffly.

She took the phone and in the coldest voice possible said, "Hello."

"This is Agent Fennigan. I'm five feet behind you at a table with another man. Is the man squatting down between you and Mr. Luckadeau the man we're looking for?"

"That's right," she said.

"Do whatever he says. Where's he taking you?"

Jane pretended she was talking to Celia and hoped the agent would understand her form of code. "Celia, you think you're so damned smart letting him find out about where I was. With friends like you, I damn sure don't need enemies. You'd shoot a woman in the back as they were leaving, you bitch," she said as hatefully as she could. Her hands were clammy and she had the sudden urge to hum. She'd never forgive herself if John pulled the trigger and shot Slade or that child that reminded her of Lizzy Luckadeau. She handed the phone to the waiter and said, "Here, take this damn thing and if she calls again, don't bring it to me."

John told them in a very conversational tone to stand up and walk to the front door. Jane was to loop her arm in Slade's, to remember that John got trigger happy when he was spooked and that he didn't have any qualms about shooting Slade in the back. She envisioned gun battles and dead bodies on the short walk from the pool to the front lobby.

The takedown was so anticlimactic, she was almost disappointed. Two agents simply walked up behind John and put a gun barrel in each side of his back. He dropped his gun and raised his hands slowly.

"John Farris, you are under arrest for attempted murder, conspiracy to commit murder, and…" the agent rattled off a long list of infractions. When he finished, the other one read John his rights.

"You still want some time with him?" the first one, a short man with a bald head and heavy jowls, asked.

"No, I found out what I wanted to know already. It wasn't personal. It was just business," she said.

John smiled sweetly at her. "Darlin', I don't know what this is. I love you. I just wanted to take you home and marry you. Tell them the truth. I made a mistake. Forgive me. I love you, Ellacyn."

"Don't let him get in touch with Paul Stokes. I want him to think that John is still chasing me," Jane said.

"I am darlin'. I will chase you until the day I die. I never forget a woman who does me wrong." His eyes were lifeless and cold as ice.

"Get him out of my sight."

"You got it, lady. And thanks."

They put him in the car and Jane shivered in spite of the humid heat trying to suffocate her. She began to hum and then everything started spinning. Slade caught her as she fainted.

"I'll take her up to the room. She'll be fine. You've got my number," he told the men. He didn't watch as they drove away with John in the car.

He laid her gently on the bed and went to the bathroom, where he wrung out a cloth in cold water. He laid it gently on her forehead and whispered, "Jane."

She shut her eyes even tighter and shivered. "Is it over?"

"It's over. Are you all right?"

She began to hum again.

He recognized the tune as one from the Martina McBride CD they'd been listening to earlier: "Help Me Make It Through the Night."

Slade stretched out beside her and took her hand in his. "I thought for sure he was going to get trigger-happy and put a hole in my gut. How in the hell did he slip up on us so slick?"

She made no effort to remove her hand, glad for the warmth of his touch. "He was dressed like a waiter. It's his job to be slick."

The words to the Martina tune came to his mind. The singer talked about it being sad to be alone and asking for him to help her make it through the night. She said she didn't want to be alone. At that moment, Slade could think of nothing scarier in his own world than being alone. He didn't know who was going to help who, but they both needed another soul and a warm body to get through the night. Tomorrow would be a different story. Time would have done its job in getting them past the experience, but right then, they both needed each other.

He drew her close to his side and held her tightly. Her heart raced even yet and she continued to hum as if that would erase every single horrible memory from her mind. He kissed her gently on the lips, drawing a bit of her lower lip into his teeth and nibbling ever so gently.

"Slade?" she mumbled.

"Yes," he said.

"What are you doing?"

"I'm making love to you."

"Why?"

"Because I want to."

"Slade?"

"Yes?"

"I want you to."

The very warmth of his breath made her insides quiver. She knew what they were doing was one hundred percent wrong and the consequences would be horrible but she couldn't stop it; didn't want to.

"You kiss really good," she said between fast heart-beats and quick short gasps as she tried to control her fevered body, still in shock from the ordeal.

The next time his mouth claimed hers she tasted beer and steak mixed together from the meal they'd shared. She forgot all about John and Paul and Ramona as he removed her bathing suit top so gently that she wondered how he'd gotten it over her head without breaking the kiss. His breath on her bare skin brought a soft moan. When he picked up her fingertips and kissed each of them separately she thought she'd die with wanting him.

Her imaginary guardian angel perched on her shoulder and told her that she was making the biggest mistake of her life, that she should put a stop to what she and Slade were about to do. She reminded herself again that she hadn't used birth control in more than a week, but nothing seemed to matter except satisfying that dull, aching need filling her whole being. The one telling her that she was alive; that she could live without looking over her shoulder even if just for a few days; that she needed to be loved to prove that she was truly alive.

He slipped her bathing suit bottom down slowly from her hips, kissing her belly button on the way. When he planted kisses from her inner thighs to her toes she gasped. Jane wanted him to get on with the job, not play around, but at the same time she wanted him to go slow so she could savor every single moment of the experience.

She sat up and for a moment he thought she was going to call a halt to the whole procedure. One part of him wished she would; it would be awkward to spend every waking moment with her afterwards. The other part wanted her to be in his bed every day for the rest of his life. Two opposing forces and both terrified him.

"It's my turn," she whispered. She buried her face in the soft brown hair on his chest, nuzzling there until he moaned.

"I could love you," he tangled his fingers in her hair.

She heard him but chose to ignore such a crazy idea. It was a line he probably used on all the women he bedded from Texas all the way to New York City. Love was an overrated, overused, four-letter word. She pulled the string on his bathing suit and peeled it off his slender hips. "Oh my, I do believe you could hold up your hat," she whispered with a giggle.

He smiled and she trailed kisses up his neck and chin, finally finding his lips. She didn't love Slade and she wouldn't say such idiotic words. She didn't intend to ever love anyone again and this was definitely a one-night stand just to release all the adrenaline still racing in her veins.

Later, Slade propped up on an elbow. "The next time will be better. It's been a while."

She wrapped the bed sheet around her and started for the shower. "If it's any better than that, I wouldn't be able to stand it. There won't be a next time, Slade."

"Why?"

"Because… I can't put it into words. It just can't happen again, is all."

"So this is what a one-night stand feels like," he said.

"I wouldn't know. I've never been one until now. It was a heat of the moment thing, Slade. One of those,

I'm-alive-I-have-to-prove-I'm-alive moments. It didn't mean anything lasting or real."

He lay on his back staring at a blank television screen while she took a long shower. Emotions rattled around inside him like marbles in a quart fruit jar. He was elated that she wouldn't expect more out of him than a one-time performance. Now that her would-be assassin was in custody, he could take her to Greenville and get on back to his hayfields.

Then again, Slade was just plain sad.

He made no attempt to cover his nakedness when she returned, dressed in her faded old nightshirt, a towel around her wet hair and a blush on her face. "Your turn," she said.

"Sure thing. Then we can check out. I can have you back at your ranch before midnight and be on my way back to Ringgold."

"No!" she almost shouted.

"Why? The boogerman is in custody. This meant nothing. What else is there to do?"

"One more week. We don't have to travel but I've got to be somewhere hidden for another week. Damn it, Slade—don't you see? If Paul has to do it himself, he'll pull the trigger or commit me to keep that oil company. I can't go home until I'm twenty-five years old. Even the fancy-smancy lawyer you put me in touch with said for me to stay away until the Monday after my birthday."

"Why the Monday after? Why not the very day?"

"Company offices are closed on Saturday and Sunday. Please find a place for me to hide for another week. I don't have to be on the ranch but..."

"I know just the place. We'll leave in the morning. It'll take a couple of days and when we get there, I'm going home."

"Where?" Lord, she wished he'd cover up or at least put his bathing suit back on. Desire was beginning to melt her hormones into a puddle in the middle of her stomach.

"You are going to Milli and Beau's place until your birthday. I'll go on back to the Double L and take care of my own business. You can fly home on Monday. I'll even drive up there and take you to the airport in Dallas."

"I wasn't invited."

"No, you weren't. You can pay them."

"You sure are a cold sumbitch when you are mad," she said.

"I'm not mad, Jane. I'm tired of running all over creation with you. I'm ready for this to be over and go home."

She nodded. "Me, too."

"Pick a movie or read your romance book. I'm going to take a shower and go to the bar downstairs for a few drinks."

"Can I go?"

"Not with me. You can go before I do or after but not with me," he said.

"Why? Are you interested in a one-night stand with another woman?" Her heart dropped to the floor and flopped around in pain.

"I'd say that was my business."

"After what we just did?"

He stretched and stood up, towering above her. "I think your exact words were 'It was a heat of the moment thing. One of those, I'm-alive-I-have-to-prove-I'm-alive moments. It didn't mean anything lasting or real.' Correct me if I'm wrong. But there might be a woman in the bar who's looking for something lasting or real, now that I don't have to baby-sit you or put up with your whining."

"Whining!" she shouted and threw her wet towel at him.

He caught it mid air. "Yes, whining! I'm mad. Feed me. I'm not dead. Make love to me. I own you because I'm in trouble so do everything I say but it doesn't mean shit."

"You are a pig from hell."

"You stole that line from that stupid chick flick, *Steel Magnolias*. Come up with something original or keep your mouth shut."

"You don't tell me what to do. And I don't care if that line is straight out of your sorry ass, it's the truth. Besides that movie is *not* stupid and what were you doing watching it? Suffering through something without blood and guts to get in a woman's pants?"

He grinned. "Oh, darlin', I don't have to do anything like that. I just have to be a damn good bodyguard and they fall at my feet."

"Go to hell," she said.

"If that's what they call the bar, that's where I'm headed. I'll call your curse and meet you in hell, Ellacyn Jane Hayes, but you stay out of the bar. I don't want any more of your company tonight."

She shot him her meanest look and slammed the door between the bedroom and sitting room. Damn his black soul to the devil's back forty for all eternity. There hadn't been a man in her entire life, and that included John, who could make her so mad. So he was going to the bar, was he? Well, she'd beat him there and be one drink ahead of him when he arrived.

She jerked her T-shirt over her head with such force that she ripped the neck binding and kicked it over next to the wet towel. She fished one of her sundresses from the duffel bag, glad that it was that new fabric that could be left on the highway, run over by a semi, and then thrown in a dog bed for a week, and still wouldn't need ironing. Her bra went into the duffel bag and she pulled the dress up from the bottom, tying the halter top at the nape of her neck. She ran a brush through her semi-wet hair and applied a little makeup. She was just shutting the door when he stepped out of the shower.

"Well, damn it all, anyway," he grumbled. Surely, she hadn't taken off on her own. Granny would kill him on the spot if he'd lost her precious friend's granddaughter. He sure couldn't tell her they'd had a knock-down, drag-out after the best sex he'd ever had.

He hurriedly dried his hair, put on jeans, a shirt, boots, and splashed on a bit of cologne. He wasn't really looking for a woman. God knew he wasn't even interested in anyone but a feisty little wench who fought like a tiger and had a bend toward arguing. But he'd be drawn and quartered before he let her know such a thing.

He found her sitting on a barstool with several men already staring their fill and a look in their eyes that said they were about to go in for the kill. Considering how enraged she was, they had no idea how much a one-night stand would cost them. Dinner alone could run into three digits. A romp in the bed would have them yanking out whatever hair they had left. That bald-headed fellow winking at her from the end of the bar would have to bite the bullet and tear the earring out of his earlobe just to pay for part of her dinner.

He propped a hip on the barstool right next to her and ordered a beer. She'd already downed one and was on her second. She didn't even look at him.

He looked into the mirror behind the bar instead of at her. "What's a nice girl like you doing in a place like this?"

"That's cliché and about as old as my grandmother," she said.

"Okay then, what's a good-lookin' broad like you doin' in a high-class joint like this?"

"This would only be high class to a piece of redneck white trash like you."

"Thank you ma'am. I *am* a redneck piece of white trash but remember I can hang a hat on the family jewels without using my hands to hold it there."

"Prove it."

"Right here?" He made as if to stand up.

"Chicken?"

"Not at all. You don't mind the ladies seeing the trick, I damn sure don't mind. Remember Ellen is my aunt."

She actually blushed.

He stood the rest of the way up, slowly pulled his shirt from his pants and unbuckled his belt.

She put her hands over her face. "Stop!"

He refastened his belt and sat back down on the stool, leaving his shirt hanging free.

"What's your name, pretty lady?"

She glared at his reflection without bothering to turn her head and actually look at his profile. He smelled wonderful. Water droplets still hung on the curls just beginning to hang on his shirt collar again from the last haircut. She wanted nothing more than to drag him back upstairs and undress him.

"Jane Day," she answered belligerently. No man was going to talk to her like he did and expect to make up in the mirror above a bar. Whining indeed!

"Pretty name for a pretty girl. Could I buy you a drink?"

"You're buying all of them. I'm charging everything to the room. Including a tray full sent to that table over there where all those good-looking preppy types are sitting."

He bit back the acid remark begging to be let loose from his mouth.

"Remember what Pepper said to the lady at the party?"

"Before he danced on the tabletop?" she asked.

"That's right. I believe the line was 'I can ride anything with hair and dance with anything that has two feet.' Well I can add one to that. I can ride anything with hair better than you can, dance with anything with two feet better than you can, and I can damn sure drink your sorry ass under the table," he said.

"You're on, cowboy."

"I was an hour ago," he said.

She blushed again.

"What's the stakes?" she asked.

"No stakes. Just a contest. Winner wins. Loser loses," he said.

"Set 'em up bartender. And bring a bottle of Jack Daniels to chase 'em with."

"You crazy, lady?" the bartender asked.

"No, I'm a winner."

She declared she was still sober enough to make it up all seven flights of stairs and to hell with the elevator. He said he'd be carrying her before they made it to the third floor. By the middle of the second floor they were kissing while they caught their breath. On the third floor she threw up in a huge pot with a fake tree of some kind. On the fourth, Slade did the same in a trash can. Fifth floor: it took three tries to get the quarters into the soda machine for a Sprite, but they finally managed and washed the bad taste from their mouths. They had to rest on the sixth floor steps and that's where she lost her dress and gained his shirt. Finally, they made it to their floor and stumbled down the hall leaning on each other, slipping and falling, giggling and kissing. By the time they had their room door locked she was wearing nothing but his shirt. Her bikini underwear was hanging out his back pocket like a victory flag and her dress was thrown over his shoulder like a towel.

They awoke the next morning in bed together, snuggled up in each other's arms wearing nothing but birthday suits and severe headaches, with the memory of proving that Slade could wear a hat in a most conspicuous place and that Jane could make love with his boots on her tiny feet.

She awoke humming "Don't Call Him a Cowboy."

Slade tried to smile but it hurt too badly.

"I'm going to the shower. When I come out I don't want to hear a word," she whispered.

"Don't worry, neither do I," he said.

Chapter 13

IT WAS FIVE HUNDRED AND FIFTY MILES FROM BATON ROUGE to Beau and Milli's ranch southwest of Ardmore. Slade had every intention of unloading Jane that night. He could make it in nine hours, even allowing time to stop for food and potty breaks. But he hadn't counted on hangovers and headaches. He kept hoping she'd set up a whining moan, wanting to stop so she could sleep off the hangover. He couldn't complain—not after the whining accusation he'd made the night before. She didn't and he made it to Shreveport before he took an exit advertising Economy Inn. To the devil with waiting for her to want to stop; he was driving. She was simply sitting there.

"Thank God," she muttered. She would have curled up in a ball beside a farm pond and used a dried-up cow patty for a pillow just to get out of the truck. The wheels turning on the highway sounded like a brass band marching through her head. Every time Slade sighed she wanted to slap him for making so much noise. She figured he was stopping for a cup of coffee or a potty break. A few minutes inside the bathroom at a McDonalds would be heaven. She might sit on the toilet for an hour, lean her head against the cold steel of the stall, and sleep.

"Did you say something?" he asked.

She shook her head and even that hurt.

"Two rooms or one?" he asked when he stopped under the hotel awning.

"Two," she answered.

She could have kissed him but she'd already proven where that could and would lead. And she damn sure didn't want a drink to celebrate having her own bedroom.

Early birds that they were, he was able to get them ground-floor rooms with outside entrances. Side by side with a connecting door, which he had no intention of opening. He tossed a couple of room keys toward her when he opened the truck door.

"We got two right around the corner toward the back," he said.

She didn't care where they were as long as the ice machine wasn't close enough that she could hear it dumping every few minutes. A bed with clean sheets and dark drapes were the only things she required.

He grabbed his suitcase and she reached for her duffel bag at the same time. Their fingertips touched and sparks flew but neither of them even looked up. There would be time enough to think about the future once the present pain was gone.

There was plenty of hot water and she stood under it for a long time. She wrapped a white towel around her body, brushed her teeth, and turned back the bed. The sheets were crisp and cool, the air conditioner turned down as far as it would go, and she wallowed for about thirty seconds before she looked at the digital clock beside the bed. It was three minutes past three p.m. when she shut her eyes.

She felt a presence, slowly opened one eye, and checked the clock. Six forty-five. She popped both eyes open to see Slade sitting on the bed right beside hers. He was a dead man. She'd only had a three-hour nap. No way was she ready to go again. He could go find something to do and let her sleep some more.

"Hungry?" he asked.

She put a pillow over her head and rolled away from him. "Still sleepy. Go away."

"You've been sleeping almost seventeen hours."

She sat straight up and her stomach set up a growling howl that could have been heard halfway to Georgia.

"You're lying to me just to get me awake," she said. Her head was free of pain. She was hungry. Was it really morning? She grabbed the remote control and turned on the television to find the morning news complete with a weather report for Shreveport. Hot and dry. Surprise!

"Sounds like you are hungry. Get dressed while I check out and we'll find a Denny's. I could eat a Grand Slam breakfast this morning," Slade said.

Jane was beautiful with her hair all tousled and it was cute the way she kept the sheet tucked around her when she sat up. Evidently when he wasn't around she slept in the nude just like he did.

"Give me ten minutes to brush my teeth and get my hair in a ponytail," she said.

He didn't move.

"Get out of here. I'm starving."

"I've seen you naked. Go ahead. Besides I've already checked out. My stuff is in the truck."

"You are a pig from hell," she said.

"We've already established that. I think it was before I showed you who could drink the most."

"I outdid you, cowboy. You fell asleep before I did."

"That's only because you wore me out. So crawl your ass out of bed and get dressed. I'm sittin' right here. It's my prize for winning."

"You did not win," she argued.

"Sure I did. I woke up before you did, which means it didn't take me as long to get over the drunk, so that makes me the winner."

She drew her brows down into a fine line above her squinty eyes. One swift toss of the covers landed them over his head and she was in the bathroom with her duffel bag in her hands before he fought his way out of them.

"You are the pig from hell," he shouted.

"Find your own lines. That one is mine. I'm layin' claim to it and you can't use it the rest of the time we are together," she yelled from the other side of the door.

They found a Denny's on their way out of town and both ordered the Lumberjack Slam, which consisted of pancakes, sausage, bacon, ham, eggs, grits, and biscuits. Slade decided on hash browns instead of grits and snarled when she stirred over easy fried eggs into her grits.

"That's as disgusting as sugar and pepper on buttered biscuits," he said.

"When the waitress comes by, ask her for half a dozen more biscuits. Nothing like chasin' beer with Jack to bring on the hunger, and I'd forgotten about pepper biscuits."

"Or sleeping sixteen hours. How do you stay so slim?"

"It makes me poor to carry it around. That's what my grandmother told me when I was a little girl. I never did look like anything but a beanpole. When the other girls got all fluffy and pretty, I looked like a boy in a skirt. It sure was frustrating."

"You must have one high metabolism," he said.

"Basically, I like food and I work hard."

The waitress came by to refill their coffee cups and Jane asked for six more biscuits and another bowl of grits.

"And you sir?" The waitress turned her charm on Slade.

"Just a large cup of coffee to go."

"You ever look at the nutrition guides for a breakfast like this?" Jane asked.

"It would give me a heart attack. Don't tell me."

"Suffice it to say that there's two hundred percent of cholesterol right here even before she brings my biscuits. There's more than a thousand calories with another thousand tacked on if I eat all six biscuits and don't share with you, enough salt to plug your veins and arteries like an old man, and you don't even want to get me started on the fat grams."

"Then why do you eat it? Why not a cup of yogurt and dry toast?" he asked.

"Because I like it and the women in my family don't run to fat. Not like Kristy or Elaine."

"Are you trying to start a fight? Here I was being nice and you are starting a jealous fight."

"I'm not jealous. I'm stating fact."

"No ma'am, you are jealous and trying to get me to say how they look without clothes. Sorry. I don't kiss and tell. When we get back to Ringgold I won't tell them how you look, either, so don't worry about them looking at you with pity."

"You are a…"

"…pig from hell. Find something new and fresh. That one is getting old," he grinned.

She buttered two of the new biscuits the waitress set before them and proceeded to sugar and pepper them. He buttered two and filled them with strawberry jam.

Just goes to prove how different we are, she thought. *He eats his plain old strawberry jam and I have something exotic and different. I'm not jealous. I was just making a comment and I don't give a rat's ass what those two women look like naked. Why would I? I don't have to compare me to them. I'm going home in one week and never looking back.*

By eight thirty they were back in the truck headed north to Texarkana. It was hard for Slade to believe that a week ago they'd spent their first night in that town and now they'd come full circle and found themselves headed there again. Only this time, they'd bypass it and keep driving northwest to Beau's ranch, the Bar M. He had called Nellie the night before and she'd told him in no uncertain terms he was to stay on the ranch with Jane. She'd get in touch with Beau and Milli to tell them they were about to have a week's worth of company. She was sure that they'd be glad for the help during the busy season. Jane could help Milli and Rosa cook for the crew and Slade could help Beau take care of the hay and cattle. Everything on the Double L was under control. She'd see him the Sunday after Jane's birthday. He could take her to Mississippi on Saturday, leave her at her ranch, and come on home on Sunday. She was a big girl. She could take care of her own business on Monday, and Slade would have his job finished.

If she's such a big girl, why in the hell am I in this truck with her headed toward the Bar M for a week? he argued with the memory of his grandmother's voice. *I got my two cents in on the phone too, but it was only a token argument because down deep inside I don't want to leave her just yet. Give me a week to convince myself I don't even like her and it'll be a whole lot easier.*

"Setting the record straight: I didn't have sex with Elaine or Kristy. The kids were always in the way with Kristy and I just plain didn't like Elaine," he said.

Jane stiffened her mouth to keep from smiling. "Why are you setting the record straight? What does it matter?"

"It probably doesn't but I don't want you thinkin' I'm a whoremonger."

"I didn't sleep with John, either, just for the record."

"But you were about to marry him," Slade said.

"And he said that we should wait so it would be special. I had no idea that I was waiting and he was sleeping with Ramona."

"You didn't have to tell me that."

"Same back at you."

A ring tone went off in the console beside them. He could have gladly tossed the cell phone out the window. For the first time they'd been about to carry on a conversation that didn't start and end with bickering and it felt right. She picked up the phone, flipped it open, and handed it to him.

"Hello," he snapped. "I see."

A long pause. Slade's brows drew down in a frown.

"We were on the way to my cousin's ranch in southern Oklahoma."

Another one. He looked bewildered.

"How old are they?"

A short pause. Slade smiled.

"That's a bit amusing. You'll understand later."

He snapped the phone shut and dropped it.

"How old are who and what's funny?" she asked.

"John Farris is an alias. Of course, you'd probably figured that out. He injured an FBI agent this morning with a fork. The man is in surgery and they expect him to live but he's lost a lot of blood. John left a print on the fork before he escaped. Turns out he was in the Air Force, special ops, went rogue and they booted him out. He's been trained in combat and to kill. Nice thought, ain't it?"

Cold chills raced up and down her spine like kids playing chase on a hot summer day. "He's loose?"

"He is. Agent August has assigned two agents to stay at the Double L just in case he shows up there with intentions of hurting Granny or Ellen. They'll be living there in the house for a week."

She giggled. "How old are they?"

"Both retired. This is just a favor to Agent August. Seems the two of them go to a working ranch once a year for their vacation. Have been doing it for years. Funny, ain't it?"

She couldn't contain the laughter. It bounced around in the truck for a few minutes then, as if on cue, she went deadly silent. "He'll come after me. What are we going to do? I can't put Beau and Milli in danger."

"Don't suppose we can. It's your day to pick. Where do you want to go?"

"Home, but that's not possible."

The phone rang again and he answered it, saying "Okay" several times before he hung up again.

"That's the last time we use that phone, since anyone can trace calls made from it. The agents are already at the ranch posing as hired hands. Milli is picking us up in Texarkana. That's all I know right now."

"Milli is picking us up? Why would she drive to Texarkana to pick us up there?" Jane asked.

"She owns her own plane. She flies back and forth to west Texas all the time. I expect she's going to take us somewhere."

"This gets weirder every minute. How far is it?"

"An hour. There's a Luckadeau ranch south of town. She'll be waiting. I guess we leave it in the hands of the FBI now. You aren't bait anymore, but you are on the run until they catch him. And he won't be talking his way out of the situation when they do. Not when he tried to murder an agent. They'll get him and you'll be safe," he said.

Safe? Right. But how do I ever trust anyone again? Even you, and you're a good man, Slade. But I'd always have a doubt, wouldn't I?

She swallowed hard and nodded. She wanted to cry but she turned and watched the tall pine trees sweeping by at seventy-five miles an hour.

In forty-five minutes Slade pulled the truck into a gravel lane leading back to a ranch house. Kids played outside. Two ladies sat on the porch. Men were working round and about everywhere. He didn't stop but kept driving down a path to the back where a small plane sat on a short concrete runway. Milli waved at them and motioned the truck closer.

"Beau's momma will be taking your truck to a barn and hiding it away for a week. Leave the keys under the floor mat. She'll come and get it later today. She's the only one who knows what's going on here, so everything should be safe. Get your gear and we'll get going," Milli said.

Jane had flown since before she could walk, but she hated small airplanes. Give her a big old jet with wide aisles so that she felt as though she was traveling with the comforts of a condo and she was fine.

"You look a little pale, Jane," Milli said. "Don't worry. I've been flying for years and I've got the manual right there in the cockpit with me in case something goes wrong. Slade can read big words, can't he?"

Jane blanched.

"Hey, I'm only teasing. Slade, you sit up front with me. Jane, I'm sorry the back is so crowded. I had this one adapted for just me and Katy Scarlett. That little seat accommodates her car seat just fine but it's going to be a tight fit for you. Thank God you're not as big as that Amazon Slade was dating at Granny's party."

That brought out a smile as Jane practically folded her legs against her shoulder bones to sit down.

"Okay, crew, here we go," Milli said.

"Where do we go?" Jane asked.

"I'll tell you a story. Believe it or not, my maternal grandmother was a blonde before she went gray. She's English as they come. Grandmother came from Rio County, one of the border counties over in Texas. Anyway, she came to the University of Mexico to study Spanish, and she met Grandpoppy. She made friends with his sister and went home with the girl for a weekend and there was her older brother. She says it was love at first sight, and they were both thunderstruck. She says he looked like a darker version of Clark Gable and he says she looked just like a goddess with her blonde hair and blue eyes.

"They were in love, but do you know what it was like in the '40s for a rich white Texas girl to fall in love with a full-blooded Mexican boy? Even if his parents were every bit as rich as hers? Well, I can tell you, it wasn't easy. I guess her father came close to a heart attack when she wrote them she was marrying my Grandpoppy. He disowned her and refused to have her name mentioned in his house ever again. So they lived in Mexico; then her parents were both killed in a house fire and since she was the only child, the property was hers. So she and my Grandpoppy took the girls… all five of them… to Rio County to raise them in the United States. They kept their place in Mexico and went back to see that side of the family for vacations and holidays. Sometimes Grandpoppy came back to settle business ventures, and now that they're retired, they spend a lot of time there and less in Rio County. It's their cabin on the beach where you'll be spending the next week. Few people even know about the cabin, since it's on a private stretch of beach property. I can't think that the man who is after you will ever find you. Oh, I've got a cell phone here. It's to be used only in emergencies. That means dial the number taped on the back, which is your agent's number, or leave it alone."

Slade rolled his eyes. Just what he wanted and needed. A week on a deserted beach with Ellacyn Jane Hayes. Life couldn't get any more complicated.

Jane sighed. Maybe John wouldn't be able to locate her there. Hopefully, his resources didn't include the whole Luckadeau family.

"After I drop you off, I'm going to Momma's. She's got Katy Scarlett and I'm picking her up and taking her back home tomorrow morning. As far as anyone knows, I'm simply flying in and out to get my daughter," Milli said.

"Thank you," Jane finally remembered her manners.

"Yes, thanks, Milli," Slade added.

"Hey, family sticks together. You know that, Slade. Took me a while to figure it out but I sure do like the concept now that I'm getting on to it."

"How long have you and Beau been married?" Jane asked.

"Less than a year. This is my last flight until the baby is born. I promised Beau I'd give it up after the first trimester. He's holding me to my promise."

"Had this plane long?" Slade asked.

"A few years. I had a Cessna-172 at first and loved that little bitty plane, but this old bird took my eye at an air show when I was in college and I had to have one like it. So I sold the Cessna and with the money I had saved from stunt shows and a season of crop dusting, I bought this old Yak-52. It was one of those old Russian war buzzards that was customized with room for the pilot, copilot, and just enough room to put the baby's car seat behind me. I loved the bubble of glass over my head and felt like the Red Baron the first time I took it up. My very first plane was painted candy-apple red with thin red pin stripes and spectators said it looked like a ball of fire when I put it through the acrobatics in a show."

"You fly stunt?" Jane was intrigued.

"Sure. Want to fly upside down or close enough to the trees down there to count the oranges on them?"

"No, thank you," Jane laughed.

"Tell Beau next time you see him. He hates to fly and is just a notch above Katy when it comes to nausea. I swear she got her daddy's genes in everything."

"Really?" Jane asked.

"She really did. I thought I'd kept him a secret and did pretty good until we came to Oklahoma last spring. One look at her and him together and it was plain who her father was. Someday when you and I have lots of time we'll find a quiet corner and compare Luckadeau stories," Milli said.

"Here now!" Slade said.

Milli cocked her head to one side, fiddled with controls, and listened intently. "Yes, sir," she finally said.

"Change of plans. A hurricane is developing off shore and headed toward the beach. I'm taking you straight to Hereford, Texas. There will be an agent at the ranch to take you elsewhere."

"Mercy!" Jane said.

"That must be a wicked man you are running from," Milli said. "Thank goodness you've got Slade with you. Luckadeau men are good at protecting their women."

It was on the tip of Jane's tongue to tell her that she was in no way Slade's woman and never would be, but she didn't say a word.

A Cadillac and a black van were waiting when Milli landed the plane. The lady in the Caddy brought a squirming, blonde-haired little girl to Milli, who kissed her all over her face and told her how much she'd missed her that week. The man in a black suit leaning on the van waited a few minutes and then motioned Jane and Slade over.

"Milli, thank you," Jane said before she obeyed.

Milli hugged her with the arm that wasn't holding the child and whispered softly, "When it's all over, come and see me. I'd love to hear the whole story. I'll show you mine if you show me yours."

"You got a deal," Jane whispered back.

"Thank you, Milli," Slade said.

"You are very welcome. Take care of her."

"Will do," Slade waved as they crossed the pasture.

One agent was tall and slim and wore jeans, a three-button knit shirt, and boots. He had a nose slightly too big for his gaunt face and a receding hairline. The other one had carrot-red hair cut in a burr, a round face, and tight lips that gave him a serious appearance.

"I'm Agent August," the red-haired one said. "This is Agent Jones. We moved your truck from the Luckadeau ranch. I hope you don't mind but if you do, rest assured we did it with legal papers. There's a blond-haired man driving it—from a distance he looks like you—and a small dishwater blonde is riding with him. We feel sure that John has already identified you, Slade, and has your truck license number. He has lots of resources. We hope to catch him in the next two or three days when he finds that truck parked at a motel. Now if you two will get into the van, we'll be on our way."

"This has been a hell of a day," Jane said when she was buckled in beside Slade in the backseat.

"Hopefully it will get better. We are taking you to a safe house about two hours from here. The only thing you have to do for the next week is stay within the borders we'll give you. Sorry about the beach holiday. It would have been a good place."

"I'm confused," Jane said as she watched Milli get into the van with her mother and drive away. "If you want to catch him, it's easy. Just let me call Celia. He'll be in touch with her for sure."

"Think you can bring my truck back to me without bullet holes?" Slade asked seriously.

"Do our best—or else fix the holes before we do," Agent August said.

Jane leaned her head back and fell asleep. It had been a long day. Thank goodness it hadn't come on the heels of the drunken night in Baton Rouge. One thing for damn sure, she was going to have stories to tell her grandchildren… if she ever had any. She awoke with a start when the van stopped and could hardly believe she'd been asleep two whole hours.

"We're here," Agent Jones said. "Home sweet home for a week. Try not to kill each other. Familiarity breeds contempt, you know." He chuckled.

"Ah, it's not such a bad place. Can see for miles in any which way. A man would be a fool even to attempt to sneak up on this place. And the last time I brought a witness here to stay a few days, we left a deck of cards and a few books, so you won't get too bored," Agent August said.

"Here're the keys and the phone," Agent Jones handed them to Slade.

"You're not coming inside?" Jane felt as if she'd been thrown to the wolves as she stared at the small cabin set in the middle of nowhere with nothing around it but a pole bringing electricity from God knew where.

"Got to get back to Amarillo and catch a plane. Dial the number on the back in an emergency. Other than that, don't use it. We'll be in touch with your grandmother, Slade. Don't worry about her. We've got two good agents there to protect her." Agent Jones handed him a cell phone and crawled into the passenger side of the car. Evidently it was his turn to ride and August's turn to drive.

"Who's going to protect the agents from Nellie and Ellen?" Jane asked.

"Oh, I reckon those old buzzards can take care of themselves. We'll come get you next Saturday morning, take you to Amarillo, and put you on a plane to Greenville and you to Dallas." He pointed first at Jane and then Slade.

"Where in the hell are we?" Jane asked when the dust settled from their leaving.

"I think New Mexico, but I fell asleep. Did you notice any highway signs?" he asked.

"Hell no," she quipped.

"Well that's just great!" He marched toward the house with her following on his heels.

"I hope there's enough food in there to last a week."

"I hope you don't get mad or there might not be."

The porch stretched the length of the house. The whole place looked to be about twenty-four foot square with the last dregs of paint long since gone. Two windows and a door faced out onto the porch. Slade used the key to open the door and stepped inside ahead of her. She followed, eyes darting around every which way, making sure there were no spiders or mice to greet them.

It was pristine clean and looked more like an army barracks than a house that real people occupied. Two twin beds, one on either side of the room, were made up military tight with olive drab blankets and sheets folded down neatly from the top. A small kitchenette was comprised of a two-burner stove, a small, stainless-steel sink to the left of it, and a tiny refrigerator underneath, all in one unit. Beside that was a chest-type freezer about the size of a computer desk. The orange floral sofa was outdated and worn but looked comfortable. The old Formica-topped table and two chairs looked like something Lucy and Desi Arnaz had eaten on back when they first got married.

A door opened at the end of the bed on the right into a fair-sized bathroom. Toilet. Sink. Old claw-foot tub. A tiny apartment-sized washing machine tucked into a corner with cabinets above it. Jane opened the doors to find a healthy supply of toilet paper, towels, washcloths, soap, laundry soap—all the comforts of home.

Another door opened at the end of the bed on the left into a pantry. It was about a third as big as the living/bedroom area with shelves on three sides. They were stocked full of canned goods and plastic containers marked dried eggs, flour, cornmeal, sugar, brown sugar, powdered sugar… Whoopee yeah! They weren't going to starve, but someone had to cook from scratch.

He moaned. "A whole week in this place. I might be tempted to kill you myself just to go home."

"If you are still breathing next Saturday when they return, it won't be because I haven't thought about doing you in, either," she said.

"Welcome to hell, Jane Day."

"Same to you, Slade Luckadeau."

Chapter 14

JANE UNPACKED HER DUFFEL BAG AND CARRIED THE DIRTY clothing to the bathroom. No dryer anywhere in sight, so she opened the back door to find a clothesline stretched from the porch post to a small, lonesome old mesquite tree not much bigger than a bush. There were a few clothespins still stuck on the line but her jeans would have to be doubled over the wire to keep them from dragging in the dirt. Grass grew here and there in strange clumps—not like anything in Greenville, where it was green and plush as a carpet underfoot. She shaded her eyes with the back of her hand and looked out across acres and acres of desert that didn't stop until it met up with the sky. It reminded her of the ocean in Florida. Water and sky in that peaceful paradise. Dirt and sky in this leftover from hell.

Sweat beaded under her nose and ran down her forehead into her eyes, making them burn. She swiped at it with her hand and then wiped it on the rear end of her jeans. Before the week was out, she might consider cutting the legs from her jeans and turning them into Daisy Mae shorts.

"Air conditioning?" she asked aloud.

"None. But there is a swamp cooler in that window." Slade answered with a nod of his head toward the far end of the back porch. An old water cooler, rusted around the bottom, sat on concrete blocks. The padding on the sides looked fairly good and it would provide moisture in the heat of the day.

"No phone, so no internet. Electricity and a well for water. Looks like the potty flushes out into a septic tank. Pretty basic," he said.

"Why didn't they bring John out here instead of us?" Jane asked.

"Now that's a question worth pondering. He's so mean and tough he could probably walk out of here naked with his eyes closed and not step on a single rattler. Reckon this is the area where they found the aliens fifty or sixty years ago?"

"If you see a big saucer coming down from the sky, you better start running toward it because I'm calling the first seat, especially after that comment about rattlesnakes," she said.

"What's for supper? I'm hungry," he said.

"There's plenty of food in there and you are a big boy. Go cook it."

"Are we going to work together on the meals or do we take turns?" he asked.

She thought about it for several seconds before she answered, "Let's work together. We haven't got much else to do but eat and sleep and read whatever books are on that shelf. Let's do a big breakfast, leftover or light dinner since that will be the hottest part of the day and we won't want to start up the stove, and a big supper."

He nodded. "It's suppertime, so this one will be meat and potatoes like dinner is at home. I'll thaw out some meat in the microwave. I checked that freezer and there must be a quarter of beef in there."

"First wet down that swamp cooler and let's get some air flowing."

"You askin' or bossin'?"

"Out here, darlin', there ain't no boss," she said.

"Then I'll take it that you're askin'. And there is one other thing we could do to pass the time rather than read." He raised an eyebrow rakishly.

"Been there. Done that. Ain't going there again."

"Why? Wasn't it better than reading a book all day?"

"At the time, yes. But that time is done and finished. I'll read the book. Besides, we'd slide off each other, we'd be so sweaty. Hot as it is if we added sex heat to it we might ignite and burn the place down."

What she didn't tell him was that she hoped to hell her birth control was still in effect and that there wasn't a little blond-haired boy already swimming around in her womb. The first time she'd been very vulnerable; the second, very drunk. She was neither and wouldn't be again. Vulnerability ended when they dropped her in this godforsaken place and she'd already checked—drunk wasn't an option. They were so far out in the boonies it would take a man or woman more than a week to find them, and there wasn't so much as a can of beer in the place. Kool-Aid and iced tea would be the beverages of choice. And if they didn't remember to keep the trays filled and put back in the freezer, it might be lukewarm Kool-Aid and tea.

"You are a cold-hearted woman, Jane Day."

"Yep, I am. Ellacyn Hayes wasn't, but Jane Day damn sure is. Do you see what I see?" She pointed.

"The swamp cooler?"

"A propane grill right there beside that tree. If it's got a full tank, we can cook outside and not heat up the house at all."

"We sound like a married couple," he chuckled.

"More like an odd couple," she quipped.

He fired up the grill. She thawed two T-bone steaks. He sat on the porch steps and watched them cook in between times when he turned them over. She heated peas and carrots on one burner and made boxed macaroni and cheese on the other. When he brought the steaks inside, she had the table set with mismatched plates and cutlery and paper towels for napkins.

"Potatoes?" he asked when he set the steaks in the middle of the table.

"Instant all right?"

The edges of his nostrils flared.

"I figured instant potatoes would make you surly for a whole day, so I made macaroni and cheese from a box. Be grateful we have margarine. The milk is powdered and has to be reconstituted. I wouldn't recommend it for cereal in the mornings, but it'll make gravy and do to cook with."

"It ain't a five-star restaurant, is it?"

"It's edible and we won't starve in a week," she said.

"Speak for yourself."

"Don't be a baby. Eat your peas and carrots. It could be worse. They could have put us out here with a tent, a spade to make our own bathroom, and a bucket to draw water," she said.

"Dessert?" he asked when he finished eating.

She laid a package of six miniature chocolate donuts beside his plate. "Eat slowly and chew well. That's the only thing in the house other than canned fruit. They're only semi-soft and the date on the package is three weeks ago, so they're probably stale."

"Want to share?"

She shook her head. "Coffee?"

"I'd love some. Is there a pot or do we boil it on the stove?"

"I found a four-cup drip pot in the pantry and two huge cans of dark roast," she said.

She set about making coffee and he ate the stale donuts. Being in a deserted place gave him a whole new outlook. Had he been put out there with Kristy and those two girls, he would have already yanked every blond hair from his head. If he'd been dropped there with Elaine, he would have used a paring knife to stab himself to death. A month ago he wouldn't have chosen Jane for his companion for a week in the middle of nowhere, but among the three women he'd been familiar with the past six months, he had to admit he was glad it was Jane sharing the experience with him and neither of the other two.

Jane washed dishes.

Slade dried.

She found a worn paperback book and settled down on one end of the sofa.

He found a worn paperback book and settled down on the other end of the sofa.

She opened the J.A. Jance book, *Lying in Wait,* and began to read about J.P. Beaumont's grandfather's death in the prologue. That reminded her of her grandfather, dead many years, who'd left the ranch to her father, who had in turn bequeathed it to his only daughter in his will. Of course her mother continued to run it and love it until the day she died. It was the one thing that wasn't tied up in the trust fund accounts until she was twenty-five. It supported itself with the quarter horse business and Lanson, her manager and trainer, was an excellent manager of that part of the business. The cattle brought in a fair share of money also, with Grady, her foreman, taking care of that.

She shook the thoughts of home out of her head and kept reading. It would make the time go by faster until she could crawl into that twin bed on the left side of the room and fall asleep. Tomorrow it would be six days until the ordeal was over. Then five and so on. It wasn't so long if she took it a day at a time. And boring as hell, which was good after the past few days. Just lie back, eat, sleep, and waste a week.

Evidently a previous tenant had liked J.A. Jance, because Slade picked up a book by the same author. He'd never read her work before, didn't know if J.A. was Jane Ann or Jimmy Andrew until he read the brief bio inside the back cover of the book. Still didn't know, for that matter, since it just referred to her as J.A. Not that it mattered a bit. The book, about a lady sheriff named Joanna Brady investigating the death of an elderly widow, kept his attention. It was close to midnight when he finally read the last page and decided against the excerpt from the next Joanna Brady mystery, *Devil's Claw*, available from William Morrow at bookstores everywhere on July 5, 2000.

"So who'd you get out of trouble by the end of the book? Did Sheriff Brady have two black eyes in your book?" he asked.

Jane held up a finger. "Shhhh." Five minutes later she shut the book and looked at him. "Sheriff Brady was not a character in this book. I was reading about J.P. Beaumont, a detective. Miz Jance is a good writer. I'll trade you tomorrow and then we'll compare notes on which character we like best."

"Shhhh," he held up a finger.

"What?"

He cocked his head to one side, frowning the whole time. "Put your shoes on. Grab your purse. That's a chopper. And it's coming right at us."

"Agent August?"

"I have no idea but we're not taking chances. Hurry up. We're going out the back door and heading toward the wash about a hundred yards out."

He had his shoes on, phone in one hand, and shaving kit in the other by the time she'd located her purse. She turned off the lamps on her way out the door behind him. He shoved the phone into his shaving kit, grabbed her hand, and took off in a run that she had trouble keeping up with.

He gave thanks as he ran that it was a pitch-black night with barely a sliver of leftover moon hanging in a sky riddled with clouds. How in the hell had John found them, who did he know willing to work with him, and where did he get a chopper on such short notice? He hit the wash, no more than three feet deep, and pulled her down with him.

For the next fifteen minutes they listened to enough gun power noise to rival the Fourth of July fireworks show in Terral, Oklahoma. Six figures dressed in black started at the front of the house, emptied clips into the windows, reloaded in sync, began firing again as they made their way to the back. Then they repeated the process toward the front until they were back at the helicopter. They loaded up and then all hell really broke loose. Two blasts from the chopper leveled the house and sent it up in flames.

Jane stared in mute shock. If she'd had to speak or be tossed inside that burning inferno, she'd have to have taken the latter, because there were no words. Why did Paul want her dead so badly and how much was he willing to pay to get the job done?

"What do we do now?" she finally whispered hoarsely, five full minutes after the chopper had disappeared in the direction from which the FBI had brought them to the so-called safe house. Surely she was asleep and in the middle of another terrible nightmare. The smell of burning house and smoke spiraling up toward the black clouds convinced her that she was indeed awake.

Slade still held her hand in his and couldn't untangle their fingers if he tried. "I don't know. I think we should head out the back way, though. They'll be coming back for the bodies at dawn."

"You think so?" she shivered. "Damn them to hell anyway. Thank God you heard that chopper and had a few doubts or we'd be toast."

"More like grilled steaks," he said.

She shuddered and slapped his arm. "God, Slade. That's horrible. Look at that place. Why in the hell would they come back? Nothing caught inside could possibly be alive."

"Got to have a body before you can collect the money," he said.

She looked down at the shaving kit and rage boiled up from somewhere so deep in her soul that she could have ripped his blond hair out by the roots and scratched the dimple off his chin. She'd left everything that wasn't in her purse in that place. Her meager amount of clothes, her makeup on the bathroom counter, even her hairbrush, and he brought his shaving kit?

"Why?" she yelled. She didn't look up and blame God Almighty but she was so mad at Slade she could have thrown him on the flames of the house like he was a T-bone steak on a grill.

"Why what?" His heart refused to slow down and his mind did double time hoping they'd find a road or a town before dawn.

"Why'd you bring that stupid shaving kit?" she yelled.

"Because it's holding our cash. You think anyone is going to give us a vehicle or a bus station is going to let us ride for free?" He couldn't understand why she was so angry at him for picking up his shaving kit. Hadn't she grabbed her purse on the way out?

"Oh," she said flatly.

"Get over it. I'm not being vain. Hell, I don't care if I shave or not, but we will need money. We've probably got a long way to walk before morning. By then you'll be so hot and sweaty you won't give a damn about what I'm carrying," he said.

"Use the phone and call the emergency number," she said.

"No thank you. I'm not trusting anyone again. FBI can kiss my cowboy ass," he said.

She stood up, dusted the seat of her jeans, and put her hand in his. He held on to the strap of his leather shaving kit with his other hand. She carried her purse with her other one. They headed west, not knowing where they'd end up.

Three hours into the trip, Jane declared she'd sell her whole oil company for a bottle of cheap water. She'd even be tempted to drink from a mud puddle if they could just find one.

"Willing to do a stomp dance for a little rain?" he asked.

"I feel like a sweaty hog. I'd dance nude for rain right now and not even care if a policeman came along and hauled me to jail. At least a cell would have a potty and a drink of water," she said.

"You might get your wish. I saw a flash of lightning over to the southwest. That's where the big storms come from. We might be wading in the mud before morning."

"I'd wade in it gladly. Back there, I would've figured that was Agent August coming to take us home. It would never have dawned on me that John could have found us so quick. Good Lord, we left Baton Rouge, went to Shreveport, flew to Hereford, and were driven to hell. How did he follow that trail?"

"Good question. You come up with an answer that makes sense, we might call that emergency number on the back of the phone. Uh-oh!" he exclaimed.

"That didn't sound good."

"It's not good. Matter of fact, it's damn bad and I don't know what to do about it," he said.

"Agent August and Agent Jones knew about the phone." Jane tried to think about nothing but that cell phone and where she'd seen it. "And Milli. Remember she had the thing and was going to give it to us to take to the beach place. Where did she get it?"

"From whatever agent sent her to Shreveport." Slade stopped and dropped Jane's hand. He took the phone from his pocket along with a pocket knife.

"She handed it off to Agent August. I saw her do it," Jane said.

He pried the back of the phone off and held it up. "Here's the sorry culprit. John or Ramona has an inside man. I'll eat my socks if this isn't a tracking device. They know exactly where we are, that they didn't kill us in the house, and believe me, they'll come running when we stop walking."

"What are we going to do?"

"Think right hard and keep walking," he said.

Two hours later they crossed a barbed wire fence with a No Trespassing sign painted on a tire and hung on a fence post. On the other side of the fence, across a ditch, was a highway. Jane stared at it as if it were a mirage that would disappear if she blinked.

"Which way?" she asked.

"I see a highway sign way down there. Let's go that way until we see what it says. We can always turn around," he suggested.

At that moment, Jane was scared out of her mind, wondering what they were going to do with that damned tracking telephone, and wishing she was back at the safe house with another week of boredom ahead of her. She wished Slade had taken her hand back in his after he'd dismantled the phone. Just the warmth of his touch had brought her a measure of comfort, but she didn't have the nerve to make the first move.

"It says Childress three miles," Slade said when they reached the sign. "I've been to Childress. It's in the eastern edge of the Texas panhandle. There's a couple of motels there. We can be there by daybreak."

"Then let's keep walking. Knowing that those people are sitting in air conditioned comfort with a beer and a hamburger makes me so mad I could spit."

An old pickup truck approached them from the west, slowed down to a crawl, and went on past. A car sped by from the east going so fast the driver probably didn't even see them on the shoulder. Then a black van slowed down in front of them, and Jane's blood ran cold. A red-haired lady stopped beside them and leaned out the window, "Y'all have car trouble somewhere back there? Need a ride into Childress? I could take you back there."

"No thanks. We know some folks just up ahead. They'll go get the car out of the ditch for us. We were nearly home anyway. Thanks for the offer," Slade said.

"Anytime. I been where you are and it's good when someone offers to help," she said. "Want a bottle of water?"

"We're fine," Slade told her. "Where you headed?"

"On my way to Dallas."

"Want a cell phone?" Jane asked.

"What?" The lady asked with a quizzical expression.

"My ex-boyfriend is stalking me. He put a tracking thing in this cell phone and ran us off the road back there. We just found the device. You want the phone? You can call whoever you want. Run up his bill to a million dollars if you want to. I don't give a damn. Then toss it in the backseat of a truck headed for

Montana. That should teach the sorry sumbitch to stalk me," Jane said.

"Give it here, honey. I don't cotton to men acting like that. I'll make a few phone calls between here and Vernon. I usually stop at a truck stop there for coffee. This phone is going to be traveling all day."

"You are a doll," Jane said.

"Just a sister protecting another sister," the lady said with a smile.

Slade peeled the number from the back of the phone and handed it to the driver. "Thanks, lady. I've been trying to protect her but that ex is a fiend."

"Well, may his soul rot for abusing you. Rest assured he's going to be chasing his tail end by the time he finds this. I'll slide it up under the seat of the meanest, toughest truck driver I can find."

She drove away and they walked on. Even if the woman used the phone to call her friends and relatives then threw it in a bar ditch somewhere near Wichita Falls, that would buy them some time. They came into Childress from the east on Highway 287 just as the light began to shine through the trees and the town was waking up. When they saw a sign that said Super 8, Jane could have really done that stomp dance. She vowed she'd never take a soft bed and a shower for granted again.

The lady at the desk said that check-in wasn't until three o'clock and if they wanted to check in they'd have to be out by eleven o'clock, which was only five hours away.

Slade assured her that he was willing to pay for two days. Then he went into a long-winded spiel about their car breaking down and how it would take until tomorrow to fix it anyway.

"Well then, sir, we've got a room for you. I see you didn't bring a suitcase. Do you need a hospitality kit with a razor and toothbrush?"

"That would be nice. Thank you," Slade signed the register as Mr. and Mrs. Jimmy Jance.

"Got a bus station in town in case my wife needs to go on back home while they're fixing the car?" he asked.

"That'll be a hundred and thirty-nine dollars and sixty-nine cents with tax for two nights, and yes, sir, there is a bus station in town," she said.

Slade pulled several twenties from his wallet and waited while she slowly made change.

"Don't get much real money these days. Mostly it's credit cards," she explained.

"Would you rather have a card? I've got mine with me, honey." Jane started fishing in her purse.

"No, ma'am, this will be just fine," the lady said. "You are on the ground floor right around the side. Hope your car gets fixed soon. Have a nice stay. Continental breakfast from six to ten. That'll be in about ten minutes."

"Thank you," Slade said.

When he opened the door to their room and she saw two double beds she got misty-eyed. She didn't even stop but threw her purse on the bed nearest the bathroom and walked straight to the sink where she unwrapped a plastic cup from its protective sleeve and filled it three times with water before she wasn't thirsty anymore. That finished, she went into the bathroom, turned on the hot water, sat on the potty long enough to pee, and stripped down to bare skin.

No amount of washing took away the feeling that surrounded her like the sleeve on the cup. Something very, very evil—and it wasn't going to go away with hot water. She wrapped one white towel around her head and one around her body and opened the door to find Slade sitting on the end of the bed watching television.

"Your turn," she said. "I'm going to sleep until tomorrow."

"Look at this," he said.

The television anchor woman was standing in the foreground of a pile of smoldering rubble. "…hunting cabin south of Hollis just over the Red River on the Texas side of the river went up in flames last night. The person who owns the land and cabin is not available for comment. The latest news is that no one was in the cabin, which was burned to the ground, but there will be a search later for bodies when it's safe to get near the still-smoldering house. It's too early to tell if there was foul play. Stay tuned to this channel for further news on that item. Now for the weather, here's Pete Morris."

"Local station. Evidently it's not big enough news for national," Jane said.

"We'll need to buy a car and keep moving. This is Sunday so there's probably no way to get one until tomorrow. You want to chance staying here until then?" he asked.

She was so tired she wasn't sure if she had the energy to actually trust and work with Slade, but she had no choice. They'd have to work together if they wanted to come out on the other side alive and well. She could rely on the fact that he'd kept her from being assassinated for a whole week, but if they were both to live another week it was going to take serious planning. Thank goodness she'd learned to like him, maybe even love the man.

Love him! Her conscience screamed. *Love Slade Luckadeau. Never! I'm just tired. I'm not thinking straight. It's one of those damned vulnerability moments. God Almighty, love him? I'd admit I'd like to have sex with him, but I'll never admit that I love him.*

"You going to answer me or are you in total shock now that it's over?"

"I'm in shock," she admitted.

"Not quite as tough as you thought?" he asked.

"I'm tough enough to keep up with you all the way to this motel and to hoodwink that woman into getting rid of the phone, so don't be giving me any of your sass," she said.

A grin tickled the corners of his mouth but he was too damn tired to produce it for real. "Honey, I couldn't hold a light for you to go by when it comes to sass. Let's sleep and when we wake up we'll discuss the next move. I'd love to call Granny but I'm afraid to. One of those men at the ranch could be the one who's working for Ramona or John. Surely they'll tell her that we got out and there were no bodies."

"I figure they won't tell her anything. She thinks we're on some island paradise. Hopefully, they'll let her keep thinking that," Jane said. When Slade went into the bathroom she dropped the towel and slipped between the cool sheets. Tomorrow she'd find a place where she could at least purchase a change of clothing and a nightshirt.

When she awoke the room was freezing and Slade was snuggled up to her back every bit as naked as she was. One arm was thrown around her waist, the other touching her hair. She eased out of the embrace, brushed her teeth, and dressed. While he slept, she thumbed through the yellow pages and found the Greyhound bus station number. He awoke when she began asking about schedules and how to get to the station from the Super 8 motel.

"You making decisions without me?" he yawned.

"I'm making a list without you. A bus leaves at midnight—that's in two hours—for Las Vegas and points west. One goes in one hour to Denver and points north. At six o'clock in the morning, there's one heading east to Wichita Falls. What do you think?"

"I'd like to fly to get a jump on them but the only airport this place will have is a little municipal one and it wouldn't take ten minutes to find out where we went if they find we stopped here—and they will, Jane." He threw the sheet on the floor and padded barefoot and naked to the bathroom.

Her breath caught in her chest at the sight of him. "Name your poison and then feed me. I'm starving."

"You got any feelings about it?" he yelled through the closed door.

"How much money you got in that kit?" she asked.

"Enough for a week, I'm sure."

"Then let's buy a ticket to Vegas and get off in Amarillo and catch a flight out of there," she suggested, amazed that they were actually talking about a plan instead of arguing again.

He nodded. "How far is the bus station from here?"

"Four blocks, and that bus leaves in two hours."

"It's ten o'clock on a Saturday night. What's open between here and there?"

"I have no idea but we could order out pizza. I could probably eat two big ones," she grinned.

"Then what are you waiting on? I want meat lovers or supreme. Call it in and pay for it out of the shaving kit. Count the money if you want to so you'll know exactly what is in there." He used the hospitality kit and shaved, dressed, and repacked his billfold with money, all without putting on a stitch of clothing. He did have his jeans on when the pizza was delivered.

Before he could jerk his shirt over his head, Jane was on her second piece.

"This is the stuff movies are made from. I wonder if Random House will buy our story and give us a million dollar advance?" she said.

"Don't hold your breath until that happens. I would have been very satisfied with a week of boring reading."

"And instant potatoes?" she asked.

"If I had to eat those nasty things I might have torched the place myself. Scoot that box on over here."

At midnight they headed for Las Vegas with a whole busload of gamblers with money in their pockets and winning on their minds. They were loud, boisterous, and excited beyond words. In three days they'd be on their way back to Childress, broke and talking about going again the next year. Any one of the women with their big hair and loud clothing could have been Ellen. Jane missed her terribly as she listened to several conversations at once.

Jane and Slade got off the bus in Amarillo and caught a taxi to the airport, where Slade purchased two tickets to Nashville, Tennessee with a stopover in Houston, Texas.

They had two hours to waste before the flight so she bought a capri outfit in one of the airport shops and changed in the ladies' room. Slade purchased a T-shirt with an Armadillo on the front and changed in the men's room. Their old clothes went into a gift bag they carried on the flight. Dirty clothing shoved in the trash could be a clue that they'd been in the airport if anyone was looking really close.

"So what do you say, Mrs. Jance? Do we fly all the way to Nashville or get off in Houston, rent a car, and go over to Galveston for a day?"

"You been there before?"

"Yep, to a restaurant that serves pretty good gumbo right on the beachfront with a hotel right beside it. We could drive down the coast to Brownsville and turn the car back there or go to San Antonio. Be thinking about it while we are in the air."

"We can't rent a car. They have to have your driver's license," she reminded him.

"Then we'll take a taxi to the nearest car dealership and I'll buy a damn car," he said, annoyed that he hadn't thought of that.

"Good grief, Slade. How much money are you carrying in that kit?"

"I told you to count it. There was fifty thousand dollars when we left the house. You got that much to repay me when this is done?"

"With interest. The beach in Galveston sounds wonderful. But why on earth did Nellie have that kind of money in the house?"

"She grew up in the Depression. She keeps at least fifty thousand in a concealed safe just in case we hit another one."

"Sounds like a smart lady to me."

"I always thought it was dumb and just humored her until now. Guess the Depression hit in a different way."

They had gumbo and shrimp for supper and spent the night on the second floor of the hotel right next door. The next day Slade purchased a used, eight-year-old Mustang with only forty thousand miles on it. He paid with cash and the dealer put a thirty day tag on it, reminding him to change the license and put the title in his name within that time. They drove from Galveston to Brownsville and ferried over to Brazos Island for a day. From there they went to San Antonio and stayed on the river walk for a night. Then on Thursday they drove to Beaumont and spent a day swimming in the hotel pool and reading two J.A. Jance books they'd picked up at a Wal-Mart store where Jane shopped for T-shirts and shorts.

Friday found them in Shreveport, where they stayed in a Day's Inn and watched old *Law and Order* reruns on TV all evening. Saturday morning Slade drove to a nearby Wal-Mart and bought a birthday cake and roses.

Jane fought back tears when he carried them into the hotel room. Watching him leave her in Greenville, Mississippi the next evening was going to be the hardest thing she ever did.

They'd made it. She was twenty-five and the oil company was hers. Now all she had to do was learn to live without Slade.

"Please stay until Monday morning. I'm still scared out of my wits until I sign the papers tomorrow morning before the board meeting," she begged Slade on the way to the ranch on Sunday afternoon.

He nodded. Leaving was going to be difficult no matter when. Today. Tomorrow. It didn't really matter.

"Besides, I'd like you to see where I live."

"Maybe I'll buy a horse from you with what's left of our Depression money."

"Honey, you pick out whichever one you want and it will be delivered to the Double L on Tuesday morning."

Chapter 15

ON MONDAY MORNING JANE DRESSED CAREFULLY IN A black power suit with a short skirt and hip-length jacket over an ivory silk blouse. She wore her grandmother's pearl earrings and bracelet and her mother's pearl and diamond ring. Her lawyer and Slade had stayed at the ranch the night before.

Slade left at the break of dawn, taking her heart with him. She hadn't known what to say or do when he threw his new duffle bag into the Mustang. "Call me when you get home," she'd said.

"I will. You could call Nellie and tell her I'm on the road."

"I'll do it—and Slade..." she'd stopped because the words wouldn't come out past the lump in her throat.

He took two steps forward and hugged her fiercely. "You don't have to say a word. Just remember that phone line works both ways. You call me when you have time to catch your breath. You're going to have a lot of decisions to make. Good luck today." And then he was gone. She watched the tail end of the silver Mustang until it turned at the end of the lane and was gone. Then she went to her room and got the crying jag over with all alone.

James, the lawyer, would go to the board meeting with her, taking a whole briefcase full of papers. He'd managed to get done in two weeks exactly what she wanted, which was just short of a miracle.

She was ready two hours before time to go, so she paced the floor, talking herself out of going to the board meeting and going after Slade. The doorbell rang and she took off downstairs without putting on her spike heels, hoping that Slade had turned around and come back for her.

Agent August waited on the other side of the door, a serious look on his wide face. "Ellacyn Hayes, I need to talk to you."

"There's nothing to say. I'm twenty-five. It's over and my life can get back to normal. I'm mad as hell at you for that phony safe house, but I'll get over it."

"I owe you an explanation. May I come inside?" he asked.

She stood aside and let him enter her home but didn't offer him a chair. The foyer was wide with doorways showing a sitting room, a dining room, a formal living room, and a winding staircase wide enough for six people to walk down together side by side. Shiny hardwood floors, crystal chandeliers, and the aroma of fresh flowers in sparkling vases all attested to the fact that the man who'd put the contract out on Ellacyn had indeed had his eyes on her physical worth. Too bad he hadn't seen the strength the little lady had beforehand or he'd have known she was a fighter.

Agent August was intrigued by the house but his business wasn't a tour of an old plantation home. "You have a lovely home."

"Thank you but I don't think you came all the way to Mississippi to take a look at the house," she said.

"You are right. I came to tell you that Agent Jones and John were distant relatives and both served on the same special ops team in Iraq. He was Ramona and John's inside man. He and John are both dead.

Jane gasped. One was a son-of-a-bitch, the other his accomplice, but still death was so final. Besides she'd pictured them both in prison for the rest of their lives, not dead.

Agent August went on. "It's probably best because he authorized government equipment to set up the safe house bombing. If he wasn't dead, he'd be on the run or spending the rest of his life in prison. Ramona used her lawyer to send out a message to an accomplice who took care of John and Agent Jones the day after the bombing. If you would have called in, we could have saved you a lot of running and hiding. John is dead so he can't talk, and Agent Jones is also dead so there's no one to talk there, either. She won't hang for the crimes against you because there are only dead ends, but we've got her for previous crimes."

"The lawyer?" Jane asked. It was hard to wrap her mind around the fact that John was really dead and that the nightmare was over.

"His only crime was being an idiot. She slipped the note into his pocket and someone slipped it out. The only way we discovered it was when we watched the surveillance tape from her cell for the hundredth time. She sneezed. He offered her his handkerchief. She put a small piece of paper in it when she handed it back. He stopped at a convenience store on the way home and got his pocket picked. Handkerchief, wallet, and comb all in one swift motion. He reported it to the police. Found it all crammed down into a trash can not a block from the store. Money gone. Everything else intact," the agent said.

"How'd she get paper and pencil or pen?"

"She is very good. It had to be from the lawyer but neither he nor we can figure out how. She's still up for previous crimes and they'll put her away for a long, long time. But I thought you deserved to know what happened out there and that John is dead."

"Thank you," she murmured. She had loved the man enough to give him her heart and soul and all she felt was immense relief. A rock had been lifted from her heart and she was free at last but somewhere down deep lurked a guilty feeling at the news of his death.

"I'll be going now. Hopefully, I'll never have contact with you again."

"That would be a good thing. Good-bye." She showed him to the door and watched as he drove away.

She met her lawyer, James, coming down the stairway as she started back to her bedroom located on the ground floor of the huge house.

"You are ready early," he said.

"No, I'm not ready at all, but I will be shortly. Have you had breakfast?"

"Yes, ma'am. You have a wonderful cook. I tried to steal her away from you. I've been out to see the horses and talked to Lanson. You want to sell this place?"

"You want to buy it?"

A wide grin split James' face. "Always wanted a horse ranch but thought I'd settle in Texas. Got any good-lookin' women around these parts?"

"Few," she answered.

"Let's take care of the oil company and when that's done have a serious talk about your ranch."

She couldn't believe what she was hearing. "You serious?"

"Could be if the price was right. Besides you owe me enough for the down payment already."

"I'll think about it," she said.

Her mind raced as she took off the expensive suit, threw it on the bed, and pulled on a pair of faded jeans and a T-shirt from San Antonio with a dolphin on the front. She kicked her panty hose and high-heeled shoes into a corner and picked up the cowboy boots she'd worn the night before when she showed Slade the horses. She wished she would have slipped into his room and spent the night making love to him until dawn.

The cheval mirror at the foot of her bed was a reflection of Jane, not Ellacyn. Jane had survived the six-week experience, and Jane would walk into the boardroom and deliver her news. *Burn the house down,* like Bob Lee said in the movie she'd watched with Slade. Paul had put out a contract on Ellacyn; Jane would bring the consequences.

James didn't even raise an eyebrow when she declared she was ready to go to the board meeting. She looked a lot more confident in her jeans and boots than she had all nervous in that black power suit, anyway. That stepfather of hers would run and hide if he knew what kind of woman was on her way to the office.

The conference room at the Ranger Oil Building was long and narrow with raised panel oak siding stained a rich cherry and enough glass on the east side to make the department heads around the table feel as though they were sitting outside beside the river. The glass-topped oak table had twelve padded chairs around it, eleven filled and one empty chair waiting on Ellacyn to fill it.

When Jane slung open the double doors, Paul had just stood up at the head of the table and begun to talk. He stopped mid-sentence and turned an ashy gray when he saw Ellacyn with several serious-faced men and women behind her, taking up places around the room like sentinels in a castle. Paul had always been handsome beyond words with his premature gray hair, angular face, and clear blue eyes. Everything about him said, "Trust me. I would never take advantage of you or hurt you in any way."

He opened up his arms and smiled brightly, "Ellacyn, darlin', you've come home. I've been so worried. What are you doing here, though? You need to be resting. I'll call Dr. Harrison to come take a look at you. You have dark circles under your eyes and my God, Ellacyn, you've never come to the office looking like that."

"Paul, this is my company now. I intend to fire your sorry ass, but I've got a few things to say first."

"I'm sure you are under duress still. Take a few days. Are you sure you don't need professional help? Are you mentally stable, Ellacyn? You're acting crazy and you never come into the office looking like that," he repeated himself, groping nervously for something solid to convince everyone that she was insane. "I'm thinking maybe I should send you to a psychiatric hospital for evaluation."

"I said sit down and I don't mean in my chair," she said.

With a wave of the hand meant to tell eleven other people that he was merely appeasing his stepdaughter, he took the empty chair midway down the table. "Oh, by the way, happy birthday, Ellacyn. I'd planned a company party, but you were gone. Maybe later you can tell me what happened between you and that nice man you were supposed to marry. He was devastated."

Any other time Paul would have intimidated her. Everyone else around the table looked confused. Eight women in black suits with their makeup and nails done to perfection; three men in various shades of custommade suits and power ties.

"That nice man I was supposed to marry is dead. You hired him and his girlfriend to kill me before my twenty-fifth birthday, but he's dead and she's in prison," she said.

"Hey, that's a pretty heavy accusation. Can you back it up with facts?"

"Yes, I can. You put out a hit on me. Ramona gave the job to John, who took out a million dollar life insurance policy on me so he could get paid double. He's dead so he's not talking. Ramona is in custody and she's not saying a word about the assassination attempts. Yes, there were many this past six weeks. I overheard John and Ramona talking about it the night before the wedding and believe me, your name was brought up."

"I didn't…" Paul started.

Everyone else was deadly silent.

She shook her head. "No excuses necessary. While I was running away from bullets and bombs I hired a lawyer and gave him access to everything in the company. Even though I couldn't legally have it all until I was twenty-five, I still had a password and enough clout to look at everything. It's amazing what I *can* prove, isn't it Paul? And I am filing charges against you for embezzlement. I'd love to file on you for murder because I'm sure you had my father killed as well as my mother, but I can't prove it at this late date. This morning I signed the papers and this oil company is now a part of Tex-Okie oil out of Houston, Texas. Please meet the new staff. Heads will roll. Heads will stay. It's up to them, not me."

"Ellacyn, this is your legacy. Your great-grandfather founded Ranger Oil in the boom days. You can't just sell it. I don't know what you think you've found, but…" Paul started again.

She held up her hand. "I'm twenty-five as of Saturday. I can do anything I damn well please without anyone's signature. This oil company and the ranch are both mine, Paul. Or at least the oil company was until this morning, when I signed all the papers selling what's left of it to Tex-Okie. And I don't *think* anything. I know everything. Phone records show multiple calls between you and Ramona. An audit shows that you've been using company funds for your personal high-dollar lifestyle, including paying out half a mil for the first half of the money to have me killed."

"You can't do this. I've given this company thirteen years. You owe me."

James stepped up and opened the briefcase. "What I have here is proof that she owes you nothing. It's also proof that you have just about run this company into the dirt. Tex-Okie is buying a flailing whale, and you're the one who killed it."

Paul took a deep breath and started across the room. He wouldn't stop at his office or make a detour through the penthouse, but would go straight to the private parking lot, get into a low-slung, sleek black Porsche, and drive toward Jackson to implement his backup plan. A con man always had an exit, and he was a professional. The nest egg in his foreign account was at the lowest it had been in years but it would get him by until he could find another scam to work. Damn it all, he thought he had this one in his back pocket. What had gone wrong? He'd have to think about it and not make the same mistake twice. One thing about Steven Ferrell, he learned from his mistakes, and with all his identities he would never get caught. That young man who pulled his first con in northern Arkansas had learned a lot in the past forty years.

But even the best laid backup plans can go to hell in a handbasket. When he opened the door it was in the face of two uniformed officers with handcuffs. They read him his rights and escorted him out to a black-and-white police car instead of a nice, shiny black Porsche. Paul was on his way to prison, not some exotic hideaway where he could conjure up another scam.

After Jane formally turned the business over to the new buyers, she and James left the building. She didn't even look back.

"It's amazing what shows up when you start turning over rocks, isn't it?" Jane said on their way to the elevators. "Who'd have thought that his name wasn't even Paul Stokes? It was a stroke of luck that you thought about running his fingerprints through the system. I'll be ordering a new tombstone for my mother's grave that has her real name on it. Stokes indeed! Wonder where he came up with that name? It's not even close to Steven Ferrell."

"Who knows where a person gets a fake name? I understand you used Jane Day when you ran away," James reminded her.

"Yes, I did. Jane is my middle name and probably what I'll go by the rest of my life. I like the Jane I've become better than the Ellacyn I was. Day is what happens when you almost say Hayes and stutter."

James grinned. "I imagine you feel like you've been duped your whole life."

They both got into the steaming hot truck and buckled up.

"Not really. Momma and Daddy were both very honest. And my grandmother was a jewel. No, I can't say I've been duped my whole life... just the past few years and especially the past six weeks. Even then, there was a good honest man beside me."

"Slade is a good man. Now you want to talk about selling your ranch or not?"

"Let's talk about it over dinner," she said. "I'm buying. What do you want?"

"I've got a four o'clock flight out of Jackson. I won't be here for dinner."

"Dinner on the ranch is at noon. Supper is in the evening. And I've had enough selling for one day. But I'll either buy you dinner or have my cook fix whatever you want. As far as the ranch, give me a few weeks to get my bearings. If you are really interested after you have time to think about it, and I'm still in the mood to sell when I've had time, we'll negotiate. When we do, you'd best have a banker with a lot of money."

"Why? I was thinking of paying cash."

❖ ❖ ❖

Slade had been home a week and still hadn't put the Mustang up for sale. He parked it beside the hay barn where he and Jane had worked together those weeks that seemed like a hundred years before. Every evening he sat on the hood and watched the sun go down.

Sometimes he smiled.

Sometimes he frowned.

Always he missed Jane.

He'd picked up the phone a dozen times to call her, but every time he flipped it shut before he dialed the complete number. She had things to take care of, decisions to make concerning her properties. If she wanted to talk to him, she'd call. After a week, he gave up hope.

"You drivin' us to the Silver Saddle tonight?" Nellie asked Slade at the dinner table.

It had been another hot August day, sun beating down, no clouds in sight, work to be done from daylight to dark. The hands drank more tea and lemonade than they ate food.

"It's so hot I saw a lizard totin' a canteen on one shoulder and a machine gun on the other," Marty had said.

Everyone had laughed except Slade, who had a flashback of machine gun fire at the safe house. Agent August had come by the ranch a few days before and told him how things had gone down.

"So, are you taking us or not? We've got to have time to pretty up." Ellen poked Slade, bringing him back to the present.

"Guess so."

"Why in the hell don't you just call that woman? You can't tell us you weren't thinking about her," Marty said.

"Don't have any idea who you are talkin' about," Slade growled.

"Yes, you do. Call her and sell me that Mustang. I've drooled over it a whole week. I've got money saved for a down payment and I'll work for the rest or go to the bank. Dad says he'll co-sign for me," Vincent said.

"Why don't the whole bunch of you leave me alone?" Slade said as he carried his plate to the trash can and went back to work.

"Think he'll get over her?" Marty asked.

"I hope not," Ellen said. "I hope it eats at him until one morning we wake up and that Mustang is gone to Mississippi."

"Well, if it is, I hope it comes back and he sells it to me. That is one sweet little car," Vince said.

"Boy, you need a pickup, not a *sweet little car*," one of the other hired hands said. "In my day if we'd talked like that someone would have brought out some starch for our wrist."

"What? Oh! You are crazy. I'm a ladies man. That's why I want the car. Just think how many chicks I can pick up in that ride. Every kid in this area has a truck. I'd be special with that car," Vince said.

"Dream on," Ellen said. "Until he gets over Jane that car won't budge."

"Where does she live? I'll go bring her back here myself if it'll help old Slade stop that mooning around every night. Sometimes I expect him to start howling at the moon, the way he just sits there," Vince said.

"Come on, kid. Let's go back to work. Cars or trucks don't have a thing to do with how them cows are going to get from one pasture to the other before dark," Marty said.

Nellie wore a flowing broomstick skirt in a red bandana print with a matching red T-shirt and red kid leather sandals. Her gray hair was freshly washed and curled around her face. Ellen was dressed in her trademark "loud, cheap, and sassy," as she called it with her hair done up in a red puff with lots of hairspray.

Slade took a fast shower and put on a pair of soft jeans, the T-shirt with a dolphin on the front that he'd gotten in San Antonio, and his old worn boots. He combed his wet hair with his fingertips and didn't even bother with cologne. He settled into a recliner in the living room and read a J.A. Jance book entitled *Failure to Appear* while he waited on the ladies to make their appearance.

"Is our chauffeur ready?" Ellen asked as she swirled into the living room in a gauze skirt of bright orange with yellow lilies.

"He is."

"And what is he going to do while we are dancing the leather off our shoes?" Nellie asked.

"He's going to read in the truck. It's a fairly pleasant evening and I've got this new contraption Jane picked up in Galveston. It's a booklight. You just snap it on the top of the book and it sheds enough light to read by. So you ladies can flirt to your hearts content, and I'll get old Jonas Beaumont out of this predicament."

"Sounds like a real excitin' evenin' to me," Ellen groaned.

"Why don't you just call her?" Nellie asked.

"She knows my number and where I live. She's got a lot on her mind to work out. It could be that we were just drawn together because we damned near got killed so many times. We sure didn't like each other before that, so who's to say we would afterwards? Time will tell," he said.

"Sure, for you. But we're two old women who might not have so much of that precious commodity called time. Humor us and call her," Nellie said.

"Tell you what. If in six months she hasn't called me, I'll humor you and call her. That's my final word on it. Now are we going to go to the Silver Saddle, or stand here fussing about Jane?"

He drove them to the dance hall and watched as they went inside. He was the adult and his grandmother and aunt were the youngsters. The roles had reversed and he felt old. They'd dance, have a few drinks, and talk about the fun they'd had for days. He'd sit in the truck and wait to drive them back home like a dutiful father figure.

Opening his book, he found the right page, clipped the light to the cover, turned the switch, and presto, enough light to read by. It was an ingenious invention that Jane assured him was not anything new but had been on the market for years.

He sighed and tried to read but his mind wandered. He really should sell the Mustang to Vince. The boy wanted it and it was crazy to just let it sit out there under the stars. But every time he looked at it he remembered all the good times they'd had that week living on the edge, running from an assassin. Who would have thought Slade Luckadeau would be a knight shining Mustang? Maybe in six months he'd be ready to get rid of it.

He made himself look at the words and read. He liked the J.P. Beaumont better than the Joanna Brady series and had picked up every one he could find as he traveled home the previous week from Mississippi. He wondered if Jane was reading a Jance mystery that evening.

It took a few minutes of severe concentration but soon he was in the middle of the book following every move Jonas made. An hour later the words began to blur and his head drooped down on his chest. The little light burned on but Slade was dreaming of a burning house out in the corner of Oklahoma and Texas. Jane had kept up with him, her hand in his, and she'd even stepped up and helped get rid of that cell phone. They made a good team when they were scared out of their wits and on the run. When it came to plain, routine, everyday living, the story might be altogether different. In his dream he replayed the whole night up to the time he crawled into bed with her in that motel in Childress.

They were both too tired for anything to happen after they went to bed but his dream played in a different way. He could feel Jane's body plastered next to his, could smell the beer on her breath and her hands slipping up under his T-shirt to touch the hair on his chest. His eyes fluttered. God, he didn't want to wake up. Dreams were at least better than the nothing he'd have if he opened his eyes.

"Oh, darlin', I've missed you. I'm so sorry I was so mean," Jane said.

"I missed you, too," he whispered.

Her lips brushed across his but something didn't seem right. When Jane kissed him every nerve in his body wanted more. These kisses left him feeling like he should clean his mouth with alcohol. He opened his eyes wide but at such close quarters all he could see was double images of mascara-coated eyelashes. Her hands began to fiddle with his belt buckle. He reached up and pushed back on her shoulders and not six inches away, her back plastered against the steering wheel, was Kristy.

"Good. Now you're fully awake, we can get more comfortable. Let me get this bra off," she said.

"Don't bother," he said through clenched teeth.

"Did I upset the baby waking him up? Well, I'll make it up to you, darlin'." She kept tugging at the back of her shirt trying to pull it free from skin-tight jeans.

He opened the door and practically fell out, his book and light landing on the ground beside the truck. "I said, 'don't bother.'"

"What's the matter with you? That woman left you high and dry. Don't you realize she's too good for the likes of a plain old farmer? But I'm not, Slade. I promise I won't be ugly anymore. Come on back in the truck, honey. Let me show you how much I love you."

"Go home, Kristy. I don't love you."

"But darlin' I love you enough for both of us. Let me prove it. We just never did get to bed. Once we do, you'll see how good I can be," she giggled.

"You're drunk."

"But not so much I don't know how to please a man."

"Go home. I'm not interested."

"Well, don't ever say you didn't get one last chance. Stay on out there on the Double L and pine away for some rich bitch you can't have. See if I care." She stumbled out of the truck, stepping on the little light he'd dropped, and weaved across the parking lot to her uncle's Cadillac.

He picked up the booklight and held it in his hands as if it were a sparrow with a broken wing. In that moment he knew it was over, just like Kristy said, but it would take him months, possibly years, to get over the ache in his heart.

Jane exercised several horses that day and had a sore butt to prove it. She sank down into a deep tub full of bubbles and sighed, thinking about the day that she'd ridden with Slade all day on the Double L. She remembered verbatim the conversation they'd had and how he'd tried to trick her into giving out background information.

She shut her eyes and envisioned him riding beside her, meeting every barb she threw out with one of his own. A smile tickled the corners of her mouth when she remembered rocking Kristy's jaw. She wondered if that witch had been sniffing around the ranch since Slade had gone back home.

The phone rang and she reached across the edge of the tub to the bright red wall phone and picked it up. "Hello?" She almost crossed her fingers hoping it was Slade or at least Nellie.

"Ellacyn, this is Celia. Am I forgiven yet?"

"No, I don't think so."

"Hey, he talked you into marrying him, and you're the most stable person on the earth. If he could do that, think how he could snow me? Remember, I'm the true blonde. And besides, I didn't sic him on you intentionally. I just wasn't too smart when it came to keeping my mouth shut when you called, and I am sorry."

"Right-out-of-a-bottle blonde, you mean. The only way it's true is if the color on the box says *True Blonde*. You are forgiven but it'll take me longer than saying three words to forget that you didn't shut up when I told you to."

"Thank you," Celia said. "Now that you aren't mad at me, could we do lunch? Or better yet, my new boyfriend has a friend who'd love to meet you. He's interested in horses and we could do a double on Friday. How does that sound?"

Jane's hands went clammy and her stomach tied up in knots. She'd never trust a man again, not as long as she lived. If someone could sweet talk her into almost getting herself killed one time, it could damn sure happen again. The only man she'd ever put her trust in was Slade.

"No thank you," Jane said.

"Okay, as your newly forgiven friend, I'm going to put on my preaching robes. Ellacyn, you've got to get off that ranch. Sure, it was a sad thing that happened, but you aren't listed among the dead. You are still alive and it's time you stopped acting like the world has come to an end. You've been holed up there a whole week and not even been out to lunch with me and I'm your best friend. So I won't take no for an answer. If you are home on Friday night—that's two days away—you will be going out with me and my boyfriend. We'll pick you up at eight. Be ready and no excuses. Amen. Now you deliver the benediction," Celia said and hung up before Jane could tell her not only no, but hell no.

"If I'm home on Friday. That's what you said and so this is the real benediction, darlin'. I won't be home. Final Amen!" Jane shouted into the silent cell phone.

That word "home" is what set her to thinking. When she heard the word "home," a vision of the Double L came to mind: dinner on the deck with the hired hands gee-hawing over what they'd done or were going to do, how hot it was, how hungry they'd gotten; Nellie and Ellen arguing over the Silver Saddle dances; Slade, always Slade, exchanging barbs with her. That was home. The ranch was a place to live. The oil company a place to work. But home, like the old cliché said, was where the heart was.

She rose up out of the bathtub with such speed that the water sluiced off in great waves. "Damn that Kristy hussy. If she's been out to the Double L causing trouble she'll just think I've rocked her jaw in the past. She'd best be keeping her sorry ass on her side of the property line." She wrapped a towel around her midsection and headed for the bedroom.

She dug around in her purse for a business card. Holding the towel up by pinching it against her side under her arm, she punched in the numbers on the house phone.

"Hello," James' voice said. "Is this Ellacyn Hayes?"

"You've got caller ID—but no, this is Jane Day and I'm calling to see if you've got your money counted. I'm ready to negotiate."

Chapter 16

SLADE KEPT TIME WITH THE RADIO BY TAPPING HIS FINGERS on the steering wheel of the old work truck as he drove west toward Ringgold. Marty couldn't plow the south hundred acres with a broken-down tractor, so he'd driven to Nocona for tractor parts. When he reached the ranch, he bypassed the house and drove down to the field where Marty had taken off the broken pieces and sat in the shade of the tractor wheel.

"Well, you look like you are in a better mood. Maybe we should send you for parts more often." Marty's brown eyes twinkled, lighting up his weathered face.

"It won't last long," Slade said.

Marty picked up the tractor part and searched in his toolbox for a screwdriver. "Women can be a good thing. Don't know what I'd do without Gloria; she's been my right arm for thirty years. But there's days when a woman will drive you crazy—like when she's arguin' about every little thing. Them days I could shoot her between the eyes and feed her to the coyotes. Then I get to thinkin' and feel guilty as hell for feelin' like that about the woman who's put up with my sorry ass for all these years."

Sorry ass? That's what Jane had called Slade more than once. He'd just about sell his share in the Double L to a homeless soul for a dollar bill to see her pop her hands on her hips and call him that again. He'd consider giving the homeless fool fifty dollars to take it off his hands for a night like they'd shared after they'd had too many beers with whiskey chasers.

"You got that look in your eye, son. You was thinkin' about her. It's been three weeks. Don't you think it's time you called her?"

"She'll call me if she wants to talk," Slade said.

"Good girls don't call boys. They wait for the boys to call them. Nellie has told you that often enough that it should have soaked in. Hold this right here and don't let it slip. We'll be 'til dinnertime gettin' this thing fixed."

Slade held but he didn't comment.

The sun was straight overhead, the August heat bearing down on them like an anvil by noon. They were dirty, greasy, and hungry, but the tractor was fixed and ready to plow all afternoon.

"I'm glad for air-conditioned cabs, let me tell you," Marty said on the way in for dinner. "Why don't me and you invent a tractor with an automatic button that knows when to make the corners and keep a straight line? Then we could take a nap during the afternoons."

"That'll probably happen but I hope not in my lifetime. I like ranchin' too well to give it all up to robots," Slade said.

"Me, too, son. But today I wouldn't mind havin' a robot tractor. I feel my age."

They parked at the back edge of the yard and washed up at the pump. The cold water felt good on Slade's arms and face. A soft summer breeze had kicked up by the time he'd dried off and headed for the dinner table. He stacked sandwiches on his plate and filled a bowl with chicken and dumplings. Two pans of brownies waited at the end of the table along with a big bowl of frozen peaches.

"Will you sell me that Mustang now?" Vincent grinned from across the table.

"Why would today be any different than yesterday or last week?" Slade asked.

"More tea?" Jane asked from the back door.

Slade's sandwich stopped midair. "What in the *hell* are you doing here?"

"Working," she said. Her pulse raced. Her breath came in short spasms. It wasn't the reception she'd hoped for but it was one hundred percent bona fide Slade Luckadeau and that's the man she was in love with—not one who'd rush to her side, take her in his arms, and all but swoon. But one who couldn't get his sandwich to his mouth even though smart-ass remarks could come out of it.

"Showed up on my doorstep this morning with a duffel bag and said she needed a job. She's proven she's damn good help, so I hired her. You got a problem with that?" Nellie asked.

"Wouldn't do me a bit of good if I did, would it?" Slade asked.

Ellen cut the brownies into generous squares. "You got that right."

"More tea?" Jane asked again.

"Love some, but you aren't working here, Ellacyn Hayes."

"Ellacyn Hayes isn't but Jane Hayes is. You didn't hire me, cowboy, so you can't fire me. Move your old dirty arm over so I can set this tea pitcher down."

God, she felt good. Celia had been right two weeks before when she'd said Jane wasn't alive. Well, she was right then and by damn she didn't intend to quit living ever again.

"The Mustang?" Vince pressured.

"You can have the damn thing. It's yours. It needs a title and tag. You buy them and you can consider it your bonus for the summer's work," Slade said.

Vince shouted so loud it scared the birds from the pecan tree and two squirrels set up a chattering to let everyone know the noise had interrupted their afternoon nap. "Can I drive it tonight? I got a hot date with my girlfriend. I been telling her about that car for three whole weeks."

"I don't care what you do with it. Keys are in the ashtray. It's yours," Slade said.

Nellie and Ellen exchanged a look.

Jane bit back a grin.

"What are you doing this afternoon?" Jane asked.

"Plowing and I don't need any help," he said.

His heart hadn't stopped thumping since he looked up and saw her in the doorway wearing that dolphin T-shirt and faded jeans. Her hair was in a ponytail and she wore only a faint hint of eye makeup. Scuffed up brown work boots had replaced the Nikes. She'd never looked so damned beautiful and his mouth was so dry he didn't dare try to eat the sandwich. He wouldn't be able to swallow a damn bite of it.

"I hadn't planned on helping you but if you are plowing that acreage back in the southwest corner, don't bother. Nellie sold me five acres back there. I don't want it plowed or planted."

Slade's mouth dropped. "You did what?"

"She offered me a deal I can't refuse," Nellie said.

"I cannot believe you broke up our land to sell a stranger five acres," he said.

"Believe it. I did and she don't want the five-acre corner plowed, so leave it alone," Nellie said. "Besides, Jane's not a stranger."

Slade pushed back from the table, grabbed his hat from the back of his chair, slapped his leg with it five times and stomped out to his truck. Of all the scenarios he'd envisioned those nights he'd spent sitting on the hood of that blasted Mustang, he'd never even thought of anything like the one that had just played out.

He'd been right in the beginning. They couldn't abide each other in normal surroundings. It was only during the adrenaline rush of danger that they got along. Hell, even a spider and a rattlesnake could be friends in a situation like that. And now Nellie had sold the woman five acres. She'd be a thorn in his side forever. Hells bells, she was already telling him not to plow her five acres. He should have let John shoot her back down there in Baton Rouge.

After the meal was finished and the men gone back to work, Jane helped carry in the leftovers and dishes that needed washing. She ran a sink full of water and set about cleaning cutlery and glasses while Nellie and Ellen put away leftovers.

"Well, that went well," Jane said.

"Wasn't what I wanted," Ellen said.

"Nor me," Nellie shook her head. "He's so damn bullheaded. Just like his mother. His father wasn't like that."

"Give it time. It was a shock and I meant for it to be. I'm not in a hurry. I've got a job and five acres. It'll take a while to get the septic tank people out here and the electric company to put up a pole for me. By the time my new double-wide is delivered, I bet he's singing a different tune."

"Girl, you got more faith in that grandson of mine than I do," Nellie said. "His mother's genes are surfacing. She never could see the best thing right in front of her nose."

"He'd come unglued if he heard you say that," Jane said.

"Unhinged is more like it," Ellen said. "Lord, I'm glad you're back. Things were getting so dull around here, I was thinking about going back to Wichita Falls forever. Now I'm thinkin' maybe I'll talk Nellie out of the five acres on the other side of this place and put me in a double-wide. Things are poppin' again. I don't care if he don't never come to his senses, this is so damn much fun—I love it."

"Maybe I shouldn't have surprised him like that," Jane said.

"No, siree, that was just the ticket. Let's go shopping for something to wear to church tomorrow morning," Ellen said. "We haven't had a driver to take us anywhere since you left."

"Oh, come on, don't give me that line. You two have been to the Silver Saddle every week."

"Yes, but Slade hasn't got time to take us to the outlet mall and I'm naked for clothes," Ellen said.

Nellie rolled her eyes. "Your closet here is packed and you've got three closets in Wichita that wouldn't hold another hanger."

"I'll give them all away if you'll take us shopping. We could stop in that defunct food court and have one of them giant cinnamon buns. I'll even pay for it," Ellen begged.

"I'm working for Nellie," Jane said.

"Then I guess we'll go shopping," Nellie said. "I'll never hear the end of her whining if we don't. Want to shop for things for your new home?"

"Not now. One step at a time," she said. She felt like singing just to be back home. She was in no hurry to make big decisions such as what color towels to put in the bathroom.

At Burke's Outlet, Ellen bought two new outfits and Nellie goaded her into giving away two old ones when she got back home. "Nothing else comes in the house unless something goes out."

"That mean we have to throw Slade out to keep Jane? I vote we toss him out in the heat on his ear, the way he acted today. He could have at least been cordial instead of so damn stubborn," Ellen said.

"No, we're keeping both of them," Nellie said. "I'm already making plans for a swing set for the backyard."

Jane blushed.

"Isn't that why you came back? Why is your face red?" Ellen asked.

"I simply came home. I admit I love that rough-edged man, but if he doesn't love me then I'm still home."

"What are you going to do if he decides to stay a cantankerous old bachelor?" Ellen asked.

"Then I'm still home."

"What if he marries someone else?"

"Still home. Brokenhearted, but at home. I found my place and I'm not leaving. If it makes him uncomfortable, he can stay out of my way," she said.

"A woman with a mind of her own. I like it," Nellie said. "What do you think of this little dress for church tomorrow?"

"Good Lord, Nellie, we're old women. We can't wear sleeveless. We have bat wings." Ellen held up her arm and pointed at the flapping flesh.

"Well, I'll be hung from the nearest pecan tree with a rusty length of bailing wire. You just admitted that your body doesn't look like a teenager's," Nellie laughed.

"I most certainly did not. I just said we had flabby old bat wings and sleeveless dresses weren't our style," Ellen backtracked.

"How about this one for me?" Jane held up a sleeveless sheath the same color as her golden brown eyes. It had wooden buttons down the front and slits up to the thigh on both sides.

"Very nice and it's got a dot on the tag. Let's see it," Ellen said. "Yep, forty percent off the price."

Jane draped it over the cart. "Good buy. I think I should have it for church tomorrow."

"What all did you leave out there in Mississippi? Bet you left some dresses you could be wearing to church," Ellen eyed her carefully.

"No, my closets were cleaned out. What had been in them is now in the church closet for the needy. Wasn't anything there I wanted except my five horses, which will be arriving in a week. James tried to talk me out of them, too, but I couldn't part with them. Besides, Slade liked those five when he looked through the stables."

"What about keepsakes? Things your grandmother or mother had that were precious?" Nellie pried.

"They'll be coming along with the horses. Few boxes of things I didn't want to part with. Other than that, James bought it—lock, stock, and barrel."

"You had it all, girl."

"No, I had material things. Now I've got it all," Jane said.

Almost all. If I can talk that stubborn-headed mule of a man into believing I love him, then I'll have it all and never look back.

Chapter 17

THEY SAT SIDE BY SIDE IN THE CHURCH PEW, BOOKENDED with Nellie beside Slade and Ellen beside Jane. They sang a hymn, the choir sang something special, the preacher talked about the duties of a Christian soul in the community. The whole while all Jane could think about was how she'd like to drag Slade down to the Sunday school rooms and do things that would make the angels blush.

Stubborn mule of a man that he was, he hadn't spoken to her all morning beyond a cursory good morning. He hadn't even had a sharp barb to sling her way when she deliberately put sugar and pepper on her buttered biscuit.

Slade's mouth went dry when he sat down to the breakfast table that morning. Just to have her sitting there, even eating that ridiculous combination on her biscuit, was wonderful. But it stuck in his craw that she'd snuck into his life without one word of discussion.

He listened to the preaching with one ear and endured a severe lecture from his conscience with the other. The preacher talked about setting a Christian example. His conscience talked about the sorry bastard he'd been to Jane ever since she walked back into his life.

Nothing had been put to rest by the time the last amen was said. He told Nellie he'd meet them at the truck when they got through with their gossiping.

She shot him a dirty look. Ellen grinned and Jane ignored him.

"Where you going to feed us?" Jane asked when they got into the truck with him.

He just shot her a mean look.

"Feed me and then take me home. I'm reading a book all afternoon or until I fall asleep, whichever one comes first, and then the ladies are coming for a card game at five o'clock," Nellie said.

Slade raised an eyebrow. "Poker on Sunday?"

"We didn't have it on Friday, so God will have to avert His eyes," Ellen said.

"Where do you want to eat? Dairy Queen or Sonic?" he asked.

"Neither. Take us over to the Cracker Barrel in Gainesville. I didn't buy a new outfit to eat at the Dairy Queen in Nocona. I want something a little nicer. Besides, I've got a hankering for turkey and dressing," Ellen said.

He nodded and turned east at the red light.

"You still mad at me?" Jane asked right out of the blue.

How was he supposed to answer a question like that with his grandmother and aunt in the backseat?

"Never was mad at you," he said.

"Well, you got a strange way of showing you're not mad."

"You got to care to be mad. I don't give a damn what you and Granny cook up. You won't be here that long anyway. You don't put any value on things your ancestors worked their asses off to leave you. You'll get tired of us country people and move on. Lord knows you've got enough money to do whatever you want," he said.

"How do you know what I did with the money? Maybe I gave it all to charity," she said.

"She gave me seventy thousand," Nellie said. "I put it in the safe against the day when the government runs us into another damned Depression. I'm not losing my land just because a bunch of politicians get in a pissing contest."

"You did what?" Slade said.

Jane looked across the seat at him. "I paid my debt. I believe you said you had fifty thousand dollars in the shaving kit when we left. I added interest plus your time to that and came up with seventy. I don't owe you jack shit, Slade Luckadeau."

Nellie tapped him on the shoulder from the backseat. "And she gave me a hundred thousand for that five acres. I told you she made me an offer I couldn't refuse. Land sellin' for two thousand an acre at the top and she offers me ten times that. I'm buyin' a new John Deere next year."

"What'd you do with the rest of it?" Slade glanced at Jane.

"That, darlin', is my business. If I burned it in the fireplace before I left Mississippi or gave every last nickel to the college for scholarships or if I had it rolled into toilet paper and intend to wipe my ass on it for the next twenty years, it's my doings. And you just said you don't care enough to be mad, so there." She folded her arms across her chest and stared out the side window.

"I guess the show is over. I thought it would last at least until we got to the Cracker Barrel," Ellen said.

"Guess so. Y'all got any more fight left in you? If not, me and Ellen got things to talk about. If you do, we'll put ours on hold so we can watch the fun," Nellie said.

"We're not two-year-olds," Slade snapped.

"You're acting like it," she said.

Slade set his jaw.

Jane didn't even blink.

Ellen and Nellie went to work on every bit of gossip they'd gleaned in the after-church fellowship with their acquaintances. They'd covered everything twice or three times by the time Slade parked at the Cracker Barrel north of Gainesville, in the same parking lot as the outlet mall. Neither of them acknowledged the tense silence in the front seat.

The hostess had a table for four and seated them immediately. Everyone ordered sweet tea when the waitress arrived. Jane studied the menu while Ellen and Nellie decided which vegetables they'd order so they could share.

The waitress brought the tea and a platter of biscuits and cornbread along with a dish of assorted jams and butter. "You need a few more minutes?" she asked.

"No ma'am, we are ready and we are hungry," Nellie said.

Ellen decided on turkey and dressing, fried okra, and hash brown casserole.

Nellie opted for turkey and dressing, carrots, and greens.

"And you?" The waitress turned to Jane.

"I'll have the ham steak, pinto beans, and fried okra. Then I'll have the chicken and dumplings with steak fries and corn. And get an apple dumpling in the oven for when I get finished."

"You want the first or the second one in a to-go box?" the waitress asked.

"I want all of it right in front of me. I plan to eat every bit of it. And I'll be picking up the ticket, so don't let that sorry-assed old cowboy over there have it. He'll bitch for hours if he has to pay for my anger—which he caused, by the way," Jane said.

Ellen slapped her leg and grinned. "Act Two coming up."

The teenage waitress was visibly uncomfortable and for that Slade could have gladly turned Jane over his knee and given her the spanking she was asking for. That visual caused a reaction behind the zipper of his jeans that made him stifle a moan.

"I'll have the fried chicken platter. Green beans, corn, and a dinner salad for the sides. I'll have to eat part of what she's ordering, I'm sure. And honey, I'll take that ticket."

"Tell you what. I'll just put it on the table. Y'all can fight over it," the waitress said.

"You won't touch a bite of my food, Slade Luckadeau. I'll stab you with a fork if you try and I know exactly where the right vein is to do the most damage. You'll be dead before you fall out of the chair, and there'll be blood everywhere," she said.

He grinned at her.

She blinked to be sure she was seeing clearly. *God Almighty in Heaven, the man smiled.*

"What are you laughing about?" she snapped.

"You. You're pretty damn cute when you are mad. Did you girls know that when she's angry she can eat a whole steer? Just wipe its nose and ass, slap it on the grill until it's hot, and bring it to her. She's got a hollow leg when she's upset."

"Then don't upset her if you plan on feeding her," Ellen said.

"I didn't. All I did was state the facts. She upset herself," he said.

"You are a pig from hell," she reminded him.

He passed the platter across the table to her. "Biscuit? Jelly or sugar?"

"Cornbread. Honey."

"No endearments necessary," he continued to grin.

"Believe me, there was none intended."

She buttered a cornbread muffin, slathered it with honey, and ate it while she waited for her food. If she and Slade ever did get together, she sincerely hoped her metabolism didn't fail her. If it did, she'd weigh six hundred pounds before their first anniversary.

When the ticket arrived, he had to scramble to get it before she did. There was no way he would let her or any other woman pay for dinner when he sat up to the table with them. His ego couldn't survive that kind of blow, and he didn't give a damn if she got mad and cleaned out the refrigerator when they got home.

When he parked in the front yard, the older women crawled out with declarations about taking naps before their poker buddies arrived. Neither of them asked Jane and Slade what they planned to do with the remainder of their day of rest. Hopefully, they'd get their fighting over with and learn to make love instead of war.

Jane headed to her room to change out of her Sunday finery and he did the same, both of them hell-bent not to care what the other one did. She hung her new dress in the closet, pulled on a pair of cut-off jean shorts and a tank top, picked up a romance book, and stomped out into the hallway. She met him coming out of his room. He wore flip-flops and the bathing suit they'd bought in Florida, carried a towel and a book, and gave her a dirty look.

"You going swimming?"

"I am."

"Where at?"

"Nocona Lake."

"I'm going with you," she said.

"I didn't invite you."

"So what. I'm going."

"You got a bathing suit?"

"Nope, but I can swim in what I'm wearing. Let's go."

"It's a lake. It's not a nice clean chlorinated swimming pool. You'll get moss around your ankles and dirt on your feet."

She rolled her brown eyes and led the way down the hall to the front door. "Wait a minute. I forgot a towel."

"If you can make it to the truck before I get it in reverse, you can go. I'll leave you behind if you don't hurry," he threatened.

She pointed her forefinger at him. "You do and I'll make your life miserable. You'll have to watch every bite of food you take for the next week, because I'll put something in it that will make you puke worse than the night I drank you under the table."

"I won that bet. You didn't."

"You better wait on me or you'll wish you were dead," she threw over her shoulder as she ran as fast as she could down the hall toward the bathroom.

The truck was moving when she grabbed the passenger door and hauled herself and her towel into the cab. "You better be careful. I can get mean."

"Do you eat as much when you're mean as when you are mad?"

"Don't test me."

Mercy but he felt good. Every nerve was on red alert. Every emotion jumping around like worms on hot ashes. He tapped his fingers on the steering wheel to the beat of the music from the radio. He'd made her just as angry as she'd made him by turning up at his ranch without so much as a "let's talk about this situation between us." Not even a phone call to see what his thoughts were on her buying a corner of his land. What in the hell was she going to do with five acres, anyway? Grow a vegetable garden?

He turned north on Clay Street in Nocona and followed the road several miles to a sandy bar where they could swim. It wasn't the ocean and the sand didn't resemble sugar, but it was wet and the day was hot. Sometimes a person got rib eyes; sometimes bologna sandwiches.

"This is beautiful," she said. "I'm calling that spot over there under the shade tree and reading for a while before I go in the water."

"You'd sink like a rock if you went in now, with all that dinner in you," he said.

"My, oh my, but aren't you complimentary today. Did you never learn how to sweet talk a lady?"

"You're not a lady."

"Go swim but be careful, honey. If you drown, I won't save your sorry ass," she said.

"What makes my ass sorry?" he asked.

"It talks when it should let your mouth do the talking," she shot right back at him.

He turned quickly so she wouldn't see him smiling and walked out into the warm water until it was deep enough to swim. She pretended to read but kept an eye on him, growing more nervous by the minute when he got so far out toward the distant shore that she couldn't see him anymore.

They fought like tigers. They made love with such passion it was scary. She didn't want to lose a single moment of life with him. He'd come around to her way of thinking eventually, if he didn't drown first.

Finally he reappeared, coming up out of the water like a Greek god, all wet and muscled. Jane didn't blink for fear he would disappear. He grabbed the towel, dried his hair and face, and spread it out beside her. "Okay, I'm ready to talk. What are we going to do about us?"

"I'm reading," she said.

"Hey, you're the one who started this. You came to me; I didn't go to you. You tagged along today when you weren't even invited. So we're going to talk," he declared.

"Don't order me around. I'm not one of your clingy, gold-digging bimbos with big boobs and too much hair. I don't care if you've got money or not. I've had it. It don't buy happiness."

"What does?"

"Being home."

"What are you talking about? You left your home," he said.

"It hasn't been home since Mother died. It's been a place to live. A place where folks were paid to do what I wanted. Home is where they love you and take care of you even when you aren't nice."

He began to understand the edges of what she was talking about. He'd never thought of her being so alone and lonely in that big house. There were people everywhere, just like on the Double L, but his hired help were more than just employees. Take Vince, for instance. The boy was like a younger brother to him. Marty was an uncle for sure and the rest made up the family.

"You never have to worry about family, Slade. You could kick any mesquite tree between here and Louisiana and find a Luckadeau relative who'd stand up for you. The only place I've felt at home since that whole fiasco is at the Double L. So you tell me, what are we going to do about us?"

"Would you go to dinner with me next Friday night?"

"You askin' me for a date?"

"I am. We could try the courtin' process and see if it will endure us," he said.

"Then yes, I will go to dinner with you."

"Okay, we've been nice five whole minutes. We've got a date and a week of hard work ahead of us. Nice is over. Now I'm going to pitch you out in the middle of that lake," he said.

She was on her feet in seconds and running so fast she lost her flip-flops. But her speed couldn't match his. He caught her up in his arms, but he didn't toss her out into the water from the edge of the lake. He kept walking when he reached the water's edge, laughing the whole time she screamed that he was the product of a filthy swine and a whore. He carried her out into the deep water and pitched her as far as he could throw her. She remembered to suck in a lung full of air before she hit the water so she came up ready to fight rather than trying to survive.

He was back on the bank stretched out on his back by the time she swam to shore. Life was good now and he was as happy as he'd been in years. Not to say that in ten minutes she'd have him ready to drop-kick her all the way back to Mississippi. But in that few minutes when he was honest with himself, he realized that he'd never be happy with a clingy woman who needed his opinion on every single item. Jane was his kind of woman—but he'd have to be very careful not to let her know. With that kind of power, she could lead him around like a boar hog with a ring in his nose.

She picked up her towel and carried it to the edge of the water, away from the grassy knoll right off the road where the scrub oak trees were located. She laid the towel out as though she was going to let the sun dry her and her clothing, sat down, and began piling handfuls of sand in the middle of the towel. She'd teach him to throw her into the water.

When it was full enough that she could barely drag it, she looked back at him. He was snoring. Things didn't get any better than that. She picked up all four corners and eased it up beside him, carefully pulled his bathing suit open, and dumped all the sand inside. He came up from a dead sleep kicking and screaming.

She beat him to the water that time and was halfway out into the lake before he got free of the sand in the lining of his suit. It had been years since she'd played. She'd dated and even fancied herself in love a few times before John. But the dates had been dinner and movies or dinner and a play. Never had she had so much fun just plain playing. She really was growing up to be like Ellen.

"You have to come in to the shore sometime," he yelled.

"Don't go to sleep or I'll do something worse," she yelled back.

He chuckled. She would. There wasn't a doubt in his mind. Would they always have fun together? He hoped so. He hoped that when he was eighty he'd still be trying to figure out a way to get ahead of her. It might take that long to find a way to get the job done, but what fun the journey would be.

Chapter 18

THEY WORKED HARD ALL WEEK AND HAD LITTLE TIME TO talk, passing in the hall in the morning and evening. Slade was in the fields until after dark and she drove the ladies to their Thursday night dance, then went on in to Wichita Falls to do the weekly grocery shopping at the Wal-Mart super center.

She'd worried about "the date" all week, dreading it one minute and looking forward to it the next. When Friday finally ended, she wasn't sure how to dress for a date with Slade. Were they going back to the steak house in Wichita Falls, or perhaps to the lake with a picnic basket?

He opened the back door at six thirty that night, dirty, greasy, his eyes two white holes in a mass of grime, protected only by his sunglasses all day. She was in the kitchen making peanut butter cookies for the next day's dinner.

"I thought we had a date," he said.

"We do. You didn't tell me what time and this is the last dozen cookies. Are we in a hurry?"

"Evidently not," he said.

"By the time you get cleaned up I'll be ready. Where are we going?"

"Your choice," he said. "But I'm hungry."

"For what?" she asked.

"Food."

He came out of the bedroom dressed in starched jeans and a white shirt, his face clean shaven, and smelling so good she had second thoughts about going anywhere but the nearest motel.

He took one look at her in soft jeans, a T-shirt with Tinker Bell on the front, and sandals. Her hair was washed. The flour was gone from her face and he could smell expensive perfume.

"You said you'd be ready."

"I am. You said it was my choice and you are hungry for food. That means something to fill your belly, not tease your palette. I want to go to the Dairy Queen in Nocona for supper. Then I want to take a blanket to the Nocona park. That way we can play for a while and then watch the lightning bugs."

He couldn't believe his ears. Surely she hadn't worked all week and looked forward to an evening out to eat at the Dairy Queen and lie on a blanket in the park. But hey, if that's what the eccentric lady wanted, he could provide it.

"I'll change into something more comfortable. Give me five minutes and I'll be ready," he said.

She breathed a sigh of relief that he hadn't fought with her. She'd worried all week about the date and whether it would make or break their delicate relationship. She didn't want a dinner, movie, kiss good night, and I'll-see-you-next-week date. She wanted to make beautiful memories that would keep her warm in her old age.

He returned in a few minutes dressed in faded jeans, a T-shirt, and boots. That was her Slade. Not that he didn't make her heart beat like a native drum when he was all dressed up, but her Slade was comfortable with her, not just dating her.

"So what made you decide on a night like this?" he asked.

"Dating scares the hell out of me."

"Wow! You're scared of something."

"Don't tease. You've seen me scared shitless. When that house was bombed the only thing I thought was that I couldn't pee my pants because I didn't have any to change into."

He chuckled.

"Don't laugh. You were scared, too."

"Amen, sister."

"Slade, I'm not your sister. Let's get that straight right now. If things never work out between us I might be your friend but don't you ever call me your sister."

"Are we fighting? Tell me why you are afraid of dates."

"We aren't fighting. I'm stating facts. I'm afraid of dates because..." she paused, not knowing whether to trust him with the information.

The way she'd gone pale and her chin quivered scared him far worse than a burning house. "Hey, you're the one who's thrown her past away and started a new life. You don't have to tell me anything if you don't want to," he said.

"I had dates with John. I had dates with other men. I don't trust any of them. You are the only man in the world I'm willing to put my trust in, Slade Luckadeau."

"Wow," he whispered. "That must have been hard to spit out."

"You will never know," she said.

He felt his chest swelling and his ego inflating. She trusted him, did she? Well, she damn sure better.

He'd put his fanny on the line for her so many times he couldn't even count them.

Yes, and you enjoyed every minute of the adventure. It took you out of the vacuum you created for yourself. So don't go getting all big-headed. Besides, she's the only woman you've trusted since your mother left you crying your eyes out on the front porch. You going to tell her that?

"Well, thank you for the compliment," he said.

"It's not a compliment. It's a fact."

The Dairy Queen was hopping that evening. They ordered hamburgers and milk shakes, found the last available booth, and sat across from each other. The walls were decorated with every Coca Cola tray ever put on the market or so it seemed. Some had ladies from the last century pictured on them; some had polar bears and Santa Claus. The waitress brought their burgers and fries in a red plastic basket and shakes in disposable cups.

"So, does this feel like a date?" he asked.

"It feels like a fun time. No pressure. Just burgers and then the park. This might be a good time to tell you that there are five horses coming tomorrow morning. Nellie said you wouldn't have a problem with letting them have some pasture with your horses. I thought I'd better clear it for sure."

"No problem," he said. "What five horses?"

"The ones that you liked. The stallion and four mares. Thought we might do a little horse trading on the side."

"You mean you might do some horse trading. Those aren't my horses."

"Oh yeah, they are. At least they belong to the Double L as soon as they get here."

"Are you serious? Why did you do that?"

"Because you liked them and because I didn't want to get rid of those five. And just because..." she stammered.

He bit into the hamburger. "I can't believe you don't have a catty comeback."

"Hello, Jane Doe," Kristy said right at her elbow.

"It's Jane Day."

"Whatevvver," Kristy drawled. "So your rich bitch did come back, did she?" she looked down at Slade.

"You didn't learn your lesson the first time about calling me names," Jane said.

"You wouldn't start something right here in the Dairy Queen," Kristy said.

Jane slowly laid her hamburger down, slid out of the seat and stood up, her nose only inches from Kristy's when she stood on her tiptoes. Kristy took two steps backward and fell over a chair, barely righting herself before she tumbled all the way to the ground.

Jane sat back down, picked up her burger, and bit off a chunk.

"Lady, one of these days you are going to meet me in a dark alley," Kristy whispered loudly.

"I'll bring the disinfectant spray because if you're in a dark alley, you'll either be pissing on the trash can to mark your territory or something equally as smelly," Jane said.

An elderly man in the next booth laughed so hard he had to wipe his eyes on a paper napkin. "Momma, that girl fights like you used to," he told his wife.

"Oh, hush, you old fool. She's just protecting her rights. When you was a good-lookin' husband like that, I'd have fought Bette Davis for you," she said.

Jane started giggling. It turned into a full-fledged infectious laugh that had Slade and everyone around joining in. Kristy flaunted out the door in a huff, which made everything even funnier.

"Are we ever going anywhere that one of your women don't show up?" she asked Slade.

"Hey, you don't get to answer that after what your fiancé did."

"I'd love to hear that story," the lady behind them said.

"It would take too long," Slade assured her. "You finished?" he asked Jane.

"I'll take the milk shake with me."

"I'm just glad she didn't make you mad. I didn't bring that much money with me," he said when they were outside.

"She don't get to make me mad anymore. That would give her power and she's not worth it," Jane said.

"You are a strange woman, lady," Slade said as he drove west a few blocks and turned back south toward the park. The night was hot and humid with no wind. The sun had barely set and the stars were starting to pop out around the half moon like little pieces of diamond. He parked and retrieved the blanket from the backseat.

She'd pondered on the statement he'd made about her being strange for several minutes and decided he was simply stating a fact. She *was* strange when compared to other women her age. Life's twists and turns had made her that way and she made no apologies and offered no excuses. If she was strange, then so be it.

A whole hoard of bugs met her when she opened the truck door. She stepped out into oppressive heat and became instant supper for a dozen blood-sucking varmints.

"It's too hot to swing. I'd be a sweaty mess in ten minutes, and the mosquitoes are already eating me alive. Can I change my mind?"

"This is your date. What do you want to do?"

"Go home, Slade. I want to go home. The girls are playing poker so I don't want to go to the house. Can we take our blanket and go to my five acres?"

He pitched the blanket back where he'd found it. "We can do that. Tell me what you intend to do with five acres? It's not enough to keep five horses on."

"The horses have several sections of land to roam around on with your horses. I didn't even think of the horses when I asked Nellie to sell me the land."

"What did you think?"

"That if I had a piece of the Double L, I would belong there."

That blew his mind out of Montague County and somewhere near the Gulf of Mexico. "Why would you want to belong there? I know you said you felt at home, Jane. But is this a passing thing or is it for real?"

"It's the most real thing I've ever experienced, Slade. Take me to the five acres and I'll show you what I'm going to do."

For that bit of information he would have carried her there on his back. He drove too fast and was lucky the highway patrolmen were busy eating donuts or having supper with their wives. When he reached the corner of the Double L that she'd paid Nellie an exorbitant fee for, she got out of the truck and inhaled deeply.

"It's mine. It wasn't my grandmother's. It wasn't my mother's or my father's. It's my land and I'm putting a double-wide trailer on it." She spread the blanket out on the grass in the pasture and laid down on her back.

"A trailer. You're shittin' me."

"No, Slade, I'm not. I told you at the beach in Florida I wanted a little house."

"Why?"

"Because if I have a little house, then by damn my husband can't get mad at me and go pout in the den while I'm a mile away in the east wing of the mansion. If I'm at home all day cooking his meals and helping run a ranch, he can't spend every other night in a penthouse with the excuse he's working late. In a little house, we have to live so close that we have to make up when we fight because there's no room for the tension and anger."

He stretched out on the blanket beside her. "You got it all figured out, don't you?"

"Pretty much. My trailer is going right here facing that way. You are stretched out on my sofa right now," she said.

"Pretty damn wide for a sofa," he said.

She tugged at the corner of the blanket. "Move the damn thing this way about six feet."

"Why in the devil would I do that?"

"Because if it stays here it's in the spot where I envision my living room and it's too damn wide for a sofa, so we'll move it to where the bedroom will be. Looks like it's about the right size for a queen-size bed to me," she grinned.

He moved the blanket, laid back down, and laced his fingers behind his neck.

She snuggled up next to him and laid her head on his chest. "Okay, cowboy, we had really good sex when we were scared shitless and when we were piss drunk. We're both sober and there's nothing out here to scare the bejesus out of us, so let's see if the third time is the charm. Will we find that we don't like it when things are normal or that it's just as good as ever? My five acres is far enough out here that no one can see us making love on this blanket. I don't care about a couple of mosquito bites on my naked ass. How about you?"

She straddled his chest and leaned forward until her mouth found his. He wrapped his arms around her, letting his fingers slip under her shirt to feel bare skin. No one had ever made him feel like Jane did—but what would happen if they had sober sex and she declared it wasn't as good as scared or piss-drunk sex?

"You sure about this?" he whispered hoarsely.

"You?"

"I'll show you sure!" He tumbled her over on her back and kissed her until she couldn't breathe. He slipped the shirt over her head and removed her bra then tugged her pants down and tossed them off the blanket. Another dozen kisses and she deftly flipped him over and returned the favor.

Under the moonlight with only the lightning bugs and one stray raccoon peeping around a fence post to watch, Slade made love to Jane. The emotional explosion that would put an atomic bomb to shame was for their benefit only. The raccoon didn't see it and the light from the fireflies wasn't dimmed a bit. But it was there on their pretend queen-size bed, proving they didn't need adrenaline or liquor to fuel the sparks. It was the meeting of souls and hearts, the kind that would never diminish, no matter where or when.

"So?" She bit his earlobe gently. "That all you got or is there an encore?"

He groaned. "You're a vixen, lady."

"Yes, I am and don't you forget it."

The night breeze chilled the slick sweat on their bodies and she pulled the edge of the blanket around them. "Well?"

"Give me ten minutes and I'll show you an encore that surpasses the main performance."

"I think you are a real cowboy," she giggled.

"What's that mean?"

She sang part of the old song about not calling him a cowboy until you've seen him ride. She laughed aloud 'cause she could tell he was blushing.

He pulled her closer to him, liking the way she fit into the crook of his arm.

"So when does the trailer arrive?"

"You want to talk about the trailer? You only got eight more minutes. Don't you think you'd best be thinkin' about something else?" she asked.

"I'm just catching my breath. Don't you worry about the second round. I can keep up with you, Jane Day Hayes!"

"Okay then, trailer will be here in about a month. The septic tank people are coming next week and so are the folks who'll be putting in the well. After that, it's the electrical folks and then the house can be brought in. James has taken care of all of it for me. He's my lawyer on call now."

"A month, huh?" he asked. He'd miss her being down the hall from him every night. There was something about knowing that she was close that brought peace, if you could call any proximity to Jane Hayes peaceful.

"So are we coming out here to this blanket-on-the-ground bed thing during that month?" he asked.

"Here. My bedroom. Your bedroom. The hay loft. Wherever, whenever we can find time. I hear a bell in the distance. I think that means round two is about to start." She kissed his eyelids.

He groaned.

"You've got a month to propose to me. If you're too damn bashful or can't seem to get the job done by the end of a month, then I'll propose to you," she whispered.

"What?" he stammered.

"You'll get used to the idea. I'm not losing you, Slade. You're the only man in the world I trust with my heart and soul. So take your choice. You can propose or I will. Oh, by the way, I don't want a diamond. A plain gold band like Nellie wears is what I want."

"Good grief! You're telling me how to propose and what kind of ring to buy?" he raised his voice.

"That's right, Slade Luckadeau. You couldn't run me off the first time around and you damn sure ain't goin' to this time, especially after tonight. Now shut your mouth and let's do something other than talk."

He wrapped his arms tightly around her and kissed her hard. By damn, he would propose within the next month. He'd never live it down if he didn't.

Chapter 19

IT WAS A GLORIOUS SEPTEMBER MORNING. NOT TOO HOT, but sunny and bright with no rain clouds in sight. White cloths covered tables in the backyard. Centerpieces of fresh wildflowers arranged in Mason jars with wide orange ribbons around them were scattered down the tables. The deck had been transformed into a stage for a wedding. Illusion and ivy intertwined on an arch, and rows of white folding chairs lined up to accommodate the early birds. The rest could sit around the tables.

Caterers were busy putting last-minute details into play.

The preacher waited in the living room with Slade, Beau, and Griffin.

Jane paced the floor of her bedroom in the shirt she'd borrowed from Slade. The hairdresser who'd arrived earlier suggested she wear a button-down shirt to keep from messing up her hairdo and the veil that fit over a crown of curls and hung down her back.

No doubts plagued her. She was doing the right thing. She was home. Her heart was here. Her house was in place. She and Slade had picked out the furniture and it had arrived the day before. But she was so nervous she could hardly be still. Finally she picked up the box from the dresser and went into the bathroom.

She took a deep breath and opened the box. The actual test only took long enough to pee on a stick. The next sixty seconds lasted five days past eternity. She sat down on the potty and shut her eyes tightly. When she opened them, she was only mildly surprised.

That done, she tossed the stick in the trash can and went back to her bedroom, where she found Celia and Milli getting dressed in matching orange floral sun dresses. Celia's was halter-styled, fitted to the waist, with a short straight skirt. Milli's was an empire with a fuller skirt that stopped at her knee.

"It's about time. Did you pee one last time? That dress is so snug it'd take a bottle of Vaseline to get it up if you have to go again," Celia said.

Jane nodded. "How much time have I got?"

"Enough to crawl out that window and be gone in five minutes. I've got a rental out there. We could be in Paris, France, not Paris, Texas, by tomorrow morning. You sure about this, Jane?" Celia asked.

"More sure than anything I've ever done in my life," she said.

"That's the spirit," Milli said. "By wedding time I was sure, too. It was the weeks before I had my doubts. I even ran away and had to eat crow when I came back."

"We've *got* to have a shopping trip and exchange stories," Jane said.

"Anytime. Call me. We'll meet in Gainesville and have a day," Milli said.

"Okay, let's get her melted into this dress," Celia said.

"It's not that tight," Jane smiled.

"I'm teasing. I can't imagine you choosing such a simple thing. The last one was big enough that six little girls were going to carry the train," Celia said.

Milli giggled. "So was mine. The second one was very simple. I think we do have similar stories."

Jane removed Slade's shirt and carefully slipped the ankle length sheath of white, lace-covered satin over her head. Sleeveless. Simple neckline that looked wonderful with her grandmother's pearls. Slit up one side to the knee. Ultra plain.

"Shoes?" Celia asked.

Jane shook her head.

Milli looked around for lace-covered bridal boots like she'd worn at her wedding. "Boots?"

Jane shook her head again.

"Barefoot?" they chorused together.

"That's right. I did have my toenails done. Aren't they pretty?" She wiggled the toes on her left foot.

"So when's the baby due?" Celia asked.

Jane cocked her head to one side.

"Barefoot and pregnant—isn't that what the old adage says? So you are barefoot. Are you going to do the pregnant half of the saying on the honeymoon?"

"Maybe."

"Don't bet on it. Took us six months to get pregnant the second time. I teased Beau that Katy Scarlett was conceived because he was drunk. Thought for a while there I was going to have to get him drunk again just to get a second child. You got a bottle of champagne hiding? That might help." Milli zipped up the dress and brushed a sponge across Jane's upper lip. "Little sweat there. Methinks me sees nervous."

"Little bit," Jane agreed.

Ellen poked her head in the door. "Music is playing. You all ready? Pick up your flowers in the kitchen and let's get this show on the road."

Ellen wore a bright yellow satin dress with a fitted bodice and flowing skirt. She'd declared that she was playing the mother of the bride and she'd have a dress fitting for the title. "Okay, Jane, let's go make this official. Me and Nellie will breathe a lot easier when you are really ours. We live in fear every day that you'll call it off."

"Why would I do that? I love Slade. Loved him even before I knew I loved him. Loved him before I was willing to admit it. Love all of it, even the fighting. Know what's the best part of a rousting good fight?"

Ellen shook her head.

"The making up. I start fights just so I can haul his ass back to the bedroom and make up with him."

"You really might grow up to be like me. Bless your baby heart," Ellen said. "Now get your shoes on and let's go."

"Ain't wearin' shoes. They pinched my feet and my work boots don't match the dress."

Ellen nodded. "It's your day, honey. You do it the way you want to and to hell with anyone who says a word. Anyone don't like your bare feet, you send them to me and I'll straighten out their ass."

On the right cue the preacher took his place under the arch. A minute later, while the band played "The Dance" by Garth Brooks in the background, Beau and Griffin took their places beside the preacher. Nellie and Slade stepped out of the kitchen door, arm in arm. She wore a yellow dress that matched Ellen's and he wore black Wranglers, a starched white shirt, a black hat, eel boots, and a western-cut tux jacket with a daisy in the lapel. Nellie kissed him on the cheek when they reached the arch.

"You finally got that lucky break you've talked about your whole life. Don't ever let her go," she whispered.

"I promise," he whispered back.

Then the traditional wedding march started and Milli made her way slowly down the aisle. The look in Beau's eyes said that if he could, he would repeat his vows to her again that day. He winked when she passed.

Celia made an entrance at the back of the church and Griffin watched her as she strolled down the aisle, a tall, graceful blonde who looked as though she was walking down a model's runway. She smiled at him and he smiled back, but he wasn't interested. Blond-haired women reminded him of his ex-wife.

Everyone stood when Ellen escorted Jane down the aisle. The crowd, both those in the chairs on the deck and the ones gathered around the tables, smiled at her bare feet. Slade grinned the biggest. This was his bride. His Jane. She'd always do things her way and to hell with everyone else. The world disappeared when she put her hand in his and they were the only two people left in the world.

"Dearly beloved, we are gathered here today in the sight of God and this multitude of witnesses to join Ellacyn Jane Hayes and Lester Slade Luckadeau in holy matrimony…" the preacher began.

Multitude of witnesses was right. Jane was marrying into one enormous family and she loved it. Today she was no longer just the maid at the Luckadeau ranch; she was part of it.

"Slade?" the preacher prompted.

"Jane, I've got to admit I did not like you in the beginning."

A universal chuckle went up across the yard.

"I had a whole set of vows memorized but while Granny was walking me down the aisle she reminded me of something. For years I said I could never catch a lucky break. Well, I still didn't catch one. To catch something you have to chase after it. At least that's what Granny said when I whined. I didn't catch you. I tried to outrun you, not catch you. But I was wrong because you are the best thing that ever happened to me. You bring me happiness and joy, and I vow to love and cherish you the rest of my life. You truly are my lucky break. Today I give you my name."

"Jane?"

"Slade, I got to admit, I damn sure didn't like you either."

Louder snickers that time and a few little girls put their hands over their mouths at such a word coming out of a fairy princess bride.

"Talk about a lucky break? When I got off that bus in Wichita Falls, Texas, I was running scared, not trusting anyone. But I found a man I could trust, who would protect me with his life and love me with his heart. Slade, I promise you a life of roses, complete with thorns. The sweet smell of roses will keep us in love. The thorns will make us strong. Until the day I die, I will love you passionately. I gave you my heart a long time ago, even before I knew I had. Today I take your name and give you my soul."

The ceremony went on as the guests wiped at their eyes.

"Rings?" the preacher asked.

They exchanged plain, wide gold wedding bands.

Then the preacher pronounced them husband and wife and told Slade he could kiss his bride. When they turned to face the crowd he said, "I give to you for the very first time, Mr. and Mrs. Slade Luckadeau. They came in as separate people. At this point they will dance their first dance together as a couple."

She melted into his arms. He swept off his hat and held it on her fanny. The band began to play "So Are You to Me," by eastmountainsouth. The female singer with a high soprano voice sang about the simple things, like the wind blowing over the plains, being like him to her.

"Barefoot?" he whispered while they danced to the lovely music.

"Pregnant, too. How do you like that?"

He was so stunned he stopped dancing and looked down into her brown eyes.

"Upset?" she asked.

"Elated." He dipped her deeply and then swung her around. Then he kissed her, hiding their faces with his hat. "I'm the happiest man alive."

"I think it's a girl. Her name is Susan Jo Ellen. Susan was my mother's name. We're going to call her Ellie," she whispered.

"Luckadeau's throw boys."

"Are we fighting? If so, can we go to our trailer and make up?"

"All in due time, Mrs. Luckadeau, all in due time. We've got a lifetime together, and I intend to enjoy every minute of it."

The End

About the Author

Carolyn Brown, an award-winning author who has sold more than forty books, credits her eclectic family for her humor and writing ideas. She was born in Texas but grew up in southern Oklahoma where she and her husband, Charles, a retired English teacher, make their home. They have three grown children and enough grandchildren to keep them young.

Read on for more from Carolyn Brown and the
Luckadeau cowboys

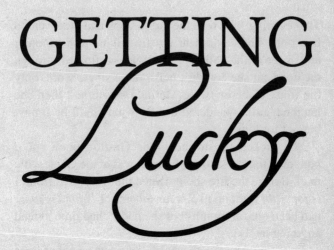

GETTING
Lucky

Coming in January 2010 from
Sourcebooks Casablanca

GETTING *Lucky*

That evening Julie read the kids a book and then went to her room. She could hear Griffin talking to his mother and sister in the hallway. Their voices floated through the door but she couldn't make out a single word, only the tone. Once or twice Melinda swore and then she laughed. Julie wondered briefly what could be funny, but not for long.

She picked up the new Sue Grafton book she'd bought at the bookstore when she was at the Gainesville mall. Before the fire she'd owned the whole set, from *A is for Alibi* right up to *S is for Silence*. *T is for Trespass* had been out for months but she hadn't had time to read anything lately.

Footsteps came up the stairs. Two sets went to rooms across the hall. One set stopped at her door for a moment then continued on to Griffin's room. She wondered if he was aching for a fight about that kiss. Well if he was, then he should have it, right?

She peeked out into the hallway. She could hear Melinda and Laura moving around behind closed doors. She tiptoed to Griffin's door and raised a hand to knock, then thought better of it. One little noise and at least two doors would open in the hallway, with the possibility of a third, if Annie heard it. Explaining to Annie would be easy compared to Laura and Melinda if they caught her going into Griffin's room. Melinda's temper would ignite into flames and she'd do a dance right there in the hallway for being right about the red-haired, white trash gold digger.

She turned the knob and eased into the dark room. Griffin was stretched out on the bed, his hands laced behind his head. He figured Lizzy was sneaking into his room to ask for a midnight snack. When he looked across the room and saw Julie lit up from the moonlight flowing through the window, he sat up so fast it made him dizzy.

"Which kid needs me?" he whispered.

"Nothing is the matter with the kids. Something is the matter with us," she said.

"Please tell me that kiss didn't spook you into leaving Saint Jo for the holidays…"

"I'm not leaving. Wild horses couldn't drive me away and let your sister win this silly war she's declared on me," she said.

He threw himself backwards with enough force to make the bed bounce. She pulled up a rocking chair to the side of his bed and slid into it, drawing her knees up, propping her forearms on them and her chin on her arms.

"Okay, then what *is* the problem that you'd invade my bedroom without even knocking?"

She was suddenly tongue tied. What had seemed like a perfectly good idea five minutes before was suddenly sophomoric and silly. She wasn't a teenager and Griffin wasn't the first man she'd kissed.

"It was the kiss, wasn't it?" he asked.

She nodded.

"Well, rest assured it was just something that

happened. Kind of like a knee-jerk reaction to a situation. It won't happen again."

"Why?" she asked.

"What do you mean?"

"Why won't it happen again? Am I ugly? Do I repel you?"

He sat up again. "You most certainly do not!"

He was careful to keep the sheet over his lower body. Just looking at her in that silly nightshirt with Betty Boop on the front had flushed him with desire that wasn't easy to cover up, even with a sheet.

"Then why?"

"Because you…" he stammered.

"Because I was with your brother, Graham?"

"That, and the fact that you and I could never have a relationship, Julie. Number one, you are not my type. Number two… I can't think of what number two is but give me a day or two and I'll have a whole list."

She was on her feet in flash and put one hand on each of Griffin's cheeks. She leaned forward and kissed him soundly and passionately. When she broke away she ran her tongue over her lips to get the final taste.

"Number one," she said, "you aren't my type either. Number two, I'd rather be your friend. Number three, you kiss damn good and your brother and I were both so plastered that night I can't even remember what his kisses were like. Good night, Griffin. Rest assured, it won't happen again. I just wanted to make sure the first kiss I'd had since my divorce really was as good as I thought it was."

"And was it?" he asked hoarsely.

"I don't kiss and tell." She slipped out the door.

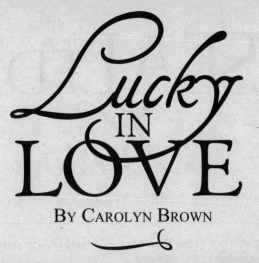

Lucky IN LOVE

By Carolyn Brown

BEAU HASN'T GOT A LICK OF SENSE WHEN IT COMES TO WOMEN

Everything hunky rancher "Lucky" Beau Luckadeau touches turns to gold—except relationships. Spitfire Milli Torres can mend a fence, pull a calf, or shoot a rattlesnake between the eyes. When Milli shows up to help out at the Lazy Z ranch, she's horrified to find that Beau's her nearest neighbor—the very man she'd hoped never to lay eyes on again. If Beau ever figures out what really happened on that steamy Louisiana night when they first met, there'll be the devil to pay...

Praise for Carolyn Brown:

"Engaging characters, humorous situations, and a bumpy romance... Carolyn Brown will keep you reading until the very last page." —Romantic Times

"Carolyn Brown's rollicking sense of humor asserts itself on every page." —Scribes World

978-1-4022-2435-5 • $6.99 U.S. / $8.99 CAN

SEALED
with a *Kiss*

BY MARY MARGRET DAUGHTRIDGE

**THERE'S ONLY ONE THING HE CAN'T HANDLE, AND ONE
WOMAN WHO CAN HELP HIM...**

Jax Graham is a rough, tough Navy SEAL, but when
it comes to taking care of his four-year-old son after
his ex-wife dies, he's completely clueless. Family
therapist Pickett Sessoms can help, but only if he'll
let her.

When Jax and his little boy get trapped by a hurricane,
Picket takes them in against her better judgment.
When the situation turns deadly, Pickett discovers
what it means to be a SEAL, and Jax discovers that
even a hero needs help sometimes.

*"A heart-touching story that will keep you smiling and
cheering for the characters clear through to the happy
ending."* —Romantic Times

*"A well-written romance... simultaneously tender and sen-
suous."* —Booklist

978-1-4022-1118-8 • $6.99 U.S. / $8.99 CAN

SEALED
with a
Promise
BY MARY MARGRET DAUGHTRIDGE

NAVY SEAL CALEB DELAUDE IS AS DEADLY AS HE IS CHARMING.

Professor Emmie Caddington's quiet intelligence and quirky personality intrigue him. When he discovers that her personal connections can get him close to the man he's vowed to kill, will their budding relationship be nothing more than a means to revenge... or is she the key to his salvation?

Praise for *SEALed with a Kiss*:

"This story delivers in a huge way." —Romantic Times

"A wonderful story that will have readers experiencing a whirlwind of emotions and culminating with an awesome scene that will have your pulse pounding." —Romance Junkies

"What an incredibly powerful book! I laughed and sniffled, was turned on and turned inside out." —Queue My Review

978-1-4022-1763-0 • $6.99 U.S. / $7.99 CAN

Romeo, Romeo

~ BY ROBIN KAYE ~

Rosalie Ronaldi doesn't have a domestic bone in her body...

All she cares about is her career, so she survives on take-out and dirty martinis, keeps her shoes under the dining room table, her bras on the shower curtain rod, and her clothes on the couch.

Nick Romeo is every woman's fantasy—tall, dark, handsome, rich, really good in bed, AND he loves to cook and clean...

He says he wants an independent woman, but when he meets Rosalie, all he wants to do is take care of her. Before long, he's cleaned up her apartment, stocked her refrigerator, and adopted her dog.

So what's the problem? Just a little matter of mistaken identity, corporate theft, a hidden past in juvenile detention, and one big nosy Italian family too close for comfort...

"Kaye's debut is a delightfully fun, witty romance, making her a writer to watch." —*Booklist*

978-1-4022-1339-7 • $6.99 U.S. / $8.99 CAN

Too Hot to Handle

BY ROBIN KAYE

He sure would love to have a woman to take care of...

To Dr. Mike Flynn, there's nothing like housework to help a guy relax, while artist Annabelle Ronaldi doesn't have a domestic bone in her body.

When they meet at her sister's wedding, Mike is sure this is the woman he wants to take care of forever. While Mike sets to work wooing Annabelle, she becomes determined to sniff out the truth of the convoluted family secret that's threatening to turn both their lives upside down.

978-1-4022-1766-1 • $6.99 U.S. / $7.99 CAN

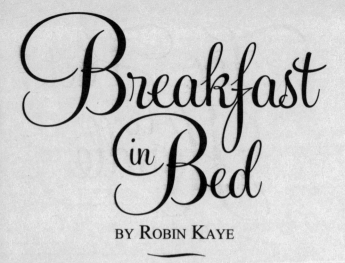

Breakfast in Bed

BY ROBIN KAYE

He'd be Mr. Perfect, if he wasn't a perfect mess...

Rich Ronaldi is *almost* the complete package—smart, sexy, great job—but his girlfriend dumps him for being such a slob, and Rich swears he'll learn to cook and clean to win her back. Becca Larson is more than willing to help him master the domestic arts, but she'll be damned if she'll do it so he can start cooking in another woman's kitchen—or bedroom...

PRAISE FOR ROBIN KAYE:

"Robin Kaye has proved herself a master of romantic comedy," —*Armchair Interviews*

"Ms. Kaye has style—it's easy, it's fun, and it has every–thing that you need to get caught up in a wonderful romance." —*Erotic Horizon*

"A fresh and fun voice in romantic comedy." —*All About Romance*

978-1-4022-1895-8 • $6.99 U.S. / $8.99 CAN

HEALING LUKE

BY BETH CORNELISON

She can't escape her past...

Occupational therapist Abby Stanford is on vacation alone, her self-confidence shattered by her fiancé's betrayal. Romance is the last thing on Abby's mind—until she meets the brooding and enigmatic Luke...

He won't face his future...

Scarred by a horrific accident, former heartthrob Luke Morgan is certain his best days are behind him. Abby knows how to help him recover, but for Luke his powerful attraction to her only serves as a harsh reminder of the man he used to be. Abby is Luke's first glimmer of hope since the accident, but can she heal his heart before Luke breaks hers?

"*Beth Cornelison writes intriguing, emotionally charged stories that will keep you turning the pages straight through to the end. Fabulous entertainment!*" —Susan Wiggs

"*Healing Luke is a breath of fresh air for romance fans... a stirring novel and a five star read!*"
—Crave More Romance

978-1-4022-2434-8 •$6.99 U.S. / $8.99 CAN

Line of
SCRIMMAGE

BY MARIE FORCE

SHE'S GIVEN UP ON HIM AND MOVED ON...

Susannah finally has peace, calm, a sedate life, and a no-surprises man. Marriage to football superstar Ryan Sanderson was a whirlwind, but Susanna got sick of playing second fiddle to his team. With their divorce just a few weeks away, she's already planning her wedding with her new fiancé.

HE'S FINALLY FIGURED OUT WHAT'S REALLY IMPORTANT TO HIM. IF ONLY IT'S NOT TOO LATE...

Ryan has just ten days to convince his soon-to-be-ex-wife to give him a second chance. His career is at its pinnacle, but in the year of their separation, Ryan's come to realize it doesn't mean anything without Susannah...

978-1-4022-1424-0 • $6.99 U.S. / $8.99 CAN

Love at FIRST FLIGHT

BY MARIE FORCE

What if the guy
in the airplane seat next to you turned out
to be the love of your life?

JULIANA, HAPPY IN HER CAREER AS A HAIR STYLIST, IS ON HER
WAY TO Florida to visit her boyfriend. When he tells her
he's wondering what it might be like to make love to other
women she is devastated. Even though he tries to take it
back, she doesn't want him to be wondering all his life. So
they agree to take a break, and heartbroken, she goes back
to Baltimore.

Michael is going to his fiancee's parents' home for an
engagement party he doesn't want. A state's prosecutor,
he's about to try the biggest case of his career, and he's
having doubts about the relationship. When Paige pulls a
manipulative stunt at the party, he becomes so enraged that
he breaks off the engagement.

Juliana and Michael sat together on the plane ride from
Baltimore to Florida, and discover they're on the same
flight coming back. With the weekend a disaster for each of
them, they bond in a "two-person pity party" on the plane
ride home. Their friendship begins to blossom and love,
too, but life is full of complications, and when Michael's
trial turns dangerous, the two must confront what they
value most in life...

978-1-4022-2006-7 • $6.99 U.S. / $7.99 CAN

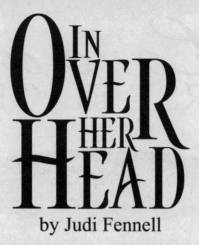

IN OVER HER HEAD

by Judi Fennell

"Holy mackerel! *In Over Her Head* is a
fantastically fun romantic catch!"

—Michelle Rowen, author of *Bitten & Smitten*

○ ○ ○ ○ ○ ○ **HE LIVES UNDER THE SEA** ○ ○ ○ ○ ○ ○

Reel Tritone is the rebellious royal second son of the ruler
of a vast undersea kingdom. A Merman, born with legs
instead of a tail, he's always been fascinated by humans,
especially one young woman he once saw swimming near
his family's reef...

○ ○ ○ ○ ○ **SHE'S TERRIFIED OF THE OCEAN** ○ ○ ○ ○ ○

Ever since the day she swam out too far and heard voices
in the water, marina owner Erica Peck won't go swimming
for anything—until she's forced into the water by a shady
ex-boyfriend searching for stolen diamonds, and is nearly
eaten by a shark...luckily Reel is nearby to save her, and
discovers she's the woman he's been searching for...

978-1-4022-2001-2 • $6.99 U.S. / $7.99 CAN